Why am I getting myself into this mess?

After going through countless pieces of evidence, this question still gnawed at me. I felt bad that the Moyers had been murdered and I owed Donald Moyer a debt of gratitude for bringing my daughter into my life–making it possible to adopt her. But a more pressing reason for getting involved had nothing to do with the Moyers. Murder or anything else that reflected badly on the day-to-day operation of the marina couldn't be ignored. If I didn't do something, our professional reputation could be ruined.

But bottom line: Police matter or not, the marina's approval or not, I was involved. It was just something I had to do. And it felt right.

"An impressive debut. I look forward to seeing Kellie again. And again and again and again."
—Stephen Greenleaf, anuthor of *Past Tense*

"I'm looking forward to reading more of her work."
—*Earlene Fowler*, author of *Dove in the Window*

MORE MYSTERIES FROM THE
BERKLEY PUBLISHING GROUP . . .

CAT CALIBAN MYSTERIES: She was married for thirty-eight years. Raised three kids. Compared to that, tracking down killers is easy . . .

by D. B. Borton

ONE FOR THE MONEY

THREE IS A CROWD

FIVE ALARM FIRE

TWO POINTS FOR MURDER

FOUR ELEMENTS OF MURDER

SIX FEET UNDER

ELENA JARVIS MYSTERIES: There are some pretty bizarre crimes deep in the heart of Texas—and a pretty gutsy police detective who rounds up the unusual suspects . . .

by Nancy Herndon

ACID BATH

LETHAL STATUES

TIME BOMBS

WIDOWS' WATCH

HUNTING GAME

C.O.P. OUT

FREDDIE O'NEAL, P.I., MYSTERIES: You can bet that this appealing Reno private investigator will get her man . . . "A winner."—Linda Grant

by Catherine Dain

LAY IT ON THE LINE

WALK A CROOKED MILE

BET AGAINST THE HOUSE

DEAD MAN'S HAND

SING A SONG OF DEATH

LAMENT FOR A DEAD COWBOY

THE LUCK OF THE DRAW

BENNI HARPER MYSTERIES: Meet Benni Harper—a quilter and folk-art expert with an eye for murderous designs . . .

by Earlene Fowler

FOOL'S PUZZLE

KANSAS TROUBLES

IRISH CHAIN

GOOSE IN THE POND

DOVE IN THE WINDOW

HANNAH BARLOW MYSTERIES: For ex-cop and law student Hannah Barlow, justice isn't just a word in a textbook. Sometimes, it's a matter of life and death . . .

by Carroll Lachnit

MURDER IN BRIEF

A BLESSED DEATH

PEACHES DANN MYSTERIES: Peaches has never had a very good memory. But she's learned to cope with it over the years . . . Fortunately, though, when it comes to murder, this absentminded amateur sleuth doesn't forgive and forget!

by Elizabeth Daniels Squire

WHO KILLED WHAT'S-HER-NAME?

MEMORY CAN BE MURDER

IS THERE A DEAD MAN IN THE HOUSE?

REMEMBER THE ALIBI

WHOSE DEATH IS IT, ANYWAY?

SINS OF SILENCE

VALERIE WILCOX

BERKLEY PRIME CRIME, NEW YORK

SINS OF SILENCE

A Berkley Prime Crime Book / published by arrangement with the author

PRINTING HISTORY
Berkley Prime Crime mass-market edition / July 1998

The Penguin Putnam Inc. World Wide Web site address is
http://www.penguinputnam.com

ISBN: 0-425-16396-2

Berkley Prime Crime Books are published by
The Berkley Publishing Group, a member of Penguin Putnam Inc.,
200 Madison Avenue, New York, NY 10016.

The name BERKLEY PRIME CRIME and the BERKLEY PRIME CRIME
design are trademarks belonging to Berkley Publishing Corporation.

PRINTED IN THE UNITED STATES OF AMERICA

10 9 8 7 6 5 4 3 2 1

For Dave and our daughters,
Maryanne, Julie, Linda, Dawn, and Joann
with my love

ACKNOWLEDGMENTS

MY SINCERE THANKS to the following people for their invaluable assistance and support: Jack Zufelt, for teaching me how to achieve my "core desires"; Rita Gardner, for editing the early drafts of the manuscript; Sharon Svendsen, Penny Peabody, Robert Schumacher, and my instructors and fellow students in the writing classes at the University of Washington and Centrum, for their suggestions and encouragement.

I'm especially grateful to the following people for answering my many questions with patience and professionalism. If there are errors, the fault lies not with what they shared with me but with how I interpreted it. Julia M. Stroud, Ph.D., of Shrink Write, for her psychological insights; Nicki Ehrlich DeBoard of Blue Heron Sailing, Linda Glein of Tacoma Women's Sailing Association, Gary Baillargeon of Yacht Sales International, and Robert Morrow of Elliott Bay Yachting Center, for their sailing expertise, instruction, and guidance; Jerry Evans, Ret., of the Port of Seattle Police; and Officer P.B. Nicholls and Lieutenant Al Gerdes of the Seattle Police Department, for giving so freely of their time and knowledge.

A special thanks to my agents, Anna Cottle and Mary Alice Kier of Cine/Lit Representation, and my editor, Judith Stern Palais, for believing in me.

Shall I present my first-born for my rebellious acts,
The fruit of my body for the sin of my soul?

—MICAH 6:7

"... Before I built a wall I'd ask to know
What I was walling in or walling out,
And to whom I was like to give offense.
Something there is that doesn't love a wall,
That wants it down. ..."

—FROM "MENDING WALL"
BY ROBERT FROST

SINS OF
SILENCE

ONE

ON THE WATER everything is quiet. It doesn't hit until you're out of the marina, beyond the breakwater and well into the bay, sails hoisted and motor cut. In the distance, the city witnesses your escape like a jealous lover. Traffic, pollution, people, and, if you're very lucky, the noise in your head are all beyond reach. The rushing water against the hull and the light wind against the sails calms and soothes your troubled soul. The crisp winter air feels spiritual, and you lean your body into it as if in prayer. You feel so strong, so vibrant, and so alive that you want to shout just to hear the power of your own being. But you don't because nothing feels as good as the quiet.

So you listen and watch, knowing full well that it is nothing more than an illusion—this quiet, this feeling of power that surges within you. For it is the wind that is powerful. It is the wind that determines everything. It is the wind that gives lie to the presumptuous notion that because we're human we are in control, that we have dominion over the world and its elements—because we don't own our world, the sea doesn't belong to us, and we have nothing in firm control. The sailor knows this, and responds to what the wind requires of her. She changes course, she trims the sheets, she sails into the wind, against the wind, with the wind, sideways to the wind, or, if the wind so chooses—she sails not at all.

Measured against the tremendous forces of nature—the hurricane, the typhoon, the squalls—the sailor knows that we are nothing, that our well-being, our very lives, are as tenuous as sea foam, subject to the whim of an unseen fist rising up at any moment to strike us down. Death, accident, and disease are as inevitable as the wind. The sailor knows this. And responds.

The sea is unforgiving, Kellie darlin'. Didn't I say that? Didn't I say you gotta keep your eye on her? Didn't I say you gotta pay attention to everything? See those streaks of white in the sky, see how they're trailing clouds of gray, see the way the wind is shifting, rippling the water across your bow—now what's all that telling you?

I didn't see it coming, Grampy. Not the wind or anything that came later. It was a mistake, of course. And for this error in judgment, this miscalculation, this failure to heed the warning signs, the consequences were irrevocable, absolute—and deadly.

THE WIND WAS a chilling winter wind out of Alaska that blew in fast and hard, turning a peaceful, early morning sail into a rough and rowdy dance across a seething mass of whitecaps. Within minutes, the wind-strafed waters of Elliott Bay had become a churning, boiling cauldron from the breakwater at Larstad's Marina to the Seattle waterfront two miles away. I was aboard *Second Wind*, a sturdy forty-foot sloop that had taken on far rougher waters in Puget Sound without a problem. Ordinarily I'd have reefed the sails and enjoyed the ride, but I was nursing a bum ankle from a nasty fall earlier in the day and didn't feel up to the challenge. Reluctantly I started the engine, dropped the sails, and headed back to the marina.

I'd just approached Larstad's mile-long breakwater when I spotted a boat in trouble. I couldn't tell if she was disabled and adrift or piloted by a raw beginner, but the result was the same—she had a problem and needed help. I've been around boats ever since I can remember—from tiny rowboats to racing sloops twice the size of *Second Wind*—but I couldn't handle a rescue by myself in these conditions without endangering my own craft. So I kept one eye on the boat, switched the VHF to Channel 78, and called the harbormaster.

"Larstad's Marina, Larstad's Marina. This is *Second Wind,* Whiskey-Bravo-Romeo, 4-5-5."

"Larstad's Marina. Go ahead, *Second Wind.*"

"Bert, I'm at the south end of the breakwater. There's a fair-size boat in trouble out here."

"What kind of trouble?"

"She's drifting toward the rocks."

"You see anyone signaling for help?"

"Not a soul. It's possible no one's aboard."

"OK, I'll get Danny to check it out. Thanks, Kellie."

"Better hurry. It doesn't look good." I signed off, confident that Bert got the picture—if the boat stayed on her present course, she was doomed. A boat hitting the massive rock wall of the breakwater would be like a parachutist hitting the ground without a chute. Even if the boat didn't immediately sink from the violent jolt of the crash, she'd be destroyed soon enough from the action of the waves grinding her against the 400 pound boulders.

I maneuvered *Second Wind* so that she was headed into the wind and waited for the rescue crew. Within minutes, Danny and another kid named Joe rounded the breakwater in the marina's small work skiff and headed directly for the troubled craft. I held *Second Wind* as steady as I could and watched their progress with a pair of binoculars, realizing as I did so that it wasn't the rescue I was drawn to, but the boat's almost certain demise. The insight made me feel sheepish, as if I were some bloodthirsty hockey fan hoping for a good fight. But I could live with sheepish. Hell, I could live with bloodthirsty.

Even with binoculars, the fancy gold lettering inscribed across the boat's stern was difficult to read. It took a moment, but when I finally figured out the name—*Merry Maiden*—I had to read it a couple more times before I was sure that I'd gotten it right. In the three years I'd lived aboard my sloop at Larstad's, this was the first time I'd seen the elegant, sixty-five-foot Hatteras outside the confines of the marina.

There didn't seem to be anyone aboard, but as soon as I readjusted the focus, I spotted someone slumped over the helm on the flybridge. Based on size alone, it could've been the yacht's owner, Donald Moyer. Then again, it could just as well've been his wife, Miranda, an attractive but rather portly woman. It was impossible to tell for sure who it was, particularly since the face was obscured by an oddly skewed hat. I could tell the person wasn't moving, though, and in light of the boat's predicament, he or she was most likely unconscious—or worse.

Another pass around the deck with the binoculars and I discovered a second person aboard. I'd missed the sighting on the first go-around because he or she was partially hidden by a dinghy dangling at a precarious angle from its davit. This person was sprawled facedown on the deck and was also unidentifiable.

When the skiff finally reached the yacht, Danny struggled to get close enough for Joe to throw a tow line. The wind had picked up, and the Hatteras was bobbing even more erratically than before. The wake from a passing Washington State Ferry didn't help matters. Every time Danny got close enough for Joe to throw a line around the cleat at the bow, *Merry Maiden* heaved in the opposite direction, and the tow line fell into the water.

Realizing at last that the bow cleat wasn't going to work, Danny spun the skiff around so fast that Joe was taken off guard. Only by grabbing the gunwale did he manage to save himself from falling overboard. Danny, meanwhile, had quickly maneuvered the skiff amidships where he should've been in the first place. This time Joe looped the line over a cleat without a problem.

As soon as he had their craft secured to the yacht, Joe scampered aboard and hauled the line to the forward cleat so Danny could tow the boat from the bow. It would be a slow trip back to the marina. Besides the wind and the rough water, the Hatteras must have outweighed the small work-boat by twenty tons or more.

The show over, I exchanged a thumbs-up with Danny and Joe and set my course once again for Larstad's, where—if the folks aboard *Merry Maiden* were as bad off as they appeared—all hell was about to break loose.

TWO

AS FAR AS marinas go, Larstad's wasn't the largest in the Seattle area, but it was unquestionably the ritziest. And, with mooring space at a hefty ten dollars per linear foot, it was the priciest. The facility's on-site amenities included a yacht brokerage, an upholstery and sail repair shop, a yachting apparel outlet, a sailing school, and two restaurants—the Topside Bar and Grill for casual dining and the elegant Pacific Broiler for more formal occasions.

In spite of the cost, folks were so eager for moorage at Larstad's that there was a three-year waiting list for a slip. It wasn't uncommon to reserve a spot on the list before you'd even bought a boat. Having not much money and even less patience, I came to moor my sloop at the marina via the old-fashioned route—I knew someone who had pull. Bert Foster, the harbormaster, was married to my older sister for more than twenty years. They divorced five years ago, and, much to Donna's displeasure, Bert and I have remained friends. He not only moved my name to the top of the waiting list—no small feat in itself—but also arranged a substantial discount for the slip due to a job he finagled for me at the sailing school.

Even with the cold and windy weather, there were more than a few hearty souls out and about when I got back to the marina. I knew it wouldn't be long before word of *Merry Maiden*'s rescue-in-progress had made the rounds. Sure enough, I'd no more secured *Second Wind* and headed up the mooring ramp than Bert came running out of his office with half the marina's staff and a number of inquiring-minds-want-to-know types hot on his heels.

Within seconds, the others had left him behind, hurrying off to A dock on their own. Bert was a big man and definitely not accustomed to running, which was understandable, considering he was carrying an extra hundred pounds on his six-foot frame, mostly around the belly. I'd seen him struggle to tie his shoes, so running would be nearly impossible. Despite that, he made it to the repair dock before I did. My ankle hurt like a son-of-a-gun, and a gimpy walk was about the best I could muster.

A substantial number of looky-loos had gathered along the dock to witness *Merry Maiden*'s impending arrival. Front and center was Todd L. Wilmington, a.k.a. the Weasel. He'd easily beaten Bert to the repair dock and was busy doing what he always did—trying to look important. The *L* in his name stood for Larstad. As in Larstad's Marina. As in owner's nephew. Meaning he was like an itch you couldn't get rid of.

A couple of fellows had come over from the fuel dock to help with the yacht's mooring lines when she arrived, but they'd made the unfortunate mistake of standing too close to the Weasel. The next thing they knew, they were on the receiving end of a lengthy lecture. Namely, how they should handle the tie-down—something they'd only been doing half their lives.

Meanwhile, Bert, whose normally ruddy complexion had turned a mottled shade of reddish purple, stood off to one side of the dock and tried to catch his breath. He doffed his official harbormaster's hat and wiped the sweat from his forehead with the back of his jacket sleeve.

"You call an ambulance?" I asked.

"Police," Bert gasped, still breathless.

"There are a couple stiffs aboard the yacht," added the Weasel, sidling up to us uninvited. He delivered this news in a thin, high-pitched voice, like an adolescent who never made it through puberty. Some people around here think that's not far off the mark. At thirty-five, he still had the long, lanky body and pimply face of a teenager. I stared at him blankly, momentarily overcome by an urge to send the guy to the principal's office.

When I didn't respond, he tossed out what he must've thought was a real zinger: "I caught Danny's radio call while Bert was in the john."

I pointedly ignored him, addressing Bert instead. "Did Danny say who they are?"

"Nope. Joe was too shook up after he found them. He just said they're a man and woman."

"And deader than doornails," the Weasel offered.

"Most likely the owners, Donald and Miranda Moyer," I said. "You know them, Bert?"

He shook his head. "Only by reputation. I met them officially when they signed up for a slip a few years back. I haven't had much contact with them since. Have you?"

The Weasel jumped in before I could answer. "I have," he said. As old man Larstad's nephew, Todd L. Wilmington was on the marina's payroll, but he had no job description or official duties to perform, which left him with plenty of time to butt into everybody else's business. When he wasn't busy doing just that, he was fawning over the marina's wealthiest clients. And the Moyers, with their seven-figure luxury yacht, were undisputedly wealthy. That Wilmington had had contact with them was about as surprising as a rainy day in Seattle.

"In fact," he said, warming to the subject, "Don and Miranda were very good friends of mine. Very good friends, indeed."

I tried. Honest to God, I tried. I even gave Bert's warning

look fair consideration. But the Weasel's thin-lipped, full-of-himself smile did me in. "Really, Todd," I said sweetly. "Did the Moyers know you were such good friends?"

Bert groaned.

The Weasel didn't get it. "Well, of course, they did." He held up two fingers tightly crossed. "We were like this."

I was all set to fire back another remark—one that he was damn sure to get—when a commotion at the other end of the dock distracted me. No doubt a career-saving moment. As Danny's work skiff with *Merry Maiden* in tow pulled alongside the dock, I joined Bert and the other fellows to lend a hand with the lines.

When we had the yacht safely secured, I asked Bert about going aboard. Ever since I'd first spotted *Merry Maiden* in trouble, I knew it would come down to this. Worse than any of the looky-loos lining the dock, I was determined to find out who was aboard and what had happened to them. Preferably sooner than later, before the police arrived and put all such notions permanently to rest.

Bert hesitated, looking around at the crowd that had by now grown even larger. He was a "by the book" type of guy, the kind who follows all the rules, written and unwritten—never tipping less than 15 percent, never drinking milk straight from the carton, never speeding up to make a yellow light, and, God love him, never coloring outside the lines. Judging by the size of the frown working its way across his brow, my request to go aboard the yacht had him rattled. After all, there were definite rules about such things. I expected a flat no, but he waffled instead. "Gee, Kellie, I don't know," he said.

"The police aren't going to like you going aboard," advised the Weasel. He'd faded into the background when the yacht came in, but now that we had the dock work finished, he was in our faces again.

"He's right," Bert agreed.

The Weasel flashed me a self-satisfied look.

"Oh, come on," I pleaded. "Let's both go see what's

up. You're the harbormaster. You have the authority."

Bert didn't say anything. I knew he was weighing the need to appear decisive and in charge against the possibility of making some kind of mistake. He'd been harbormaster for more than ten years, but, like a lot of jobs nowadays, it wasn't a secure thing. Old man Larstad was seriously considering selling out to Nakito Enterprises, a Japanese conglomerate that had been hankering after the marina for some time.

"And just what gives you the right to go aboard, Kellie?" asked Wilmington. The question was valid. I had no right at all. I was just the manager of the sailing school—a fledgling side business that was barely holding its own. If Nakito made any cuts when they took over, the school would be a likely candidate. Making a mistake wasn't exactly in my best interests either.

Sirens wailed in the distance. Decision time. "What's it going to be, Bert?" I asked.

He shrugged. "Well, I suppose it wouldn't hurt to take a quick look around. We don't know for sure if the bodies aboard really are the Moyers. I guess we should find out."

Merry Maiden was one of those fabulous luxury yachts that most folks can only dream about owning. Although I was prejudiced against "stink pots," as we sailors call motorized craft, there was no denying that the Hatteras was sixty-five feet of sheer yachting excellence. She had a dazzling array of electronics and navigational aids that would've made even the U.S. Coast Guard jealous. Modern, sleek, and fashionably European in overall appearance, this was one classy vessel. Based on her stunning exterior, I could only imagine how grand the main salon and other quarters were. I would've liked a tour, but there was no time for sightseeing.

While Bert climbed up the ladder to the flybridge, I checked out the body sprawled facedown on the deck of the cockpit. It didn't take an expert to determine that Joe's assessment was correct—the man was dead. The gaping hole in his temple and the attendant blood and gore left no room for doubt. In spite of the shocking mess, I still recognized Donald Moyer.

I didn't know much about guns, but it was obvious that whatever was used to kill him was powerful. Blood, brains, and skull fragments were splattered all across the deck and gunwale. Rust colored splotches and streaks covered his Helly Hansen rain gear like some kind of macabre fashion design.

I stood upwind of the body and took a couple of deep breaths, thankful that he hadn't been killed inside the cabin. Even with the brisk wind, the stench of death was suffocating. Time stopped as I crossed myself, and half-forgotten words from my youth tumbled from my lips: "Hail, Mary, full of grace . . . The Lord is with thee . . . Holy Mary, Mother of God, pray for us sinners now and at the hour of our death."

I once did a two-year stint as a volunteer paramedic with the King County Fire Department, so I've seen a lot of gruesome stuff—heads through windshields, severed limbs, bodies burned beyond recognition—but violent death still unnerves me. Especially when it involves someone I knew. Stifling the urge to upchuck my breakfast, I turned from Donald Moyer's body to take in the rest of the death scene.

The dinghy was suspended from the davit just as I'd seen it through the binoculars, the lower half still angled in its cradle. Judging by the remote control device alongside Moyer's right hand, it appeared that he'd been trying to release the small craft when he was interrupted by the bullet.

I was wondering how Bert was faring on the flybridge when he shouted for me to get myself up there. I wasn't sure if I'd be able to manage the ladder with my bad ankle, but curiosity is a powerful painkiller.

I hobbled onto the bridge just as the cops arrived at the dock. "Hey! You there!" The shout came from a uniformed patrolman with a standard-issue black mustache and a scowl the size of Texas. A couple of his brothers in blue, stiff and wooden-looking in their crisp uniforms, stood by his side. The Weasel promptly joined the group.

Bert's moaning diverted my attention from the dock. He could hardly stand upright, and his face, so red a few minutes ago, had turned chalky white. Since he appeared to be on the verge of passing out—or, God forbid, suffering a stroke—I quickly grabbed his arm. "Here, Bert, sit down before you fall down." I helped him ease his bulky frame onto a bench seat, which was remarkably untouched by the blood bath at the helm. At the same time, the officer who'd shouted at me uttered a few colorful adjectives and climbed aboard the yacht, leaving his compatriots, along with the ever-helpful Weasel, to stand guard on the dock.

By the looks of the body at the helm, it was easy to determine why Bert was in such difficulty. Like her husband, Miranda Moyer had been shot. The bullet's impact had blown her rain hat almost completely off, giving me a perfect, albeit unpleasant, view of her blood-matted blond hair and what was left of her head. She was slumped over the wheel, her arms casually draped against the console panel as if she had simply taken a moment from her piloting duties to rest. The console panel and windshield resembled a bloody Rorschach test with brain matter and pieces of what looked like teeth thrown in for added horror.

Bert leaned over the railing and retched. I searched through my jacket pockets for a handkerchief, but could only come up with a flimsy little tissue. It was better than nothing, so I handed it over. By then, the mustached cop had climbed onto the bridge.

"What the hell's going on here?" he demanded.

"He's sick."

"Look lady, don't get smart with me. Tell me something I don't already know."

The possibilities were mind-boggling. "Like what?"

"For starters, I want to know who you two are. Why you're on board. Why you're in the middle of a crime scene—a double homicide, by the looks of things. And I damn well better like your answers.''

Bert gave it a valiant try. ''I'm the harbor—'' he began. Then, grabbing for the railing, he bent over and heaved again.

''Jesus!'' muttered the cop. He held a gloved hand over his nose while barking orders to the men stationed on the dock. ''Foley! Gilbretti! Get up here on the double. I want this man off this goddamn boat *now*.''

As Foley and Gilbretti helped Bert down from the fly-bridge, the officer turned his attention back to me. ''Okay, lady. Start talking.''

I figured I had two choices here. I could play it straight and cooperate with the man. After all, he was just doing his job. And doing it damn well, if you consider the tough cop routine convincing. Or, I could give him some of the sass I usually reserve for the Weasel. I opted for cooperation. ''The man you just ordered off the boat is Bert Foster, the harbormaster. He's the one who called you.''

''And just who might you be?''

''She's Kellie Jean Montgomery.'' Homicide Detective Allen Kingston swung his long legs over the top rung of the bridge ladder and added, ''Also known as Larstad Marina's resident snoop.''

I do so love a compliment. ''Hello, Detective. Nice to see *you* again, too.'' Not that he was such a pretty sight. His raincoat—a dirty, frayed-at-the-cuffs, torn-pocket affair—and his equally scroungy suit and dress shoes didn't make him a likely candidate for Seattle PD's best-dressed detective. But Allen Kingston's impressive, twenty-year record with the department hadn't gone unnoticed. As long as he continued to produce results, the brass seemed willing to cut him some slack on the dress code issue.

I wouldn't say Kingston and I were old pals, but we did have a history of sorts. Despite his outstanding record, I've bailed him out of the fire on more than one occasion, the most recent being the eyewitness I located in a drowning case. The effort saved Kingston and his partner, Brian Saunders, from wasting valuable time chasing after the wrong suspect. I looked at it this way: He could call me snoop or any other old name he wanted, but sooner or later he would have to appreciate, if not welcome, my smarts and moxie.

"I'll take it from here, Benson," said Kingston. The officer paused just long enough to toss me another scowl before scurrying off.

"Where's Brian?" I asked.

"Giving me a reprieve."

"What's that supposed to mean?"

Brian was a bright young man, not long out of college, who hadn't exactly endeared himself to Kingston since becoming his partner.

"He got himself shot. Probably be out a month or more."

"My God, I didn't know. That's terrible!"

"Don't fret yourself. The kid's got a lock on the fast track. A little bullet's not going to stop him from making sergeant right on schedule." He looked over at Miranda's body. It wasn't difficult to guess what was coming next.

Kingston sighed and shook his head. "Kellie, Kellie, Kellie."

"Yes?"

"How many times do I have to tell you that you're not supposed to compromise a crime scene?"

"I haven't compromised anything."

"Is this a crime scene?" he asked, pointing at Miranda's body. Without waiting for a response, he carried on the conversation without me. "Yes, Detective, this is definitely a crime scene," he said, mimicking my voice. "And are you standing in the middle of the crime scene? Yes, Detective, I certainly am. Then the goddamn fucking crime scene is goddamn fucking compromised!"

"Are you quite finished, Detective?" I asked.

"No, but you are." He took my arm, presumably to escort me off the boat.

"Wait a minute," I said, twisting out of his grasp. "Don't you want to know who she is?"

"You know the victim?" he asked.

"I know both victims."

He sighed wearily. "Okay, Montgomery. I guess I'll have to talk to you."

"Hey. Most men would fight for the privilege."

He glanced at Miranda's body again and then down at the crowd gathered along the dock. "The only fighting that'll be going on around here is over who's gonna get the case." Besides the uniforms who were providing crowd control, representatives from the King County Sheriff's Office and the Port of Seattle Police had now arrived on the scene. Due to the unique location of the marina, jurisdictional boundaries between the various law enforcement agencies weren't very well defined. As a result, you could have as many as three or four different groups vying for the same case.

"I forgot. Men and dogs—they're so territorial," I said, immediately regretting the remark. Kingston looked tired. He often looked tired, but this was something different—a weariness that enveloped him like smoke, altering and softening him somehow.

"Listen, Kellie," he said after a moment, "I really would like to talk to you about the victims. How 'bout meeting me at the Topside in an hour?"

Touched by the almost tender way he'd spoken, I smiled and told him I'd be there. Then, feeling I had to reassure him, I said, "Don't worry, Kingston, I promise I won't interfere with your case this time."

"Damn straight, Montgomery. Now get out of here," he growled, shrugging off any lingering hints of tenderness. "I've got a crime scene to secure."

THREE

AFTER LEAVING ALLEN Kingston to his official duties, I decided to check on how Bert was doing. His office was on the top level of the three-story building that housed the marina's administration offices. Like the rest of the marina, the harbormaster's office was a grand event. With its profusion of oak and brass, Oriental carpeting, oil paintings, and leather furniture, it looked like the office of a CEO from some Fortune 500 company. Actually the office used to belong to old man Larstad, who let Bert take it over when he decided he'd rather spend his time on the golf course.

The Weasel's been bent out of shape over the arrangement ever since. He had a little cubbyhole down on the first floor behind the employee lounge, which he claimed didn't properly reflect his station in life. Everyone agreed. A broom closet would've suited him much better.

When I walked in, Bert was stretched out on a white leather couch with his eyes closed and a damp cloth draped across his forehead.

"How're ya doing, Bert?" I asked.

He removed the cloth and, struggling a bit, pulled himself upright. "Okay, I guess."

I found a comfy-looking chair and sat down, relieved to be off my feet for a while.

He noticed my limp and asked, "What's the matter with you?"

"Nothing to worry about."

Bert rubbed his temples. "Jeez, Kellie, I don't know how you do it."

"Do what?"

"Look at all that bloody gore without feedin' the fish."

"You forget, Bert, I've seen much worse."

"Huh?"

"Fifteen years teaching in Seattle public schools."

He let that groaner pass without comment and walked over to the floor-to-ceiling windows, where he had a bird's-eye view of the marina.

I slipped off my shoes and socks and rubbed my ankle a moment, then propped both feet atop Bert's desk.

Still peering out the window, he asked, "What's going on down there now?"

"Detective Kingston showed up after you left and started barking orders at everyone. Ran me off."

He took a deep breath and let it out slowly. "Has the medical examiner arrived yet?"

"I don't think so. They'd just started stretching that yellow police tape all over the place when I left."

"We could have a big problem over this thing, Kellie."

"What do you mean?"

"One of the Nakito guys called me a few minutes ago. He wanted to know about our security procedures. Apparently Wilmington told him 'it leaves a lot to be desired.' "

"Wilmington leaves a lot to be desired." Fearing that his own meal ticket might be in jeopardy if the Nakito deal went through, he'd ingratiated himself with the advance team sent to check out the marina by personally escorting them around as they examined the books, interviewed employees, and generally got in everybody's way.

"Maybe so," Bert said and sighed. He folded his arms

across his chest, as if trying to hold himself together. "But he's got them so spooked that they've asked for a briefing tomorrow morning. Besides the security info, they want me to give them some kind of damage control plan."

"Damage control?"

"You know, how to deal with adverse publicity. They think the murders might affect business at the marina."

"Listen, Bert, I'm really sorry. I shouldn't have made such a fuss about going aboard *Merry Maiden*. I didn't think things would turn out like this."

"Neither did I." He turned from the window. "Well, I suppose I ought to head back down there and try to act like a harbormaster," he said without enthusiasm. "At least while I still am one."

Aw, Bert. He hadn't been this down on himself since Donna chewed him up and spit him out. I didn't feel so great myself. My little stunt at the dock was just the sort of thing the Weasel lived for. Bert didn't deserve that. Catholic guilt. It was moving in faster than a cold front. "What can I do, Bert?"

"Short of solving the murders, you mean?"

"Hmm. That's not such a bad idea."

"Now, hold on, Kellie. I wasn't serious."

"Think about it. If I helped out with the investigation, this whole mess might be cleared up real soon."

"That's Allen Kingston's job, not yours."

"Don't sweat the details. The important thing is, the Nakito boys need to be reassured that we're on top of the situation. It could save both our jobs."

"Or put us out on the street."

"Face it, Bert. The way things have been going, we're practically there already. The Weasel hasn't exactly been giving Nakito Enterprises a flattering picture of us."

He sighed and glanced out the window again. "You're right about Wilmington." After a moment, he asked, "But what about your job? Do you really have time to get involved? For that matter, what makes you think you can solve this case?''

"Time I've got. There aren't any sailing classes scheduled until after the holidays.'' That wasn't exactly true, but I saw no need to confuse Bert with the facts. "As for solving the case, I do have a pretty good track record.''

"Suzie was family,'' he said simply. I knew what he was implying. I'd known his sixteen-year-old niece since she was a baby. Her death had hit me as hard as it had him. In Bert's view, her being family was the only reason I'd been so motivated to locate her killer.

"The Weasel never gave me a chance to answer your question about how I know the Moyers.''

"It doesn't matter. I checked the records. They weren't live-aboards like you, but their yacht has been moored across from your slip ever since you've been here. You and the Moyers were dock neighbors.''

"It was much more than that. Donald Moyer was the attorney who handled Cassie's adoption.''

"Good Lord, Kellie, that was almost twenty years ago. Are you saying that you've kept in touch with him ever since?''

"Well, no. Not more than a casual hello whenever we happen to run into each other, but I've always felt grateful for what he did for us. I owe him a lot—because of Cassie, I mean.''

We tossed the subject around for a few more minutes. Finally Bert agreed that it wouldn't hurt for me to see what I could find out about the Moyers. "Just be careful, Kellie,'' he warned. "Wilmington is already trying to turn these murders to his advantage.''

"I can handle the Weasel.''

"What about Detective Kingston?''

"That may take a little finessing.''

He laughed for the first time. "Good luck!'' He gave one last look out the window and then crossed the room. "The crowd's getting pretty big. Guess I better go.'' He stopped at the desk, where he picked up his hat and a clipboard. "You coming?" he asked.

"No. If you don't mind, I'd like to stay put. Rest my ankle here for a few more minutes."

"Sure, no problem," he said, heading for the door.

"Oh, Bert. Before you go, where do you keep those files for visitors?"

His face wrinkled up in a confused look.

"You know," I explained, "the ones where the boat owners list all the people they want the marina to let through the security gates."

"The Visitor Access List?"

"That's it."

He eyed me suspiciously. "What do you want that for?"

"Oh, just an idea I have. It's probably nothing, but I'd like to look at the list anyway."

He pointed to a five-drawer filing cabinet. "Help yourself. If you find anything useful, let me know. How we deal with visitor access is going to be a top item at tomorrow's briefing."

Whatever the state of marina security, Bert's filing system left, in the Weasel's words, "a lot to be desired." After spending thirty frustrating minutes rifling through all five cabinet drawers, I finally discovered the folder with the information I wanted. If I hurried, I'd be able to make it to the Topside just in time for my meeting with Detective Kingston.

FOUR

THE TOPSIDE BAR and Grill used to be a warehouse. It was purchased several years ago by old man Larstad, who hired a high-priced California designer to transform it into a trendy watering hole with a big mahogany bar, mirrors, brass ceiling fans, and an elaborate marine motif. But the place retained enough vestiges of its former roots to give it a casual, working-class atmosphere. The food and drinks were good, the service fast, and the price tag cheap—all factors that attracted customers not usually associated with Larstad Marina's upscale image.

Today's crowd was a mixed bag—marina "regulars" like myself, tourists who'd wandered in from several of the small shops along the waterfront, a sprinkling of blue-collar types fresh from a construction project nearby, and a sizable number of the looky-loos I'd seen earlier down at the dock. The noise level was something akin to the trading floor at the New York Stock Exchange.

I paused at the entry to get my bearings and scan the cavernous room for Detective Kingston. The air was heavy and warm with smoke and grease, beer and lively talk. It made me feel good, as if some need I had to dispel the horror surrounding the Moyer murders was fulfilled by the sensory overload.

The bartender ran a thin, damp rag over the counter, mopping up the residue of an overturned pitcher of beer. When he caught sight of me, he stopped and waved. "Hey, there, Mrs. M!" he shouted. Like most of the kids who worked at the marina, Austin Reynolds was a college student. Somewhere along the line, he'd dubbed me "Mrs. M." The other kids soon picked up on it, and, for better or worse, the nickname stuck. But lately, whenever I'd hear it, images of myself as a doddering old woman flashed through my mind. Bert claimed that was because I was so sensitive about turning the big 4-0 in a few days. Maybe so.

I bellied up to the bar and squeezed out a spot between a couple of well-heeled yachting types who weren't what you'd call Topside regulars. People with money to flash around usually hung out at the Pacific Broiler, where the beer costs twice as much and you have to pay extra for peanuts. I greeted Austin with the obvious. "Looks kinda busy today."

"Yep." He grinned. "Even the A-list showed up."

"Not that he's A-list material, but have you seen Detective Kingston?" Almost everyone at the marina knew the detective. When he wasn't working a case, he hung out at the Topside a lot. Kingston claimed it was because of the coffee, but I think the bevy of cute college girls waiting tables was a more likely draw. Rumor had it he was married once a long time ago. If so, I didn't know any of the particulars.

Austin shook his head.

Allen Kingston wasn't the type you'd have difficulty spotting. At six foot four, he stood out in any crowd, but it was much more than a height thing. Kingston was one imposing guy. In his mid-forties, he had the tight, well-honed body of a thirty-year-old. I'd heard he was part Native American, but it wasn't something that he talked about, and I wasn't sure if it was even true. His dark complexion could've just as easily been due to an Hispanic or Italian background. What you noticed first about him wasn't his skin tone anyway. It was his eyes. Dark and impenetrable, they were capable of making you confess to just about anything—not a bad attribute in his line of work.

A fellow at the end of the bar raised an empty beer mug in the air and signaled Austin impatiently. "Hey, kid, how 'bout some service down here!"

Austin tossed aside the counter rag and nodded. "Comin' right up!" He filled a beer mug from the tap and asked, "Is there something I can get for you while I'm at it, Mrs. M?"

I ordered a hot buttered rum and pushed my way through the throng to a corner booth, amazed that such a choice spot was still available. While waiting for my drink, I noticed for the first time just how much the diner had been spruced up for the holidays. Strands of red and green lights twinkled at the windows, and small candles ringed with holly lit up each table. In keeping with tradition, the staff had decorated a big Christmas tree with photos of the Topside's regulars.

Janey caught me looking at the tree when she brought my drink. "We haven't forgotten you," she said. A Polaroid camera hung from a strap about her neck. She set my drink down and aimed the camera. "Say cheese, Mrs. M."

"I can do better than that," I said. Showing more teeth than Carol Channing, I blurted out Grampy's favorite tongue twister: "Sexy sailors smell sumptuous." Try that after a round of drinks.

The camera whirred, buzzed, and spit out a hazy, soon-to-be color print. Janey removed the still-developing photo from the camera and set it on the table. "I'll be back in a moment to hang it on the tree."

I studied my image as it began to materialize and felt my mood darken. My husband would've gotten a kick out of posing with me. Wendell had never been one for hamming it up the way I'd done with Janey, but he was very sentimental. He'd have treasured the Topside photo and asked for a copy to keep. Even after three years, life without him by my side was difficult, especially at Christmas and other holidays.

In the aftermath of his death—coming so soon after Grampy's—I vowed never to love again, for to love was to risk more than I could bear to lose. It took a while, but I've finally come to realize that it is love that truly heals. Vows such as mine—to live without love—will wither the soul if not broken. Besides, it's damn lonely.

The photograph was a dud. I looked startled, as if I'd been caught by a hidden surveillance camera in the act of doing something unspeakable. My blue eyes were red from the flash and much larger than usual. The old felt beret I'd hurriedly put on earlier in the day sat atop my head like a soggy waffle. A look that did nothing to set off my expensive new hairdo—a short bob that the stylist had assured me would keep my naturally frizzy red hair under control. Waste of money. I shook my head and turned the photo over.

"Why so glum, Red? 'Fraid I stood you up?" Detective Kingston slid into the booth and shrugged out of his raincoat, which he wadded into a tight ball and then tossed onto the seat next to him. His suit jacket was a rumpled mess, which led me to believe he'd played ball with it a few times, too. He was good-looking enough with his thick black hair just starting to gray at the temples and his engaging, toothpaste-ad grin, but if clothes make the man, he was in serious trouble.

I took a sip of my drink, relieved that his mood seemed more upbeat than in our earlier encounter. I suddenly felt upbeat myself. When Kingston wasn't grousing at me about compromising a crime scene or something, he could be kind of fun to be around. I had to admit he had a certain appeal. Sort of like a mangy dog that follows you home. You don't want it, but you can't bear to get rid of it, either.

"What'll it be, Detective?" asked Janey, who'd returned as promised.

Kingston hesitated, eyeing my rum. "Coffee," he said

finally. "But none of that espresso crap. Just plain black coffee. And make it strong."

She turned to leave, but stopped midstride and whirled around. "Oh! I almost forgot." Pointing to the Polaroid print still lying facedown on the table, she asked, "How'd it turn out, Mrs. M?"

I groaned and rolled my eyes.

"It can't be all that bad!" She laughed, reaching for the print.

Kingston slapped his big hand over it first. He picked up the snapshot and held it at arm's length, studying my image like an art critic judging a fine oil painting. "Well, Janey," he said after a beat, "I don't want to tell you what to do, but you're gonna have a serious problem if you put this thing on the tree."

"How come?"

"All the needles are gonna fall smack dab onto the floor."

Janey giggled.

"Hey, I'm serious. You put Red's mugshot on that tree, and it's gonna be stripped bare as a baby's butt in a matter of seconds."

Did I say the man was fun to be around? I snatched the print from his hand. "Here, Janey. Take this away before the detective gets hurt."

"Aw, Red, I was only joking."

I tossed him a "spare me" look and said nothing.

He gave it another shot. "Besides, everyone knows you're a damn sight prettier than any old photo they got on that tree."

"Come on, Kingston, a simple apology is sufficient. You don't have to sugarcoat it."

He waved his hand dismissively. "Photo Christmas tree . . . lamest idea I ever heard of."

I eyed him over the rim of my mug.

"What?"

"I didn't say anything."

"Well, you've got something on your mind," he said. "And I don't think it's that damned photo. So go ahead, lay it on me."

"Okay, here's the deal. I want to poke around a bit and see what I can learn about the Moyer murders."

He gave me a strained look that pretty much said it all: I'd crossed the line—again.

Janey returned with his coffee, and I waited until he'd taken a couple of sips and declared it drinkable before I completely obliterated the line. "I've already found out something important. I'm willing to turn it over to you right now. I'll do the same with anything else I come across."

"This is supposed to make me happy?"

"You have to admit I have good instincts about things."

He took a noisy slurp of coffee. "I have to admit squat."

"What about the Suzie Hoffman case?"

"What about it? You got lucky and stumbled across an eyewitness. Big deal. We'd have eventually located her ourselves. A murder investigation isn't for amateurs, Montgomery, and it's sure as hell not like what you see on TV. Poking around—following your instincts, as you call it—can get you hurt. Not to mention the damage you can do to the real investigation."

"I'm fully aware of the risks. And I promise I won't do anything to compromise your investigation."

"You're real good at making promises. An hour ago you promised that you weren't going to butt in to this case at all."

"Things have changed."

"What things?"

"We don't need to get into all that right now. I thought the purpose of this conversation was for me to tell you what I know about the victims."

"Then let's hear it." He leaned back in the booth and loosened his tie, an ugly blue polka-dotted thing that made the rest of his outfit look almost classy. "I'm all ears," he said.

"If what I say is useful, you'll agree to let me pursue things on my own?"

He sighed. "Don't push it, Montgomery. Let's just hear what you have to say. Then we'll see about what I will or will not agree to."

I figured that was the best I was going to get from him. "All right. To start with, the victims aboard *Merry Maiden* are Donald and Miranda Moyer."

He shot me an exasperated look. "You're going to have to do better than that. They both had plenty of ID on 'em, so we know all the vitals—height on the shorter side, weight on the higher side, age in the mid-fifties, and an address in the most exclusive area of town."

"Do you know that Donald Moyer was a lawyer?"

"Get outta here."

"It's true."

"Well," he said, throwing his hands into the air, "talk about job security—I'll be interrogating suspects 'til the day I retire."

"It could've been much worse, you know."

"They don't tell lawyer jokes for nothing."

"But Moyer could've been a tax lawyer."

That got a laugh out of him. "What was his gig, then?"

"He specialized in family law. Adoptions, domestic issues, things like that. In fact, Wendell and I hired him when we adopted Cassie. His office is in the Columbia Center downtown."

"Along with about a jillion others. Do you know there're more lawyers in that building alone than all the lawyers in Japan?"

"I don't know about that, but I do know that Moyer had a partner. His name is R. James Preston."

Kingston took out a pad and pencil from his suit jacket and scribbled some notes. "What's the *R* stand for?"

"I don't know."

"R. James Preston. F. Lee Bailey. What is it with lawyers

and initials anyway? Are you sure Moyer didn't have a *P*
or a *Q* tacked on in front?"

"Far as I know, he was just plain Donald Moyer."

Kingston shook his head. "Amazing. Well, what about
Preston? You know him, too?"

"Never met him. I just know about him because his name
is on the marina's records as being a co-owner of *Merry
Maiden.*"

Janey stopped by the booth long enough to refill Kingston's coffee cup. He downed a big gulp and grimaced.
"Now *that's* coffee," he said. "OK, what else have you
got?"

I pulled my jacket off the hook where I'd hung it earlier
and reached inside the pocket. "Here," I said, unfolding a
computer printout onto the table. "Take a look at this."

Kingston quickly scanned the printout. "What am I looking at?"

"It's the Visitor Access List for *Merry Maiden.* It gives
you the names of everyone whom the Moyers authorized
the marina to let through the security gates."

"How'd you come by it?"

"The harbormaster's office."

Kingston shook his head. "I just don't get it, Red."

"Don't get what?"

"Why you're at it again. Fiddling around at the crime
scene, rummaging through Bert's records—God only knows
what else you've been up to in the last hour. I thought you
ran a sailing school. Business all that slow?"

"I told you I had good instincts about things."

"That's not the point," he said, tossing the printout aside.

"It's precisely the point." I jabbed my finger at the page.
"It's quite possible that the name of whoever killed the
Moyers is right here in front of you."

Kingston heaved an exaggerated sigh and examined the
printout again. "Hmm," he said, running his finger down
the page. "It's a long list. They must have done a lot of
entertaining."

"*Merry Maiden* was one of those party boats, the kind that corporate executives own to impress important clients."

"You were a client of Moyer's. Were you impressed?"

"He didn't have the boat twenty years ago. When we adopted Cassie, Moyer was just starting out. I was impressed by his ability, not his possessions."

"Looks like he's done all right for himself since then. *Merry Maiden* ain't no working man's boat."

"It's not a boating man's boat, either."

"What do you mean?"

"This was the first time I've ever seen the yacht outside her slip. There was always a party going on, but it was always a dockside party. As far as I know, the Moyers never took *Merry Maiden* out for a cruise."

"What do you make of that?"

"Not much. It isn't unusual to use a yacht like that strictly for entertaining. I know a couple who own a much smaller boat, and they never go boating, either. They just spend their weekends on it. Like a floating cabin or something."

"So what happened? Why'd the Moyers suddenly decide to go boating?"

"Beats me. Maybe they had a compelling reason—like whoever killed them forced the issue. When I first noticed that she was gone from her slip, I just assumed they'd moved the party elsewhere for a change."

"When was this?" he asked, picking up his pencil again. "It's important."

"For establishing time of death parameters?"

Kingston nodded. "The medical examiner can only give us a range. We need to consider other factors as well. Like when the victims were last seen."

"I didn't see them leave, but the boat was gone from her slip by eight-thirty this morning."

"How're you so sure of the time?"

"I'd just checked my wristwatch. I was going sailing and wanted to get an early start. Anyway, when I stepped onto the dock to untie the mooring lines, I noticed that *Merry*

Maiden wasn't in her slip. I was so distracted that I slipped on some ice and wound up on my rear with a twisted ankle.''

"Ouch," he said, shaking his head. "You were that surprised to see the boat gone?"

"Well, yeah. Like I said, I'd never seen her out of the slip before. A winter cruise dodging heavy winds can be a challenge the first time out. But then, maneuvering a sailboat on rough waters isn't exactly like cruising with twin screws and every automatic convenience that money can buy."

"All the fancy equipment didn't do them much good."

"I'd have to say so. Now, what do you say about letting me check out things on my own?"

Kingston refolded the printout and tucked it inside his suit jacket. "Well, Red, I say this: If you have to snoop, then snoop with discretion. If I find that you're compromising the investigation in any way, any way at all, then you're through. Do you understand what I'm saying?"

I nodded vigorously, like a good little girl. I thought about giving him a salute, too, but didn't want to risk pissing him off. If things ran true to form, though, I'd wind up doing just that sooner or later.

FIVE

I STAYED AT the Topside after Allen Kingston left and had an early dinner of barbecued salmon kabobs, lentil salad, and another hot buttered rum. As I ate, I thought about the Moyers and what they could've done to make someone want to kill them. I examined a copy of the same computer print-out that I'd given Kingston, as if the names listed there might somehow contain the answer. That I didn't recognize any of the names wasn't so surprising—we hardly traveled in the same social circles. Still, there was something about the lengthy list that bothered me. I pushed the skewered salmon around on my plate, appetite taking second priority to the puzzle in front of me.

I was still perusing the printout when Janey stopped by the booth to ask if I'd like some dessert. The Kahlúa cream cheesecake was tempting, but I passed. I'd already had enough guilt for one day. Prodding Bert to go aboard *Merry Maiden* had been a dumb thing to do. His getting sick was one thing. Putting his job on the line because of my curiosity was something else again. I did penance for whatever guilt still lingered by leaving a generous tip for Janey.

It was raining lightly when I left the Topside, but within

just a matter of minutes even the ducks were scurrying for cover. As soon as I was aboard *Second Wind,* I turned on the cabin's electric space heater and stripped off my wet clothes and hat. When I'd gotten myself all warm and comfy in a long flannel nightgown, robe, and slippers, I brewed a cup of tea.

Space on a sailboat is naturally limited, so, out of necessity, most things serve a dual purpose. Even at forty feet, *Second Wind* was no exception. The dining table doubled as my office and a handy catch-all for books and a host of odds and ends. I took one look at the table—piled even higher and deeper than usual—and groaned. A stack of folders I'd bought a week ago during a fit of organizational frenzy lay in a heap, still in their original packaging; so, too, did the Christmas cards I'd yet to address and mail, the latest Sue Grafton mystery I'd yet to read, and some bills I'd yet to pay. Lots of bills I'd yet to pay.

It took a moment to clear away the mess, but eventually I had a clean spot about the right size for a notepad. I sipped the now-cooled tea and thought about the questions rattling around in my head. I jotted them down just as they came to me:

1. Who had a motive for killing the Moyers?

2. Was the killer(s) invited aboard or did he/she/they force their way onto *Merry Maiden*?

3. How did he/she/they get on and off the yacht without being seen—or were they seen?

4. What is bothering me about the Visitor Access List?

5. Why am I getting myself into this mess?

Of all the questions on the list, number five gnawed at me the most. I felt bad that the Moyers had been murdered and I'd meant it when I told Bert that I owed Donald Moyer a debt of gratitude for bringing Cassie into my life. But the most pressing reason for getting involved had nothing to do with the Moyers. Murder or anything else that reflected badly on the day-to-day operation of the marina couldn't be ignored, especially in light of the precarious situation Bert and I were in with Nakito Enterprises. If I didn't do something, it was a sure bet that the Weasel would. And I was certain that whatever he did wouldn't be good for either Bert or me. Bottom line: Police matter or not, Kingston's approval or not, I was involved. It was a lot like how I felt about sailing—it was just something that I had to do. And it felt right.

As I pondered the cosmic significance of all this, the telephone rang. At least I thought it was the phone. The cordless had a muted, faraway sound to its ring. But nothing's very far away in the cabin of a sailboat, so I figured I'd buried the dang thing in my rush to find a suitable writing spot. I rummaged through an assortment of pillows, books, newspapers, and whatnot until the ringing got louder and louder.

"Hello?"

"Hi, Mom."

Since she hardly ever called, Cassie's voice took me by surprise. Pleased, but surprised nevertheless. "Hi, yourself," I said, recovering quickly. I waited a beat, thinking she'd say something further. When she didn't, I asked, "Uh, how're you doing, hon?"

"I'm fine."

"Are you sure?" It was a dumb question. One of those mother questions that no kid appreciates hearing, but you can't help asking anyway.

Cassie responded true to form. "I *said* I'm fine." Then, as if to make up for how irritated she'd come across, she added, "How're you doing?"

"I hurt my ankle a bit this morning, but I'm okay."

"Hmm." She paused a moment, and I thought she was about to say something more, but the line was silent.

"When are you coming home for Christmas break?" I

asked. Cassie attended college at Rensselear Polytechnic in Troy, New York—which was just about as far away from me as she could get.

"That's what I'm calling about. I want to give you the flight info."

Oh. So that was all. I don't know whether I felt relieved or a bit irritated myself. Probably both. I grabbed the notepad I'd been scribbling on and took down the particulars as she gave them to me. Afterward, I asked, "What've you been up to—besides studying for finals?"

"Not much. What've you been up to?"

A regular chatterbox, this child of mine. I tried to be more forthcoming—a role model of sorts—and told her about spotting *Merry Maiden* adrift. "When she was finally rescued and towed ashore, we found the Moyers aboard. Murdered."

"My God." She was quiet a moment, as if considering how this news might affect her. It didn't take long. "Mom, you're not going to act like Jessica Fletcher again, are you? It's so embarrassing." Cassie had about as much use for my sleuthing as Allen Kingston.

"I don't know why you insist on comparing me to that TV character. We're nothing alike."

"Ha! You're like her in every way possible—you're both widows, you're both busybodies, you're both—"

"Enough, already. You've made your point. And just for the record, I'm younger than Jessica Fletcher. A lot younger!"

"Whatever . . . Mom, will you do me a favor?"

"Of course."

"Don't get so caught up in solving the murders that you forget to pick me up at the airport."

"Oh, please. What kind of mother do you think I am?"

"I wouldn't touch that one with the proverbial ten-foot pole."

The implication stung, even in jest, and I didn't laugh. Perhaps sensing my discomfort, she quickly changed the subject. "Mom, I have something important to talk to you about when I get home."

"What is it?" I asked.

"Not now. When I get home, okay?"

It wasn't okay. I knew I'd toss and turn all night wondering what was up, but I didn't press further. After we said our good-byes, I poured myself another cup of tea and went over our conversation, carefully analyzing each word we'd spoken. Something I now find myself doing on those increasingly few occasions that we talk with one another. I keep thinking I'll figure out a way to mend the rift that's developed between us.

Cassie was a challenge from the start, an angry baby who only seemed content when Wendell held her. The father-daughter bond developed early and grew stronger as the years passed. Cassie was only sixteen when he died, and, as some kids do when their parents divorce, she blamed me for not having her father anymore. No matter how hard I've tried to right things between us, our relationship has been strained ever since.

I was only eighteen when I married Wendell, but we knew we'd never have children. The previous summer I'd had emergency surgery that, while life-saving, had ended any hopes of motherhood. We'd accepted our fate as much as you can accept something like that, and then, two years into our marriage, Cassandra was born. At the time, Donna was working as a receptionist for an obstetrician who'd delivered a baby girl to an unwed mother. When the mother said she'd be unable to keep her child, Donna told her about us. And just like that, Wendell and I were parents.

The last three years on my own had been difficult enough without Cassie's resentment and distancing tactics. That she actually wanted to talk to me about something important was a hopeful sign. Nevertheless, I stewed about the possibilities for a while. Was she flunking out of college? Was she sick? Pregnant? Breaking up with her boyfriend, Tyler?

And then it hit me. Tyler and Cassie. Cassie and Tyler.

Couples. Yes! That was it. That's what had been bothering
me all afternoon. I grabbed the computer printout and took
another look at the Moyers' Visitor Access List.

> Bill and Theresa Adams
> Corbin and Betsy Ames
> Stan and Diana Atwood
> Robert and Susan Bates
> David and Laura Beeson

Couples. From A to Z, each of the three columns of
names on the page were couples, most likely married couples. Didn't the Moyers know any unattached males or fe-
males? You would've thought such party people would've
invited a few single folks once in a while—for no other
reason than to liven things up a bit.

I turned to the list of questions I'd jotted down earlier
and scratched out number four, *What is bothering me about
the Moyers' Visitor Access List?* In its place I scribbled, *Why
only couples?*

SIX

MOST PEOPLE THINK living aboard a sailboat is carefree and romantic. But three years into the live-aboard lifestyle has more or less ruined any romantic notions I might have had. Don't get me wrong. I like my floating home. It's just that I'm a lot more realistic about what's involved than I was in the beginning.

Trading my house for a boat didn't make the responsibilities of home ownership suddenly disappear. They were just different, that's all. And not necessarily any simpler. Instead of mowing the lawn, I have to empty the sewage holding tank each week. Instead of throwing a load of laundry in the washer on my way out the door, I have to trek back and forth to the Laundromat. Instead of an instant source of running water, I have to refill the tanks once a week. The instead-ofs are lengthier than most people realize.

This morning was sewage pump-out day. I'd just motored *Second Wind* back to K dock when I heard a commotion at the next dock over. A man—I judged him to be about thirty or so—fiddled with the combination lock on one of the large dock boxes near *Merry Maiden*'s former slip. By the sound of things, he wasn't having much luck. With each unsuccessful effort to open the lock, he exploded with profanity that, while not terribly original, was certainly attention-grabbing.

When he started hammering at the lid with his fist, I decided to go see what was up. The slip was located directly astern of *Second Wind* on J dock, which meant I had to walk halfway around K dock to get there. By that time, he'd stopped his attack on the storage unit long enough to light a cigarette. He sat atop the dock box, his legs casually draped over the side. I figured he was maybe five foot seven at the most, considering how his spiffy suede shoes didn't reach all the way to the dock. He wore pleated, cream-colored gabardine slacks, a similarly colored turtleneck, and a brown leather jacket. Besides a Rolex, he sported several gold chains and a diamond as big as the Kingdome on his pinkie ring. Everything about his attire said money. Everything about his face said stay away.

I stared at him with the most direct, authoritative look I could muster. "Who are you?" I demanded.

"Who wants to know?" he countered.

"The harbormaster's office." I never hesitate to throw around what power I have, usurped or not.

He didn't say anything, but his expression was something akin to, "Wow, I'm impressed." He took a couple of puffs on his cigarette and flicked the butt into the water. So much for the direct, authoritative approach.

Continuing to ignore me, he scooted off the dock box and rummaged through a bulky sports bag. When he pulled out a crowbar, I stepped back a couple of feet in keeping with my policy to avoid surly men with crowbars whenever possible. As he pried at the lid of the dock box, I had a fleeting thought about stepping back even further. Until I was out of there altogether. But my curiosity got the best of me, and I stuck around.

Once he got the lid pried open, he began to swear again. I don't know what he expected the box to contain, but it obviously wasn't the boat-cleaning supplies he found.

Within seconds he'd yanked out a hose, a plastic five-gallon bucket, a few old rags, a couple of scrub brushes, soap, rubbing compound, and boat wax. He pitched them one by one onto the dock. Some of the smaller items missed the dock altogether and sailed directly into the water.

I couldn't take it anymore. "Looking for anything in particular?" I asked. As before, he ignored me and continued rummaging through the box, discarding each item he found until the growing heap on the dock looked like a yard sale gone awry. I tried a different tactic. "That's private property, you know."

He slammed the lid shut and spun around. "No shit, Sherlock."

I checked to see where the crowbar was, then continued. "I don't think the owners would like you rifling through their things."

"For your information, Miss Harbormaster's Office, this property is mine."

"How so?"

"If you must know, I'm Donald Moyer, Jr." He paused briefly to let that information sink in. And then, as if the thought had just occurred to him, he said, "But I guess it's *senior*, now."

Oops. Now that he mentioned it, I could see something of a family resemblance. He had his mother's sandy blond hair and rather stout build, but his ears stuck out more like Clark Gable's than the formerly senior Moyer's. He was younger than his father, of course, but he had the same receding hairline and the same crooked nose. His eyes were blue like Miranda's, but he had such dark shadows under them that his pudgy, unshaven face seemed almost gaunt. The sports bag notwithstanding, I doubted he worked out much. He had the soft, unmuscled look of a man unaccustomed to labor of any sort.

I knew the Moyers had a couple of kids—a son and a daughter. I'd never met them, but I had seen the son. He was about eight or nine years old at the time and he'd accompanied his father to court the day our adoption of Cassie was finalized. I remembered how he seemed to idolize his father, following him around the courthouse like a junior associate, watching his father's every move, hanging on his every word. I couldn't picture whether the man in front of me was the grown-up version of that little boy, but I was willing to concede the fact. So I backpedaled a bit and told him how sorry I was about his parents' untimely deaths. He brushed my condolences aside with a casual "shit happens" and lit another cigarette.

"Do you know of anyone who might want to harm your parents?" I asked.

"The police asked the same thing. What's it to you?"

"Since your parents were murdered aboard their yacht, the harbormaster's office is cooperating with the investigation. I'm assisting Detective Allen Kingston." It was the truth. Sort of.

"Then I'll tell you the same thing I told him," he said, pointing his cigarette for emphasis. "Everybody fucking loved my parents. Fucking loved them."

I came at the question another way. "Are you sure your father didn't have any disgruntled clients?"

"Shit, lady. Are you deaf or what? I said he was loved by everybody. And that includes his clients. *Especially* his fucking clients."

"Especially his clients?"

"Yeah. The old man was the fucking answer to their fucking prayers."

"What do you mean?"

"Christ, you're worse than the police. It was the adoptions. You know, parenthood shit." He took a final drag on his cigarette and, as before, tossed it into the water. "Time to stop playing copper wannabe, lady. I've got a question for you. Are there any other storage units at the marina?"

"Storage units?"

"Jesus. Are you brain impaired, too? You know, lockers,

tubs, boxes, anything that my folks might have kept stuff in.''

''Not that I know of.''

''Great. Just fucking great.'' He fumed, kicking the side of the box. He had a few more comments to make, but the point had been made—he was not having a nice day. His interest and anger seemingly spent, he turned from the dock box and walked away.

''Wait,'' I called after him. ''When's your parents' funeral?''

He merely shrugged and kept on walking.

I headed for the harbormaster's office. My intention was to track Bert Foster down and tell him about what had happened, but I was saved the trouble. Just as I got to the administration building, he came barreling out the double doors like a beach ball on a mission. ''Hey, Bert,'' I called, ''where're you off to in such a hurry?''

''Rocky Point Beach.'' Rocky Point was a somewhat isolated area, located half a mile from Larstad's Marina. Technically speaking, the beach was not within Bert's jurisdiction as harbormaster, but it was so close to the marina that Bert had long considered the goings-on there his responsibility. That mostly amounted to nothing more than periodically running off groups of teenagers whose partying had gotten out of hand. I fell into step alongside him. ''What's up?'' I asked.

''They've found *Merry Maiden*'s shore boat.''

''But the dinghy was aboard the yacht when she came in. It was still on the davit.''

''That was the Achilles inflatable. The craft at Rocky Point is a fiberglass jet boat.''

''You mean *Merry Maiden* had two shore boats?'' I asked. I couldn't believe I'd missed the second davit when we were aboard.

''I thought you knew. There were two davits aboard the yacht, one for each shore boat,'' Bert explained. ''*Merry*

Maiden was a custom boat. Moyer wanted two davits, and that's what he got.''

I pictured the yacht when she came in, her inflatable still dangling from the davit and Donald Moyer's body and remote control lying beneath it. "Whoever killed the Moyers, then, must have used the second davit to launch the jet boat."

"And abandoned it at Rocky Point."

At the parking lot, Bert unlocked his Jeep Cherokee and hoisted himself inside. I sprinted around to the passenger's side, pleased to note that my ankle offered no protest. "Hold on, Kellie," Bert said as I climbed in. "Where do you think you're going?"

"With you, of course," I said. "I've got something to tell you that can't wait. And I need to talk to Kingston, too." Although he'd agreed yesterday that it might be helpful to our cause if I looked into the murders, Bert still had his reservations about my involvement. Especially in front of the police. The fact that his morning briefing with Nakito Enterprises hadn't gone well only made matters worse. "Kingston is at the beach, isn't he?" I asked.

"Yeah." He sighed. "He's there."

En route, I told him about my encounter with the young Donald Moyer. Bert used the car phone to contact a dock attendant, instructing him to inspect and clean up the area. When he hung up he asked, "What do you think Moyer was looking for?"

"Beats me," I said. "But one thing's for sure."

"What's that?"

"He hadn't been down to his parents' boat slip for a while."

"How do you know?"

"Because the dock box he pried open wasn't theirs. It was the Talbots'."

"You're kidding."

"Nope. You know how all the marina's dock boxes look alike? Apparently he either didn't know or failed to notice that the Moyers' box is number twenty-two, the same as their slip. The box he pried open is number twenty-three, which corresponds to the Talbots' slip twenty-three. Of course, there is another explanation for the mistake.''

"What's that?"

"He wasn't Donald Moyer, Jr."

I CHEWED ON the possibility that I'd been duped by an imposter while Bert and I watched a three-person forensic team examine the jet boat. We stood at a discreet distance, impressed with the way they went about their business. The Weasel was also at the scene. Why did this not surprise me? He carried a clipboard and appeared to be taking copious notes, looking more official than the officials. He inched his way closer to the boat until he was directly alongside, chatting up the technicians as they snapped their photos and dusted for prints. Kingston was on him like dirt on a five-year-old. He bellowed at the Weasel to back off. To make sure he did, he showed him exactly where he could park himself. It was vintage Kingston and a terrific show.

I'd replayed the entire scene with "Moyer, Jr." half a dozen times before Kingston finally wandered over our way. He nodded. "How're ya doing, Red? Bert?"

Whether it was his run-in with the Weasel or something else, he was in remarkably good humor. I seized the opportunity to tell him about my encounter with the man I thought was Moyer. When I got to the part about the wrong dock box, Kingston burst out laughing. "That's Junior all right. That stupid SOB couldn't find his dick if . . ." He caught himself and paused a beat.

I stifled the urge to grin at Kingston's newfound concern for my sensibilities.

"Well, let's just say," he continued, "that sounds like the guy I know. What was your impression of him?"

"What's this? You're actually asking for my opinion?"

"Don't let it go to your head."

"First of all, the Moyer I met definitely had a limited vocabulary, adjective-wise."

"Ha! We're tracking so far. Go on."

I described his physical appearance and how he looked somewhat like his parents—close enough, anyway, to satisfy me. Then I added, "The main thing is, despite his tough-guy routine, I thought the man was truly hurting."

"Now you've lost me, Red. Moyer hurting? No way. More likely he's scared."

"Scared?"

"As of right now, Junior is our number one suspect in the murder of his parents."

"Why?" I asked, glancing at the jet boat. "What did you find?"

"For starters, the guy's a loser. But since that doesn't count for anything in a court of law, we have to go on evidence. And we've got plenty of it."

"What are you talking about? What evidence?" I asked.

Kingston smiled and proceeded to make his case against Moyer. "Number one," he said, holding up his right index finger, "Moyer stood to inherit quite a bundle with his parents' death. Like an estate that's worth, conservatively speaking, well over ten million dollars."

"So? Lots of kids have rich parents. That doesn't make them killers."

"Right, but in Junior's case, he was about to be disinherited. He's turning thirty next month. His parents have been carrying the guy financially for years, hoping that he'd eventually get his act together and make something of himself. For years Junior has disappointed them. Hell, he's been kicked out of more exclusive schools than I knew existed. As far as work is concerned, he's never been able to hold a job for more than a few weeks at a time. Not a good habit to get into if you have his expensive tastes. Anyway, his folks had had enough. They told him that come his thirtieth birthday, he was off the familial payroll, so to speak. On top of that, they threatened to add a codicil to their wills, preventing him from collecting any inheritance from them at all. That is, unless he got a decent job and proved to their satisfaction that he'd changed his ways for the better. He knew they'd do it, too."

"Why's that?"

"Because they'd already done it once before—to his older sister. Kicked the little princess out of the castle without a penny when she failed drug rehab one too many times. Junior wasn't about to let that happen to him."

"Okay, I'll concede he had motive. What else have you got?"

"Number two," said Kingston, holding up his second finger. "The M.E. figures the Moyers were killed sometime between seven and eleven A.M. yesterday, December fifteenth. Junior has no alibi for that time period."

"Let me guess what's coming next," I said. "You found his fingerprints all over *Merry Maiden*."

"Bingo!" He pointed to the jet boat. "And my hunch is that the latents they're busy lifting over there will be Junior's also."

"That doesn't prove anything. *Merry Maiden* belonged to his family. He's probably been on it, as well as the jet boat, lots of times. His fingerprints could've been left there months before the Moyers were killed."

"True, but we also know that they were killed with a large bore firearm—probably forty-five caliber—and wouldn't you know, Junior just happens to own a Colt .45. And guess what?"

"It's missing," I answered.

"You got it."

"But, Kingston," I protested, "everything you've just told me is circumstantial evidence at best."

"I can live with circumstantial. It's even better than an eyewitness sometimes."

"Surely you're not going to arrest the guy?"

"Well, not yet," he admitted, "but it won't be long."

He was smiling broadly now, clearly pleased with the turn of events.

Bert was ecstatic. "Our problems are over, Kellie!"

I nodded and for once refrained from voicing how I really felt.

SEVEN

THREE DAYS LATER. Donald Moyer, Jr., was still a free man. I awoke well before dawn on the morning of his parents' funeral to the sound of sleety rain pelting the deck of the *Second Wind*'s cockpit. Since the cockpit was directly over my sleeping quarters, the noise was worse than a hundred halyards clanging against the masthead. But it was the noise inside my head that kept me awake—disjointed thoughts about the Moyers' murders, their funeral, their soon-to-be-arrested son, and Cassie's arrival at SeaTac airport later in the day. The sudden realization that Christmas was just days away (and the fact that I hadn't done a whit of shopping) didn't help matters. Still, I tried to go back to sleep. An hour later, I was still trying. At six o'clock, I finally conceded defeat and struggled out of bed.

After I showered and got ready for the day, I had a cup of tea and a bagel for breakfast and mulled over the possibilities behind Junior's non-arrest. The fact that he wasn't sitting in the King County Jail suggested that the case against him wasn't as airtight as Detective Kingston would've had me believe. The more I thought about what Kingston had said about his background, the more convinced I became that Donald Moyer, Jr., was one troubled guy.

I'd seen kids like him when I taught at Horace Mann High. Kids who had everything Daddy's money could buy—designer clothes, a Porsche when they turned sixteen, even a nose or boob job. And if the kids got into any kind of trouble, Mom and Dad were right there to bail them out. As a result, the kids never learned to assume responsibility for their actions, nor did they know anything about the responsibility that comes with earning what you want.

Donald Moyer, Jr., had probably been spoiled from the get-go. No wonder he didn't know how to take care of himself as an adult. Much as I'd hate to have someone second-guessing my parenting efforts, I couldn't help but think that Junior's parents had failed him big time. Whether that failure is what got them killed remained to be seen.

I pushed aside my breakfast things, flipped through my case notes, and figured out a plan of attack for the day. I've never been one for detailed planning, preferring instead just to go with the flow, but I had a full day on tap and needed to get myself organized for a change. The first item I put on my "to do" list was an appointment with Donald Moyer's law partner, R. James Preston. Figuring it wouldn't hurt to see what he had to say about his partner's death, I'd finagled an appointment under the pretext of being from the harbormaster's office. His secretary bought the story that I needed to talk to him about his yacht and scheduled me to see him at nine o'clock.

From the extensive write-up about the murders in the *Seattle Times*, I'd learned that Donald and Miranda's funeral was to be held at St. Charles Episcopal Church in Woodinville. Since the Bellevue Square Mall wasn't too far from there, I figured I could squeeze in an hour or so of Christmas shopping and still make it to the funeral by one o'clock. Then it was on to SeaTac in plenty of time to pick up Cassie at three.

So that was my plan. An excellent plan—even if it wasn't

jotted down in one of those fancy scheduling books. I should've known that it wasn't going to work.

FINDING A PARKING spot in downtown Seattle under normal circumstances is difficult, but at Christmastime it's nearly impossible. I drove around for several blocks, dodging early-morning shoppers, distracted drivers, and traffic lights timed to hinder progress as much as possible before finally giving up and springing for an underground garage. Even then, finding a garage that still had space available took another fifteen minutes. I pulled my Miata into a space marked for motorcycles and called it good 'nuff.

The two-block trek to Preston's office wasn't bad. My ankle didn't bother me a bit, which I took as a good sign since I was wearing a pair of low-heeled pumps instead of my usual deck shoes. I'd gone all out with this morning's wardrobe. Besides the pumps, I wore a camel-hair coat and my favorite dress, an all-purpose black shirtwaist with a large gold belt. Of course, I only owned two dresses, so my choice was naturally limited. I'd downsized my wardrobe out of necessity when I moved aboard *Second Wind*, which suited me just fine since I prefer mostly jeans and sweatshirts anyway. And since I'd limited my wardrobe to the bare minimum, I didn't have to store anything in the trunk of my car like some live-aboards do.

Preston's office was on the forty-second floor of the Columbia Center, an imposing all-glass monolith in the heart of Seattle's business district. At seventy-six stories and twice the height of the Space Needle, the Center is the tallest building west of the Mississippi River, and, judging by the number of power suits hustling about the lobby with their briefcases and cell phones at the ready, it's also the busiest.

The fashionably thin receptionist behind the counter at the Moyer and Preston Law Office was perched on an ergonomically correct chair, pecking at her computer keyboard like a hungry bird. I gave her a moment to reach a stopping-off point, cleared my throat, and said, "Excuse me. I'm Kellie Montgomery and I have a nine o'clock appointment with Mr. Preston."

The woman kept on typing with a dogged single-mindedness, never glancing up from her keyboard or giving even the slightest indication that she'd heard me. I gave it one more try. "Hello? I'm Kellie Montgomery . . ." No response. Not even a flicker from her perfectly arched, perfectly painted-on eyebrows.

I plunked my shoulder bag on the counter. "And I have a bomb in here."

That got her attention.

"Just kidding."

She was not amused. For a moment I thought she was going to call security, but she directed me to a seat in the adjacent waiting area. "I'll let Mr. Preston's secretary know you're here," she said with as much warmth as a Mafia hit man.

Forty-five minutes later, I was still waiting. Finding the reading material and all other sources of diversion exhausted—not to mention my self-control—I stood up and stretched. I glanced over at the receptionist, who was still typing her heart out, and entertained thoughts of wrestling the woman to the floor. Or whatever else it took to see Mr. R. James Preston.

"Kellie? Kellie Montgomery?" A petite, dark-haired woman, dressed in a smart gray suit and carrying a leather Day-Timer, stood at the entryway.

"Yolanda?" She looked somewhat like Yolanda Rodriguez, a teacher's aide who'd worked for me at Horace Mann. But this woman was about thirty pounds lighter with a short, gender-neutral bob instead of the long hair Yolanda favored. She had none of Yolanda's jangly costume jewelry, either. Just conservative, small gold hoops at her ears and a round pin that secured a rose-colored designer scarf at her neckline.

She rushed into the room and hugged me. "I can't believe

this! When Debbie said there was a Ms. Montgomery here to see Mr. Preston, I had no idea I'd find you out here. Gosh, what's it been? Ten years?''

"About that," I said with a smile. "It's good to see you again, Yolanda. Do you work for Preston?''

"I'm a paralegal for the firm. Technically I work for both partners, but mostly I handle Mr. Moyer's cases." She hesitated. "Handled, I should say."

"You're a paralegal now? That's great, Yolanda!''

She shrugged. "It's not exactly what I had in mind when I went back to school. I'd originally planned to become a lawyer. Even got admitted to the University of Washington Law School."

"What happened?" When I knew Yolanda she was the single parent of a four-year-old boy, struggling to keep body and soul together. I was amazed that she'd been able to go to school at all.

"Oh, the usual. I got married," she said with a tight smile. "My name's Yolanda Vanasek now. I met my husband, Richard, in law school. He's an attorney with Dutton, Hoffstedder, and Grimm, right here in the building." She seemed about to say more but tossed the ball into my court without elaborating further. "And what about you? Still teaching?''

I gave her the same spiel I gave to everyone I hadn't seen in a while—a sixty-second update that glossed over the low spots like Wendell's death and highlighted the positive. Some days this was easier to do than others. The fact that I could so quickly summarize ten years of my life left me feeling a little funky. I mustered a passable smile and checked my watch. "I hate to cut this short, but I had a nine o'clock appointment with James Preston. Do you know if he's in?''

"Oh, Kellie, I'm so sorry. That's what I meant to tell you when I came out here. He had to leave, but I'm not sure why. He's not due in court or anything, but . . ." She glanced at the receptionist and lowered her voice. "Things around here haven't been the same since Mr. Moyer's death. He was murdered, you know.'' She seemed on the verge of tears.

"Yes, I know.'' I briefly explained my connection to the Moyers and that I was planning to attend their funeral later in the day.

"Then I'll see you there,'' Yolanda said. "The whole office is going.''

"Listen, Yolanda, do you have a few minutes for coffee? I'd like to talk to you about something.''

She opened her Day-Timer and checked her schedule. "I'm free right now but I've got a meeting at ten-thirty. I wish I could get out of the meeting, but—''

"That's fine. What I want to talk about shouldn't take long.''

The Columbia Center has three atrium levels with assorted retail shops and fast food outlets available at each one. We rode the elevator to the first atrium and joined a long line of caffeine-starved folks in front of Starbucks. Yolanda ordered a latté—something called a double tall vanilla skinny while I stuck with my usual tea.

I waited until we'd found a table and got settled before easing into the point of our meeting. "Yolanda, I couldn't help noticing your reaction when you told me about Donald Moyer.'' The tears she'd held in check earlier spilled freely onto her cheeks. I handed her a tissue from my bag.

"He was a wonderful man,'' she said, dabbing at her eyes. "His wife, too. I just can't believe they're both dead.''

"You knew his clients. Do you think any of them had reason to kill him?'' Allen Kingston might be convinced of Junior's guilt, but I wasn't quite ready to abandon other possibilities.

"No! There's just no way. Everyone was so happy and grateful for what he did for them—arranging adoptions, helping them become parents and all.''

"I just wondered if there might've been a client who

wasn't entirely happy. Perhaps an adoption that didn't go through as planned or something."

"No, there was nothing like that."

"What about his kids? I understand they have some problems."

She rolled her eyes. "Losers, both of them."

"How did they get along with their parents?"

"It's so sad," she said, shaking her head. "Donald and Miranda loved those kids. They would've done anything for them—and they did, too. But it wasn't enough. Terri and Junior were never satisfied, always demanding more, more, more. And what did Donald and Miranda get in return? Nothing but a lot of grief."

"Maybe it went beyond grief."

"Wait a minute. You're not suggesting that Terri and Junior might've had something to do with their parents' murders, are you?" she asked.

I shrugged. "Just exploring possibilities."

She sipped on her latté as she considered the idea. "Terri's been out of touch with reality for years—self-induced, I might add. Thanks to drugs and booze. From what I've seen of her, she isn't capable of harming anyone other than herself. Besides, she's been locked up in some rehab place for the last six months. And Junior's too lazy. All he cares about is spending money—his parents' or whoever else's he can get his hands on. Both of them are totally messed up. But could they have committed murder? No, I don't think so."

"Can you think of *anyone* who could have?"

"No, but . . ." She paused and looked around the coffee shop.

"But what, Yolanda?" I prompted.

She leaned over the table, her voice barely audible. "There was some trouble with Mr. Preston."

"Preston? What kind of trouble?" I asked.

"I'm not sure if I should say. It's probably nothing, anyway."

"If that's true, then what can it hurt?"

She hesitated, but I got the impression she wanted to tell me. I decided to make it a little easier for her. "If it'll help you any, I'll keep anything you say confidential."

"I hate to spread rumors."

"Hey, are you forgetting Rumors-R-Us?" Horace Mann had a principal who thought his true calling was to see just how miserable he could make his staff. The only way we all survived was to keep each other informed about his comings and goings.

"Well, actually, this isn't a rumor," she said. "Mr. Moyer practically carried the partnership himself. Mr. Preston doesn't come in half the time, and when he does, he doesn't get anything done. He's always wandering off without telling anyone where he's going. Just like he did today."

"Do you have any idea why?"

"I know exactly why. Mr. Preston is a hard drinker, a very hard drinker."

"Did Moyer know about Preston's drinking problem?"

"Oh, definitely. Mr. Moyer tried to get him help, and when that didn't work, he threatened to break up the partnership."

"How?"

"I suppose by buying him out. Mr. Moyer had plenty of money to do it, too."

"Why didn't he?"

"I'm not sure. All I know is that they had a terrible argument just a few days before the Moyers were killed."

"What kind of an argument?" I asked.

"It was mostly one-sided. By Mr. Preston, I mean. I'd stayed late to do some research in the law library and I didn't think anyone else was still around. Then I heard Mr. Preston shouting. It sounded as if he was right outside the library, but he was actually down the hall in Mr. Moyer's office."

"What was he shouting?"

"Nothing that made much sense. He accused Mr. Moyer

of ruining people's lives, crazy stuff like that.''

"Ruining lives? That's a rather curious view of the adoption process.''

"Like I said, he wasn't making much sense.''

"Then what happened?" I asked.

"I heard a door slam. After that, everything was quiet again.'' She started to take a sip of her latté but set it back on the table. "Gosh, Kellie, you don't think this has anything to do with the Moyers' deaths, do you?''

"I don't know. Have the police questioned you?''

"That's the meeting I have at ten-thirty. A homicide detective—Allen Kingston, I think his name is—wants to talk to me. Do you think I should tell him about this?''

"By all means, Yolanda. Tell Detective Kingston everything.''

We chatted a few minutes longer before saying our goodbyes and promising to stay in touch. We both knew, of course, that we wouldn't. Too much time had elapsed since we'd worked together, time that had brought too many changes to each of our lives. In Yolanda's case, a new hairdo, a new wardrobe, a new career, and a new husband. Those were the obvious changes, but there was something else about her that had changed, too. It nagged at me all the way back to the parking garage, but after I'd recovered from shelling out the seven-dollar ransom for my car, I'd forgotten all about it.

EIGHT

TWO FLOATING BRIDGES connect Seattle with what is commonly referred to as "The Eastside," a patchwork of smaller cities and towns that stretch from Lake Washington eastward into the foothills of the Cascades. Thanks to the success of Microsoft and the influx of similar high-tech industries hoping to emulate Bill Gates's magic, the area has experienced an explosive growth rate. Inevitably, that has brought more people, more housing developments, more strip malls, more traffic, more everything. But especially more traffic.

I took my chances with SR-520 rather than the newer I-90 bridge and, as usual, I chose wrong. I got stuck in traffic twice due to a construction project and by the time I finally got to Bellevue Square, I just had time to grab a quick bite before heading to Woodinville for the Moyers' funeral. Christmas shopping was out of the question.

I decided I could make better time if I stayed off the freeway and took Highway 202 to Woodinville. The winding road passed through land that, while in transition, still had enough rural flavor to make you believe it just might escape the ravages of urban sprawl after all. Traffic was light, and, as I expected, I made good time.

Then came the snow. Seattleites are experts when it comes to driving in the rain, but let Mother Nature throw a little snow at us and we fall apart. The traffic suddenly got nasty, and I found myself behind a long line of cars creeping over the snow-dusted highway like a gigantic inchworm.

By the time I finally made it to the church, the parking lot was full. I finally wound up on a side street, squeezing the Miata into a tiny spot between an obscenely big Cadillac and an equally monstrous Lincoln Continental. I doubted the roadster was legally parked, but I figured no one would notice with those bookends.

The service had already begun when I slipped into a pew at the back of the chapel. I felt strangely out of place, as if I'd popped into the middle of a foreign film. Although I call myself a Catholic, I'm really a religious hybrid. Dad was the Catholic in the family, while Mom was a Salt Lake City Mormon and direct descendant of Brigham Young himself. Even without their religious differences, my parents were a volatile combination. The only thing they ever agreed on was making babies. Mom was carrying number seven when a semi jack-knifed and slid into their car, killing her and Dad instantly. I was thirteen at the time and mad at the world in general. After the accident, God bore the brunt of my rage and I've followed my own brand of spirituality ever since. For the most part, that simply involves being on the water. I feel far closer to God sailing *Second Wind* than I've ever felt sitting in a hard-backed pew.

I'd almost forgotten how beautiful some churches can be. St. Charles was large and cathedral-like with high, arched ceilings, stained-glass windows, and an intricately patterned terrazzo entry. Donald and Miranda Moyer's twin white oak caskets sat side by side at the front of the chapel near the altar. A funeral bouquet of red and white roses adorned the top of each casket, while two large, multicolored floral displays stood like sentries on both sides.

The air was hot and heavy with the scent of candles, flowers, and too many people. I had a hard time keeping my eyelids from drooping and would've drifted off completely if it hadn't been for the fussy baby in the arms of the woman next to me. I smiled sympathetically at the embarrassed mother, recalling the many times Cassie had caused me similar discomfort in public.

A lot of folks had come to remember the Moyers, almost filling the spacious chapel to capacity. The law offices of Moyer and Preston took up an entire pew. By contrast, the front pews reserved for family members were practically empty. Donald Moyer, Jr., wasn't seated there, nor could I see him anywhere else in the chapel. I didn't know what his sister, Terri, looked like, but as far as I could tell, an elderly couple and a handful of others were all that represented the Moyer clan.

A thin, silver-haired man on the downward side of sixty came in late and paused briefly at the chapel entry. Impeccably dressed in a classic, charcoal-gray suit, he had a distinguished air about him. So, too, did the striking young woman at his side. She wore a tailored black silk suit accented with a single strand of pearls and a broad-brimmed black hat. The couple took a seat in the pew occupied by the law office staff. James Preston perhaps? If so, he didn't so much as nod in the direction of Yolanda and the others.

For a funeral, this was a glamorous gathering—furs, jewels, and designer everything. The notable exception was a slender woman standing all alone at the back of the chapel. Her outfit was what Cassie would call "trashy Victorian": lots of black lace, velvet, and leather. She wore a floor-length black velvet skirt, a long-sleeved white blouse with enormous ruffles at the cuffs and neck, and a tight-fitting leather bodice tied at the sides. Her face and most of her hair and shoulders were hidden by a black lace mantilla and veil. I waited to see who she'd sit with, but when an usher offered to escort her, she just shook her head and remained standing.

There were many children present, from tiny babies like the one at my left to teenagers looking bored and uncomfortable. And across the chapel, in the very last pew, sat Detective Kingston scanning the crowd like a human radar antenna.

As soon as the white-robed minister began the eulogy, the baby at my left began to cry in earnest. The mother tossed me an apologetic look. Nestling her child in her arms, she stood up and hurried out of the chapel. I waited a moment then slipped out after her.

I found her pacing back and forth in the carpeted foyer, gently rocking the infant in her arms. She appeared to be in her late thirties with the worn, frazzled look of a new mother in over her head. Her efforts to comfort her child had succeeded only in escalating the crying to an all-out wail.

"I know something that might work," I said, approaching the woman.

"Please! I've tried just about everything." She thrust her daughter into my arms with a huge sigh of relief.

I carried the baby to a nearby bench and sat down. "I used to do this with my daughter all the time," I said, crossing my right leg over my left thigh and forming a little pocket with the folds of my dress. I placed the baby inside the makeshift cradle and gently rocked my legs back and forth. Her little scrunched-up face was red and splotchy from crying, and her eyes were tight slits above a button nose. I cooed at her, "It's all right. It's all right now, little one. Hush, hush . . ."

Maybe it was just another's voice and nothing more that calmed the child, but whatever the reason, her crying stopped. I continued to hold her, cuddling and loving her as if she were mine. Soon she was asleep with a contented, relaxed look on her delicate face. I smiled at her mother. "I guess I haven't lost the touch."

"How many children do you have?" she asked, joining me on the bench.

"Just one, but she's nineteen now and in college." I lifted

the sleeping child from my lap and carefully handed her to her mother. "Enjoy this little doll while you can. They grow up way too fast."

"That's what everyone says, but Phil and I treasure every moment. We tried to have a baby for years and years. Took a million tests and spent just about the same amount of money, but I still couldn't get pregnant. Finally we decided on adoption." She looked down at her daughter. "You just can't imagine what having her in our lives means to us after all these years."

"I think I can. My daughter was adopted, too." We talked for a few minutes about the wonder of adoption and how the experience had changed our lives. "By the way, my name's Kellie Montgomery."

"Glad to meet you, Kellie. I'm Sara Zimmerman, and this little angel is Anita."

I recognized the Zimmerman name from *Merry Maiden*'s Visitor Access List. I'd looked at the computer printout so many times that I almost had it memorized. "Did Donald Moyer handle Anita's adoption?"

She nodded. "And just about half the kids in there," she said, glancing at the chapel. "We're all friends."

"Who?"

"The adoptive parents. All of us who had the legal arrangements handled by Don Moyer. He used to have these terrific parties aboard his yacht, *Merry Maiden*. That's where we first got acquainted with each other."

"Those parties on Moyer's yacht—were all the partygoers clients of his?"

"Now that you mention it, I guess we were. We were all hoping to adopt a child and the Moyers were helping us. But later on, after we had our babies, quite a few of us got together on our own and started our own adoptive parent support group."

When Wendell and I adopted Cassie, there weren't any groups like that. Other than our family's support, we were pretty much on our own. Nowadays you can find a support group for just about anything. "Tell me something, Sara. From all that I've heard, it sounds like everybody really loved Donald Moyer. Were there any parents in your group who didn't feel so loving toward him?"

"What do you mean?" she asked, frowning.

"Were there any adoptions he arranged that didn't turn out as wonderfully as little Anita's here?"

She hesitated a moment. "I can't think of any. Why do you ask?"

I briefly explained my connection to the Moyers' murder investigation and asked for her cooperation. She didn't think that she knew anything, but agreed to answer whatever questions I had. "The least I can do for the Moyers," she said.

I started with a question that had been on my mind for a while. "I suppose adopting a child these days is pretty expensive?"

"Oh, my heavens, yes. There were the legal fees, of course, which were just out of sight. Then we paid the birth mother's expenses, too."

"What kind of expenses?"

"Medical, temporary housing and transportation during her pregnancy, things like that. We also paid for her to go back to school."

"That was generous of you."

"The woman had made us so happy, giving us a new life and all. We felt it was only right that we helped her get back on her feet and start over."

"How 'bout Moyer's other clients? The ones in your support group. Did they feel the same way?"

She smiled. "To be perfectly candid, most of us in the group can well afford to help our children's birth mothers. There was one couple, though . . ."

"Yes?"

"I don't want to say they were poor or anything, but I do know they had quite a hard time just covering Don's fees, let alone anything else. The wife was real nice, but sort of embarrassed by their situation, especially her husband's attitude."

"What about his attitude?"

"A real pill. Always grousing about the cost of the adoption, as if that were more important than the joy of getting a child."

"How're they doing now?"

"I don't know. They left the group shortly after Phil and I joined, so I have no idea what happened to them."

"Do you remember their names?"

"Hers was Betty. Betty and Robert, or Raymond, something like that. I can't remember exactly, but their last name is Chapman."

"Do you know where they live?"

"Across the Sound. In Bremerton or Silverdale somewhere. I think the husband works for the Navy over there."

"He's in the military?"

"No, he just works for the military—in the naval shipyards. I think he's a pipefitter or maybe a shipfitter. One of those anyway."

We both looked up as the chapel doors swung open, and the minister, followed by twelve men accompanying the Moyers' caskets, led the procession of mourners into the hallway. I dug into my handbag and retrieved a business card for Sound Sailing. I scribbled my home phone number on the back of the card and handed it to Sara Zimmerman.

"It was nice talking to you, Sara. If you think of anything else that might help with the investigation, please call me. I live at the marina, so I can usually be reached there, either at the sailing school or on my boat. If you call me at home, be sure to let it ring for a while. A long while."

"Why's that?"

"I lose the phone a lot." I grinned. "Maybe I'd better put my boat slip number on the card, too."

She handed me the card and said, "I hope they find whoever did this terrible thing real soon."

"That's my hope, too, Sara." As I stood to leave, the

contingent from the Moyer and Preston law offices filed out of the chapel. I gestured to the silver-haired gentleman and young woman I'd seen earlier. "You know them?"

She nodded. "James Preston and his wife."

I had a hunch the guy was Preston, but I'd assumed the woman with him was his daughter. She couldn't be much older than thirty. "His wife?"

Sara smiled at my obvious surprise. "A May–December romance."

"What can you tell me about them?"

"Not much, actually. I've only seen him once or twice at the law firm. He was Don's partner. His wife's name is Nancy, and they have two little boys. That's about it."

"They never attended your parties with the Moyers?"

She shook her head. "Never. I'm sure I'd remember if they had." As the couple walked past us, she added, "They're kind of hard to miss."

"What about the Moyers' son and daughter? Have you ever met them?"

"No, I haven't. I'm sorry."

"That's okay. I appreciate your help." I patted Anita's head and smiled. "She's a real beauty. Thanks for letting me play mom."

Sara stayed behind to change Anita's diaper while I followed the crush of people heading downstairs to the reception hall. I spotted Yolanda standing off to one side of the crowded room chatting with a strikingly handsome man in a dark brown suit. When I caught up with them, she introduced her companion as her husband, Richard Vanasek.

He had the tanned, fit look of an outdoorsman rather than the pasty-faced corporate attorney I had imagined when Yolanda first told me about him. He pulled at his collar with a grimace. Yes, Richard Vanasek was an REI or Eddie Bauer man. Probably wishing he were wearing hiking clothes right now. "I understand you and Yolanda work in the same building," I said as I shook hands with him.

He glanced at his wife and smiled. Yolanda didn't return

the gesture. "That's right," he said. "But we hardly see each other these days."

"Oh, Rich, stop it," Yolanda snapped. An awkward moment passed before she shrugged and said, "It's just difficult right now."

He put his arm around her shoulders. "I know, I know. I'm sorry."

Yolanda wriggled out of his embrace. "Rich, I'd like to talk to Kellie for a few minutes. Why don't you go get us some refreshments?" After he left she said, "God, he's so impossible!" Tears began to well up in her eyes, and she dabbed at them with a handkerchief from her purse. "He just doesn't understand what I'm going through." She took out a compact and checked her makeup. "Nobody does."

"I'd like to try."

She shot me an apologetic look. "I must seem like a horrible wreck."

She seemed worse than that, but I kept the observation to myself and offered a benign comment. "Death and funerals tend to affect people that way."

"Yeah." She sighed. "The office is a mess. And thanks to James Preston, everything is on my shoulders now."

"I see he's here today with his wife."

"The golddigger, you mean." She caught my raised eyebrows and added, "Don't let that refined air fool you. Fancy Nancy acts like she was born with a silver spoon in her mouth, but her background is very sketchy. I don't think she knew what a social register was until she married Mr. Preston."

"Sounds as though you don't like her very much."

"Or trust her."

"Oh?"

"Now that Mr. Moyer is gone, she's—"

"Here we go, sweetheart." Richard Vanasek had returned, juggling two cups of punch and some cookies. I took one of the cups and a cookie while Yolanda declined the refreshments with a dismissive wave. I wanted to hear more about Nancy Preston, but Yolanda had essentially clammed up, leaving me to make small talk with Richard. I stuck around long enough to finish the punch and cookie and then excused myself.

Across the room, Detective Kingston had James Preston cornered. The conversation looked serious. I kept one eye on them and wandered over to the refreshment table where I indulged myself with a second helping of punch and cookies.

"Hickey Freeman."

I hadn't seen him approach, but the Weasel's high-pitched voice was unmistakable. He stood next to me, punch glass in hand, pinkie extended.

"Definitely a Hickey Freeman," he said again. "Hand tailored, soft shoulders, center vent in the jacket, pleated trousers with cuff. It's gotta be a thousand, minimum."

"Huh?"

He gestured toward Preston and Kingston. "I hope your detective is taking pointers from the man."

"*My* detective?"

"Style. That's what it's all about. Of course, your detective would never be able to afford a Hickey Freeman on his salary. But then, almost anything would be an improvement over that old raincoat and rumpled suit he always wears." He shook his head. "Good Lord."

I grabbed another cookie and took a big bite.

"Anyway," he said, focusing his attention on me. "It's fortunate I found you. I need your plans for the marina's booth on my desk ASAP."

I stared at him blankly. What plans? What booth? The Weasel would be out of his depth in a puddle, but I was the one struggling to keep up this time. "Todd, so help me, I haven't understood a single thing you've said since you first started talking. So, if you'll excuse me, I have to be somewhere else. Anywhere else." I turned to leave.

He laid a bony hand on my arm. "You know, Kellie, it is just that kind of attitude that alarms Mr. Kano."

I shrugged out of his reach. "Who?"

"Mr. Hiroshi Kano. From Nakito Enterprises. He's the advance team's head man. I thought you knew that."

"I haven't exactly been palling around with the team, Todd."

"Larstad's booth at the Kingdome Boat Show next month is a valuable publicity vehicle. I have gone out of my way to reassure Mr. Kano that the Moyers' murders were an anomaly. And, in spite of the marina's serious security problems, I have convinced him that, with my direction, we'll be able to take care of things. Bert is working on it as we speak. I should think you would want to do your part as well. Handling the boat show booth would prove to Mr. Kano that you care about Larstad's future."

Damn. He had me and he knew it. "You'll have the plans." I sighed. "But it'll take me a few days to put something together."

"Just don't dilly-dally," he cautioned. "Mr. Kano likes promptness."

I scooped up a handful of cookies. "And my detective likes cookies. Gotta go."

Kingston had finished his little talk with Preston and was still standing in the middle of the room when I caught up with him. I shoved the cookies into his hands.

"What's this?" he asked.

"I see you've been working the crowd. I figured you'd need nourishment."

"Thanks." He tossed one into his mouth. "But if I know you, Red, you've been doing the same thing."

I wanted to give him a snappy comeback, but I couldn't think of anything. The Weasel had drained me dry. "I don't see Junior here. Did you finally arrest the guy?"

"Nope."

"How come? Doesn't the D.A. think as much of your case as you do?"

"It's kind of hard to arrest a dead body."

"Junior's dead?"

"Yep."

"Oh, my God. How'd it happen?"

"The maid found him at the Moyers' estate early this morning. Looks like he was killed by the same person who did his folks."

"Why do you say that?"

"The initial report indicates that the bullet's caliber was the same as the weapon used to kill Donald and Miranda."

"Hmm. Guess that brings you back to square one. What about his prints?"

"What about them?"

"Were they on *Merry Maiden*'s shore boat at Rocky Point like you thought?"

"Nope."

"Did you find *any* prints on the boat?"

"Yep."

"Donald and Miranda's?"

"Nope."

"Well, if they aren't the Moyers', then whose prints are they?"

"Don't know."

"Aren't they readable?"

"They're readable."

"So you've got prints of someone who's never been arrested, worked for the government, or anything else that requires fingerprints. In other words, there's no record of the prints on file."

Kingston nodded but said nothing.

I tried a different approach. "I saw you talking to James Preston earlier."

"Yep."

"I heard that he had quite an argument with Moyer right before he was killed."

"Yep."

"Well?"

He merely shrugged. My irritation with him was exceeded only by my curiosity. "Come on, Detective," I prodded, "you must have an impression of the guy. What do you think?"

"I think you're one nosy woman."

I hated it when he got like this. He'd tagged the wrong suspect and, too embarrassed to admit his error, he patronized me with "yeps" and "nopes" and flippant remarks. I popped another cookie in my mouth and hustled out of the reception hall before I said something I'd regret. Keeping my mouth shut was fast becoming a habit.

When I came upstairs to the church foyer, I spotted the "Victorian" woman again. She was sitting on the same bench where I'd met Sara and baby Anita. I decided to play a hunch and join her. She took no note of me as I sat down. "Excuse me," I said, "I'm Kellie Montgomery."

"What do you think is the ultimate intimacy?" she asked, ignoring my outstretched hand.

Her face was partially obscured by the mantilla and veil, but what I could see was as curious as the question she'd asked. She wore heavy white foundation like a clown, and her lips—full and sensual and pierced with two small silver rings—were outlined in black. A pair of matching black lines extended from the outer corner of her eyes, across her temples to the hairline, then down each cheek, ending in a cluster of tiny tears.

"I mean, don't you think it's blood?" she asked.

"Blood?"

"You know, giving blood to someone you love. That's real intimacy. It's like, I'm not just giving you my fluids, I'm giving you my life."

"I guess you could look at it that way, Terri."

"But then, it's not something we're supposed to talk about. It's not even an idea that's promoted or anything. Drinking blood is strictly against the rules. I mean, it's sort of a cross-over thing between . . ." She let the sentence trail off and suddenly turned to face me. "How do you know my name?" she asked.

I shrugged. "Just a guess." From what Yolanda had said

about the Moyers' troubled daughter, it wasn't much of a stretch. "I'm very sorry about your parents and brother."

She pulled back her veil. "Why?"

"Because I knew them and death can be difficult on those left behind."

She nodded.

"How are you doing?" I asked.

A single tear slowly rolled down her left cheek and joined the painted-on cluster. "You just have to remember that everyone is either a source of blood or a threat," she said. "I mean, who would you trust? And how much? Try walking around like that for a day and then you'd know exactly how I'm doing."

As strange as her rhetoric sounded, it struck a familiar chord. "How long have you been a Goth, Terri?"

Her mood shifted, and she gave me a tentative smile. "About six weeks is all, ever since I went to the Catwalk. You know the scene?"

The Catwalk was a nightclub. And the scene, as she referred to it, was Gothicism. A few of Cassie's friends from high school had been Gothics, members of a subculture that encompasses a style of dress, music, and role playing that takes its inspiration from the macabre world of vampires, fallen angels, witches, and other creatures of the night. When Cassie started wearing the black clothes they favor and hanging out at the Vogue and other clubs the members frequent, I became concerned enough to investigate what she was getting into. What I found was a movement that's been around at least fifteen years. It has its own symbols, fashions, and a brand of role-playing where aggression and eroticism are pervading themes.

At one end of the spectrum were people who couldn't care less about vampires but dressed up in Gothic black to show that they're unique; at the other were those who claimed that they really were vampires and possibly even drank blood. From the way she talked, it seemed as though Terri might belong to the second group. Or, like Cassie, she was merely saying whatever she thought would shock me the most.

"My daughter was associated with some Goths a couple of years ago," I explained. "Before she went to college."

The revelation seemed to intrigue her. "Really? Is she still into it?"

I shook my head. "I don't think so."

"Well, probably not. I'm actually rather old for it myself—I turned thirty-three a couple of months ago. But I love being a Goth—it's fun, it's different, and very erotic. I'll never give it up." The foyer had begun to fill with people as we talked, and Terri looked around nervously. "Just think," she whispered. "The person who killed my family could be in this very room."

"That's what I was hoping to talk to you about." I explained my interest in the case and gave her one of my business cards. "Do you have any idea why your family was murdered?"

She tugged on the mantilla. "Why should I? We weren't close, you know. Mama and Daddy wrote me off as a lost cause years ago. And Donny always acted as if his big sister never even existed. "

"I understand."

"Do you?" she asked, clearly skeptical.

"My daughter and I've had our share of problems, too."

She took that in and then said, "What about her father?"

"He's dead."

"How does she feel about that?"

"It's been hard on her."

Terri shrugged. "He was probably a good father."

"I believe he was. And your father? Was he good to you?"

"That's something I'd prefer not to talk about, if you don't mind."

"Of course." I pointed to the card she still held in her hand. "But if you ever change your mind, I'm a good listener."

She looked down at the card. "You own a sailing school?"

"I don't own it, just manage it."

"But you give lessons?"

"That's right."

"Cool." She tucked the card inside a black beaded purse. "Does it cost a lot? I mean, do you have to be rich to learn how to sail?"

I laughed and said, "If money was a requirement, I'd never have learned. No, our rates are very competitive." Then a thought occurred to me. "Are you interested in sailing, Terri?"

She considered the question a moment. "Sure. I mean, maybe . . . if I can get out of Coleman on a pass or something like I did today."

"Coleman?"

"Coleman Rehab Center. I'm just about through with the program." She grinned. "Looks like it's gonna take this time. I've been clean and sober for six weeks now."

"Congratulations," I said. "I'd be happy to have you as a student, Terri. In fact, I have just the class for you. It's an all-woman group. I don't think any of them are Gothics, but I have a hunch you'd like them."

"How much would it cost? I've got a part-time job lined up, but it's just minimum wage."

"Don't worry about that. If you're really serious about sailing, we can work something out." I gave her the course schedule and other particulars and then said good-bye. If I hurried, I'd have just enough time to make it to the airport before Cassie's plane landed. I was anxious to see my daughter, but my thoughts were on Terri Moyer. I didn't know what to make of her. Yolanda had said she was out of touch with reality, and at times our conversation certainly seemed to dance around the fringes, but she still struck me as intelligent and cogent. I had a feeling that there was a lot more to this woman than drugs, vampires, black lace, and leather. I wasn't sure if I could tap into her world or not, but I hoped the sailing lessons might be a start.

NINE

"YOU'RE LATE!" CASSIE wrenched out of my embrace, folded her arms across her chest, and glared at me.

Moments ago, she'd been slouched against a wall next to the United counter, her nose buried so deep in a paperback that she hadn't even noticed I'd arrived. "Take a look out there, Cass," I said, pointing to the terminal window. The snow flurries I'd encountered on the way to the Moyers' funeral had developed into a major storm. "I'm sorry I'm late, but traffic on four-oh-five was a mess. It's a wonder your plane could even land in this stuff."

"The plane landed just fine," she said, swinging her knapsack off her shoulder and jamming the paperback inside. "An hour ago!"

Great. So far today I'd dealt with a funeral, marching orders from the Weasel, a patronizing tête-à-tête with Kingston, and a snow-clogged freeway. I'd even snagged a ticket while at the funeral—my creative but illegal parking spot for the Miata hadn't gone unnoticed—to the tune of twenty-five dollars. And now, to top it all off, a nineteen-year-old with an attitude. It wasn't the kind of welcome that warmed this mother's heart, and I wasn't about to let it pass.

"So I'm late." I shrugged. "I told you I was sorry. Cancel my birthday if it'll make you feel any better."

"Fine, Mom. Be sarcastic." She stared out the window. A 747 sat on the runway, immobilized by a swirling blur of white. No planes would take off or land for the rest of the evening. "I was worried," Cassie said, her eyes downcast. "That's all."

I took a deep breath and let it out slowly. "OK, Cassie. Why don't we start over? Welcome home." I smiled and added, "I've missed you a lot."

She hesitated, then tossed me a tentative smile. "Yeah, I've missed you, too."

I embraced her again, and while she didn't return it, neither did she pull away. "Now that we've got that settled," I said, "how 'bout we get something to eat?"

We decided to eat at the airport cafeteria and claim her luggage after we were done. That way, we reasoned, the snow-snarled commuter traffic would have time to ease off before we entered the fray.

As we walked our trays through the cafeteria line, I found myself studying Cassie. It had only been four months since I'd last seen her, but I couldn't get over how different she looked. It wasn't the clothes, for she was wearing basically the same outfit she had on when she left—baggy jeans, a scruffy pair of Doc Martens, a sweatshirt with an I ♥ NY logo, and a tan bomber jacket. Underneath the Mariners baseball cap, her thick, blue-black hair was styled the same—hanging straight to the shoulders with over-the-eyebrow bangs. Dorm food hadn't affected her weight. At five foot ten, she was still as slender as any model. Now that her anger had subsided, she was responsive and cordial. The difference was less tangible. Sophistication? Confidence? If pressed to explain it, I'd say she seemed more sure of herself somehow; as if she'd finally figured out what she wanted from life and nothing was going to stop her from getting it.

Short on staff, the grill cook—a gangly youth with long

hair slipping from a loosely tied ponytail—doubled as espresso operator. The faster he danced between stations, the more hair fell into his face. We made his life easier by heading for the salad bar where we filled our plates to overflowing and grabbed two cans of Diet Pepsi. After paying for our food, we found a small table next to a Japanese family who, judging by the eight Nikon cameras stacked on their table, took their sightseeing seriously.

The cafeteria was as short on ambience as it was on staff. The holiday decorations that adorned the rest of the airport's public areas were missing. Instead, an international theme prevailed, consisting primarily of maps, flags and photos of children in traditional costumes. A map of the world covered the entire south wall while the children's photos dotted the other three.

Considering our shaky start, Cassie and I chatted amiably, each of us trying to avoid repeating the harshness of our earlier encounter. And perhaps trying to avoid resurrecting the strain we'd felt around each other since Wendell's death. So we had no heavy discussions or revelations, although I was surprised to learn that Cassie had become a vegetarian.

I kept thinking about our phone conversation earlier in the week. For the hundredth time, I wondered what could be so important that she had to wait to tell me in person. I wanted to bring it up, but I decided to let her pick the moment.

"So, Cassie. How many suitcases do you have?"

"Don't worry, I only brought one. It'll fit in the Miata with room to spare."

I laughed. "That's a relief."

"And you don't have to worry about room on the boat, either."

"What do you mean?"

"I'm staying with Aunt Donna."

Cassie didn't like *Second Wind*. She was furious when I sold our house, the house she'd grown up in. "The house where my memories are" was how she'd put it at the time.

I wasn't able to make her understand that I had to sell the house for the very same reason. Buying *Second Wind* had been my chance to start over after Wendell's death. A chance to do what I really wanted. Within months, I'd sold the house, cashed in the life insurance, bought the sailboat, and quit teaching. The change was too much and too fast for Cassie. She said the boat should be called *Second Childhood*.

"Aunt Donna said I was more than welcome to stay with her. She has a huge house."

"I know how big her house is, Cassie. But why do you want to stay there?" Donna had never been particularly close to Cassie. Or to me, for that matter. Three brothers, a sister, and eleven years separated Donna and me. It might as well've been the Grand Canyon. The chasm between us was too deep and too wide to be bridged, especially since I'd remained friends with Bert after their divorce.

"Well, Mom, that's part of what I wanted to talk to you about." She took a deep breath, and I knew instantly I wasn't going to like what was coming next. "Aunt Donna is going to help me with my search."

"What search?"

"I'm going to find my birth mother."

So there it was. For years I'd dreaded something like this. Cassie's adoption, like most adoptions twenty years ago, had been confidential. Sealed records and altered birth certificate with Wendell's and my names listed as parents. We didn't know who the birth mother was, nor did she know who had adopted her baby. That was the way it was supposed to be. Forever.

I'd heard of adopted children who searched for their birth parents when they got older, but I wasn't sure what drove them to do it. Could it be they didn't love their parents—or didn't feel loved by them? I knew for a fact that Cassie and Wendell had loved each other very much. She and I had had our differences over the years, as all mothers and daughters do. Maybe we'd even had more than our share, but in spite of everything, I'd always believed deep in my heart that she still loved me. Maybe I'd been wrong.

"Why, Cassie?" I asked.

"It's hard to explain. It's just something I have to do."

"Did your father and I do something to disappoint you, fail you in some way?"

"Mom, it has nothing to do with you and Dad. You've been good parents, the best. Really."

"Then what is it? I don't understand."

"I don't know if anyone who isn't adopted can understand. It's like a part of me is missing. I don't know who I am when I look in the mirror. There's just so many questions. Where did I get my nose? Whose genes are responsible for the dimples I have in both cheeks? Do I have any sisters or brothers who look like me?"

"So it's a matter of who you look like?"

"Not exactly, though you have to admit I've been odd man out in this family. You with your curly red hair and freckled face, Dad with his blond hair and blue eyes." She pulled the cap from her head, tossed her hair back, and ran her fingers through it. "I want to know where I get this mane of straight black hair, my dark skin and brown eyes. And, of course, my height."

She sipped her drink, twisting the straw as she talked. "Remember when you went to Ireland and looked up your ancestors' records in that parish register in Galway? Why'd you do that?"

Uncovering our family's roots had been my mother's passion, not mine. It was an aspect of her Mormon heritage that she truly loved. When she died, Donna managed to get everything of value, but I somehow wound up with her genealogy records. Since it was all I had of my mother, I hung onto them. It wasn't until much later that my own interest in genealogy surfaced. "I guess I was curious to see where my family came from."

"That's the difference between you and me. You know where you came from—Ireland, your country of origin, your people. I don't know a thing about my family." She glanced at the wall photos of the children in their native costumes. "I mean, am I Hispanic? Native American? Italian? Some combination?"

"But, Cassie," I argued, "the Montgomerys and the O'Connells are your family. That's what adoption is all about. Being a mother and father has nothing to do with blood relationships. It's about getting up in the middle of the night to care for a sick child; it's about praising and pinning your child's drawings on the fridge door; it's about making sure your child is safe and warm and loved; it's—"

She waved her hand in front of me. "Mom, stop. I know all that. I'm talking about something else. Remember when I had that school assignment? The one where Mrs. Sampson had us make a chart showing our family lineage? For social studies class?"

I remembered exactly what she was talking about. The assignment had caused Cassie a lot of tears. She'd argued that because she didn't really know what her true lineage was, she shouldn't be required to turn anything in. Mrs. Sampson had disagreed and told Cassie to use her adoptive family's lineage for the assignment. In the end, Cassie turned in a chart with big question marks all over the page.

"I think," said Cassie, "it's about time I filled in the question marks."

"How? Does Donna have access to the clinic's medical records or something?"

"No, all of the records were destroyed."

I'd forgotten about the fire. The obstetrician who'd delivered Cassie retired shortly after her birth, and the physician who took over the practice had the clinic remodeled to suit his needs. The fire broke out during construction—a faulty wire or something—and the whole building went up in flames.

"So what's your plan?"

"Well, it would be easier if Aunt Donna could remember

my birth mother's name, but she can't. The woman was young and unmarried, that's all she can tell me. Besides, she's probably married by now and going by a different last name. So, I'll have to resort to other resources." She unhooked her knapsack from the back of the chair, unzipped the main pouch, and pulled out a book and some papers. She pushed them across the table. "This book was written by an adoptee who made a successful search. She gives all kinds of information on how to do it."

I thumbed through a few of the pages. I'd heard of the author, a strident advocate of opening sealed adoption records. "What's all this other stuff?" I asked, setting the book aside and trying to appear calm.

"Information on WARM."

"What's that?"

"Washington Adoption Rights Movement. It's an organization that helps reunite adoptees with their birth parents. I'm going to fill out an application for the service."

"Sounds like it might be expensive."

"There's some cost involved, but not as much as something like this." She held a glossy white business card with embossed gold lettering. Underneath the words "*The Missing Link*" was a phone number, but no address.

"The Missing Link? It sounds like some primitive ape/man thing."

"Hardly." She laughed. "It's a private search service. I met a girl at school who was from Washington. She used the Missing Link to find her birth mother, but it cost her a bundle. I can't go that route, but I thought I'd keep the card."

"You're serious about this, aren't you?" I asked.

"I am." Her eyes met mine. "But I don't want you to feel bad about it."

"What I feel bad about is that you won't be coming home with me. Do you really think this is such a good idea?"

A flicker of anger darted across her face. "I *knew* you'd be against the search."

I reined in my own rising anger and said, "Wait a minute, Cassie. I didn't say I was against your search."

"You didn't have to. It's pretty obvious how you feel."

Our conversation came to a standstill. I sipped my Pepsi and debated how to handle the situation. The Japanese family gathered up their cameras and prepared to leave. They bowed and wished us a Merry Christmas in flawless English.

"Christmas without you around is going to be hard," I said.

She shrugged. "I'm just staying at Aunt Donna's. It doesn't mean I won't see you, especially on Christmas. But I'll be pretty busy the rest of the time, going to the library, writing letters, things like that."

"I see." We talked a while longer, and I tried to be upbeat and positive, but in truth I felt miserable. Mostly I was worried. Worried about the answers to the questions I couldn't bring myself to ask: What would finding her birth mother do to our already shaky relationship? Would Cassie still love me? What if the woman didn't want to be found? What if she rejected Cassie? No matter how I looked at it, I just couldn't see how anything good could come from Cassie's search—for her or for me.

The snowstorm had gotten worse, not better, while we were at the airport, and the trip to Donna's home in Redmond—one of the rapidly growing cities on the Eastside—took a lot longer than usual. It was after dark when we arrived, and every light in her ranch-style house appeared to be on, including an extravagant outdoor display of red and green Christmas lights. Donna answered the door as soon as we rang the bell.

"Oh, my goodness gracious, you're finally here!" She grabbed Cassie's suitcase and ushered us into the foyer. Once inside, she stood on tiptoe to give Cassie a hearty bear hug and a kiss on the cheek. I rated a frown from her over my daughter's shoulder.

"Oh, Cassie dear, it's sooo good to see you again!" Donna's whiny voice was more syrupy than I could stomach. It had made me nauseous as a kid, and nothing had changed in the intervening years. I tried not to grimace, but failed.

"What happened?" she asked, finally turning her attention to me. "You forget where I live?"

Maybe it's because she's the oldest, but my sister has always had a strange effect on me. I lose all sense of myself and just sort of wilt in her presence. I apologized and started to explain about the storm, but she cut me off.

"Come on, come on," she said. "Let's get your coats off, and I'll make us some lattes. Or maybe a cappuccino."

Cassie shrugged out of her jacket and handed it to Donna. I kept my coat on. "The roads don't look good," I said. "I'd better be going."

But Donna had put her arm around Cassie's waist and was steering her toward the kitchen, whispering something I couldn't make out. Evidently it was something quite amusing, for Cassie giggled and patted her aunt's shoulder affectionately.

"Well, maybe I can stay for a minute," I said, trailing along behind them like a little lost puppy.

Cassie was right about Donna's house being big enough to accommodate her. Donna and Bert had bought the four bedroom, three-thousand-square-foot home shortly after they'd moved to Redmond. They'd filled it up with kids right away, but all of them were out of the nest and on their own now. Bert said the house was too big, even when he was living there. And yet, after kicking him out five years ago, Donna still hung on to the place. Bert said she viewed the house as if it were some kind of prize, a medal she earned for years of diligent—make that controlling—service.

On the way to the kitchen, I ran a fingertip along a picture frame. No dust, just the lingering smell of lemon Pledge. I don't know what I'd expected. Donna had always been a neat freak, a *Good Housekeeping* poster child who would've made her bed before getting up if she could've figured out how. I thought of the cabin on *Second Wind* and winced. Never in my wildest dreams would it be this clean.

Besides over-the-top cleanliness, the home looked about as lived-in as a furnished model you'd see on a Street of Dreams real estate tour. And a well-furnished model home it was—a rich blending of contemporary pieces along with a rather extensive collection of quality antiques. Donna's spending habits were a sore spot with my other sister, Mary Kathleen, and our three brothers. As our parents' survivors, we received a substantial settlement from the trucking company whose driver was legally drunk when he hit my parents' car. Donna was appointed executrix of the trust fund that was set up and, as such, controlled all of our investments. Based on her lavish lifestyle, Mary Kathleen and the others think she's been siphoning off more than her fair share of the proceeds for her own personal use.

Donna's kitchen was at least ten times the size of my galley and had all the conveniences—a gas range with double oven, microwave, Jenn-Air grill, subzero fridge, trash compactor, dishwasher, and walk-in pantry. Lining the counter next to the espresso machine was a blender, a bread machine, a pasta maker, and a KitchenAid mixer. God only knows what was parked in the appliance garage in the corner.

Donna directed Cassie to sit at the dinette table, a built-in, wrap-around unit that could easily seat a family of eight. I stood near the French doors and watched Donna, the hostess with the mostest, set to work making lattes. At five foot eight, she was the tallest of all us kids, even the boys. She'd been reed-thin most of her life, while the rest of us had waged a neverending battle against the bulge. Worse yet, we were all approaching middle age now—with plenty of wrinkles, bags, and sags to prove it. But not Donna. Her auburn hair had no traces of gray, her oval face no traces of wrinkles, her lithesome body no traces of flab. Whether all that was due to the luck of the gene pool, good makeup, or good surgery, I couldn't say. But I had my suspicions.

Donna hummed some cheerful little tune as she worked. As always, she kept her shoulders back and head up as if she were balancing a book atop it. Proud of her posture is what she claimed. Proud of her boobs was more like it. She was the busty one in the family and never let the rest of us forget it. The ensuing years had certainly treated Donna well, for she seemed bustier than ever. Yes, I definitely had my suspicions.

Looking like a TV mom straight out of the fifties in her dress and white ruffled apron, she fussed about the large kitchen with practiced ease. Donning a padded mitt, she took a tray of cookies from the oven and then transferred them to a large plate, which she set in front of Cassie with a flourish. A warm, spicy aroma wafted through the kitchen.

"Wow! Applesauce and raisin cookies. My favorites!" exclaimed Cassie.

Donna looked at me and beamed.

Cassie took a bite and closed her eyes. "Umm. This is sooo good."

Applesauce and raisin? What happened to chocolate chip? "Uh, look, Cassie, I've got to get going."

"No time for a latte?" asked Donna. The way she said it wasn't a whine exactly, but the words dripped with so much sweetness that it was all I could do to keep from gagging.

"You know I'm a tea drinker."

"Well, for Pete's sake. How could I forget something like that? I'll put a pot of water on to boil this very minute." She patted the back of a wicker chair in the corner. "You just sit yourself down right over here. It'll be ready in the shake of a lamb's tail."

I looked at the expansive dinette. "No room at the table, Donna?"

"Of course there is, you silly goose. I just thought this chair would be more comfortable for you." She opened the cupboard and pulled out a box of tea bags. "All I have is herbal. Would you like wild berry or peppermint?"

"Listen, let's just skip it. It's been a long day." I gave Cassie a hug. "Call me soon, OK?"

Cassie nodded, her mouth full of cookie.

"I hope you're not upset or anything, Kellie," Donna said. She sat down next to Cassie and put an arm around her shoulder. "Cassie will be just fine here with me."

"I know."

"Well, you seem upset." She glanced at Cassie. "You're not worried about this search of hers, are you? It's going to be just fine, too."

"Aunt Donna's right, Mom. Everything will be just fine."

Donna and Cassie were still huddled over their lattes and cookies when I slipped out the door and into the night. I stood a moment on the brightly lit porch and watched the snow. It didn't fall, but plunged from the sky in an angry, violent riot of white. The turbulence was so compelling that I wanted to rush back inside and grab Cassie's hand as if she were a small child who'd wandered into a busy street. I turned around and touched the doorknob. And then, hearing laughter, I pulled my hand away.

TEN

THE NEXT DAY. Seattle ground to a halt. They were calling it a repeat of the Arctic Express, a full-scale blizzard several years back that had immobilized the entire region for weeks. In a matter of hours, the current storm's sharp, pinlike flakes had covered the city with a fine, icy blanket several inches thick. Schools closed, businesses opened late or not at all, and newscasters advised everyone to stay home if they possibly could.

I ventured outside *Second Wind*'s snug cabin just long enough to make sure everything topside was secured. Afterward, I exchanged my work jeans and heavy jacket for flannel nightgown and robe, wrapped myself in a warm, cocoonlike blanket on the couch, and had myself one hell of a pity party.

For weeks I'd been looking forward to Cassie's homecoming. It was supposed to be a new beginning for us, a time to mend our differences and start over. I'd envisioned us sharing one of those mother-daughter days we'd enjoyed when she was younger—baking Christmas cookies, shopping, wrapping presents, and talking girl talk. Instead, Cassie was with my sister—baking Christmas cookies, wrapping presents, and talking girl talk. From the looks of the weather outside, I was relatively certain they weren't shopping, but it didn't really matter what they were doing— Donna was with Cassie, and I was alone.

I was still wallowing in the misery mudhole when Rose called. Rose was the marina's accountant and Bert's girl-friend for the past year or so. She was also my best friend.

"It's time to celebrate, Kellie. Bert and I want to take you out for your birthday."

"It's not my birthday."

"A mere technicality. Bert and I won't be here on Christmas Day. We're flying to Denver to spend the holiday with my family, so we thought we'd treat you to a little celebration before we left. How 'bout meeting us at the Pacific Broiler for dinner tomorrow night?"

As a kid, I always felt cheated that my birthday fell on Christmas Day. Each of my brothers and sisters had their own special day, but mine always seemed to get lost in the holiday shuffle. As an adult, I didn't mind that so much— especially this birthday.

"I appreciate the thought, Rose. But with the snow and all, why don't we just forget it?"

"No way! A birthday is special, and you're special to Bert and me. We'll see you in the Broiler Lounge tomorrow night at seven o' clock."

I tried a few more excuses, but Rose wasn't easily put off. When I finally agreed, she called me on my lack of enthusiasm.

"What's the matter?"

"Oh, nothing."

"Uh huh."

"No, really, I'm fine."

"Something's bothering you, Kellie. And don't tell me it's just because you're turning forty in a few days."

Ouch. "It's nothing. Believe me, I'm fine."

"No, I don't think so. You might as well tell me because I'm not going to hang up until you do. Maybe I can help."

That's all it took. An offer of help from my best friend, and everything I'd been feeling since Cassie's airport announcement came rushing out. Rose listened without judgment. At twenty-five, she'd already accumulated more maturity and good sense than some people do in a lifetime. She didn't tell me I shouldn't feel the way I did or that I was being foolish for worrying. She did offer a suggestion, however.

"Listen, Kellie," she said, "I know you're not into net surfing, but you really should check out CompuServe."

While I'd subscribed to the service for some time, I hadn't used it all that much. Nor did I get what CompuServe had to do with what we'd been talking about. "Why?"

"The forums. As you know, I belong to one for CPAs and I also chat regularly with folks who raise golden retrievers. But, Kellie, there's also a forum that addresses adoption issues."

"What kind of issues?"

"As I understand it, the topics cover a wide range—searches for birth parents, reunion experiences, support groups, things like that. The forum is listed in the hobbies section under genealogy. Who knows, there might be people out there who have already gone through what you're experiencing right now. You could share your concerns with them."

"I don't know, Rose. This is kind of personal. I don't mind sharing my feelings with you, but letting the whole world in on what's troubling me is another matter."

"You don't have to get into anything personal. Maybe you could talk to people who've already located their birth mother. You might learn something about the process that would ease your mind, or at least help you understand what's driving Cassie."

I thanked her for the suggestion and said I'd give it some thought. But after we hung up, I decided to spend the rest of the day working on the boat show plans I'd promised the Weasel. It was something I had to get done, and I figured the task would help take my mind off Cassie for a while. Using the laptop, I recorded some preliminary ideas for the booth's theme and sketched out a possible booth design. Before I knew it, two hours had passed and I was ready for some tea.

While I waited for the water to come to a boil, curiosity finally got the better of me. I hooked up the modem, logged onto CompuServe, and located the adoption forum. As I read through the list of available topics, I spotted a familiar name—the Missing Link. Since Cassie had made a point of mentioning it, I spent several minutes retrieving and downloading any message that referred to the Missing Link. There were a lot. So many that I forgot all about my tea. And dinner, too.

By the time I finally logged off, it was well past midnight and I was no longer dreading tomorrow night's birthday celebration. I could hardly wait to talk to Rose about what I'd learned. Looking back on it, though, the person I should've been eager to talk to was Allen Kingston. But I was still smarting from the way he'd dismissed me at the Moyers' funeral so I didn't even consider it.

THE WEATHER FORECASTERS had predicted the storm would be around for a while but, wonder of wonders, they were wrong. The blizzard blew itself out overnight. By late Thursday afternoon, the highway crews had spread enough sand and the sun had melted enough snow that the roads were passable again. Seattle was back to business as usual.

I took advantage of the weather break to lay in some supplies. Toilet paper was at the top of the list. Holding tanks on boats are rather fussy, so I made that biodegradable toilet paper. Before leaving, I took a minute to check the compressed natural gas tank. The oven runs on CNG, which can be a hassle if you're not prepared. As I suspected, the tank was nearly empty so I hooked up the spare, hauled the main tank out of its storage compartment, and took it with me to Captain Jack's Marine Supply for a refill.

I lucked out. The Captain was having a "Snow Daze Half-Price Sale." I bought a dozen rolls of TP; three big bottles of tank deodorizer; and an all-purpose, super-duper scrub brush. I even broke down and bought the salt and pepper shaker set I'd been eyeing for months. Shaped like winch handles, the stainless steel shakers cost me plenty even at half price. Since I was in a buying mood, I stopped by Safeway and loaded up on groceries. Just in case. I didn't think it likely, but Cassie could have a change of heart about staying at Donna's, and if she did, I wanted to be ready.

There's always something to do on a boat, especially following a storm. After I put away the supplies, I spent the rest of the day futzing around *Second Wind* like an old sea salt, checking for storm damage, readjusting the snow-laden sail covers and rigging, unplugging drains, and generally spiffing up the place. The cabin still looked as messy as ever, but I'd done enough work for one day. I knocked off around six o' clock so I could get ready to meet Bert and Rose at the Pacific Broiler.

Rose hadn't asked, but I would've preferred to celebrate at the Topside. I could count on one hand the number of times I'd been to the Pacific Broiler. The place was way too fancy for my taste. Not to mention too pricey. And, since dressing up was definitely expected, my usual jeans and sweatshirt wouldn't make the cut. But what the heck? As Rose had said, a birthday celebration was special. I decided to go all out for the occasion and wear my best outfit—a black cocktail number with a red bolero jacket trimmed in black brocade. The dress I'd had for a long time, but the jacket was an advance birthday/Christmas present to myself. For sentimental reasons, I added a strand of pearls that had belonged to my grandmother and matching earrings that Wendell had given me.

Rose and Bert were already in the lounge when I arrived. They stood at the bar, a broad expanse of polished oak and brass bedecked for the season with a liberal sprinkling of

holly and mistletoe. Actually, Rose stood at the bar. Bert sat
on a stool next to her, his big rear end perched awkwardly
on the small leather seat. If he was uncomfortable, he didn't
seem to notice. Rose could be very distracting.

I thought I looked pretty good until I saw her. She was
a natural beauty, the kind of woman who causes men to
write large checks. Even when she wasn't wearing makeup,
Rose turned heads. Dolled-up as she was this evening, she
turned whole bodies. You usually see a woman like Rose
on the arm of some equally striking young man. Or, as in
Nancy Preston's case, some rich old man. I don't know what
kind of reaction Nancy gets when she's out with her husband, but the fact that Rose was with big Bert, stuffed into
a Brooks Brothers suit that had seen better days, caused
more than a few inquisitive stares.

Even without the twenty-year age difference, they were
an unlikely couple. Rose was pure elegance in a silky black
sheath that moved with the curve of her slender body like
ribbons dancing in the breeze. Her long blond hair was
swept into a chignon, and except for a pair of small diamond
earrings, she wore no jewelry. Her perfume was an inex-
pensive but pleasing blend of jasmine and gardenias. And
Bert was . . . well, Bert was just Bert. Yet, as odd as they
looked together, you knew they belonged with one another.
It was as if the two of them had somehow discovered what
everyone else had missed: You have to stop frantically chasing that elusive thing called love and just let it happen. Rose
says the real reason is that Bert is the only guy she's ever
met who doesn't feel he has a genetic right to the remote
control.

After we said our hellos, we moved from the bar to a
corner table that had been reserved for us. Although located
behind the main dining room, the lounge still had a sweeping view of Larstad's Marina and Elliott Bay. In the distance, the lights from the Space Needle and the city sparkled
in the clear night air like ornaments on a brightly lit Christmas tree.

The lounge was packed—a room full of loud, boisterous folks desperate for human contact and the need to celebrate the end of their snowbound existence. The storm had shut the city down for only a day, but the lounge patrons embraced one another like long lost buddies. Their gladhanding and back-slapping was matched only by the music, a lively medley of rock 'n' roll hits from the 60s and 70s. A moonlighting deejay from some oldies station had coaxed a dozen couples onto the postage stamp dance floor with a recording of Donna Summers' *Bad Girls*.

Despite the upbeat atmosphere and Rose and Bert's peppy chatter, I found my mind wandering. I couldn't stop thinking about the Moyer case and the questions I'd jotted down in my notepad. Was the killer a client with a grudge against Moyer? Did Miranda just happen to be in the wrong place at the wrong time? Why was their son killed? Did he find whatever he was looking for that day at the dock? Was it something that identified the killer? What about Moyer's law partner, James Preston? Why were he and Moyer at odds with one another? Was the business in trouble? And how much, if anything, did Terri Moyer know about her family's deaths?

A poke from Bert brought me back to the moment. "Kellie, take a look at who just walked through the door. Isn't that Detective Kingston?"

I followed his gaze to a couple entering the lounge, arm in arm. It was Allen Kingston, all right, dressed for once in a decent suit, unrumpled and clean. The young woman clinging to his arm like Saran Wrap was a bleached blonde with enough curves to require road signs. The tight piece of short red fabric posing as her dress was a low-cut bosombragger. And she had plenty to brag about. Kingston pushed his way through the crowd like Moses parting the Red Sea and led his jiggling, wiggling companion to the bar.

"That's the detective," said Rose. "Question is, who's that with him?" She turned to me. "Kellie?"

"Don't ask me. I've never seen her before."

"She's quite a looker," observed Bert.

"Did you say hooker?" I asked.

Rose hissed.

"Claws in, ladies," Bert said with a laugh.

All the stools at the bar were taken, but Kingston and the woman squeezed out some standing room next to a preppie-looking college guy. As soon as the young guy saw the blonde, he promptly stood up and offered her his stool. She flashed him a sexy smile and lifted her so-called skirt an inch or so higher before sitting down.

Once she was ensconced on her pedestal, Kingston and Joe College both competed for her attention, sidling up to her like star-struck fans. She took them both on. Zeroing in on their ears, she nibbled and whispered and giggled like a teenager in the back seat of a Chevy. Kingston and the kid fawned all over her, vying for the privilege of buying her drinks and lighting her cigarettes. Kingston kept one arm draped over her shoulder and the other resting on the counter, a bottle of Jack Daniel's at the ready.

I stood up and said, "Rose, let's go to the ladies' room."

"What is it about restrooms and women?" asked Bert. "Is there some kind of rule that says you can't go by yourself?"

"That's right," I said. "Like nuns and Mormon missionaries, we always travel in pairs."

We passed the bar on the way to the restroom, but we might as well have been invisible. Kingston only had eyes for his sweetie and the drink in front of him.

"Don't you want to stop and say hello?" teased Rose.

The restroom was occupied. "They've only got two stalls, honey." Our advisor was a tall black woman who stood at the end of a long line of women waiting their turn to use the facilities. She looked at the elaborately carved white oak door with its brass POWDER ROOM sign and shook her head. "You'd think a fancy-dancy place like this would have a few more stalls. I bet there aren't any men standing in line to pee."

I nudged Rose and pointed to a bench at the end of the hall. "Let's wait over there. I've been wanting to talk to you alone."

"What's up?" Rose asked as we sat down.

"Remember how you said I should look at the adoption forum on CompuServe?"

She nodded.

"I took your advice and spent several hours yesterday reading through the messages people had sent to one another about searching for their birth parents."

"Good. Did it help?"

"Sort of. Most of the messages had to do with an exchange of information on how they were going about their search, what agencies were cooperative, which were not, things like that. But there was something in some of the messages that caught my eye."

"What was that?"

"A service called the Missing Link. Ever hear of it?"

She shook her head. "I'm sure I'd remember such an odd name. It sounds like an anthropology term or something. You know, like a primitive man/ape connection."

I laughed. "That's essentially what I said when Cassie told me about it. Actually it's an exclusive service that helps you locate your birth parent in record time—days, in some cases."

"That's sort of unusual, isn't it?" she asked.

I nodded. "From what I've been able to gather about the search process, it usually takes much longer—months, perhaps even years before a birth parent is located. That's especially the case if the information you have about your origins is sketchy."

"How do they do it so fast?"

"I'm not sure, but there's something else. The Missing Link was printed on a business card that Cassie showed me at the airport. For some reason, numbers seem to stick with me. When I saw the phone number on the card, I knew I'd seen the number before. It didn't hit me where until I saw the messages on CompuServe.''

''And?''

''The phone number for the Missing Link and the phone number for the Moyer and Preston Law Office is one and the same.''

''You mean Moyer and Preston handle birth parent searches as well as adoptions?''

''Apparently. What really intrigues me, though, is why the firm's name isn't on the Missing Link business cards. And why Yolanda Vanasek never mentioned anything about the service.''

''Who's Yolanda Vanasek?''

''A former teacher's aide I knew at Horace Mann. She went on to become a paralegal and wound up working for Donald Moyer. I went to the law firm to talk to James Preston and ran into her instead. She told me plenty about Preston but, as I said, nothing about the Missing Link.''

''Maybe she didn't think it was important to the case.''

''Maybe, but I have a feeling my old chum wasn't being totally honest with me about the goings-on at the firm.''

''You think she's hiding something?''

''Not necessarily. I just don't think she's told me everything she knows.''

''Why don't you go see her again?''

''Because I have a better idea.''

''Uh oh. Why do I feel like Ethel Mertz to your Lucy Ricardo all of a sudden?''

Like Bert, I'd gotten Rose involved in some of my other investigations. Unlike Bert, though, Rose was sympathetic to my sleuthing. She was willing to go along with my ideas, even if they got a little crazy at times. Like the time we dressed up as bag ladies to follow a suspect around Pioneer Square in downtown Seattle. For a CPA, she had a highly developed sense of adventure.

''Don't worry, I won't ask you to do anything crazy.''

She gave me one of her raised eyebrow looks.

"Well, maybe just a little bit crazy."

Rose grinned."Okay, Kellie, let's hear it."

I told her about the argument that Preston and Moyer supposedly had prior to the murders and about Yolanda's concerns over Preston's drinking and uncertain work performance. "From what I've gathered so far, Moyer's clients think the guy could walk on water. I have a hunch his partner didn't feel quite the same way. In any event, now that I know that the firm is connected to the Missing Link somehow, I think their business dealings need more looking into."

"And this involves me somehow?"

"I can't get Preston to meet with me. And Yolanda wouldn't or couldn't talk about the Missing Link. I don't think I can uncover what's going on there simply by asking. But you, on the other hand, could pull it off."

"Here comes the crazy part, right?"

"Not really. I just want you to do a little play-acting."

"And my role is?"

"An adoptee searching for her birth mother. You heard about the success rate of the Missing Link. You call and make an appointment. You go talk to them. You keep your eyes and ears open while you're there. See what you can pick up."

"That's all?"

"Yep. I'm interested in whom they schedule you to see at the law firm, what the process involves, the kind of questions they ask you, and how much it costs. That sort of thing." I waited a beat. "Well, what do you think? Will you do it?"

Rose shrugged. "I guess I'm up for it, but just what do you expect to find out?"

"I'm not sure, but I—"

"You gals can go in now." The black lady we'd met earlier stood in front of us. "The line's not so bad anymore. Better get in the can while you can," she said, laughing.

Our restroom sojourn over, Rose and I returned to the lounge.

"Oh, no. Look who's at our table," I said.

Allen Kingston, sans blonde, sat at our table talking to Bert.

"Where's his date?" Rose asked.

"I don't know and I don't care."

"Hey, chill out, Kellie."

"Sorry," I said. "I don't care whom the man dates. I just thought he'd have better taste, that's all."

"Methinks the lady doth protest too much."

"Think whatever you like. Just don't say anything about the Missing Link or our plan, okay?"

"No problem."

As I sat down at the table, Kingston patted me on the shoulder. "Well, well, well," he said. "How's it feel to be turning forty, old gal?"

ELEVEN

MY HEAD HURT. My gut hurt. Even my toes hurt.

Kingston's teasing the night before had been unmerciful. He'd dredged up every "over the hill" joke he'd ever heard, but I successfully ignored his pointed barbs—until he started calling my hot buttered rum the "old fuddy's drink." After downing two glasses of the nasty stuff he recommended, I discovered why the drink was called a B-52. One drink, much less two, and you're bombed. Rip roaring. Falling down. I had only a vague recollection of the evening's events, but I knew it couldn't have been good. The morning after certainly wasn't.

Desperate for some tea, I stumbled out of bed and dragged myself into the galley. I leaned against the counter a moment and forced my bloodshot eyes to open wide enough so that I could locate the tea kettle. With one hand holding onto my throbbing head, I used the other to rummage through the stack of dirty dishes in the sink. The task was simply overwhelming. Finding a clean cup, clean spoon, clean anything in that mess would take a far better woman than I. OK, God, here's the deal: Just put an end to this headache, and I really, really will get my housekeeping act together.

Maybe trying to bargain with God hadn't been such a good idea. I suddenly felt uneasy, a strange feeling that was nothing like my queasy stomach or throbbing temples. An odd, shiver-up-the-spine kind of feeling. I turned from the sink and blinked.

"Wendell?" He sat at the dining table, a newspaper in one hand, a cup of coffee in the other.

I blinked again. "Wendell?"

He put the paper down and grinned.

I reared back, almost stumbling. "What are *you* doing here?"

"She walks, she talks." Allen Kingston's deep voice bounced off the walls of the small cabin like an echo chamber.

"Quiet! Can't you see I'm in trouble?"

"Hell, yes, woman," he said, standing up. "But not as much trouble as you were in last night." He was clad in the same suit pants he'd worn the night before, but his jacket and tie were missing, and his shirttails drooped over his belt like sails in a windless sky. Barefoot. The man was barefoot.

I was still dealing with the sight of his naked toes when he grasped my arm and helped me to the table. "Want some coffee?" he asked. "It's not that good. All I could find was instant decaf."

"Tea! Just get me some tea. And quickly." I groaned.

"You'd be better off with the hair of the dog that bit you."

"Please. The tea."

He shrugged. "OK, Montgomery, if you insist." He grabbed a pan and filled it with water.

"What're you doing?"

"Making you the damn tea. Whadda ya think?"

"Don't use a pan to boil the water. The tea kettle's quicker."

"Only if I can find it." He eyed the sink. "I suppose it's

in there with everything else.'' He found the kettle without further comment and opened the silverware drawer. ''I still think you should have a good stiff one,'' he said as he opened a second drawer. He rummaged through it a moment, then scratched his head. ''Uh, where do you keep your tea bags?''

''Oh, for heaven's sake,'' I snapped. ''I don't use tea bags. Just put the water on to boil like you did for the decaf. I'll take it from there.''

He dutifully filled the kettle with water and set it on the stove.

If I hadn't been in so much agony, I might've appreciated his help. As it was, his awkwardness in the galley—he had to keep his head bent at a slight angle to avoid hitting the ceiling—merely irritated me. When he came back to the table and sat down, I said, ''You never answered my question. What are you doing here?''

He ran his fingers over the salt-and-pepper stubble covering his jaw and yawned. ''Someone had to make sure you got home last night,'' he said.

''And you got elected? What happened to Bert and Rose?'' For that matter, what about his blonde cutie pie? Why was he busy escorting me home instead of her?

''Oh, Bert and Rose helped. You weren't up for a walk, so we loaded you into a dock cart. Wheeled you down the mooring ramp like a babe in a stroller.''

I stared at him as he sipped his coffee, not knowing what to make of him. Or myself. Getting snockered and waking up with a hangover was bad enough. Waking up with Detective Kingston at my dining table was downright bizarre. I was dying to know what had happened to his date, but I was too chicken to ask. I came at the question another way. ''Obviously, my recollection of last night is a little hazy. Did we ever have dinner?'' I asked.

''We did.''

''And your friend? Did she join us?''

He cocked an eyebrow. ''My friend?'' he asked.

He knew exactly who I meant. I cocked an eyebrow back at him. "Yes, your friend."

He shrugged. "Oh, her. She got a better offer."

"So just the four of us had dinner, then," I said, feeling strangely relieved.

"Yep, but you didn't eat much. Just sort of sat there and giggled your way to dessert."

Oh my God. I'd taken over where the blonde had left off.

The tea kettle whistled, and Kingston started to get up.

"Wait," I said, clutching at the neck of my bathrobe and staring at the floor. The dress, bolero jacket, and underwear I'd had on last night lay in a heap alongside Kingston's necktie, suit jacket, and socks. "Did you . . . did we . . . how did I . . . ?"

Kingston laughed. "Don't worry, old gal. Rose got you undressed and into bed. I only stuck around because I passed out on the cabin's sofa."

"Oh."

"Do you want me to finish fixing the tea or what?" he asked. The tea kettle was screaming at us now, boring into my head like a drill.

"No, no. I'll take care of it."

I got up from the table as quickly as I dared and rescued the kettle from the burner. I felt as wobbly on my feet as a toddler learning to walk, but I managed to find what I needed in the galley without any embarrassing mishaps. I measured out two teaspoons of Twining's Irish breakfast tea and placed it in a teapot. To do it right, I should've warmed the pot first, but at this point I wasn't concerned with form. After I poured the boiling water over the leaves, I added a lid and let the tea steep in the pot. When I came back to the table, Kingston had put on his tie and jacket. He tugged on his socks, a brown argyle and its mismatched black companion.

"Leaving so soon?" I asked.

"Duty calls, you know. Got a murder or two to solve. Hell, maybe a dozen by now."

"Speaking of which, what's the latest on the Moyer case?" I asked.

"You never give up, do you, Red?"

"What's that supposed to mean?"

He studied his socks. "Damn, how'd that happen?"

"Come on, Kingston. You put me off at the Moyers' funeral and now you're doing it again. I thought we had a deal. You said I could be in on this case, remember?"

"Oh, I remember exactly what I said—you had my permission to snoop around on your own. I don't remember saying anything about giving you a show and tell every time I saw you."

"But—"

"But nothing. What's this case to you anyway?"

"I just thought I could help."

"The trouble with you, Red, is that you think too much. Why don't you just leave the investigation to the professionals?"

"I notice that the professionals have yet to arrest anybody."

"It's only a matter of time."

"Then what does it hurt if you share your findings with me? As I've assured you many times before, I won't get in your way or compromise your investigation."

"It's only a matter of time."

"Is that so? I think it's a matter of something else."

"Like what?"

"Like the amateur showing up the professional."

"Bull. The amateur could show up dead."

"Are you saying you're worried about my safety? That's very considerate of you, Detective, but I'm one woman who's perfectly capable of taking care of herself."

"Yeah, I know," he said with a grin, "just like you did last night." He looked down at his socks again and then glanced around the cabin. "Now where'd I stash those bunion builders?"

I spotted the tips of his black Florsheims poking out from

underneath the heap of clothes on the floor. Like a faithful old dog, I fetched them for him and said, "Let's just forget about last night, OK?"

An amused grin spread over his face like warm butter on toast.

What's that about a snowball's chance? "Never mind," I said. "Have you interviewed anybody on the Visitor Access List I gave you? And the Moyers' dock box, the one Junior was so eager to open? You find anything interesting in it?"

"Listen, Montgomery, I said I'm not—"

The hatchway door opened. We both watched in awkward silence as a pair of jean-clad legs inched their way down the ladder and into the cabin. When she saw us, Cassie put her hands on her hips and said, "Well, if it isn't Jessica Fletcher and Lt. Columbo."

"Cassie! What are you doing here?" I asked.

She nodded at Kingston, who was tucking in his shirttails. "I was just wondering the same thing about him."

"Hey, kid. Your mom's forty now. Old enough to have a man over, wouldn't you say?"

"Kingston!"

"Well, ex-cu-se me!" said Cassie. "I didn't know I was interrupting something."

"You're not interrupting a damn thing," I said quickly. "The detective was just leaving."

At the hatchway, he stepped around Cassie and grabbed hold of the ladder. "Better take good care of your mom, kid. She's feeling her age this morning."

Cassie watched him climb up the ladder before sitting down at the table. "What was that all about?"

"Nothing," I said, pouring myself a cup of the freshly brewed tea.

"Yeah, I'm sure. You can level with me. Have you and the detective been doing the wild thing?"

"The wild thing?"

"You know, the big nasty, the old bump and grind."

"Oh, Cassie, please. I'm sick enough as it is."

THINKING I WAS finally going to get some use out of the groceries I'd bought, I started mentally planning our lunch menu—until Cassie told me she'd just stopped by to pick up her birth certificate. Donna was waiting for her in the car; they were on their way to the library to do some research. The news didn't do much for my headache. Or any of my other aches.

It was probably just as well that she hadn't stuck around. I felt rotten. If my body was trying to get my attention, it was doing a pretty good job of it. I toyed with the idea of going back to bed, but my Catholic/Mormon upbringing kicked in, demanding that I pay for my night of sin. What better way than with a stint of vigorous, physically draining, body-punishing exercise at the Sports Center? Besides, I hadn't had a good workout since I injured my ankle. It was time.

Wendell and I joined the Sports Center ten years ago. It was a large recreational facility that included just about everything that the sports-minded person could want: tennis, racquetball, swimming, basketball, aerobics, Nautilus, and probably a whole lot more if I thought about it some. Other amenities included a bistro, day-care center, tanning salon, massage therapists, and a bevy of personal trainers. The entire facility was hoity-toity, posh—from the white marbled entryway to the lush carpets and leather upholstery in the bistro.

The club membership was one of Wendell's employment perks at DataTech. The computer firm believed that healthy employees were long-lasting employees. Unfortunately, in Wendell's case, exercise hadn't done a thing for his life span. A brain tumor wasn't something you could prevent no matter how strenuous your exercise regime. As his widow, I was allowed to keep my membership at the Center. Even after all these years, though, I still felt like an interloper—as if I'd wandered into an exclusive country club by mistake.

Since I hadn't been doing anything remotely strenuous since my fall, I took it easy my first day back. I still had a splitting headache and was moving rather slowly so I bypassed the rows of treadmills and StairMasters and headed for the Nautilus equipment. I huffed and puffed my way through the circuit and then hit the free weights. I'd just finished a set of bicep reps when Rob Gravetsky stopped by to say hello.

"Kind of short on weights, aren't you, Kellie?" Rob was a personal trainer I'd worked with right after I bought *Second Wind*. He'd set me up on a program specifically designed to increase my upper body strength. Rob had been a hard taskmaster, but I found I could hoist the sails by myself a whole lot easier after I followed his program for a few months.

I grinned sheepishly and toweled my sweating forehead. "Yeah, I'm a slacker. What can I say?"

He gave me a gentle punch on the shoulder. "Naw, you just need me around to keep you on the straight and narrow. I've missed you, Kellie."

Rob was pushing forty himself, but he had the look of a guy half his age. As you'd expect, he was muscular. Not a bulging Mr. Universe type, but definitely fit. Even dressed in the Center's garish trainer's uniform—purple shorts and green tank top—Rob exuded sex appeal. An older, better-looking Tom Cruise. But what set Rob apart wasn't his looks. He had a sincere and caring nature, plus an infectious laugh that drew you in like a magnet. No matter how crummy your mood, Rob could lift your spirits. Rough as I felt, having him tell me he'd missed me made everything okay.

"I've missed you, too, Rob. Are they keeping you busy these days?"

"Yeah, too busy," he said, shifting his weight from one foot to the other. Rob's energy level was hard to rein in. Like some of the hyperactive kids I used to have in class, he had difficulty standing still for very long. He rocked back and forth in an odd little two-step as he talked. "But I lost one of my clients the other day."

"Oh? How's that?" I asked.

"He was murdered—and his wife, too. Damn shame."

"You must be talking about the Moyers."

Rob nodded. "You knew them?"

I briefly explained our relationship. Although I'd never seen them at the Center, it didn't surprise me that the Moyers were members. The Center had developed a reputation as one of the "in" places around town. A "see-and-be-seen" type of place catering to the upwardly mobile, professional crowd. The Moyers fit the profile. "How well did you know Donald Moyer, Rob?"

"I was his personal trainer for . . ." He paused to consider. "Gosh, it's probably been over a year now."

"He was really into fitness, huh?"

"I wouldn't say that exactly."

"What do you mean?"

"The way he told it, he'd been quite the athlete in his younger years. Played rugby in college, a little basketball, some track. Said it bothered him that he'd let himself go for so long. He wanted me to help him get back in shape, but the thing is, when he came to work out, he spent most of his time schmoozing."

"Schmoozing?"

"You know, working the room like an Amway dealer or something. I guess it's called networking."

"Looking for potential clients, huh?"

"Right. And from what I saw, he managed to snag quite a few."

"Really?"

"Oh, yeah. For an adoption attorney, he did all right. You wouldn't believe the number of folks here that he got babies for. He was one popular fellow."

"Ever hear about anyone he wasn't so popular with?"

"Someone who might want him dead, you mean?"

"Exactly."

Rob stopped rocking and looked me square in the face. "I should've picked up on it sooner. You're into the Moyers' murder investigation, aren't you?"

Rob and I had gotten rather close during the time he'd been my personal trainer. We'd even tried dating a few times, but it hadn't gone anywhere. I'd broken my vow of celibacy by then, but I think it was still too soon after Wendell for me. Anyway, Rob had been around when I was investigating Suzie Hoffman's murder. He knew me well enough to guess that my interest in the Moyers' murders went beyond simple curiosity.

"The murders took place aboard their yacht. When it was towed to the marina, the harbormaster's office got involved. I'm the harbormaster's representative in the case, you might say."

"I see." He selected some bicep weights that were about ten pounds heavier than what I'd been using. "Then let me give you a little tip," he said, handing me the weights. "If you want to build muscles, add the weight and the reps. If you want to build a case, talk to Sissy Donovan."

"Who's she?"

"She runs the juice bar in the bistro. Also runs the gossip mill. If anyone knows about the Moyers around here, it'll be Sissy."

"Thanks, Rob. I'll go see her."

"You better go prepared."

"How so?"

"Tips. Sissy likes to gossip, but if you really want to get the lowdown, bring money. As they say, it talks."

I gave him a thumbs-up sign. "Gotcha."

I used the weights he'd given me to do a few more bicep curls before calling it a day. Back at the locker room, I took a quick shower and dressed. Then I grabbed my shoulder bag, checked my wallet, and headed for the bistro. Gossip mill or not, without Kingston's help I had to get my leads wherever I could find them.

TWELVE

AS THE NAME implied, the Center Court Bistro was located directly across from the tennis courts. It had a trendy, art-deco look that was supposed to pass for sophistication but came off merely jarring. The wildly geometric pattern in the apricot and plum-colored wallpaper looked as though it had been designed by someone who'd flunked his eye exam.

The floor plan consisted of two levels connected by an open stairway. The first level housed the juice bar, grill, and a host of self-service snacks. The main eating area was on the upper deck, or mezzanine, and had plenty of tables as well as a row of booths upholstered in soft leather. The best tables were along the windows overlooking the six tennis courts.

It was three o'clock in the afternoon when I arrived, and business was slow—too late for lunch and too early for the dinner crowd. The place was empty except for a couple of short-skirted ladies fresh from a round of tennis. They were drinking Italian sodas at a window table and arguing over who was responsible for the match they'd just lost.

Two women were on duty at the juice bar, and if it hadn't been for their name tags, I'd have pegged Carmen as Sissy

Donovan. She was a dead ringer for Sissy Spacek, the skinny movie star with the freckled face and strawberry-blond hair. Sissy Donovan, on the other hand, looked as if she favored the milkshakes at Dairy Queen over the bistro's lowfat juices. Thick at the waist and heavy in the hips, she was nevertheless valiantly sporting the Center's bistro uniform—a skimpy pair of tan shorts and a plum-colored polo shirt. Her ample bosom strained against the thin fabric of her shirt, and the thighs peeking out from underneath her shorts were saddled with more baggage than an around-the-world traveler.

It would've been a compliment to say that she was plain in the face, but she had artfully applied her makeup, drawing you to her expressive brown eyes rather than her beaklike nose. I guessed Sissy Donovan's age at about thirty and holding.

She nodded when I sat down at the juice bar, and continued to rinse off some strawberries in a large metal colander. Carmen was on the second level, replenishing the napkin dispensers at the courtside tables. While I waited for Sissy to finish with the berries, I checked out the drink menu on the chalkboard above the counter. There were a lot of choices.

"What can I get for y'all?" Sissy's soft drawl was accompanied by a big, toothy smile.

"I can't make up my mind. I'm torn between a pineapple banana smoothie or one of those vegetable combos."

"They're all good."

"What's that?" I pointed to the last drink scratched on the chalkboard sign—"The Green Thing."

She laughed. "Well, honey, that's George Bush's worst nightmare. It's nothing but green veggies, mostly broccoli."

I told her I'd stick with fruit, thank you very much. She set to chopping and tossing pineapple chunks and banana slices into the blender as if she were auditioning for a slice and dice commercial. In a flash, she set the smoothie in front of me. "There ya go. Enjoy." Another toothy smile. Her eyes were on me like a little child eagerly awaiting Mom's approval.

"This is good. Really good."

Sissy nodded. "I thought y'all would like it. Smoothies are my specialty."

I downed some more. "You've got the touch, all right."

Satisfied that I was satisfied, she picked up a second colander of strawberries and turned toward the sink.

"Uh, Sissy, do you have a minute to talk?"

"Honey, I always have time to talk. That's my other specialty." She set the colander down and leaned against the counter, casually folding her arms on top. "What's on your mind?"

I eased into the subject by introducing myself and complimenting her on her accent. When I asked where she hailed from, she picked up the ball and ran with it for a while, sharing a hilarious story about how she happened to wind up in Seattle when she took a wrong turn out of Dallas. Before long, though, she'd had enough. The smile faded and her mouth tightened up, forming creases around the edges of her lips that hardened and aged her on the spot.

"I can jaw all day about my southern roots, sugar. My guess is, though, that you tagged me for somethin' else. And this little chitchat we're having ain't it."

Some sleuth. I held my hands up in mock surrender. "You got me. I'm really looking for some information. Rob Gravetsky said that you might be able to help me."

"Rob." The smile was back. "Now there's a guy for ya. Most of the musclemen in this place don't give me the time of day. Always chasing after those skinny little gals in their pasted-on leotards. But Rob . . ." She paused to brush a strand of hair out of her face.

". . . isn't like that," I said.

"You got that right. He treats me like I'm a queen or something." She patted her chest. "Makes my little ol' heart go pitter-patter just looking at 'im."

"I know what you mean."

"What kind of info are y'all interested in?"

"I'd like to know what you can tell me about Donald and Miranda Moyer."

"This have something to do with their murders?"

I nodded.

"You with the police?"

"No, the harbormaster's office." I gave her a brief explanation. "But this visit is completely unofficial. Anything you tell me will be just between us."

She straightened herself up from the counter and took a long look at me without saying anything. Sizing me up. Or waiting for me to push some money her way. I was just about to pull out my wallet when she leaned on the counter again. Apparently satisfied that I was legitimate, she asked, "What do y'all want to know?"

"As I said earlier, I knew Donald and Miranda, but we weren't close. I'd like to know how they came across to you."

"That's easy enough. Don't like to speak ill of the dead, but the truth is, I had about as much use for the two of them as I have for a pound of horseshit. Pardon my French."

"Why such strong feelings?"

"To start with, they were both money grabbers—of the worst kind. But Donald Moyer—he was one of them good ol' boys. Believe me, I seen plenty of his type back home. He had balls for brains."

"Everyone else I've talked to says Donald was very well liked. Very successful, too."

"Oh, I'm not saying he wasn't liked. Whenever you deliver to folks what even God can't do, you're bound to be popular."

"I guess you'll have to spell it out for me."

"He was a politician, honey. All show and no substance. The front man. He could talk a good game, but it was Miranda who was the brains behind the adoption business."

"What about his partner, James Preston?"

"Ha! A real weenie, from what I hear. And a lush to

boot. No, Miranda Moyer was the driving force behind the Moyer and Preston Law Office.''

"Like how?"

"Like she was the one who got all them babies for folks.''

"What do you mean?"

"Lord knows I'm not an expert on babies. Or adoption, for that matter. But you'd have to have your head in the sand not to know that white, healthy babies are in rather short supply these days.''

I nodded. "The Pill and legalized abortion have taken a toll.''

"That, plus having a baby out of wedlock ain't the big deal that it used to be. A lot of young gals are keeping their babies nowadays, whether they're married or not.''

I confirmed her assessment with another nod. I was well aware that the supply of babies had fluctuated dramatically during the past three decades. During the fifties and sixties there were plenty of babies available for adoption. By the seventies, when Cassie was born, there was definitely a baby shortage, and the situation had only gotten worse in the years since. It was either get on a long, indefinite list or accept older or "hard-to-place" children. It wasn't surprising that some couples felt desperate enough to resort to illegal, black-market adoptions.

"Are you saying that Miranda Moyer had a way around the shortage somehow?"

"Bingo!"

"Baby brokering?"

"Bingo again, honey. I don't know how she got hooked up with all them young gals, but Miranda had a way. Like some heat-seeking missile or something, she found them. The younger and poorer the better.''

"Because they were more likely to give up their babies for a price?"

"Yep. Donny Boy's job was to find prospective parents who could cough up the dough. And believe me, when he found them, they paid dearly for their sweet bundle of joy.''

"How dearly?''

"The figure I've heard bandied about is in the fifty-thousand-dollar range. I know for a fact that Lily and John Lathrum—they're members here at the Center—paid sixty-five thousand for their baby. 'Course, that was chalked up to legal fees for handling the adoption. Buying babies being against the law and all.''

"Of course. Do you know how much the young girls were paid?''

"Naw, but I'll guarantee you it wasn't in no fifty-thousand-dollar range.''

"Sissy, are you aware of anyone who might have wanted to kill the Moyers?''

She straightened up and glanced around the room. Carmen had finished with the napkin dispensers and was headed back to the juice bar. The tennis ladies had left, but the room was beginning to fill up. The grill crew had reported for duty and was handling orders from a group of fellows fresh from a pickup basketball game.

"Tell you what,'' Sissy said. "Let me get Carmen to handle the juice bar for a few minutes. What I have to say will take a little more privacy.'' She eyed the tip jar. "And a contribution to my Hawaii fund.''

She told me to wait for her in the employee break room in the back of the bistro. Although the room wasn't much bigger than a closet, someone had crammed an overstuffed sofa along one wall and a chrome dinette table with four chairs in the center. The wall decor was sparse—just a huge NO SMOKING sign and several posters extolling the virtues of daily exercise, healthy eating, and a drug-free lifestyle. A small sink and counter with a coffee pot and a rack of mugs took up the rest of the available wall space.

I sat down at the table and tried to make some sense out of what Sissy had told me. When Donald Moyer handled Cassie's adoption, there'd been no hint of anything like baby brokering. The legal fees we paid were quite reasonable and, even allowing for inflation, were certainly nowhere near the figures Sissy said they charged now. Miranda wasn't even in the picture back then. My sister was the one who told us about the birth mother's intention to relinquish Cassie for adoption.

Although it was true that we adopted Cassie without the aid of a licensed adoption agency, everything had been above board and legal. Even when you adopt independently as we did, you have to be interviewed and approved by a state adoption worker. They investigate everything—and I mean everything—about your life. Anyone who is physically able can have a baby with no questions asked, but if you're going to adopt you have to prove that you're fit to parent. I wondered how Moyer's clients hid the payment of fifty thousand dollars in legal fees from the social worker investigating them. A sum that high should've caused the caseworker to raise more red flags than a bullfighter.

Sissy bustled into the room and grabbed the coffee pot. "Y'all want some?" I declined, but she poured herself a mug before joining me at the table. "Lord almighty, these chairs are harder than my boss's heart." She pointed to the sofa. "Let's sit over there."

After we'd settled ourselves, she retrieved a pack of Winstons and a Bic lighter from her shorts pocket and lit up. "I hope the smoke don't bother you none," she said. "But without my nicotine fix I don't have nothin' to say."

I glanced at the NO SMOKING sign above her head. "Your boss doesn't mind?"

"Oh, I don't worry about him. He's always trying to get me to do something I'd rather not. I'm like a challenge." She snorted. "The doofus thinks of me as a 'before' photo."

"A 'before' photo?"

"You know, like in those magazines." She waved her cigarette at the health and beauty magazines scattered across the tabletop. "He's always tryin' to get me to take the hint. Go on a diet, exercise, become an 'after' photo. But, honey, he's just pissing in the wind if he thinks I'm gonna do any such thing."

So why work in a fitness center? I left the question unasked and waited patiently as she sipped the coffee between drags on her cigarette.

"I bet you're wondering how I wound up working in a place like this."

I smiled. She ought to hire herself out as a mind reader.

"It's a long and sorry tale. And anyways, that's not why we're sittin' here." She flicked an ash onto the floor. "Let's just say I'm outta here as soon as I get enough in my tip jar."

Figuring this was her way of telling me to pay up or she'd shut up, I took a twenty from my wallet and handed it to her. "I hope this will help."

She tucked the bill into her shirt pocket. "It's a start." She finished her cigarette and dropped the butt into the coffee mug, where it hissed momentarily and died.

"Back to the Moyers," I said. "You think you know who might have wanted them dead?"

"I don't think so. I know so."

"Why so confident?"

" 'Cause Miranda was being stalked."

"Stalked?"

"That's what I said, sugar. A stalker. Hung out here at the bistro all the time, waiting for Miranda to come in after her tennis match. Followed her everywhere else, too, from what I hear."

"Do you know why he was stalking her?"

"Oh, I know all about it. No one hangs out here that much without me finding out what's up. But the stalker wasn't no man. It was a woman, a woman who wanted her baby back."

"Someone Miranda had paid to relinquish her baby for adoption?"

Sissy nodded. "The girl was just a scared seventeen-year-old at the time. Her boyfriend had dumped her, and her parents didn't want no part of her. She was all alone and penniless. Just the way Miranda liked it. She sweet-talked the girl into signing away her rights, and after the delivery, Miranda whisked the baby away from the hospital, leaving an envelope stuffed with cash in its place.''

"When did the stalking start?"

"Six months later, after the girl got back together with her boyfriend. They wound up getting married after all, and so she gets in touch with Miranda to find out who has her son so she can get him back. 'Course, it's a done deal as far as Miranda is concerned. She tells the girl to get lost. But the girl, she won't let it go, keeps on hounding Miranda. Got so hysterical here at the bistro that we had to have security come escort her off the premises.''

"When was that?"

"The day before the Moyers were murdered."

"You think the girl did it?"

"Well, she's just a tiny thing, but her husband looks like he could play defense for the Seahawks. Maybe he did it— or the both of them together.''

"What're their names?"

Sissy smiled, drew another cigarette from the pack, and took her time lighting up. I got the hint and pulled another twenty from my wallet, which she promptly snatched out of my hand and tucked inside her shirt pocket. She still didn't say anything.

I had ten dollars left. "Just how much do you think their names are worth?"

She eyed my wallet. "How much more do ya'll have in there?"

I showed her the ten spot.

"Well, this is your lucky day, honey." She held out her hand. "Ten dollars, please."

I handed the bill over.

"Darla and Steve Schuster."

"Do you know where they live?"

"Just the city."

"Which is?"
"Out of your price range."

I WAS TIRED and hungry—not to mention broke—when I left the Sports Center. After stopping at an ATM to replenish my empty wallet, I pulled into a dashboard diner to replenish my empty stomach. I maneuvered the Miata into an empty stall and popped up the headlights for immediate service, already deciding that nothing short of Cholesterol City would do. I ordered a cheeseburger with all the trimmings, french fries, and an extra thick chocolate milkshake.

As I waited for my order, I replayed the conversation I'd had with Sissy, trying to sort through what she'd said. If it hadn't been for Rob Gravetsky's recommendation, I'd have dismissed what she'd told me altogether. Her condemnation of the Moyers as money-grabbing opportunists, while simultaneously demanding money for information about them, struck me as blatantly hypocritical.

Still, there could be something to what she said. Perhaps the killer had been after Miranda all along. Maybe it was Donald who had simply been in the wrong place at the wrong time. My mind was so busy pondering that possibility that I wolfed down the burger and fries on automatic pilot, hardly tasting a thing. I should've ordered a salad.

It was after eight o'clock when I got back to the marina. A full moon danced across the dark waters of Elliott Bay, bathing the entire area in a shimmering, silvery glow. I'm the only live-aboard on K dock, but several boats besides mine were decorated for the holiday season. *Forever Young*, a thirty-six foot sloop moored in the slip next to mine, had more Christmas lights lining the mast and deck than most houses. I hadn't gotten around to stringing any lights on *Second Wind*, and she was just a dark shadow in the moonlight. Resting in the slip, she looked gloomy and sad—like an abandoned ghost ship.

Only she wasn't abandoned. Someone was in the cockpit.

THIRTEEN

BOATING ETIQUETTE IS fairly simple. Never question the skipper's decisions and never go aboard a vessel without permission. That someone had boarded *Second Wind* without my knowledge or approval was, for me, more than mere breach of etiquette or trespass; it was a personal violation. My boat wasn't an object outside of myself, but a part of me, an extension of who I am. *You want to know how to sail, Kellie, darlin'? Then know your boat—know how she responds to your touch at the tiller, how she dips and soars in the water, how her rigging whistles in the wind, how her sails swell and luff, how her hull sounds when the water rushes past her. Then know yourself—know your dreams, your strengths, your values, and your beliefs. And when you reach that moment when you and your boat and the wind are at one with each other—only then will you know how to sail.*

I stood rooted to the dock where I'd first spotted the interloper and tried to get a better look at him, but the moonlight was at his back, and his face was hidden in the shadows of a large-brimmed hat. It didn't matter. I felt as though my entire body was caught in some sort of sensory web that absorbed and intensified everything—the salt in the water, the cool breeze on my cheek, the shadows in the moonlight, the slap-slap of the rigging against the mast, the thunderous beating of my own heart. Within seconds, the dark figure aboard *Second Wind* had become so indelibly imprinted in my mind that I could've closed my eyes and I'd still have seen him.

He sat in the cockpit as if he belonged there, self-possessed and relaxed, like a mariner enjoying a brief respite in the cool night air at the end of a pleasant day at sea. I had the sudden urge to shout, to rush down the dock, to climb aboard and confront him with his impudence. But before I could take any action, he stood up and waved, almost hitting himself on the boom. I could think of only one person that tall.

"Kingston? Is that you?" I shouted.

He waved again, but did not speak.

If he thought he could come aboard any old time he wanted just because he was a hotshot homicide detective, he had another think coming. I trudged up the dockside steps and climbed aboard. "Damn it, Kingston, you could've called."

I stumbled as I came into the cockpit, and he grasped my hand. "Here," he said. "Let me help you." The voice was husky, but definitely feminine—the hand soft and cool.

I shrugged out of her grasp, momentarily confused. "I'm OK."

Keeping my eyes fixed on her, I inched backward to the hatchway. When I got to the cabin door, I grabbed the emergency basket stowed under the dodger, fished out a flashlight, and shined the light in her face. Despite the glare, she had a friendly, dimpled smile.

Besides the large-brimmed fur hat, she wore a black turtleneck under a dark leather jacket trimmed in black mink around the collar and cuffs. Her tight-fitting gray pants were tucked inside a pair of chic, black leather boots. She was even taller than I had first thought, and I felt like a little kid looking up at her. I didn't think I'd ever seen her before, but she seemed very familiar.

"Kellie Montgomery?" she asked, still smiling.

"That's right, but who're you? And what the hell are you doing on my boat?"

"Oh, dear, you're upset." She held out her hand again. "I'm Emily Cummings. Please forgive me for coming aboard when you weren't here. I waited on the dock for quite a while, but the wind picked up, and I got cold. I thought I'd be warmer in the cockpit. I'm so sorry."

I didn't take her hand. "What do you want?"

"This is turning out all wrong. I really meant to call first. You see, I saw you at the Moyers' funeral. You were talking to Sara Zimmerman. She told me about how you're investigating the murders and gave me your card. I tried to get your attention in the church reception hall, but you were talking to some man in a rumpled raincoat. After that you seemed in a hurry to leave."

"You wanted to talk to me about the Moyers?"

She nodded. "I knew them fairly well. My husband and I belong to some of the same clubs, have many of the same friends as they did. Sara said you wanted to talk to anyone who knew them. I was visiting a friend in Magnolia earlier this evening, and since the marina is so close, I decided to stop by."

"How'd you know which slip was mine?"

"You'd written the number on the back of the card you gave Sara. I just took a chance that you'd be home."

I was starting to relax a bit when the implication hit me. "How'd you get through the security gate?"

"I used the intercom to announce myself, but they wouldn't open the gate since my name wasn't on your visitor list. I just waited until someone came along with a pass key and followed him on through the gate. No one questioned me." She shrugged an apology.

Aw, Bert, so much for your beefed-up security. I studied her a moment and decided she seemed sincere enough. She might even be of some help. As far as coming aboard *Second Wind*, her explanation made sense. And, given the circumstances, I'd probably overreacted. After all, most landlubbers don't have a clue about the relationship between sailors and their boats. I conjured up a more civil attitude and said, "Well, as long as you're here, why don't we go inside where it's warmer? I'm definitely interested in anything you can tell me about the Moyers."

I put the tea kettle on the stove and scrounged up some clean cups while she made herself comfortable at the table. There was a tenseness about her despite the graceful way she crossed her long legs and leaned her shoulders against the back of the dinette. Her dark eyes roved about the cabin, never settling on any one thing for more than a second or two. *Second Wind*'s interior was fairly standard for a sailboat—no-frills galley, small dining table, built-in sofa, and a few stowage cabinets. The decor was even more limited— a lighthouse poster on the forward bulkhead and a combination brass clock, thermometer, and barometer on the aft. As far as personal touches go, there was just the laptop, books, magazines, a stack of unopened Christmas cards, and a bunch of other junk piled on the table. I watched as she took it all in, a rapid, cursory survey that nevertheless hit on everything, including my clothes from last night still lying in a tangled heap on the floor.

I couldn't tell if she was disgusted, impressed, or amused. Her face was as composed and enigmatic as the Mona Lisa's. Except for a splash of bright red lipstick, she wore no makeup. I guessed her to be in her early thirties, but she could just as easily have been in her late twenties, for her warm olive skin had no visible wrinkles or other signs of aging. The thick black tangle of curls that had been covered by her hat now fell artfully about her shoulders. Despite the obvious differences in coloring, her stunning model-like beauty reminded me very much of Rose. I was positive now that I'd seen her somewhere before, but try as I might, I couldn't place where. Probably at the funeral just as she'd said. I knew it would bug me until I remembered so I busied myself with the tea to keep from staring.

"How long have you been living here?" she asked.

"Three years."

"Do you like living on a boat?"

"I'm still here."

She took another quick survey of the cabin. "I don't mean to pry, but I've always wondered about living on a boat. Some friends of ours have a forty-seven-foot Bayliner. One summer we went on a week-long cruise of the San Juan Islands with them. It was a lot of fun, but I really can't imagine living on a boat year round." She frowned and added, "*Especially* a sailboat!"

I was amused by her reaction. It was refreshing to meet someone who didn't have a romanticized view of the live-aboard lifestyle. I joined her at the table with two cups of steaming tea. "I have cream and sugar if you'd like."

"No, this is fine." She blew on the tea and then wrapped her slender hands around the cup for its warmth. She didn't appear to be in any hurry to get to the point of her visit. In between the occasional sips of tea, she toyed with the ring on her left hand, twisting and turning the gold band and its striking diamond inset with her fingers. I don't know whether I was more distracted by the size and quality of the diamond—it had to be a full carat, more likely two—or the fact that her fingernails had been bitten to the quick.

"About the Moyers," I said, attempting to get things on track. "I'd like to know why you've come to me instead of the police."

"Actually, I plan to talk to the police."

"Then why contact me?"

She hesitated for so long that I wasn't sure if she was simply searching for the right words or if she'd forgotten my question. "Go on," I prompted. "You contacted me because . . ."

She blinked and refocused. "You'll have to excuse me. I was very close to Miranda. We weren't just friends; we were like sisters. She helped me get through something once that I'll never forget." She swallowed another sip of tea and shook her head. "My God, I still can't believe she's gone. Her death hit me so hard that sometimes I just lose my train of thought. It's so frustrating."

Tears welled up in her eyes, and she asked for a tissue. I got a box from the head and set it in front of her. She dabbed at her eyes a moment and then brushed a stray curl out of her face. "Anyway," she said after she'd composed herself, "I contacted you because I thought I could help your investigation. Sara and I talked. You seem to know what you're doing."

From her lips to Kingston's ears. I like a compliment as much as anyone, but there's something about getting an "attagirl" from someone I've only just met that makes me wary. "I appreciate the vote of confidence, but if anyone knows what they're doing, it's the police."

"I understand, but what're they doing exactly?"

"The usual—investigating leads and suspects."

"Do they have any? Suspects, I mean."

"If they do, they're not sharing their findings with me."

"Oh? I got the impression from Sara that you were close to the investigation."

"Not really. I discovered the bodies, that's all."

"But you knew the Moyers, too, didn't you?"

"That's right."

"I don't mean to press, Kellie, but I'm really quite concerned that everything is being done to find their killer as soon as possible. You must have some ideas about what happened, some leads of your own that you're following."

"Perhaps, but the police are the experts when it comes to ideas and leads."

"If that's true, why isn't someone in custody yet? Why was Miranda's son killed, too?"

"I can't answer that, but the police have a lot of resources at their disposal to help them find out. In fact, if you tell me anything I think they need to know, I'll be obligated to pass it on.''

"That's fair enough," she said, smiling.

Since she'd been asking all the questions, I figured it was time to jump in with some of my own. "You said you were close to Miranda. Did she ever mention anything about someone bothering her?"

She pushed up the sleeves of her turtleneck and adjusted the gold bracelets that she wore on both wrists. "What do you mean, bothering her?" she asked.

"Following her around, trying to talk to her, making a scene, things like that."

She shook her head. "But then, Miranda wasn't a complainer. If something like that was happening, she would've just dealt with it. Miranda was an excellent problem solver."

I thought of Terri and her history of drug abuse. "I understand her daughter's had some problems of her own over the years. That must have been difficult for Miranda."

"Difficult? It was agonizing. Terri was one mixed-up kid even before she got hooked on drugs. The hardest thing Miranda ever had to do was kick her daughter out of the house. But that's what all the professionals recommended— I think it's called tough love or something like that."

I'd heard of the term. "The idea is to stop enabling the child's behavior."

"Right. Only it didn't work in Terri's case. The last I heard she was still drugging and boozing."

"Did she have any contact with the family after she left home?"

She shook her head. "Terri was public enemy number one as far as the Moyers were concerned. They didn't want anything to do with her, and from what I understand, the feeling was mutual."

"Besides Terri, was there anyone else who didn't feel so kindly toward Miranda?"

"I've given it a lot of thought but I just can't think of anyone who'd want to kill her. They'd have to be even crazier than Terri to do something like that. Miranda was a wonderful person, just wonderful—so caring and loving." Emily closed her eyes for a moment as if she were trying to squeeze back the tears.

"I've heard people say the same thing about her husband."

Her mouth tightened slightly, and when she spoke, her husky voice was soft, almost a whisper. "Most people don't know what I know."

"Which is?"

She eyed me over the rim of her cup. "That Donald Moyer was a blackmailer."

"Whoa! You want to run that by me again? A blackmailer?"

"That's right."

"Who was he blackmailing?"

"Who *wasn't* he blackmailing?"

"Come on."

"No, really. Do some digging around. You'll find that he had plenty of enemies." She leaned forward, her arms resting on the table. "Even his own partner, James Preston. I don't know all the details, but they were at odds over that Missing Link business."

"What do you know about the Missing Link?"

"Just that it causes a lot of grief."

"I thought it was a service—a reunion service of sorts."

"Well, I guess you could say that. According to what I heard from Miranda, Preston thought it was unethical, a gross violation of privacy or something like that. Anyway, he wanted it stopped, but Donald had no intention of letting ethics get in the way of his pocketbook. He threatened to expose Preston's dirty linen if he tried to interfere."

"What dirty linen?"

"I really don't know, but it must have been pretty bad. Makes you wonder about Preston's own ethics, doesn't it?"

"Are you suggesting that James Preston killed the Moyers?"

She fingered her ring again but said nothing.

"From what I hear, the Missing Link is still in operation. Doesn't that strike you as peculiar? If Preston was so opposed to the service, why wouldn't he have shut it down as soon as Moyer was out of the way?"

"Maybe you should check with his assistant."

"Yolanda Vanasek?"

She nodded. "She was fairly close to Donald, if you know what I mean."

"She was his paralegal. Are you implying that there was more to their relationship?"

"Oh, I don't know. Miranda never came right out and said so. For one thing, she never had any proof. But she suspected something was going on. In any event, she didn't like the woman. I do know that."

"Did she like Preston's wife?"

"Nancy? I guess so. They played a lot of tennis together at the club. Why do you ask?"

"Just trying to get a picture of how things were."

"Well, I can say this about Nancy: She liked the good life. And James Preston would do anything to make sure she had it."

"Including murder?"

She shrugged. "Who knows? None of this makes sense to me. Except for Terri, who hasn't really been in the picture for years, the entire Moyer family's been wiped out. And for what? Money? Ethics? Blackmail?"

The boat suddenly rocked and sloshed some tea from our cups. Emily grabbed the table. "What was *that*?"

"Hazards of living aboard a sailboat. Probably a tanker pulling into Pier 91. We get some wave action in spite of the breakwater." I got a rag from the galley and mopped up the spill.

Emily looked at her watch. Her Cartier timepiece was as striking as her ring and bracelets—a brushed gold band dotted with a ring of diamonds encircling the face. "I need to get going." She gathered up her jacket and hat. "Kellie, I hope you'll think about what I said."

"Don't worry. I appreciate the information about Preston and I'll definitely pursue it."

She paused at the hatchway ladder and glanced around the cabin one last time. "You know, this is pretty nice. I always thought sailboats were cramped little boxes. Your boat is quite comfortable."

"Thank you. I like it."

"You give lessons, don't you? Sailing lessons, I mean."

"That's right. I run a school here at the marina—Sound Sailing."

"I'd be interested in some lessons myself."

"The school's closing for the holidays soon, but we'll have a full slate of classes after the first of the year." I rummaged through the mess on the table and found a business card. "Here," I said. "Just give us a call."

She fingered the card and said, "I guess I could, but I'd really like to get started right away. Something to take my mind off Miranda's death, you know?" She looked at me hopefully. "And I'd like to surprise my kids. They think all I do is run around to charity events and fund-raisers for my husband's campaign."

Now I remembered where I'd seen the woman—in the newspapers and on television. Until she mentioned her husband, I hadn't connected her with Conrad Cummings, a mover and shaker on the political scene. Some folks thought he was headed for the governor's mansion. His charming and photogenic wife, Emily, was a media darling and, in his opponents' views, the only thing he had going for him. While I didn't consider myself a big fan of Conrad Cummings—or politicians in general—I was momentarily taken with the fact that his wife, maybe our future governor's wife, was aboard my boat. And more than a little embarrassed that I hadn't recognized her earlier.

"I don't think a group lesson would work for me. Can't

you give me some private lessons or something?'' she pleaded.

"Well, I suppose I could, but—"

"Wonderful! How 'bout tomorrow?"

I WAS EXHAUSTED and annoyed with myself when Emily Cummings finally said good-bye. After I'd gotten over my initial reaction to who she was, I'd explained to her at length that I didn't give private lessons and on those rare occasions when I did, it was only for close friends or family. But she'd kept after me, offering to pay double my usual fee or anything I wanted, actually, if I'd just make an exception in her case. I finally said yes. And that was what annoyed me.

For most of my life, I'd been a people pleaser. A never-say-no, others-first type of woman. Where that role came from, I don't know. Certainly not from Grampy or Wendell. They'd both tried to tell me many times and in many ways just how self-limiting the role was. Their advice never sank in until after they were both gone. It was only then that I finally realized how short a time we have on this planet— so why not spend it doing what I truly wanted to do?

Since my first love, my only true love besides Wendell, had been sailing, I decided to go for it. But I knew that simply fitting a day of sailing in here and there wouldn't be enough. What I needed to do was to completely rearrange my life so that sailing became my life. Hence, *Second Wind*, the move to Larstad's, and the new job. And most important, the new attitude. Except for Cassie, most people have championed my decision, although I got plenty of comments about making too many changes so soon after Wendell's death. Bert still sometimes says I've gone overboard (no pun intended) on the attitude part. Meaning, of course, my sassy mouth.

Yet tonight I'd fallen right back into my same old people-pleasing pattern. I'd given in to Emily about the private lessons even though I didn't want to do it. Maybe it was her near-celebrity status, but I found myself fascinated by her, unwilling to displease her by saying no and, at the same time, kicking myself for being too weak to do so. I also felt guilty for taking advantage of her public persona for my own financial gain. For there was no denying that having Emily Cummings as a client of Sound Sailing was a publicity coup. It certainly wouldn't hurt business for the school, which, at this point, needed all the help it could get. So in the end I'd said yes. I postponed her first lesson, though, until after Christmas, explaining that I'd already made plans and wouldn't be home all day tomorrow. She was disappointed, but conceded that she had a full schedule as well, and the impromptu lesson would've required a major reshuffling of her plans.

I went to bed immediately after she left, but found it difficult to sleep. I tossed and turned most of the night, reliving the events of the day and sorting through my reactions to them. When I finally did drift off, my dreams were strange and disturbing. I woke up at five o'clock the next morning, still exhausted, but wide awake and unable to go back to sleep. Sometime during the night I'd made a mental list of everything I needed to do if the Moyer case was ever going to get solved. Five o'clock in the morning or not, there was no time like the present.

FOURTEEN

THE PROBLEM WITH getting an early start on things—at least a five A.M. start—is that no one else is inclined to cooperate. By the time I had showered, dressed, and eaten a leisurely breakfast, it was still only six o' clock. Too early to make the phone calls I had planned. I thought about spending some time working on the Weasel's project, but decided instead to keep the bargain I'd made with God and do something about my long-neglected housekeeping duties. I washed the dishes, swept up the dustballs floating around the cabin, scrubbed out the toilet bowl, and made a pass at straightening up the mess on the dinette table before finally calling it quits at eight o' clock.

The first person on my list was Detective Kingston. On the whole, I wasn't keen on enlightening him about anything after the way he'd been treating me. But I had promised to let him know if I discovered anything important even though what I considered important and what he considered important weren't necessarily one and the same. I definitely didn't intend to tell him about Rose's planned visit to the Moyer and Preston Law Offices, but I thought I'd report what Emily had said about the blackmail angle. Maybe that was the

subject of the argument that Yolanda Vanasek had overheard. Kingston wasn't in when I called, so I left my number
with the duty officer, making sure he added a note that I
had some important information about the Moyer case.

I also wanted to talk to Rose. I didn't know when she
was planning to get away from the office to check out the
Missing Link, but I thought she ought to know about Preston
before she went. She was in a meeting and couldn't take
my call. The marina was in the middle of a big audit for
the Nakitos, and as the accountant, Rose was up to her hip
boots in meetings most of the time. I left a message on her
voice mail.

The third person on my phone-call list was Norma Bailey.
Norma and I went to high school together and had remained
friends ever since. As a customer service supervisor with
Washington Power, I figured she could tell me where Darla
and Steve Schuster lived. If Darla Schuster was stalking
Miranda on a daily basis, the chances were good that she
lived somewhere in the electrical utility's ten-county service
area. Surprisingly, I got right through to Norma.

"Kellie! Gosh, it's good to hear from you. What've you
been up to?"

"Other than investigating a murder or two, not much."

"What murder?"

"Maybe you've read about the case. It's been in all the
papers—Donald and Miranda Moyer?"

"Oh, my gosh. How are you involved? Wait a minute,
scratch that. The marina. I bet you were there when they
found them, weren't you?"

"That's right. I'm trying to figure out who killed them
and I need your help. I hate to ask since your records are
confidential but—"

"Don't worry about it. Of course I'll help you. Who
knows how long I'm going to be working here anyway.
They just laid off twenty more people—long-time employees, all of them. It's unbelievable. Staffing realignment is
what they're calling it. Panic is more like it."

"Panic?"

"Government deregulation of the utility industry. It's just around the corner. Washington Power's trying to prepare for it by streamlining its operations, becoming more efficient. So says management, but we all know what it really means—more layoffs ahead. Morale is the pits."

"I'm sorry, Norma."

"I used to think I understood this company and its policies. Not anymore." She was quiet for a beat, then said, "But there's something else I don't understand."

"What's that?"

"Why you're getting yourself involved in a murder investigation again."

"Oh, Norma, I don't know, either. Believe me, I've asked myself that same question. The Moyers were dock neighbors, but Donald Moyer also handled Cassie's adoption. I feel obligated to the man. Besides, my job isn't so secure, either. Old man Larstad is being courted by a Japanese firm. If he sells the marina, it could mean my job, maybe even Bert's."

"And you playing detective is going to save things somehow?"

"Maybe not. I just hoped that if I could find out who killed the Moyers, it might make Bert and me look good—show the Nakitos how committed we are to the marina, that kind of thing."

"How does your old pal Allen Kingston feel about you stepping into his business again?"

"He doesn't want me in the picture, but—"

"You can't help yourself."

"Exactly."

"Oops, I've got another call waiting. What do you need, Kellie?"

I gave her the Schusters' names. As an afterthought, I also asked her to locate the Chapmans, the couple Sara Zimmerman had told me about. After Sissy's startling comments about Miranda and baby brokering, I'd sort of forgotten about them. Norma put me on hold while she searched the computer. I listened to the same bland Muzak for a couple of minutes until she came back.

"I found a Robert and Betty Chapman, but the computer is still searching for the Schusters. The Chapmans live in Bremerton. No phone listed." She gave me their address and then put me on hold again to check what the computer had come up with for the Schusters. When she came on the line this time, she told me she'd have to get back to me on their address. "The computer just crashed," she explained. "God only knows how long we'll be off-line."

I waited around for another hour hoping that Kingston or Rose would return my call, but when the phone finally rang, it wasn't either one of them on the line.

"Is this Kellie Montgomery of Sound Sailing?" The voice was pleasant but businesslike.

"Yes. How may I help you?"

"My name is Reba Stanton. I'm a psychiatric social worker at Coleman Rehabilitation Center and I'm calling on behalf of Terri Moyer. I understand that you've invited her to attend a sailing class?"

"That's correct. Terri said she was interested in learning how to sail but didn't know if she could leave the center. Something about needing a pass?"

"A day pass. We issue them for patients who are near the end of their treatment period."

"Right. She said she was almost through with her program."

"I'd like to talk to you about that, Ms. Montgomery."

"Please call me Kellie. We're pretty informal around here."

The social worker laughed. "And call me Reba. I apologize if I sounded officious."

"Not at all."

"Good. Before I proceed, though, I want to assure you that Terri has given me written permission to talk with you about her case."

"Written permission to talk to me? Now that sounds officious."

"But necessary. Without a release from Terri, I'd be breaching patient confidentiality if I talked to you about her."

"I see."

"So, as I said, we issue day passes for clients like Terri who are nearing the end of their treatment program. The intent is to ease our patients back into the outside world while still providing them with a structured living environment here at the center." Reba paused. "Frankly, Kellie, I'm very pleased to hear that Terri is interested in sailing. Her lifestyle choices in the past haven't always been that positive. If she follows through with the lessons, I'm sure they will be very helpful to her ongoing recovery."

"*If* she follows through? Is there some reason to think that she won't?"

"I'm not at liberty to discuss the specifics of Terri's case, but I will say that her problems go beyond drug and alcohol addiction. As a result, she has developed a pattern of behavior that consistently subverts her progress."

"What do you mean?"

"She sabotages herself. At the very moment a goal is about to be realized, Terri will crash. For example, she dropped out of high school just before graduation."

"She seems quite intelligent."

"Oh, she is. But intelligence really has nothing to do with it. Terri suffers from a personality disorder. It manifests itself in many ways, but when things are on the upswing in Terri's life, she'll typically regress."

"I still don't think I understand."

"She backslides. Relapses. Retreats. Here's another example that may help you understand: She broke off a good relationship with a fine young man just when it was clear that their relationship had a good chance of lasting. Unfortunately there have been many instances like this in Terri's past. If she completes your program, it will be a major breakthrough for her.''

"That's a lot to lay on a few sailing lessons."

"Perhaps, but sailing may be just what is needed to turn Terri's life around. We can only hope."

She ended the conversation by asking for specifics about the class—date, time, and location. When I finished filling her in, she asked if I would call her after Terri's lesson.

"May I ask why?"

"Certainly. I need to verify that Terri actually showed up for the lesson. She's used day passes in the past as a way to do whatever she wanted—which wasn't always that healthy, if you know what I mean."

I promised to call her as soon as the lesson was over, then asked a question that had been bothering me ever since we'd begun talking. "I'm curious, Reba, how Terri Moyer can afford a private rehabilitation program. From what she told me, she doesn't have much income. She was worried about paying for the sailing lessons."

Reba hesitated, then said, "I'm surprised she would say that. Terri has no money worries whatsoever. Although they were estranged, her father established a generous trust fund for her years ago. Payment for the sailing lessons will be no problem."

"Great," I said. "I can always use a paying customer." What I wasn't so sure I could use was someone who lied.

I checked for messages as soon as we said our good-byes, but no call from Kingston or Rose had come in while I was on the line with Reba. It soon became clear that I was just wasting time waiting for their calls. My answering machine could take messages as well as anyone else's. I rummaged through my handbag and pulled out a Washington State Ferry schedule to check the departure times for Bremerton.

Sometime during the early morning hours, while I'd been restlessly tossing and turning in bed, the fog had come in from the sea like a gauzy white veil, transfiguring everything it touched. The effect was surreal, as if something ethereal had wrapped the marina, the city, the mountains, the entire landscape in a gigantic burial shroud while the populace slumbered. I was unnerved by the transformation and hoped the fog would burn off before I left the marina, but it still held the landscape in its eerie grasp as I headed down Alaskan Way toward the ferry terminal.

I pulled onto the loading dock just as the last of the cars were boarding the ferry. Although its cavernous parking deck looked completely full, the deckhands waved me aboard. They must've thought the Miata was small enough to squeeze in somewhere, which is precisely where I wound up—wedged like a thin slice of bologna between a big Peterbilt truck and an old VW bus. Since I had to make a rather urgent pit stop, I struggled with the door until I finally got it open wide enough for me to hop out. I took the stairs to the passenger deck where I found the restrooms and later the coffee shop.

I carried my tea and bagel to one of the tables next to a large picture window. The sun had burst through the last wisps of fog like a child rushing outside to play. Despite the sun's bright cheerfulness, I couldn't shake the effects of the fog. It hovered about me like a gloomy aura, plunging my spirits into something close to melancholy. Once the ferry rounded Bainbridge Island and made its way through Rich Passage into Sinclair Inlet, I caught a glimpse of the southernmost edge of Bremerton and Puget Sound Naval Shipyard.

For some absurd reason, seeing the shipyard again finally lifted my spirits. Grampy had been a Chief Petty Officer in the Navy when his ship, the USS *Constellation,* came in for overhaul at PSNS. Like many Navy families who come to the Pacific Northwest, he fell in love with the area. Grampy had moved in with us after my parents' deaths but when he retired he decided to stay in Bremerton.

I wasn't so keen on leaving Maine. *It's God's country out here, Kellie, darlin'. You'll see. And the sailing's perfect.* God's country or not, it was Donna's reaction upon hearing the plans that prompted me to embrace the move to the Pacific Northwest. "You're going to live where?" she'd asked with arched eyebrows. "You know," she said, "living in Bremerton is like reading a book backwards. You can do it, but what's the point?" Two years later, she was living in Bremerton herself when Bert accepted a job at a local marina.

The address Norma gave me for the Chapmans was in a section of town that had probably been nice at one time— fifty years ago. Bremerton's boom years had been during World War II when the remains of the naval fleet, wounded and barely alive after the attack at Pearl Harbor, limped into the shipyard for repairs. Jobs, money and prosperity followed for years. But the bustling little town that greeted us twenty-five years ago was long gone. Most of the stores that had once comprised the downtown core had relocated to the new mall in Silverdale. Even the USS *Missouri,* the famous battleship from WWII and Bremerton's star tourist attraction, had left town during the Gulf War and would not be returning.

The Chapmans lived within walking distance of the shipyard in one of the small clapboard houses that had been hastily constructed during the war years. I parked the Miata across the street and left the engine idling while I rechecked the address. The house looked as if it still had its original paint, a dull, gun-metal gray that was peeling and chipped. A carpet of bright-green moss covered the entire length and breadth of the sharply pitched roof. By contrast, the front yard was nothing more than a dry patch of dirt with a few hardy blades of grass poking out here and there like spiteful relatives. The tiny yard was enclosed by a sturdy cyclone fence with a NO TRESPASSING sign prominently wired to the front gate.

It was hard to tell whether anyone was home. Faded blue drapes were drawn tightly across the lone front window, and aside from a battered Dodge van propped up on cinder blocks, there were no vehicles in the driveway. Unlike the yard next door—littered with an assortment of toys, balls, bikes, and other kid stuff—the outside of the Chapmans' house showed no evidence of a child's presence.

Thumbtacked to the middle of the Chapmans' front door was another sign warning: NO SOLICITING!! How about soliciting information? Nah, doesn't count. I couldn't find a doorbell so I rapped on the door, immediately setting off a flurry of desperate scratching and barking on the other side. A woman with weary gray eyes opened the door a crack and peered over the security chain. She nestled a snarling white dog at her bosom like a baby. I'm a dog lover from way back, but this thing looked like an ugly dust mop with teeth. It snarled and stared menacingly at me—appearing ready, willing, and quite eager to leap out of the woman's slender arms at the slightest provocation.

To the dog, she said, "Lucy, hush!" To me, she said, "What is it?" Her voice was as weary as her eyes.

"Mrs. Chapman? Betty Chapman?"

"Yes?"

"My name is Kellie Montgomery. I'd like to talk to you for a moment. May I come inside?"

She glanced at the dust mop, who was softly growling now, and then back at me. "I'm sorry, but I just can't buy anything today." Still clutching Lucy, she nudged the door with her knee.

But I blocked the door with my foot like the saleswoman she assumed I was. "Please, Mrs. Chapman," I said. "I'm not selling anything. I just want to talk to you."

"Are you from the state?"

"The state?"

I knew she hadn't heard the question mark at the end of my reply, but I didn't say anything further as she lifted the security chain and opened the door wide enough for me to pass through.

I wasn't sure who she thought I was, but it didn't matter. I'd made it inside.

FIFTEEN

BETTY CHAPMAN OFFERED me a seat on the couch, a lumpy green sectional that was more comfortable than it looked. "I'll be right back," she said. Still cradling the lovely Lucy in her arms, she trudged out of the room. And to the kitchen, judging by the distinct smell of liver and onions wafting into the living room.

While I waited, I surveyed the Chapmans' sparsely furnished home. Besides the couch, there was only a tattered La-Z-Boy recliner and one other chair in the square box living room. The couch and the recliner were separated by a mahogany coffee table and arranged to face the TV in the corner. The table was cluttered with several dog-eared issues of *Soap Opera Digest*, a large ceramic ashtray heaped with lipstick-smeared cigarette butts, a flyer for a "two for one night" at Bernie's Pizza Parlor, and a stack of unopened bills that looked as if they'd been lying around awhile. A 1940s-style floor lamp provided what little light there was in the room. No photographs or other pictures adorned the dingy, beige walls. I suddenly felt depressed, as if the early-morning fog had somehow enveloped the Chapmans' tiny living room in its gloomy aura.

"Lucy's harmless," Betty said when she returned. "It's just that she's not used to company and she gets a little excited." She slumped onto the opposite end of the couch and tucked her jeans-clad legs underneath her. I guessed her to be about forty or so, a conservative guess, given the wrinkle lines that marked her long narrow face and the stooped, arthritic way she moved. Her shoulder-length hair was gray like her eyes, and she wore it pulled back from her face in a loose ponytail.

She reached into the pocket of her T-shirt and took out an empty pack of Virginia Slims. She crushed it into a ball and threw it onto the coffee table. "Been trying to quit, anyway," she said. She looked at me expectantly. "Well, what's the word on Stevie? We going to get any help with him or not?"

"Excuse me?"

"Aid," she said irritably. "You know, financial assistance for Stevie's medicine and treatments." She gestured toward the furnishings in the room. "As you can see, we're about tapped out here."

"Is Stevie your son?" I asked.

"My adopted son. Don't you have our records?"

"Mrs. Chapman, I'm not from the state."

She sat up a little straighter and frowned. "Who're you with, then?"

"Larstad's Marina in Seattle," I said. I pulled a business card from my shoulder bag and handed it to her.

She stared at the card a moment. "I don't get it. Why are you here?"

"I'm assisting in the investigation of Donald and Miranda Moyer's deaths. I was told that Mr. Moyer handled the adoption of your son. Is that correct?"

"Yes, but . . . you say Moyer's dead?"

"Murdered."

Her eyes widened, but she said nothing.

"His wife was murdered, too."

"My God," she said, her voice barely audible. She

stroked her cheek with a flattened palm a moment before asking, "Who would do such a thing?"

"That's what I'm trying to find out. I was hoping that you might be able to tell me something about the Moyers."

"Like what?" she asked.

"Anything. Anything at all that will help me understand what they were like. I'm particularly interested in their business dealings."

"I don't know what to say."

"Perhaps you could start with Stevie's adoption."

"That would take all day and I—" She stood at the sound of footsteps on the wooden porch and ran to greet the short, wiry man who strode through the front door. I assumed he was her husband, Robert Chapman, even though he didn't return the kiss she gave him. He had an authoritative air about him—a little Napoleon who swaggered into the living room without speaking. He was dressed in typical shipyard garb—metal helmet, steel-toed boots, trousers, and a heavy pea jacket that he shrugged off and tossed to Betty as if she were a handy coat rack.

"Lunch is on the stove," she said softly as she folded the coat over her arm.

He nodded and removed his helmet, exposing a thinning mop of reddish brown hair. Without the helmet, the guy looked more like a bookkeeper than a shipyard worker. But the blue helmet with the Shop 56 insignia on the side told me he was a member of the shipyard's pipefitting crew.

He ran his fingers through his flattened hair before acknowledging me. "You from the state?"

I stood and offered him my hand. "Hello. I'm Kellie Montgomery."

His freckled hand was small and bony, but he had a take-no-prisoners grip that left my fingers smarting. This was no bookkeeper. "Bob Chapman," he said.

"She's here about Donald Moyer," offered Betty.

"Moyer! What's that no-good SOB done to us now?" he asked.

Betty glanced over her shoulder toward the kitchen. "I've got to tend to lunch. She'll explain," she said, scurrying out of the room before anyone could object.

"Well?" asked Chapman. It was more dare than question.

I met his icy blue stare and said, "Donald and Miranda Moyer have been killed. I'm investigating their deaths."

"You're shittin' me!"

I shook my head.

"Wait a minute, here. You're telling me Moyer's dead?"

"That's right."

He took a step backward and slowly eased into the recliner. "Well, I'll be damned. So Moyer's dead."

"Murdered. Hadn't you heard?"

"Hell, *The Bremerton Sun* don't print nothing but lost puppy stories. You with the police?"

"No, Larstad's Marina."

"What's a marina got to do with a murder investigation?"

"The Moyers' bodies were found aboard their yacht. I'm with the harbormaster's office, assisting the police in the investigation." By now the explanation had begun to roll off my tongue.

"So what do you want from me?"

"Information—about the Moyers and their business dealings."

"Little lady, you've come to the right place. I can tell you plenty, and none of it's good." He twisted his head toward the kitchen. "Hey, Betts!" he bellowed. "Bring me the Moyer file!" To me he said, "We have proof. Lots of it."

Within seconds, Betty Chapman bustled into the room carrying a bulging cardboard file box. She handed it to her husband and said, "Lunch is almost ready."

He took the box without comment and began to rummage through it.

"You want to eat lunch out here?" she asked.

He nodded distractedly and pulled some folders from the box.

She turned to me. "Could I bring you something, too? I've got plenty."

I was hungry, but just the thought of liver and onions—not to mention the smell, trailing after Betty Chapman like cheap perfume—was enough to quell my appetite. I shook my head. "Thanks for asking, though."

She glanced at her husband. "I'll get a tray and be right back. Okay, honey?" She waited a beat and, getting no response, hurried out of the room.

Bob Chapman tossed a fistful of papers onto the coffee table. "Take a look at these."

I thumbed through the papers, and he went back to the box, pulling out additional files and tossing their contents onto the table. As far as I could tell, the proof he claimed to have consisted primarily of billings from various doctors, clinics, and hospitals. Most were located in Bremerton, but a few had Seattle addresses. All of them were for the same patient—Steven G. Chapman.

"Stevie's only six years old, but he's in a treatment facility out in Shelton," explained Chapman.

"What's wrong with him?"

"Ha! What ain't wrong with him?"

Betty bustled into the room again, this time carrying a plastic tray with a single mug of coffee on it. I wondered where his lunch was, but Chapman didn't seem to notice. He set the file box on the floor and balanced the tray on his bony lap. He picked up the coffee mug—little finger daintily extended like a society matron—and took a sip.

"Betts makes a damn good cup o' coffee. Sure she can't get you some?"

Betty had already settled onto the couch, but she leaned forward when her husband spoke. I couldn't tell if she was intimidated by him or merely anxious to please.

I put out a hand. "Don't get up," I said. "I'm fine. Had plenty of tea on the ferry."

She glanced over at Chapman before easing back onto the couch.

"Betty," I said, "why is Stevie in a treatment facility?"

She glanced at her husband again before answering. "He's got a few problems."

"What kind of problems?"

Chapman jabbed at the air with his finger. "Listen, it was like this: Stevie's birth mother was a druggie and an alcoholic. She never shoulda been allowed to keep him in the first place. Stevie's health was bad from the day he was born, but his so-called mother only added to his problems."

"How was that?"

"Abuse. Knocked the kid around plenty. When the state finally took him away from her, his head had been totally messed up. Then he was bounced from foster home to foster home until his junkie mother convinced the state she was clean and sober. She wasn't, of course, but what the hell did they care? By the time we adopted him, he was four years old going on forty, the life he'd had."

"You were very courageous to adopt him. Given his background, most people would've found parenting such a child too risky."

Chapman burst out laughing, a bitter laugh that ended in a spasm of coughing.

Betty said, "Donald Moyer never told us."

"You mean you knew nothing about Stevie before you adopted him?"

Chapman took a sip of coffee before answering. "Moyer didn't tell us one damn thing, and we were so anxious to get a kid we didn't ask any questions."

"You see, we lost our own little boy when he was two," explained Betty. "I couldn't have any more kids. Adoption seemed like a good way to go, but the lists were so long. We'd just about given up when we heard about this lawyer—"

"Shyster, as it turned out," interrupted Chapman. "We knew a couple here in town who'd adopted a baby through

Donald Moyer. Cost them an arm and a leg, but they were thrilled with their baby. They had nothing but praise for Moyer. We had some savings—not a lot, mind you—but we were willing to give it all to him if he could help us.'' He picked up his coffee mug as if to take another sip, but waved it at his wife instead. ''Good God, Betts, when do I get some lunch?''

She jumped up from the couch. ''Oh, I'm so sorry, hon. I forgot.''

Chapman shook his head as Betty hurried off to the kitchen one more time. ''This whole thing has her acting goofier than a loon. Can't remember what she's up to half the time.''

''You were saying about Moyer,'' I prompted.

''He suckered us in but good. Even invited us out on that fancy boat of his. *Merry Maiden*, he called it. We felt like royalty, the way he and that wife of his treated us. Champagne flowing, everyone so goddamn nice.''

''Who was there?'' I asked.

''Just a bunch of folks Moyer had promised to get babies for. And, of course, the other couples he'd already gotten babies for. They told us all about their kids, how Moyer was the best adoption lawyer in town.''

''Besides party hostess, what was Miranda's role in all of this?''

''Oh, she was the deal clincher.''

''How's that?''

''Got us to talking all about our Denny. We even showed her a photo of him. Then she showed us a photo, too. Stevie was the spittin' image of Denny. Same blue eyes and strawberry blond hair. They could've been brothers.'' Chapman pulled two photos out of his wallet and tossed them onto the coffee table. He was right. The two little boys looked enough alike to be twins.

''We fell in love with the kid right on the spot,'' he said. ''Wrote out a retainer for Moyer's services that very night. Three months after that party, Stevie was ours. We had no money left, but it didn't matter. We had our son again."

"When did the problems start?" I asked.

"Almost immediately. At first, we weren't too concerned. Figured it would take the boy awhile to get used to us."

"So the adoption was finalized?"

"Oh, yeah," Chapman said. "His mother, the junkie, signed the papers right away. Everything went through, smooth as silk. We even joined one of those adoption support groups with some of the people we'd met through Moyer." He waved his hand dismissively. "High rollers, the whole lot of 'em. They were able to give money to their kids' birth mothers for medical expenses and things like that, but we . . . well, it was damn embarrassing, not being able to do the same. Especially when that wife of his kept pushing us."

"Miranda pushed you for money?"

"Big time," Chapman said. "Laid a guilt trip on us you would not believe. Said we had to do something for Stevie's birth mother. The line she gave us was that the gal needed to go back to school to get her in life in order. We had no idea at the time that his mother was barely eighteen and a junkie to boot. But she wouldn't have gotten the money in any case, knowing the Moyers."

"You figure Donald and Miranda were running a scam?"

He nodded. "Damn tootin'. They had no intention of sending any money to that gal. But back then we believed them. We shoulda been suspicious that something was up, though. Especially when they told us not to say anything about the money to that social worker lady, the one the state sent out to investigate us. We tried scraping together what they wanted out of my paycheck each month, but there just wasn't enough to go around. Then we got word the shipyard was headed for an RIF."

"A reduction in force?"

"Right, I didn't get laid off, but my hours were cut back. There was just no way we could help anyone but ourselves.

We even had to drop out of the support group; we couldn't afford the ferry trip to Seattle and back."

Lucy's wild barking stopped further conversation. We both turned toward the kitchen. "Jesus H.," said Chapman, sniffing at the air. "Something's burning." He bounded out of the recliner and raced for the kitchen like the devil was after him. But it was only me. When Chapman pushed open the door and charged into the kitchen, a panic-stricken Lucy scrambled out of his way—and flung herself into my arms.

Clouds of thick black smoke billowed out at us. I couldn't see anything, but as I backed away I could hear Chapman yelling for Betty. Coughing, I headed toward the living room with Lucy and opened up the front door. When I stepped onto the porch and tried to get rid of her, she wouldn't budge out of my arms, preferring instead to snarl and snap at me. "Go on, you little dirtbag. I have to call the fire department."

"No, it's okay," Bob Chapman said from the doorway. "I got the fire out."

"Is Betty all right?"

Chapman sweet-talked Lucy out of my arms and sat down on the porch steps. "Yeah, I guess so," he said, gently stroking the dog's backside. "She wasn't in the kitchen."

"Where is she?" I asked, joining him on the steps.

"Hell if I know." He shrugged. "She'll turn up sooner or later, though." His shoulders drooped as he added, "She was gone three days the last time. Went right out the back door just like she did today. Only it was chili that got burned then." Lucy had fallen asleep, but he continued to stroke her as he talked. "Found out later she'd gone to Seattle. Her brother lives over there."

The cocky, take-charge attitude he'd had earlier was gone. I suspected the little Napoleon act was just that—an act, something he used to hide his true emotions. Bob Chapman struck me as the type of man who kept his hurt balled up somewhere deep inside, unwilling or unable to let it go. I knew what a heavy burden that could be. Sometimes all it took was a willing listener and the burden could be lifted for a while. So I offered to listen. He was hesitant at first, but with some prompting on my part, he finally opened up and filled me in on how much their lives had changed after Stevie's adoption.

He said they used to live in a nice house over near Rolling Hills Golf Course. When Stevie started having problems, they tried to use their medical insurance to cover his medical bills. The insurance company refused to pay, claiming he had a pre-existing condition, which was eventually diagnosed as severe attention deficit disorder. They had him in and out of therapy, trying first one doctor and then another. The expenses mounted; they borrowed against the equity in their home and eventually wound up losing it altogether. The house they were in now was a rental, a cheap rental, but they still had trouble making the monthly payments.

"Why don't you have the adoption reversed?" I asked.

"We could never do that," he said. "Stevie's our son, and, in spite of everything, we love him. He's in a treatment facility now and making progress. If we can just hang on, I know he'll make it."

The shipyard whistle blew and woke Lucy, setting her off on another barking spree. Chapman hushed the dog and said, "Christ, I'm late. Gotta get back to work."

"Before you go, I have one more question. Do you have any idea who might have killed the Moyers?"

"Besides me, you mean?"

"Did you?"

Chapman laughed. "Don't pussyfoot around, just come right out and ask."

"Well, did you?"

"No! But I'll tell you this much, I did entertain the notion. Yes, ma'am, I did entertain the notion. And I wasn't the only one, either. Check around. You'll see."

"Any particular place I should be checking?"

"Try starting with Moyer's office. That assistant of his, what's her name?"

"Yolanda Vanasek?"

"Yeah, that's the one. Talk with her. She handled all his stuff. If anyone knows about motives, she does."

"What makes you say that?"

" 'Cause, little lady, she's the one Moyer had do all his dirty work, including that little side business of his."

"The Missing Link?"

"Yeah, that's what he called it." He looked at his watch. "But that's all you're gonna get from me today. I gotta get out of here. My foreman's just lookin' for an excuse to fire my sorry ass."

Before leaving, he put Lucy back in the house and left the door unlocked in case Betty showed up before he got home. I asked him to call and let me know how she was doing. But I already knew. Hanging on. That's what Chapman had said they were doing. I couldn't help but wonder just how far out on the ledge they were. Constant worry is a tiring thing. Like a rock worn flat by the unremitting motion of the sea, your strength becomes so dissipated that eventually you have nothing left of yourself to give, and you crack. They'd lost their savings, their home, and possibly their son. About the only thing Bob Chapman seemed to have left was anger and a very troubled wife.

I had some time to kill before I caught the next ferry back to Seattle so I drove around town awhile hoping to spot Betty Chapman. Then, feeling hungry, I parked the Miata and walked along the newly renovated waterfront in search of a place to eat. After lunch, I decided to stick around a little longer and get some Christmas shopping done at the Saturday Market—a hodgepodge of small vendor stands set up along the concrete boardwalk. Before I realized it, I'd missed the next ferry and the one after that. And I'd seen nary a sign of Betty Chapman.

By the time I finally made it back to the marina, it was well after dark. A crisp, gentle breeze was blowing, and the night air smelled clean and fresh. Except for a few wayward halyards clanging in the breeze, the marina was quiet and peaceful. But I had a strange feeling of déjà vu as I stepped aboard *Second Wind*. I'd had another uninvited visitor. The basket where I stow my flashlight had been upturned, its contents strewn about the cockpit like pick-up sticks. The lock on the hatchway had been jimmied, and the cabin door was wide open.

SIXTEEN

IT DIDN'T TAKE much savvy to conclude that someone had broken into the cabin. The jimmied lock was about as subtle as a flashing neon sign. Since I wasn't inclined to barge in and find out if someone was still there—at least not in the dark—I leaned through the hatchway just far enough to find the overhead light switch. My heart was pounding so hard I felt as if it might leap out of my chest. And when I hit the switch, it almost did.

The cabin had been trashed; a brutal ransacking that left nothing untouched. The telephone answering machine, its little red message light blinking furiously, had been dumped on the floor—along with the computer, TV, assorted books and magazines, and, judging by the mess, the contents of every drawer and cabinet on the boat. Nautical charts, tide tables, boating manuals, sailing school records, files, and papers had been tossed every which way. Seat cushions up-ended and ripped apart. Blankets and sheets pulled from the berth. Clothes yanked from the locker. Even the fridge had been violated—eggs splattered on top of the counter, milk and juice poured on the floor.

I'd seen enough from the hatchway to forego any idea I

might've had about going inside the cabin. I hopped off the boat and hightailed it to the harbormaster's office. Bert had already left for the day, so I reported the break-in to the security guard on duty in the lobby. He wanted to call the police, but I was reluctant to get them involved, mindful of how another breach in marina security might play out with the Nakitos. But the Weasel strolled through the lobby as we were discussing it and pounced on the idea.

"Now, Kellie," he said, "you know we can't let something like this go unreported. What if your boat wasn't the only one hit?"

Despite his condescending attitude, I had to admit the guy had a point. What's more, whoever broke into *Second Wind* could still be in the marina ransacking someone else's boat as we spoke. So for a change I found myself agreeing with the Weasel. But the guy just couldn't leave well enough alone. He leaned against the counter, pulled a toothpick from behind his ear and stuck it in his mouth. "Obviously," he said with a smirk, "Bert's beefed-up security precautions have been a dismal failure."

I should've let the remark pass, but I'd had enough of biting my tongue around the Weasel. It begins to hurt after awhile. I leaned against the counter next to him. "Tell you what, Todd," I said quietly. "Save your self-serving BS for the Nakitos, and maybe—just maybe—they won't notice what a failure really looks like." That felt pretty good, so I let him have a little more. "And take that stupid toothpick out of your mouth so you can call the police."

The Weasel directed the guard to call 911 and then wandered off to do whatever it is he does without saying another word to me. I knew I'd eventually have to pay for my sins, but at the moment I couldn't have cared less.

Two uniformed officers arrived half an hour later. They were the same officers who'd responded to the Moyer homicides, and I recognized Benson about the same time he recognized me. He pulled on his mustache. "Jesus H. What now?"

• • •

AFTER BENSON AND his partner were finished with their look-see aboard *Second Wind*, they joined me on the dock. "Yep, you had a break-in," declared Benson. He handed me an incident report to sign. "We'll also need a list of what was stolen—if anything." He gestured toward the boat. "But, from my experience, what you've got there is nothing more than a random prank. Kids, most likely."

I felt drained, not to mention cranky and very hungry. As soon as Benson and his partner left, I rambled about the cabin just long enough to find an overnight bag, a change of clothes, a nightgown, and some toilet articles. Twenty minutes later, I had a room at the waterfront Marriott and a full-course dinner from room service on its way. After I ate, I stripped off my clothes and lazed in the Jacuzzi tub for an hour, letting the hot water and bubbles massage my body until I was totally relaxed. Then I slipped on my nightgown, crawled into bed, and flicked on the TV, determined to put what had happened to *Second Wind* out of my mind—at least for one night. I watched *It's a Wonderful Life* until I fell asleep.

The next morning, I ate a complimentary continental breakfast in the coffee shop and then checked out. I'd thought seriously about staying another night. The Jacuzzi had been a treat—a luxurious, relaxing experience that couldn't begin to compare with the dab-some-soap-rinse-and-get-out showers I took aboard *Second Wind*. When I got the hotel bill, though, I knew I had no choice. All that luxury had come with a hefty price tag that just about flattened my already too-thin wallet.

Money (and the lack thereof) is always a concern when you run a sailing school. If it weren't, I wouldn't have been hustling back to the marina to teach a class on the day before Christmas. Since the class had been postponed twice due to nasty weather, I wanted to get at least one lesson out of the way before the holiday break began. That left December twenty-fourth. The rest of the sixteen-hour course would have to wait until after the first of the year.

Although sailing is technically a year-round sport, the busiest months at Sound Sailing were May to September, which, not so coincidentally, is when Seattle enjoys its best weather. The school was floundering when I took it over three years ago, and despite my attempts to build up the client base, it was still a touch-and-go operation. Besides trying to attract new clients, the biggest problem I've had to deal with on an ongoing basis is fleet maintenance and repair. For some strange reason, students expect the boats to stay afloat.

I've totally replaced the fleet since taking over the school. No small accomplishment given old man Larstad's reluctance to cough up the dough. He's never had much interest in Sound Sailing except as a handy tax write-off. But nevertheless we now have a fairly good selection of boats to choose from, depending upon the type of lesson taught. From an instructional standpoint, boat size is not particularly important, but I favor using a smaller boat with beginners. So, for our basic classes, we use the J 22 and the Santana 20. For the intermediate student, we offer the Wavelength 24 or the Cal 24. I'd love to have a larger boat, say a Hunter 27 or a Catalina 30, for those sailors interested in extended cruising experience. But until I can convince old man Larstad to spring for a bigger boat, I have to use *Second Wind*.

I'm the only full-time instructor at Sound Sailing. During the busy months, I have three other skilled instructors available on an on-call basis. My goal is to build up the school to the point where they're full-time as well. In the meantime, I teach most of the classes myself and make the fleet available for charter to increase income.

Because the sailing school wasn't the marina's main draw, it was situated in a small building at the far end of the marina just past the Laundromat and an old tool shed. As they say, location is everything. I passed K dock on the way to the school and tried not to think about last night's break-in. But when I caught a glimpse of *Second Wind,* I felt sick. I hated making her wait any longer for the clean-up she deserved. Hold on, girl. I'll be there as soon as I can.

Tom Doyle was pacing back and forth in front of the school. "Where the hell have you been?" he barked as soon as he saw me. Tom was fifty-five, tall and sinewy, and, despite an arthritic hip that acted up now and then, moved about the marina's docks with catlike agility. He started hanging out at Larstad's when he retired from the Navy, lending a hand here and there until he'd worked himself into a full-time job. Tom had a way about him that turned a lot of people off, but we'd always gotten along fairly well. Besides, he was my lead (and only) mechanic and, except for Grampy, the best all-around sailor I'd ever known.

"Why? What's wrong?" I asked, knowing full well that he'd tell me anyway.

"It's the J 22. Damn motor's busted again." He tapped the toolbox he held in front of him as if it were Exhibit A.

"Oh, well," I said. "I'll just use the Santana for today's lesson."

He chomped down on the unlit cigar at the corner of his mouth. "Like bloody hell you will."

Like I bloody needed this. "Okay, Tom," I said calmly. "What's up with the Santana?"

"I rerigged it yesterday, just like you asked. But I haven't had time to tune it yet. Been too busy workin' on the J."

"That's all right. The tuning shouldn't take much more than an hour."

He plopped his toolbox on a wooden bench by the school door. "Shit, that's not the problem." He nodded toward the door. "You already got a bunch of gals waitin' on you now. Whatcha gonna do with them while I'm on the boat?"

"Hey, Tom, don't sweat the small stuff. I'll figure out what to do with my students. You just make sure the rigging gets tuned."

"*Hmmf,*" he said, crossing his arms in front of him.

"And when you're done," I said with a grin, "go on

over to the Topside and have a Guinness on me.''

''Now you're talkin','' he said, returning my grin. He reclaimed his toolbox and padded off to the dock while I went inside to greet my class.

The bunch of gals, as Tom had called them, were two talkative, jeans-clad young women between the ages of twenty and thirty and a fiftyish-looking woman who was sporting an obviously new Helly Hansen jacket and matching pants. I introduced myself to the group and chatted with them for a few minutes while they filled out registration forms and a questionnaire about their sailing experience and expectations.

To make effective use of the fifteen-by-thirty-foot space allocated for Sound Sailing, I'd used blue partitions to divide the room into two parts. The front half was a reception area that also served as my office, while the back half was set up as a classroom with a long table and a few chairs. After the women completed their paperwork, we moved to the classroom. I'd just finished handing out their sailing manuals when Terri Moyer peeked her head around the partition. ''Sorry I'm late,'' she said. ''I got lost.''

Except for the slender build, she looked almost nothing like the woman I'd met at her parents' funeral. The heavy white foundation was gone, as was the black eyeliner, painted-on tears, and Victorian clothing. She still wore black lipstick, but that was the extent of her makeup. Casually dressed in snug-fitting jeans, Calvin Klein sweatshirt, and deck shoes, she looked much younger than her thirty-three years. The only leather she wore today was a stylish black jacket and short-billed cap. Her thick blond hair hung loosely about her shoulders in a long pageboy. The change in her appearance took me off guard a moment, but no more so than the realization that Terri Moyer was absolutely stunning.

After she took a seat at the table, I spent a few minutes giving my usual spiel about my sailing background and experience, including the fact that Sound Sailing was an American Sailing Association–certified facility. I also shared with them that I'd successfully completed the more rigorous testing required for the U.S. Coast Guard certification program. I then turned the time over to the group and asked them to introduce themselves and tell a little bit about why they wanted to learn how to sail.

The Helly Hansen–clad woman stood up and started things off. "My name's Juanita Jessup, and I'm here today because of my husband." She looked a little flustered. "I guess I should say in spite of my husband. We just got a new sailboat, and he's turned into Captain Bligh. I thought if I learned how to sail he wouldn't yell at me so much. Actually, it was either learn to sail or kill the old SOB." She quickly sat down amidst much laughter.

"Anything to prevent a mutiny at sea," I said.

Next up was Carla Dawson. "I first got interested in sailing when my boyfriend took me out on his Hunter last summer. I've been wanting to take lessons ever since, but something always came up." She shrugged. "Not that it was easy getting away this time of year. But I was determined."

"I'm Karen Fenton and I work with Carla," said the woman seated next to her. They exchanged smiles. "When Carla told me she'd signed up for sailing lessons, I just had to come, too. It sounds like it'll be a lot of fun—and a great way to meet guys," she added with a giggle.

"Glad to have you both here." I nodded for Terri to proceed, but she had her head down and didn't say anything. "Terri?"

She looked up. "Huh?"

"Can you share with us why you want to learn how to sail?"

She stood and took a deep breath. "I guess I first got the urge to sail when I was just a kid, maybe ten or so. I remember standing along the shore where I could watch the sailboats on Elliott Bay. I liked the way they'd dip, then right themselves, and dip again, their white sails billowing in the breeze like giant angel wings. I knew then that I wanted to be out there on the water more than anything in the whole world.''

She paused and looked down at the table. "But things happen. Life flips us from place to place, and childhood dreams die.'' When she looked up again, her blue eyes were watery. "So I guess you could say I'm here today because I want to reclaim my dream. For a long time now, a real long time, I've felt like I haven't really been living. Just existing, wasting breath,'' she said. "It's hard for me to explain how I feel, but I believe that the only way to live— truly live—is to have a dream green and growing in your heart. That's why I want to sail.''

A momentary silence followed. Then, as soon as she sat down, the group burst into applause. Terri responded with a shy smile.

On that upbeat note, I began the class. There are some things that are easily taught in the classroom, and I started with those—basic safety procedures, sailing terminology and nomenclature, rules of the road, and points of sail. We boarded the Santana after we were finished in the classroom. Tom had her all ready to go and was just leaving. "Have a good one, ladies,'' he said with a playful wink.

It was a great day for sailing—crisp but not cold, windy but not blustery. After a brief orientation to the boat, we donned our life jackets and cast off. A good sailor should be able to perform all functions on a boat, so I had each woman take turns practicing from both the helmsman and crew positions. This included use of the proper commands for "coming about'' and "heading up.'' I explained to the group that each time a vessel alters course and the trim of the sail is changed, certain commands are used to alert others on the boat that such changes are about to take place.

Carla was at the helm first. As soon as she shouted, "Ready about!'' I instructed the crew to get ready to put the windward jib sheet around the winch. Once they'd made sure that the jib sheets were clear and the boat was ready to change directions, they answered, "Ready." Carla, as helmsman, shouted, "Hard alee!" indicating that the tiller was being pushed to the leeward side of the boat, and the boat was starting to turn. A similar set of commands was used when "heading up" or steering closer to the wind.

I loved coming about or tacking a sailboat. When Grampy first taught me to do a crisp roll tack, I could spend hour after hour tacking back and forth. In a roll tack you use your weight and sail trim and very little rudder to change the course of the boat. You can actually accelerate because you create the wind in your sails as you rock from one tack to the other. It feels so good because your body and the boat become one as you balance from tack to tack. I watched as Terri assumed the helm and saw that she took to the skill naturally. If we'd been by ourselves, I'd have taught her the roll tack, too. It's an art form that takes years of practice, but of all the women aboard, Terri Moyer seemed the one most likely to master it.

The hour passed quickly, and soon it was time to drop the sails and return to the dock. I ended the lesson by teaching the women how to flake, or fold, the mainsail and jib and stow them so that they were protected from the weather. It was almost noon when we finished, and the group decided to have lunch together at the Topside. As often happens with a good sail, a camaraderie had developed amongst the class members. The exception was Terri. She'd talked very little to the others during our sail and held back from the group when the lunch plans were being made. She stopped me outside the school as the rest of the group headed off to the restaurant.

"Kellie, could I talk to you for a minute?"

"Sure. What's up?"

"I didn't want to say anything to the others, but I can't stay. I've got to get back to Coleman."

"Don't worry about it. We'll have lunch together another time."

"That's just it. I don't think there'll be another time."

I was confused. "You took to sailing like a natural, Terri. Didn't you like it?"

"Oh, I loved it. Sailing was everything I thought it would be—the wind, the water, the boat, everything. I'll carry this day with me forever and I want to thank you for that."

"But it's not over. This was just the first lesson."

"No, Kellie, I can't go sailing again," she said, her eyes brimming with tears.

Her sudden change of heart didn't square with the impassioned speech she'd made earlier about following her dream. I wondered if anything she'd said then had been true. Maybe she'd just been playing another role—that of the eager sailor instead of the mysterious Gothic. I found her ambiguous attitude annoying. "You want to help me out here, Terri? Why can't you go sailing again?"

She looked over her shoulder as if someone might be listening and lowered her voice. "Let's just say the past won't stay buried. I thought I could do this, I thought I could start over. But it's not going to work."

"Does this have something to do with your parents' deaths?"

She nodded, and the tears flowed down her cheeks. She looked so pale and fragile standing in the building's shadow that I was afraid she was going to collapse. Maybe I'd misjudged her. "Come on, Terri, let's go inside the school where you can sit down for a moment." Once indoors, I found some tissues and got her a glass of water. When she'd collected herself, I said, "Why don't you tell me what's bothering you? Sometimes it helps to talk things out."

"That's what my social worker keeps telling me. Reba's nice, but she just doesn't get it."

"Doesn't get what?"

"That it's a secret."

"What is?"

"Everything. My whole life has been nothing but a god-damn secret."

"Then maybe it's time for you to change all that."

She dabbed at her eyes with the tissue for a moment or two. "Maybe you're right," she said softly.

What followed was difficult to hear—a tragic story of childhood lost. Her innocence and dreams destroyed by her own father, Donald Moyer. In halting words and tears, she told how he'd sexually abused her from the time she was just five years old.

"Did your mother know?" I asked. "Did you ever talk to Miranda about the abuse?"

"I tried. Once—when I was about eight. I'd worried about whether I should tell Mama for a long, long time. Like I said, Daddy had made me promise that I wouldn't tell anybody. He said it was a secret, our special time together. A special secret just between him and me. If I told Mama, it wouldn't be special anymore. But I knew what we were doing wasn't right. I ached for Mama to know and make it stop. And yet, at the same time, I didn't want her to know. I didn't want to hurt Daddy. He loved me. Needed me, too. So it was an accident, my telling Mama. It just happened."

"What do you mean, 'it just happened'?"

Terri's eyes had a glazed, faraway look. And when she spoke, it was as if she were recalling a dream. "Mama was in the kitchen. It surprised me, her being there. She always said she was born to shop, not cook. But that day was different. She'd tied an apron around her waist and propped a Betty Crocker cookbook on the counter. She was baking cookies—the kitchen all warm and yummy-smelling, bright sunlight streaming through the window making patterns on the floor, some little ditty playing on the radio, Mama humming. I'd never heard her hum so I stood at the doorway awhile and listened. The mixer was broken, and she stirred the cookie dough with a big wooden spoon, the bowl cradled in the crook of her arm.

"I must have made a noise or something, because she stopped humming and turned around. I remember thinking how beautiful she looked standing there in the sunlight, her lips parted slightly—as if she might smile at me and tell me she loved me. Seeing her like that, I just couldn't keep it inside any longer. And so I told her, everything tumbling out so fast I could hardly breathe.''

"What did she say?"

"Nothing." Terri shrugged. "Mama just stared at me, her eyes blank, her face unreadable. What I wanted was for her to hug me or hold me or touch me or just . . . I don't know, just do something that would let me know it was okay, that she loved me and would take care of me, that she'd make everything all right. But she didn't. It was as if she hadn't even heard me. So I called her name. And it was in that instant, that instant when her eyes met mine, that I knew what a terrible mistake I'd made.''

"A mistake?"

Terri nodded. "After I'd poured out my heart to her and practically pleaded on bended knee for her to help me, she didn't say a thing. And when she finally did, it was to scream, 'You little bitch!' Then she hurled the wooden spoon at me. I turned to run, but in my terror I stumbled over my own two feet, and she grabbed me. Her exact words before she slapped me were, 'Don't you ever talk about your daddy like that again, you hear?' ''

"Do you think she believed you?"

"I don't know, but it didn't matter. I never talked to her about Daddy again—just like she said. And after that slap, Mama never touched me again. She'd never been what you'd call affectionate. If she hugged me at all, it was quick—a stingy little half hug that never satisfied. I have no memory of her ever kissing me. I was always doing something wrong, something that upset her—losing my hair ribbons, spilling milk, coming home late from playing, soiling my dress. She wasn't a mother. She was ice. A frigid stick woman who'd condemned me to hell long before she went there herself.''

We talked for a while longer, but it was clear that the anger and pain Terri Moyer was dealing with wouldn't be resolved with a few sympathetic words from me. She seemed so needy, though, that I promised to call her, perhaps even come to see her at Coleman. We left the matter of further sailing lessons open. After she left, I sat for several minutes thinking about all that she'd said. Then I picked up the phone and called Reba Stanton at the Coleman Rehabilitation Center.

SEVENTEEN

"HI, KELLIE. I'VE been expecting your call. How'd the sailing lesson go?"

"Great. Terri showed up a little late, but she made the class."

"That's good news."

"There's some bad news, too."

"Oh?"

"She seemed real enthused about sailing, but after the class was over Terri said she couldn't come back." I summarized our conversation, ending with Terri's revelation about her father and mother. "To be honest, Reba, I was sort of surprised that she would share something so personal."

"It's not typical behavior for Terri, all right. It took months of therapy before she'd talk about her parents with me. But, on the other hand, it's not unusual for people with Terri's personality disorder to be rather impulsive and emotionally labile."

"Labile?"

"Sorry for the jargon. What I meant was that Terri is emotionally unstable. She also lacks strong ego boundaries.

You might think of her as somewhat jellylike in attaching to others and overidentifying with them. That she has confided in you, Kellie, tells me that she must feel a strong connection to you. Don't be alarmed if she even takes on some of your mannerisms or speaking patterns.''

"So you think she'll come back for more sailing lessons in spite of what she said?''

"I can't be sure, but it's very likely. Particularly since she felt at ease enough around you to share one of her best-kept secrets.''

"One of her secrets? Are you saying there's more?''

"Definitely.'' Reba sighed and added, "But so far I've been unable to get Terri to that point in her therapy where she can let go of the trauma long enough to talk about it. I believe what she told you—the sexual abuse she endured from her father and her mother's indifference to her plight—isn't the most troubling issue she's dealing with.''

"It sounded pretty bad to me.''

"Oh, it was. What I'm saying is that Terri is holding something back, keeping the worst part of the experience hidden, even from herself. I believe that when she's finally able to talk about whatever that was, Terri will be well on her way to a full recovery. And you might just be the one to help her do that.''

"But I'm not a trained therapist.''

"Exactly. Terri's had plenty of exposure to professional help. Perhaps what she needs most right now is a friend.''

I assured Reba that I'd be quite willing to talk to Terri again. "I told her the same thing, but whether we become friends is something else again.'' Reba said that was all she could ask. In return, I asked her to check on something for me. She was hesitant at first but said she would search the records and get back to me.

I spent the rest of the afternoon sorting through and cleaning up the mess aboard *Second Wind*. I tried to concentrate on the task at hand rather than dwell on the tremendous sense of violation that I felt. In the process, I verified what

I'd only suspected the night before—nothing of value had been taken, unless you counted a bunch of Christmas cards I hadn't even gotten around to opening. Or the computer printout of *Merry Maiden*'s Visitor Access List with the notes I'd jotted in the margins. I figured that ruled out Benson's prankster theory. Or even a regular burglary. Why else would someone pass up a TV or a computer for some handscribbled notes? And, according to Bert, the police didn't find any other boats disturbed.

No, the way I saw it, this break-in was definitely related to the murders. Someone must've been worried that I'd hit on something important. If so, I sure didn't know what it was. And I sure as hell didn't know who could've thought I did. I mulled over the possibilities while playing back the messages that were still on the answering machine from yesterday. The first message was from Cassie: "Hey, Mom. Don't forget Christmas Eve at Aunt Donna's. Can you get here by six o'clock? Dinner's at seven."

Damn. In all the excitement, I had forgotten. Every Christmas Eve Donna coerces the entire family into coming to her house to celebrate. We'd been doing it for so many years it had become a tradition. And expected. If you wanted your share of the trust fund, that is. Although some extra cash would come in handy right now, I didn't want to go. But it looked as though trudging off to Donna's was the only way I was going to get to see Cassie.

The second call was from Rose: "Sorry I missed you. I went to Moyer and Preston's Law Office this morning. Have lots to tell you when I get back." Then, as an afterthought, she added, "Oh, I almost forgot. I saw Donna in the office lobby as I was leaving. Don't you think that's carrying the undercover business a tad too far?" Donna at Moyer's office? I could think of only one reason why she'd be there. Helping with Cassie's search was one thing. But using the services of the Missing Link was another. Not good. Not good at all.

Message number three was from Emily Cummings: "Just

thought I'd call to let you know how much I enjoyed talking with you last night. Sorry the timing didn't work out for a lesson today, but I think you can understand why I'm so eager to get started. Please call me as soon as possible so we can set a definite date.'' I jotted down the phone number she left and went on to the next message.

It was Norma Bailey with the address for Steve and Darla Schuster. There weren't any more messages. The ball was in Kingston's court, but the break-in had changed everything, and I couldn't wait for his call any longer. He wasn't in when I called the station and of course they didn't know or didn't want to say when he might be back.

"It's Christmas Eve, ma'am."

No kidding. I left another message, underscoring how important it was that he return my call. I gave my number and Donna's, too, just in case he called after I left.

The Christmas presents I'd picked up on the way home from Bremerton were still intact, although a little dented and scuffed up. I put some new bows on them and called it good. By late afternoon, Kingston still hadn't called. Since I'd missed lunch due to my conversation with Terri, I caught a quick bite at the Topside. The diner was closing early for Christmas Eve, and I was the last customer of the day.

When I got back home, I checked the answering machine again. There were two new messages. The first was from Reba Stanton. She'd checked the day pass records and confirmed what I'd been hoping wasn't the case—Terri Moyer had been signed out from Coleman on the dates her parents and brother were murdered. And on the day the *Second Wind* was trashed. The second message was from Bob Chapman saying his wife had returned. But no call from Kingston. Well, forget it, then. I had places to go.

I'd planned to drive straight to Donna's house, but the floating bridge traffic was lighter than I'd expected so I zoomed across Lake Washington in record time. It was only five o'clock when I hit the outskirts of Redmond. Rather than show up at Donna's an hour early, I decided to see if

Darla and Steve Schuster were home. If the address Norma had given me was correct, they lived only a half-mile from Donna's house.

I found their apartment complex without any problem. The all-brick, three story building was well maintained with lots of shrubbery and trees and a large fenced playground for kids. A huge Christmas wreath with a bright red ribbon hung on the front door of the Schusters' apartment. I rang the bell even though I couldn't detect any sounds of life inside. In fact, the entire building was quiet, as if everyone had opted to spend Christmas at Grandma's. I rang the bell again.

"Hold on, I'm coming."

When the door opened, I was eye-to-eye with a belt buckle. Sissy had described Steve Schuster as big, but that really didn't do the guy justice. Sort of like calling the Grand Canyon a gully. Well over six feet tall, Schuster had the tight, muscular body of a professional athlete. His massive arms literally strained against the seams of his short-sleeved shirt. I didn't think they made necks as thick as his—certainly not at the Sports Center. Next to this guy, the Center's musclemen looked like skinny schoolboys.

"Uh, Steve Schuster?"

"You got it!" He had a loopy grin and mischievous blue eyes. I pegged him at mid-twentysomething. He seemed friendly enough, but I was so distracted by the sheer bulk of the guy that I couldn't think of a damn thing to say—a first for me.

He waited a beat and then asked, "What can I do for ya?"

I rummaged through my shoulder bag and grabbed a business card. He studied it a moment, a puzzled look on his broad face. I was still trying to think of something to say when he turned the card over, as if expecting an explanation for my presence to be written on the reverse side.

"Larstad's Marina. Isn't that where the Moyers were—"

"That's right," I said, finding my voice at last. "I'm

Kellie Montgomery. I'm with the harbormaster's office and I need to discuss something very important with you."

He eyed me warily. "Like what? It's Christmas Eve, you know."

"I'm sorry to intrude, but this is important. Is your wife at home?"

"Darla? Yeah, sure."

"Perhaps I could come in?"

He hesitated briefly, fingering the card as he thought over my request. When he'd made up his mind, he turned slightly and shouted over his shoulder, "Honey, we've got company." He stepped aside so I could enter.

The Schusters' living room was sparsely furnished, but neat and clean. A pastel flowered couch and love seat were arranged around a square coffee table in the middle of the room. I didn't see a TV, but there were plenty of books. A stack was on the coffee table, another on the floor next to a lamp, and still more lined a small, makeshift bookcase in the corner. A card table in front of the window doubled as a desk. It held a laptop computer, a spiral notebook, and an opened textbook of some kind.

A wisp of a woman with blond hair and almost translucent skin stood behind the counter of a breakfast bar separating the living room from the kitchen. She was in her twenties also, but as fragile-looking as the china plates she held in her hands. Steve Schuster gently took the plates from her and set them on the counter. Then, as if she were a child, he took her hand in his and led her into the living room.

"This is my wife, Darla."

She smiled tentatively and motioned to the love seat. "Please sit down," she said.

Still holding hands, the gentle giant and his sweetheart sat next to each other on the couch.

"Now, what exactly is it you wanted to discuss with us?" asked Steve.

I looked directly at Darla Schuster. "I'd like to ask you some questions about Miranda Moyer."

She bit her lower lip and tightened her grip on her husband's hand, but said nothing. I waited, wondering who'd be the first to break the silence.

Steve withdrew his hand from Darla's and put his arm about her shoulders. "What questions?" he asked.

Once again, I looked directly at Darla. "I've been told that you were following Miranda for several weeks before her death." Darla clasped and unclasped her hands, her head down.

"Who told you that?" asked Steve.

"It's not important. What's important is whether or not it's true."

"Darla wasn't following anybody, least of all Miranda Moyer."

"You didn't try to talk to her at the Sports Center?" I asked Darla.

"No, she—"

"Steve, don't," interrupted Darla, putting her hand on his knee. "It's all right." She withdrew her hand and folded her slender arms across her chest. "It's true. I did follow Miranda Moyer. I tried to talk to her, too. A lot. But it didn't do me any good."

"Darla, you don't have to tell this woman anything. She's just from the marina, not the police."

"He's right. I'm not with the police, but I am assisting in the investigation. Whatever you tell me just may help us discover who killed the Moyers."

"Well, if you're implying that Darla had anything to do with it, you're way off base."

"I'm not implying that at all."

"Just 'cause she was trying to talk to the bitch—"

Darla put her hand on her husband's knee again. "Steve, please."

"Excuse me. The woman. Just 'cause she was trying to

talk to the woman doesn't mean Darla knows anything about who killed her.''

"Maybe not, but sometimes we know things that we don't consider important. Things that, when put in context with other things, turn out to be very important.'' I looked at Darla. "I'd like to know about your relationship with Miranda. I hear that she was involved in a baby-brokering business. Is that correct?''

She nodded and began to sob.

"Damn,'' muttered Steve. "Now look what you've done.'' He patted his wife's shoulder. "It's okay, hon. Hush now.''

I hesitated, considering whether to press on. Steve bent his head near Darla's ear and whispered something. Whatever he said, it failed to keep the tears from spilling out of her sad eyes and running down her face. I felt like an ogre.

"I'm sorry,'' I said, "but I have to know. Did Miranda Moyer pay you money to relinquish a baby for adoption?''

"Hey! That's enough. Can't you see you've upset her?''

"Darla, I was told you were following Miranda Moyer because you wanted your baby back.''

Steve jumped up from the couch. "That's it. You're outta here.'' He motioned to the door with his thumb.

The gentle giant wasn't acting so gentle anymore, but I figured he'd go along with just about anything Darla wanted. "Darla, do you want me to leave?''

She wiped her eyes with the back of her hand. "No.''

"Darla.''

"It's okay, Steve.''

"But—''

"Really. Please sit down, sweetheart.'' She patted the couch next to her. "It's time I told somebody what happened.'' When he was settled with their hands joined again, she began. "Steve and I met when we were freshmen in high school. We started dating, and it wasn't long before we were a steady item. The classic couple—football hero and head cheerleader.'' She sighed. "Our parents didn't think we should spend so much time together, but we couldn't stand it when we were apart. God, we were mad for each other!''

"And still are," Steve added.

Darla looked at him affectionately. "But for a time there we weren't so sure. You see, I got pregnant my senior year. Steve had just won a football scholarship to the University of Washington. I was planning to attend WSU in Pullman. Our folks came unglued and insisted I get an abortion. I was confused about a lot of things, but abortion was never an option as far as I was concerned."

"What about you, Steve? How did you feel about the pregnancy?"

"I was confused, too. I mean, I loved Darla like crazy, but football was my life. I wanted to be a Husky more than anything. Had dreams of playing in the NFL someday. A baby wasn't in the picture for years and years."

"So what did you do?"

"We fought," said Darla. "Everyone pushed and pulled at us, our folks especially. The pressure was awful. I finally had to quit cheerleading, then my grades dropped. Steve stopped talking to me. His parents were making his life as difficult as my parents were mine. When it finally got too late for an abortion, my folks kicked me out of the house."

"Is that when you met Miranda Moyer?"

Darla nodded. "After my parents kicked me out, I moved in with my best friend, Lori. Her mother introduced me to Miranda—they played tennis together."

"What was your impression of Miranda?"

"At first she was just the nicest person you'd ever want to meet. She even took me to lunch, bought me maternity clothes and everything. She was real supportive when I needed it the most, but I was still very confused and unhappy. Steve and I had broken up, my parents had disowned me, and I was basically alone."

"And pregnant," I said.

"Very. I was also seventeen with no money and no future. A baby was the last thing I needed."

"So Miranda offered you a way out."

"You have to understand: I trusted her completely. And she was very nice to me—like she really wanted to help. I felt close to her, especially after she confided in me about all the problems she'd had with her daughter. When she first suggested adoption, I told her I wasn't sure about doing that. I mean, I knew I couldn't take care of a baby. I didn't even know how I was going to take care of myself, but after all that time carrying it, feeling it inside me, I wasn't sure I could just give it away to someone else, some stranger. I wanted that baby very, very much."

"What changed your mind?"

She brushed a tear out of her eye. "Miranda kept pressuring me. Just a little at first, telling me how much better off I'd be by adopting the baby out, how I'd have a chance to start my life over. All my expenses would be paid, things like that. Toward the end of my pregnancy, she began an all-out assault. She told me how selfish I was to even consider keeping the baby. Then she said she knew a couple who wanted to adopt him, a couple who could offer him so much more than I could. The more she talked, the more I thought that maybe she was right. Maybe the baby would be much better off without me."

"Wore her down is what she did," said Steve.

"Did you know all this was going on?" I asked him.

He shook his head. "We still weren't talking back then. I wasn't even sure where Darla was living. By the time I did find out, it was too late."

"I'd already given our baby away."

"Miranda won you over?"

"Sort of. When I went into labor I still wasn't sure what I was going to do, not even after I gave birth. He was the sweetest, most beautiful baby I'd ever seen. When I held him in my arms, he looked right up at me, as if to say, 'Hi, Mommy.' I knew the instant I saw him that I loved him with all my heart. Then Miranda came in the room and took him from me.''

Steve shook his head. "God, I still can't get over that. What a bitch.''

"Oh, Steve, don't. The truth is, I let her take our baby.''

"And the money? How did she arrange that?''

"She gave me an envelope with enough money inside to cover my doctor bills and hospital stay plus a little extra for college. I didn't know what else to do. I needed the money and our baby needed parents. My loving him just wasn't enough, so I signed the forms Miranda shoved in front of me. She assured me everything was going to be all right, that I was doing the proper thing. After she took my baby from my arms, she waltzed out of the room before I could even tell him good-bye.''

"When did you and Steve get back together?''

"Not long after I got out of the hospital. Miranda had said everything was going to be all right, but it wasn't.''

"Darla was pretty shook up about the adoption," explained Steve. "She couldn't sleep or eat, cried all the time. Lori was so worried about her that she finally called me. I came over right away.''

"I was a sobbing, crying lunatic. Totally out of it. All I could think about was our baby and how he'd looked at me when I held him. I was so ashamed to think I'd taken money for him. It wasn't as much as Miranda had promised, but I still felt like I'd sold my baby. I should never have done it. I should never have let Miranda talk me into it.''

"What happened then?''

She looked at her husband. "Well, Steve was wonderful. Without him, I don't know what I would've done. He kept me from going completely insane.''

"This whole thing made us realize that we belonged together, no matter what," Steve said. "We went down to the courthouse and got married. That was two years ago. We're both in school now. I still have my football scholarship, but I had to get a job, too. Darla's going to Bellevue Community

College part-time. It's rough, but we're making it.''

"And you tried to get your baby back?''

"Yes, from the very beginning,'' Darla said. "The instant Miranda took him out of my arms, I knew I'd made a mistake. That's why I had such a hard time afterward. I tried to call her, but she wouldn't talk to me. I wrote her letters, but they came back unopened. Steve and I both camped out at the Moyer and Preston Law Office. No one would see us.''

"Did you seek legal counsel?''

They both shook their heads. "We didn't have any money,'' said Steve.

"Besides,'' added Darla, "we were stupid. We didn't think a lawyer was necessary. We thought if we could just talk to Miranda everything would be okay. Finally, after several months, we realized it was hopeless. She wasn't going to talk to us—period. We finally gave up.''

"So why did you start following Miranda?'' I asked Darla.

"Do you remember the Baby Richard case?''

"Sort of. Isn't he the little boy who the court ruled had to be given back to his birth parents?''

"Yeah, but not until he was four years old! We don't want that to happen to our baby, but it's already been two years. The longer this whole thing goes on, the harder it's going to be on everybody. We finally hired a lawyer, but it may be too late now. We'd pretty much left everything up to our lawyer, but after I read about the Baby Richard case, I tried to contact Miranda again. I followed her everywhere, hoping that if I could only get her to talk to me, maybe we could work something out.''

"And now she's dead,'' I said.

"But I didn't have anything to do with that! We were shocked when we heard about the murders. Without Miranda, we may never know what happened to our baby.''

"So who do you think killed the Moyers?''

"We've thought about that,'' Steve said, "and we think

it was someone with a grudge against Miranda.''

"Someone like you and Darla?"

"Get off that kick, will you? It's not us!"

"But it could be someone like you. Miranda was playing God with other people's lives and getting paid well for it."

"Money. It all boils down to that in the end, doesn't it?" asked Steve.

I shrugged, although I believed he was probably right. There was a lot of money involved in this case. There didn't seem to be much else to say after that. Darla offered me some coffee and Christmas cookies she'd just baked, but I was already running later than I had anticipated. I declined the refreshments, thanked them for their time, and left.

I was halfway to the parking lot when Darla called after me.

"Ms. Montgomery! I just thought of something."

I turned around and came back to the apartment. Darla stood in the doorway and said, "There's a woman you should probably talk to. The last time I saw her with Miranda, they were having a very heated argument."

"Who was she?"

"I don't know her name, but I saw her with Miranda at the Sports Center a lot."

"A friend?"

"I don't think so."

"Tennis partner? Business associate?"

"I'm not sure."

"Do you know what they were arguing about?"

"No, but you might try asking that woman who runs the bistro. The big strawberry blonde? She knows everybody's business."

EIGHTEEN

MARY KATHLEEN WAS standing on Donna's front porch smoking a cigarette when I pulled up in the Miata. She was the only one in the family who smoked, and it drove Donna nuts. A zealot on the subject, she preached death and destruction to Mary Kathleen every chance she got, but so far her dire warnings hadn't made an impact. I had the feeling that Mary Kathleen got as much pleasure out of bugging Donna as she did from smoking. She waved when I honked and threw the cigarette onto the porch, stubbing it out with her high-heel. Good going, sis, I thought. Donna's going to love that.

I searched for a parking spot, but the driveway and both sides of the street were lined with cars. I stopped next to my brother Paul's new Lexus and rolled down the window. "Hey, Kate! Where can I park this thing?"

She shrugged and came out to the car. "There might be a spot down there," she said, pointing toward the end of the dimly lit street.

I squinted, but couldn't see a thing in the dark. "Where?"

She opened the passenger's door and climbed in. "Good Lord, Kell, why don't you put on your glasses?" She flashed me an impish grin. "I'm here to tell you there's no point in vanity this late in the game."

A year past forty herself, Kate was a beauty with or without glasses. Although we shared a lot of the same features, she definitely got the better end of the deal—thick head of auburn hair with bounce instead of red frizz; big blue eyes with long, sexy lashes that you could actually see; a peaches-and-cream complexion with no unwanted freckles; and curves in all the right places. Definitely curves. With all her attributes, Kate had never wanted for male companionship. But so far a lasting love had eluded her. Married three times, she had just broken off an engagement with number four.

"It's about time you arrived," she said. "Donna's got her panties all twisted in a knot."

"What's wrong?"

"You."

"What'd I do? I just got here."

"Exactly—you're late."

"I'm surprised she even noticed."

"Believe me, she noticed. Everyone's here except you. Well, you and her kids."

"None of them made it?"

"Nope. But she hasn't even mentioned them. It's you she's all agitated about. Cornered me as soon as I got here, wanting to know where you were. Like I'm your keeper or something."

"Sorry about that."

"Forget it," she said. "Donna's a pain in the ass. Everybody knows it, but no one's got the balls to tell her to back off."

"Not as long as she controls the purse strings," I said.

"It pisses me off the way Donna doles out our share of the trust fund whenever the mood strikes her, but I'll be damned if I'll suck up to her like the rest of them do. You should see 'em in there, falling all over themselves to get on her good side. Our brothers, their wives, their kids—

she's got them all buffaloed. The only thing they haven't done yet is genuflect when she comes into the room.''

I laughed. "That's my role. Didn't you know?"

"The worst part is, nothing's changed from when we were kids. It's pathetic. I used to come to these yearly things because of Grampy. He enjoyed seeing the family all together. Now that he's gone, I can't believe I'm still doing it. I have enough shit to deal with. Who needs Donna's brand, too?" Kate pointed out the window. "Hey, what'd I tell you? There's a spot."

I eased next to the curb and cut the motor. After we'd climbed out, I retrieved the Christmas presents from the trunk. "Speaking of Grampy, I went to Bremerton yesterday." I handed her a couple of presents. "Help me carry these back to the house, and I'll fill you in on the latest."

By the time we'd trudged back to Donna's, I'd given Kate a quick update on my involvement in the Moyers' murder investigation and Cassie's birth mother search. I concluded by telling her about Rose's telephone message. "This whole search thing has me upset, but Donna showing up at the Moyers' office has me really worried."

"How come?"

"What I've discovered about Donald and Miranda Moyer is beginning to get ugly. I have a lot of unanswered questions about that law firm, particularly about a little side business called the Missing Link."

"What's that?"

"A search service. I suspect that's what Donna was doing there—checking it out for Cassie. But I can't imagine Donna parting with the kind of money they charge, even for Cassie. Until I know for sure what's going on at that law firm, though, I don't want anyone in the family near the place. It could be dangerous."

"You planning to talk to Donna about it tonight?"

I nodded.

"Kell, I don't want to give you advice when you haven't asked for it, but—"

"But what?"

"Donna's got something up her sleeve. Remember when we were kids and she'd get that quirky look on her face when she knew something we didn't?"

I nodded again. As the oldest, Donna always knew something we didn't and loved to hold it over us.

"She's had the same look all evening. Something's up, and I have a feeling it's not something you're going to like."

"So what's your advice?"

"Be prepared. Don't let Donna tromp on you the way she does everyone else. It's time someone put her in her place."

"Aw, Kate, I just want to find out what's going on. I don't want to put anyone in their place. It's Christmas Eve, remember? I appreciate the advice, but it's the season for love, not confrontation."

"So what're you going to do? Love Donna to death?"

"I'm going to do what Grampy would've advised: *Listen to the wind, Kellie, darlin', and let the wind tell you what to do.*"

"And what's the wind telling you?"

"To reassure Cassie that I love her very much and—even though I still don't understand or feel good about it—tell her that I support her search for her birth mother."

"Okay." She shrugged. "Have it your way, but don't say I didn't warn you."

Tummy-tugging aromas wafting in from the kitchen enveloped us as soon as we came inside. "Is that you, Mary Kathleen?" called Donna from the dining room.

The question generated an exasperated sigh from Kate. "Yes, ma'am."

"Well, hurry up. We can't wait for Kellie any longer. John Ryan is about to say the blessing."

"Donna the prima donna has spoken," grumbled Mary Kathleen.

We added my presents to the pile under the Christmas tree and headed for the dining room as ordered. If Donna was surprised to see me tagging along behind Mary Kathleen, she didn't let on. I exchanged hellos with everyone and sat across the table from Cassie. Her face was scrunched up in an angry scowl. I started to mouth an apology but she'd already closed her eyes for the prayer.

I'm not sure what John Ryan prayed for, but my prayer was simple: "Please, God, help me get things back on track with Cassie."

The dinner took forever. Donna's Christmas repasts were elaborate, impressive multicourse feasts designed primarily to show off her culinary skills. This year's effort was a corker: fresh Hood Canal oysters, wild mushroom soup, hot spinach salad, and eventually the goose. With each course she served, the talk around the table droned on and on. By the time dessert was finally served, we were doing more groaning than talking.

Donna's formal, Drexel Heritage dining table could've easily accommodated our whole tribe, but the kids were relegated to the wraparound dinette in the kitchen; Donna's way of ensuring that her Persian carpets and imported crystal chandelier would live to see another Christmas. I'd have preferred the kitchen myself. Judging by the giggles, they were having a lot more fun.

Cassie made a point of ignoring me throughout the meal. I tried joining in the conversations swirling about me, but I couldn't keep focused. All I could think about was how I'd screwed up again. Why had I stopped off to see the Schusters? If only I'd come straight to Donna's instead of playing detective, maybe my daughter wouldn't be glaring at me as if I were some irresponsible ninny. I couldn't wait until the meal was over so I could talk with her in private.

After our dessert plates had been cleared from the table, Donna tapped on her water glass with a spoon. "Please, everyone. May I have your attention?" She sounded sweeter than the whipped cream on our pumpkin pie. She put her spoon to the water glass again, tapping louder. "Quiet down. I have some announcements to make!"

Mary Kathleen leaned over and whispered in my ear. "What'd I tell you? Here it comes."

I nudged her with my elbow. "Hush."

"See her face? The quirky look is back."

All I could see was Donna frowning at us. "Stop it," she said. "Stop your incessant chattering this instant!" No whipped cream voice this time. It was a sour screech that silenced the entire room. Even the kitchen giggling stopped. Everyone turned in our direction.

Mary Kathleen shrugged. "Jeez, Donna. It's Christmas."

"Precisely," she said with a tight smile. "It's Christmas Eve. The perfect occasion for what I have to say." Donna paused, making eye contact with everyone around the table. When she was certain we were all with her, she smiled again. "As you know, it's been our family tradition to open our Christmas presents right after dinner."

At these words, the kitchen door swung open, and a passel of excited, wriggling little bodies spilled into the room. Donna turned and glared at them. "Not now! I have something to say first."

The youngsters pressed up to the table, fidgeting and fussing and generally acting like the kids they were—messy fingers and all. Donna shuddered. "Just hold your horses there. This won't take long. You can all march right back into the kitchen, and I'll call you when it's time. Shoo, now."

After they were gone, Donna glanced around the room again, her eyes settling on Cassie. "First of all, I want you to know how happy I am that the family could be here again this year. But I've been particularly blessed this Christmas." She paused, beaming now. "Cassie's been staying with me while she's on school break."

Cassie flashed a dimpled smile at her aunt.

"Now," said Donna, "since she came home from college, Cassie and I've been involved in a very exciting adventure."

"Uh, Donna," I interrupted, "I don't think this is the time or place to—"

"Mom, it's okay." Cassie nodded at Donna.

"As I was saying, we've been involved in an exciting adventure. A search for Cassie's real mother."

My face reddened as though I'd been slapped. I stood up. "*Real* mother?"

"Oh, Kellie, sit down. You know what I mean."

"Birth mother," Cassie said.

"Yes, yes. Birth mother," repeated Donna. "Anyway, we haven't been making much headway and . . . Kellie, please sit down."

I looked at Cassie in disbelief. What was she thinking, letting Donna carry on like this? Didn't she think I'd be hurt by her telling the whole family this way? Or didn't she care anymore? Had I let her down that much? Cassie avoided my eyes and turned toward Donna. Mary Kathleen grabbed my hand and squeezed it as I sat down.

"So as I said, we've been getting absolutely nowhere in our search. I've been told, though, that this isn't so unusual. After all, we've only been at it for a few days. But if you'd been with Cassie as I have, you'd know just how desperately she wants to find her real mother—oops, sorry. Birth mother."

Mary Kathleen squeezed my hand again. John Ryan cleared his throat. Someone coughed. But no one looked at me.

"So," Donna continued, "what I wanted to tell everyone is that I'm giving Cassie a special Christmas present this year." She pulled out a white envelope from her skirt pocket and set it on the table in front of her. "As you know, it can get terribly confusing when we all start opening our presents together." She held up the envelope. "Since this Christmas present is so special, I wanted to give it to Cassie in front of everyone. That way we can all share in her joy." Donna scooted her chair away from the table and stood up. "Cassie, would you come up here, please?"

Cassie joined Donna at the head of the table. "You don't have to do this, Aunt Donna."

"Nonsense. Nothing could bring me greater joy than to see you happy." She handed the envelope to Cassie. "Open it."

Cassie pulled a check from the envelope. "Oh, my gosh, I can't believe this!" She threw her arms around Donna and hugged her tightly. Donna's eyes found mine before hugging Cassie back.

"Wow! This is just unbelievable," exclaimed Cassie.

"Oh, come on. Don't keep us dangling," someone said. Murmurs from the rest of the table. "Tell us what Donna's given you."

"Aunt Donna's given me the best present I could ever get in a million years: a check for ten thousand dollars!"

There was a brief pause, then a collective gasp. I stood up again. "That's absurd!"

"Mom, please. This means that I'll be able to find my birth mother for sure now."

"That's right," added Donna. "There's a service called the Missing Link that finds birth parents in record time. My gift will cover their fee. The company practically guarantees they'll find Cassie's mother."

"*No!*" I shouted. "Cassie, give the check back this instant." Cassie and Donna looked at me as though I'd lost my mind. "I mean it, Cassie. Give it back right now."

"But, Mom—"

"*Now.*"

"Don't be ridiculous, Kellie," said Donna. "Don't you want your daughter to be happy?"

I threw my napkin onto the table. "Happy? How about alive? That's what I want my daughter to be, Donna. Alive."

"Whatever are you talking about?"

"Murder. Three murders, to be exact. And blackmail, baby brokering, and—"

"Hold it right there," Donna said. "Just what does all that have to do with Cassie?"

"The Missing Link, that's what. You're so bound and determined, for some reason, to make sure Cassie finds her birth mother that you've lost sight of everything else. You haven't a clue about what you're doing, the danger you're exposing her to."

"Danger? Come off it, Kellie. Ever since you moved onto that boat of yours, you've fancied yourself some sort of private detective. You see something sinister lurking around every corner. None of us here appreciate your foolish melodramatics. The Missing Link is a legitimate service offered by a reputable law firm. There's nothing dangerous about it."

"Right. A reputable law firm whose principal partner, Donald Moyer, his wife, and his son just happened to have been brutally murdered."

"According to the newspapers, the police haven't even located a suspect yet. Just what proof do you have that the Moyers' deaths are connected to the Missing Link?"

"Donna, trust me. They're connected."

"No, I don't trust you at all. This danger thing is just a ruse to cover up your true feelings."

"My true feelings?"

"You're afraid. Afraid that when Cassie finds her mother and—excuse me for saying it—but her *real* mother, she'll be someone who loves her and wants to be with her. A mother who cares enough to be with her daughter instead of running around playing amateur detective. Cares enough to at least show up on time once in awhile."

"You have no right to talk to me about being a caring mother." I motioned to the family members seated around the table. "Where're *your* sons and daughters? I don't see any of them here today. Could it be that they don't want to spend time with their mother? Even at Christmas? Is that why you're spending so much time with *my* daughter?"

Cassie was in tears. "Mom, Aunt Donna. Stop this, please."

"You're right, Cassie. This has got to stop. I'm leaving."

Mary Kathleen put her hand out to stop me. "Kellie, no."

"I'm sorry, everybody. I really wanted to have things turn out differently today." I turned to Cassie. "I hope you'll think long and hard about what I said before you spend that check. I do love you, Cassie. More than you'll ever know."

The rest of the family—who'd sat in stunned silence during the entire exchange—now suddenly found their tongues. "Don't go, Kellie. It's Christmas. We love you. Please stay. Donna, do something."

I barely heard them as I hurried from the room. Mary Kathleen caught up with me at the front door. "Kell, I'm so sorry."

"What for? You warned me. I just can't believe Donna would pull something like this. I should've known better."

"What're you going to do?"

"Find out for sure what's going on at that law office."

"How're you going to do that?"

"Get some proof. As I said, I'm positive the Missing Link is connected to the murders. I've just got to find out how before Cassie gets hurt."

She gave me a hug. "Be careful, sis. Okay?"

NINETEEN

I LEFT DONNA'S and went straight to bed, but it wasn't until sometime during the early morning hours that I finally drifted off to sleep, only to awake at dawn drenched in sweat and worry. It was Christmas and my birthday, but instead of celebrating with family and friends, I was alone—burrowing under the covers like a hurt and frightened child.

Life is a choice, Kellie, darlin'. You can stay safely on the shore, paralyzed with fear and uncertainty and dread, never experiencing anything, never understanding yourself or the world around you, never truly living. Or you can hoist your sails, climb into the wind, and soar.

I knew Grampy was right. I had to put my problems with Donna and Cassie behind me somehow, and the only way I could think of was to get out on the water. The sooner the better. The wind was from the south-southwest, and after raising the mainsail and jib, I fell off to the west, close reaching on port tack. The mainsail and jib trimmed nicely, propelling *Second Wind* to her top speed—a brisk seven knots. I let her go, not caring where she took me, just that I got there fast and without interference. I got my wish. The wind was steady and, except for a ferry and a Japanese tanker headed for Pier 90, I had Elliott Bay and the Sound all to myself.

Nearly an hour and several screaming reaches later, I was still on my own and fast approaching Bainbridge Island. Making a spur of the moment decision, I slipped past Tyee Shoal and headed south, hugging the shoreline on starboard tack. I passed only one other boat on the way, and it was hightailing it into Eagle Harbor. I'd assumed the lack of boating traffic was because everyone was too busy unwrapping Christmas gifts or drinking eggnog, but as I neared Restoration Point I suddenly came face to face with the real reason.

Want to be a statistic, Kellie, darlin'? Then forget about the fickle wind, forget to check where it's coming from and where it's going, forget its power, forget its superiority, forget the wind and you've forgotten everything.

Stupid. Stupid. Stupid. In my haste to get underway, I'd failed to heed the warning signs written in big bold strokes across the sky—long white streaks with gray clouds trailing along behind them. Until now, I'd been sailing in the protective leeward side of the island, totally unaware of the dramatic change in the wind's velocity. As if forced from some great bellows in the sky, a galelike blast came tearing through a notch in the land and slammed into *Second Wind*. The sloop immediately heeled over so sharply that she seemed to lie almost flat against the water. Fierce waves surged over the now nearly horizontal lifelines, spilling onto the deck and threatening the cockpit.

Reef the sails, you idiot. You're in trouble. No, I can handle this. Since the bow wasn't coming around fast enough to suit me, I needed to release the sheet—any sheet—to stem the pressure of wind and water on my sails. I'd have preferred the main sheet, but it was forward of the helm. The port jib sheet was closest, but *Second Wind* was so far over that the winch was completely submerged. This rarely happens on today's wide-beamed boats, but my sloop was an old Hinckley—a real charmer, but too narrow for the situation at hand.

Laid on her side, my rudder was completely useless and all but out of the water as she skidded sideways on her beam ends. Gripping the wheel in my right hand, I reached down into the freezing water as far as I could with my left hand, blindly searching for the sheet trailing from the cam cleat. To make matters worse, the perfect sail trim for the fast reaching I'd been enjoying in my solitude meant my boom vang—a multipulley system that helps to keep the boom parallel to the deck when off the wind—was hardened. And the traveler, to which the mainsheet is led, was eased down. Great a few minutes ago, but now the boom was buried helplessly in the water.

Before I could do anything, though, the overloaded boom vang fitting exploded, sending broken parts flying across the cabin and water as if shot from a cannon. The bad news: It would cost me a hundred bucks to replace the fitting. The good news: it relieved the pressure on the boom and gave it someplace to go besides the bottom of Puget Sound.

A mixed blessing indeed. The boom's sudden jump into the air helped relieve the side pressure on the boat and allowed *Second Wind* to begin righting herself. But I still had a problem—the force of the wind was no longer balanced between the jib and the main. With the boom leaping for the sky, shedding air like a wet dog sheds water, the jib threatened to force the boat to fall off the wind even further. Now that the jib sheet was out of the water, I grabbed hold of it and released it from the cleat—only to have it ripped from my hand by the tremendous load it was under.

It's all right. I'm in control here. The figure-eight knot I'd tied at the end of the sheet earlier in the morning had done its job—it'd kept a few inches of my line led to the cockpit while the remainder had been greedily grabbed by the sea and was now flapping and slapping at the water like a panicky swimmer. As the sloop's bow finally came around into the wind, the violent luffing of the sails was even noisier than the howling wind. But it wasn't the noise I was worried about—I had to move fast to stay in control and off the beach close ahead.

I secured the starboard sheet to its winch and, as the boat continued to come around to starboard, I made ready to let the main sheet out. This meant getting in front of the wheel so I could release the main sheet from its place on the cabin top. I locked the wheel to keep it from spinning around and made my way forward, where I quickly wrapped the main sheet around the winch four times, released the stopper, and brought the free end of the sheet back with me to the wheel. Then I unlocked the wheel and, as I steered the boat away from the wind, the boom swung toward starboard.

My plan was to get on a broad port reach so that *Second Wind* wouldn't be heeled over so much. But the sheet didn't cooperate. I'd expected it to move freely as I bore off. Instead, the main sheet was hopelessly stuck, tangled in the remnants of my boom vang; a tightly coiled knot that Hercules couldn't have pried loose.

I now had too much sail up in too much wind—with no way to trim the sails for a proper course. Breathing hard, soaking wet, and colder than cold, I tried to calm myself and take stock of the situation. Salt spray pelted my face and stung my eyes as I surveyed the carnage that, until moments ago, had been my main trim system. What a mess. *Just shoulder back, Kellie, darlin', and deal with it.*

As my breathing began to return to normal, I looked to the horizon. A grim sight. Blakely Rock was dead ahead. With my main locked and my jib cracking like firecrackers on the Fourth of July, I had to get steerage back and I had to get it back now. There was no time to trim in and try to tack. My only hope to avoid turning my beautiful sloop into another pile of splinters on the notorious rock was to bear away hard and fast. *Now!*

I grabbed the knife tied to my belt loop, opened it, and lunged for the hopelessly jammed mainsheet. In one swift motion, my razor-sharp blade tore through the stretched line, letting the main slam to leeward, all the way out to the shrouds. Turning quickly, I dove across the cockpit, cranked the wheel to starboard—and prayed I was in time. To avoid the rock, I let the sloop fall off further so that she was almost at a dead run downwind—a tricky maneuver at best. Let your boat fall off too far downwind and you run the risk of an accidental jibe, which, under these extreme conditions, would've caused the boom to swing around with enough violence to possibly dismast her.

With sails flogging and the wind driving me forward at frightening speed, I watched the depth sounder for interminable seconds as *Second Wind* came within feet of disaster. Luckily the tide was with me. Had it been just a few feet lower, all would have been lost.

Collision avoided, I finally had the boat under control. But the weather had turned even worse by this time. Big dark gray clouds, balled up like dirty sweat socks, rolled across the sky as a relentless, raging gale from the southwest whipped the water into whitecapped chaos.

I had two choices—go around Blakely Rock and turn upwind into Blakely Harbor where I could drop anchor and ride out the storm or try to get back to the marina—an almost straight downwind, twenty-five-minute run at this speed. *The only security you have, that you'll ever have, Kellie, darlin', lies within yourself. Sit high on the windward deck and watch the sail, watch the wind, and beware the jibe.* I went for the run.

To remove the chance of jibing, I had to get the main sail down. A real hassle by myself, especially under these conditions, but, hey, it was my choice to go for the run. I locked the wheel again, stepped forward, and released the halyard cleat. As I expected, nothing happened. Because there was so much force on the mainsail, it wouldn't come down by itself. Muscle time—the time when my workouts with Rob would be put to the test—had arrived. Haul down is a strenuous hand-over-hand, haul-and-wrap process that involves pulling down the sail and stopping at increments to wrap reefing lines around it. But the boom was loose and bouncing around in the wind so much that I had to pull the sail all the way down first and then wrap it. Not a tidy job, but the main was down.

Midway through the run—when I was bone tired and cold as hell and wishing I'd never heard of sailing—it began to rain, a steady, hard-as-needles downpour that soaked through my gloves and everything else within a matter of minutes. Foul weather gear would've been a big help under the circumstances, but naturally it was stowed below deck. I considered dropping the jib and motoring back to the marina, but a quick check of the fuel gauge put that notion to rest—it was at the fumes-and-a-prayer level. Since I didn't want to chance leaving the helm in the storm to retrieve the gear, I stood at the wheel, stoically braving the elements (and my lack of foresight) all the way back to the marina. I know, Grampy. I know.

Just outside the breakwater, I started the engine and turned into the wind. I let the jib sheet go and hauled in on the furling line. Both sheets were flapping in the wind and promptly got tangled in the furled jib, but by this time I couldn't have cared less. All I wanted to do was to get inside the marina and out of the storm. Since the sheets were tangled so badly, I had no fear they'd slip into the water and foul the prop. So I let them alone and headed into the marina for K dock.

The wind was still so strong that I dreaded docking *Second Wind* by myself, but I knew there'd be no one around to lend me a hand. Even if it hadn't been Christmas, no one in his right mind would be out in this weather. As I approached the slip, though, I spotted someone on the dock. It was Detective Allen Kingston, casually standing in the raging downpour as if he had nothing better to do.

When *Second Wind* was in position, I hurried onto the dock and grabbed the stern line while Kingston manned the bow line. As soon as I had my line secured, I ran to the bow and took the line from him and finished tying it off.

He stood back and let me take over, misreading my brusque manner for disapproval. Kingston thinks I'm something of a show-off when it comes to my boat. But showing off was the last thing on my mind. I was too cold, too wet, and too close to collapsing—my only thought was to get the boat secured as quickly as possible.

But my fingers were so numbed in my rain-soaked gloves that I could hardly get the lines wrapped around the dock cleats. I fumbled with the spring lines, dropped them a couple of times, and then misthreaded them through the fairlead. The wind-whipped rain beat against my face like tiny daggers and plastered my hair flat against my forehead. Water dripped into my eyes until I could hardly see. I wanted to scream. Instead I wiped my face with the back of my glove and wrestled the lines some more. Through it all, Kingston watched with a bemused expression on his face.

"You could lend a hand, you know."

He didn't budge an inch, his arms folded across his chest, one bushy eyebrow cocked at a rakish angle. "Hey, Montgomery. You're the sailor, not me."

Exhaustion turned to anger and along with it a rush of helpful adrenaline. I finished off the spring lines with a flourish and marched over to the boat steps, deliberately ignoring him. It was a show of defiance that backfired. As soon as I got to the steps, I had to sit down. Wrapping my arms about my knees, I tucked my head down to hide the tears. But my sobbing gave me away. Kingston was at my side immediately. He took off his raincoat and wrapped it around my shoulders, which caused me to sob even louder.

"Hey, Red, it's okay." He sat down next to me. "God, I'm so sorry. Come on now. It's okay."

He gently pried my arms from my knees and pulled me to him. I offered no resistance, unself-consciously resting my face on his chest as if I belonged nestled in the comforting warmth of his body. It'd been so long since I'd been held, so long since I'd been physically touched in this way that I felt myself sliding into an almost soporific state. The scent of his aftershave on the wind-whipped rain was pleasing, and I drew closer to him, feeling connected to him in a way I'd never experienced before.

He squeezed my shoulder. "Hey, Red, don't take this personal or anything. I mean, it's real sweet sitting out here with you in the rain and all, but I'm getting wetter than a goddamn duck."

We went inside.

I took a hot shower and changed my clothes while Kingston busied himself in the main cabin. With a towel wrapped around my wet hair, I came into the galley just as he was pouring me a cup of hot tea. I hadn't asked for the tea, and his thoughtfulness, while welcome, did nothing to restore the closeness I'd felt toward him before he'd ruined the moment. If he intended the tea as some sort of appeasement, it wasn't working.

He was bare-chested, having hung his soaked shirt next to the electric space heater. His jeans were wet, too, but he'd left them on and they clung to his muscular thighs in a way I found disconcerting. It was the second time in as many weeks that Allen Kingston had been in my cabin, partially disrobed and acting as if he were at home. Having him there—fussing about the galley in that awkward, stooped way of his—was beginning to feel normal. Well, almost.

He put the teacup on the table alongside a steaming mug of coffee he'd made for himself. After we'd both sat down, he asked, "Feeling better?"

"Sort of. How 'bout you?"

"As good as I can be, drinking instant decaf. When're you ever going to get some real coffee, anyway?"

"Probably when you start letting me know in advance that you're coming."

"Hey, you called me and said it was important. I couldn't get hold of you on the phone, so I hot-footed it right over here."

"Right over? I called you two days ago."

"I've been busy. But I'm here now—on Christmas Day, even."

It's weird how a stressful experience can affect you. I'd held up well when I was in trouble, but as soon as I was safely ashore, I'd come undone. All Kingston had to do was mention Christmas, and I felt myself losing it all over again. Tears welled up in my eyes, and I took the towel from my head to wipe them away.

He threw up his hands. "Now what's wrong? What'd I say?"

I shrugged him off. "Forget it. You didn't say anything."

"Damn it all, what's going on? I've never seen you like this before." He set his coffee mug on the table. "You sick or something?"

"Yeah, that's it. I'm sick. Sick and tired."

"What happened out there, Montgomery? You have some trouble?"

"Some."

A gust of wind rocked the boat. Kingston grabbed for the mug, but some of the coffee sloshed over the rim and onto the table before he could save it. He wiped up the spill with a napkin and said, "You know, I've never pretended to understand what makes you sailor types tick. To me, sailing is nothing but a lot of work. It can't be easy hoisting all those sails this way and that by yourself, especially in this kind of weather. And for what? To prove you can keep from puking while getting blown from here to hell and gone? The thrill of getting drenched?"

He wadded up the coffee-soaked napkin. "You can be damn sure you wouldn't find me out boating on a day like today. Hell, I'm getting queasy just sitting here at the dock. So tell me, Montgomery, why'd you go out there? Is there some maritime law requiring all sailors to go to sea whenever the wind kicks up?"

"Only if it reaches near gale force."

"Okay, that makes sense."

"Almost as much as you standing on the dock in the rain."

He smiled and downed the last of his coffee. After he'd helped himself to another cup, he said, "Now that we've established that we're both a little crazy, how 'bout telling me why you called?"

"*Second Wind* was broken into the other day. The place was trashed."

He looked around. "Yeah? How'd you tell?"

"Are you going to make jokes or listen?"

"Who's joking?"

"Detective . . ."

"Relax, Montgomery. I'm listening."

"Like I said, the place was trashed, but as far as I can tell, nothing of value was taken."

"So what's your point?"

"My point is, something *was* stolen. I just can't figure out why. I'm convinced, though, that the break-in and theft is connected to the Moyers' murders."

He sighed. "Okay, I'll bite. What was stolen?"

"The Moyers' Visitor Access List."

"That computer printout you gave me?"

"I kept a copy for myself to jot notes on," I said with a nod. "The funny thing is, they also stole some Christmas cards."

Kingston laughed. "Christmas cards! And you think all this somehow proves a connection to the Moyer case?"

"Why not?"

"What do you want me to say, Montgomery?"

"For starters, why do you think someone would steal the printout?"

"I haven't a clue, but the Christmas cards? Hey, that's a whole different ball game. Maybe the guy thought there was money or checks inside. Or maybe he was just a grinch. The grinch who stole Christmas."

I suddenly felt weepy again and grabbed the towel.

"Jeez, Montgomery, don't do that. I'm sorry. Jeez." He

covered my hand with his. I knew he was simply trying to comfort me, but I found myself unsettled by the gesture. The pleasing warmth of his hand on mine felt so good that I wanted him to take my other hand and draw me into his chest as he'd done earlier. I felt so embarrassed by the thought that I couldn't look at him.

He didn't seem to notice. Apparently satisfied I wasn't going to break down again, he withdrew his hand. "You say you made some notes on the printout. What kind of notes?"

"Questions, mostly. Things I'd found out that puzzled me."

"Like what?"

"Like why were Moyer and Preston arguing?"

"And you have a theory, right?"

I nodded.

"Does it have something to do with the fact that Moyer was running a profitable little side business called the Missing Link?"

"You know about that?"

"I know that Preston was opposed to the operation."

"Do you know that Moyer was blackmailing Preston?"

Kingston leaned forward. "Where'd you hear that?"

"I have my sources. So, what do you think? Is there anything to tie Preston to the murders besides the Missing Link? What about the computer printout? Have you contacted anyone on the list who might figure into the case? It's been almost a week since Donald, Jr. was murdered. Has anything new turned up?"

"Montgomery, we've been over this ground before. You know I never said I'd share anything about the case with you. I've already said too much as it is."

"No, you haven't. I know you think I'm just interested out of idle curiosity, but believe me, Kingston, I'm desperate to know what's going on."

He lifted an eyebrow. "Desperate?"

"Desperate. Cassie's involved with the Missing Link."

"What do you mean?"

"My sister gave Cassie ten thousand dollars for Christmas. She's prepared to hand it over to the law firm for whatever information they have on her birth mother. Cassie thinks the Missing Link will help her locate the woman."

Kingston leaned back from the table and stretched his long legs so that they were in front of the heater. "Then you can set your mind at ease. The Missing Link's not going to help her any. Preston shut that operation down."

"Are you sure?"

He rolled his eyes. "Yeah, Montgomery, I'm sure."

"Oh."

He downed some of his coffee and grimaced. "Damn, this stuff is bad."

"Kingston, are you positive Cassie's not in any kind of danger?"

He nodded. "But that's not the question you should be asking."

"It's the only question I really care about. And the only question that you've given me a straight answer for."

"Here's another straight answer—if anyone's in any kind of danger, it's you."

"Me?"

"Don't look so all-fired innocent. When you're not out on the water trying to kill yourself, you're out talking to God only knows who about a murder investigation. And just what has it gotten you? A break-in and trashed boat. The next time you could be the one getting trashed."

"So you *do* think the break-in was related to the case."

"Did I say that?"

"You don't have to—your meaning's clear enough to me."

"And your meaning's clear enough to me." He waved his hand. "Look at yourself, Montgomery. You're a basket case. You've been trying to drink that tea ever since we sat down, but your hand is shaking so bad you can't even get it up to your lips. It's Christmas Day—and your birthday, I hear. But are you with your daughter, the one you're so worried about? No. You're off sailing by yourself in weather so foul the good Lord should issue a recall. Not exactly a smart move for a sailing instructor. Shaking, weeping, tepid questions."

Tepid? "Listen, I just—"

He stood up, grabbed his shirt, and slipped it on. "What'd you do with my raincoat?"

"Are you leaving?"

"Come on, Red, fetch my coat and get one for yourself."

"Huh?"

"We're going out to dinner, Christmas dinner. So get a move on, or we'll be late."

"Listen, Kingston, I don't—"

"Hey! No arguments."

"But . . . I don't think there's any place open on Christmas."

"Don't sweat it. I know a place that's always open— three hundred and sixty five days a year."

TWENTY

KINGSTON'S CAR WAS a battered and bruised clunker of indecipherable make and model—sort of a trash can on wheels. McDonald's wrappers, a couple of empty soda cans, and what looked like sweat socks or something worse covered the passenger's seat and most of the floor.

"Don't worry," he said as he cleared out a spot for me. "Nothing in here will bite. Stink, maybe. Bite, no."

And he called my place trashy. "How do you get women to go out with you in this thing?"

"First date, no problem. Second, well . . ."

Five minutes later, we stopped in front of a house in Magnolia. A bungalow, actually—a cozy cliffside bungalow with an expansive view of the Puget Sound shipping lanes.

"Uh, Kingston, what're we doing here?"

"Going to dinner." He nodded toward the bungalow. "At Kingston's Kitchen."

"This is your place?" It was a house straight out of a Norman Rockwell painting complete with white picket fence and porch swing. All that was missing was a collie bounding down the walkway behind a couple of blond-haired, blue-eyed little kids.

"What's the matter? Expecting a dump?"

As a matter of fact . . . Dump. Clunker. Slob. Kingston. The words did seem to go together. "I was expecting a restaurant."

"This'll be better."

He whacked on the car door a couple of times. "It's kind of temperamental," he explained. Temperamental? There was nothing but a rusty hole where the door handle should've been. My door appeared to have all its parts, but when I reached for the handle, he said, "Sit tight. I'll help you."

"Don't be silly. I'm perfectly capable of—"

"Montgomery, forget it. I'm not insinuating that you're a helpless female. The damn passenger door only opens from the outside."

"Oh."

"Better make a run for it," he said. The rain had tapered off to a light drizzle, but the wind still howled and whipped at our backs as we hustled for cover. I shivered as Kingston fumbled with his house key. "The problem with cliffside living," he said, noticing my discomfort, "is the wind tends to blow right through you."

Stepping into the bungalow's living room was like stepping into a rustic cabin in the woods. It had all the requisite masculine features—knotty pine walls and floors, heavy beamed ceiling, and massive stone fireplace—softened by a southwest decor. A beige leather sofa, a natural shell stone coffee table, and a leather recliner were grouped facing the fireplace. The walls were decorated with colorful Navajo rugs and an eclectic assortment of fine oil paintings. The whole room was alive with color—a vivid blend of red, orange, and green with touches of pastel blues and pinks. I couldn't stop staring.

"Like it?"

"What can I say? It's lovely, it's comfy, it's warm, it's . . ."

"Not me?"

"Well . . ."

Kingston laughed. "It was my parents' home originally. I lived here as a kid. When my folks died a few years back, I inherited it. Most of the stuff you see here is theirs."

He fluffed up several of the brightly colored pillows adorning the couch before inviting me to sit down. "Make yourself at home," he said. "I'll be right back." As soon as he left, I got up to look around. Except for a limited edition Carol Griggs print above the fireplace, the rest of the artwork in the room was signed simply "R.D.K."

I ran my fingers over the spines of several dog-eared books crammed into the built-in pine bookcases on both sides of the fireplace. Hemingway and Steinbeck were obvious favorites, plus there were more than a few Louis L'Amour titles interspersed with Shakespeare and several volumes of poetry. I wondered which, if any, were Kingston's choices and which were his parents'. An old photograph album on the bottom shelf caught my attention. I picked it up and leafed through several pages of what I assumed were Kingston family photos. Although the photos in the second half of the album were in color, they were taken at least twenty years ago, judging by the hairdos and clothing styles.

"How're ya doing out there?" Kingston hollered.

I snapped the album shut and set it back on the shelf.

"Doing good," I hollered back.

As I scrambled from the floor to the couch, a small photo slipped from the album. I just had time to scoop it up and tuck it under a throw pillow before Kingston elbowed his way through the swinging doors. He carried a steaming mug in each hand.

"Here ya go. This should warm you up," he said, setting the drinks on the coffee table.

"Ah. Hot buttered rum," I said. "The old fuddy's drink."

He laughed and sat down. Holding up his mug, he said, "Here's to old fuddies. Long may they fuddy." We clicked mugs. When he saw me shivering he offered to build a fire.

While Kingston made like a Boy Scout, wadding up newspapers and stuffing them under the fireplace logs, I stole a look at the photo I'd hidden. It was a color shot of a young woman in a Seattle Police Department uniform. She was strikingly beautiful with eyes as dark as burnt chocolate and a creamy, peachlike complexion. Her blond hair was cut short, regulation style, but she wore her hat set back on her head, exposing curly bangs across her forehead. I turned the photo over. On the back someone had scribbled, "Roberta. Class of 1970."

"What kind of music do you like?" Kingston suddenly asked.

I jammed the photo between the couch cushions. "Music?"

He turned around on his haunches. "Yeah, you know. The art and science of making pleasing sounds. Usually vocal or instrumental. Melody, harmony, rhythm—"

"Okay, okay. I get it. I like most anything. Why?"

He pointed to the stereo system. With three-foot-high speakers on both sides, the stacked unit had more dials and doodads than a 747 cockpit and took up an entire wall. "My folks left me quite a record collection. Mostly big band sounds of the 1940s, but I also have some CDs that are fairly up to date. I thought you might enjoy listening to something."

"Kingston, do you have a guilty conscience?"

"What do you mean?"

"Why are you being so nice to me—my favorite drink, a fire, music . . . ?"

"Hey, I'm always nice to you."

I sipped the rum and gazed into the fire. The crumpled newspaper was long gone, and the red and yellow blaze cast the room in a soft, warm glow. "You were right earlier today when you said something must be bothering me. I'm worried about Cassie and not just because of the Missing Link."

"Want to talk about it?"

"She and I . . . well, our relationship is a little shaky right now."

He shot me one of his confession-demanding stares. "A little?"

"Okay, a lot. I'm hurt and I guess it shows, but I don't need your pity."

"Pity? Is that why you think I invited you here?"

I nodded.

He walked over to the stereo, slipped a record from its cover and put it on the turntable. A clarinet's pear-shaped tones spiraled up and burst into a sustained trill. "I played the clarinet in junior high," he said. "Elvis was big back then, but it was this sound—the sound of Benny Goodman—that grabbed me. I remember seeing a movie about his life story when I was in the eighth grade. Elvis was playing in *Jailhouse Rock* at the other theater in town. All my friends thought I was nuts for choosing Goodman over Elvis. They teased me for weeks afterward. But, hell, wild horses couldn't have kept me away from that theater."

He came back to the couch and sat down. "It's Christmas, Montgomery," he said with a sigh. "You're alone. I'm alone. You seemed like you needed to talk to someone, and I listen better on a full stomach. Don't read anything more into your being here than that."

I leaned forward and set my drink on the coffee table. "Well, I just thought—"

"Don't do any thinking for a change. Just sit back and listen to the music. After awhile I'll fix us dinner. And if you want, I'll even tell you about that photo you seem so interested in."

Embarrassed, I retrieved the photo and handed it to him. "Sorry. It fell out of the album."

"Her name was Roberta," he said quietly, "but everyone called her Bobbie. She wanted to be an artist." He gestured toward an oil painting. "That's one of hers—plus just about everything else you see here. But she joined the force to please her dad. He was a lieutenant in the West Precinct, and it was sort of expected she'd follow family tradition. Unusual for a woman at the time, but then, Bobbie was an unusual woman. We met as cadets at the academy and got married six weeks after we graduated. A year later she was dead. Killed in the line of duty.''

"I didn't know. I'm so sorry."

"Yeah, well . . . it was a long time ago."

"It's been three years since Wendell's death, but the emptiness is still there. I'm beginning to think it will never go away."

"Maybe not, but at least you have your daughter. Bobbie was three months pregnant when she was killed."

Only the crackling of the burning wood broke the silence that followed. I didn't know what to say. I'd been feeling so sorry for myself, thinking I'd lost Cassie to Donna, and perhaps some woman yet unknown, while Kingston really had lost his child—in the worst possible way.

After a moment, I asked, "Tell me something, Kingston. What do you think about adopted kids who search for their birth parents?"

"Like Cassie?"

I nodded.

"I've never given it much thought, but it makes a lot of sense."

"In what way?"

"Everyone has a right to know who they are, but adopted kids are legally denied that right." He pulled the photo album from the shelf and flipped through the pages. "Here, take a look at this." He pointed to a faded black-and-white photo of two young girls, unsmiling in their high-collared, long gingham dresses. Their dark hair was piled atop their heads and secured with big floppy white bows.

"The one on the left was my great-grandmother. The other, her sister. They were Snoqualmie. The photo was taken at the Tolt River Missionary School. They were taught religion and language at the school—white man's religion and language. They were also given new names, new clothes, new hairstyles, and forbidden by law to speak their Lushootseed language ever again.

"Their heritage was denied them, but my great-grandmother never forgot. She taught her daughter—my grandmother—to speak Lushootseed. She taught her the dances, the legends, and the myths—all the old ways, the ways of her people. And my grandmother passed them on to my mother who, in turn, taught me. If my child had lived, I'd have been the teacher. And you know why?"

I shook my head.

"Because who we are and where we came from is what spirituality is all about. It's what centers us. It's what connects us to all of those who've gone before. Without that knowledge, we're never complete. My great-grandmother knew that, so she passed our culture on, even though it was forbidden. The way I see it, adopted kids have had their culture taken from them, too. Maybe reuniting with their birth parents is their way of taking it back."

"That was quite a speech. Your great-grandmother sounds like a wonderful woman, but the analogy is flawed. I love Cassie. Wendell and I didn't try to make her into something else when we adopted her. When she came into our lives, she came into our family as well. Our family became hers—with love. Unlike your great-grandmother, she didn't have our heritage forced upon her."

"But she didn't have a choice in the matter, either, did she?"

We ate our dinner in the kitchen. Kingston had transformed the chrome dinette into a formal dining table with a white linen tablecloth, Waterford crystal, and Lenox china. He lit two green candles encircled with holly sprigs. "There," he said. "Festive enough for you?"

"Festive? This is wonderful. I must say, I'm impressed."

"Wait till you taste my cooking. It's not just impressive, it's good." He'd made lasagna, a tossed green salad, and some kind of flat bread served with a head of roasted garlic and a side of Cambozola cheese. For dessert, he brought out some spumoni ice cream, courtesy of Häagen-Dazs.

"Now it's time to open your presents," he said as we took our after-dinner drinks—coffee for Kingston and tea for me—into the living room.

"What are you talking about?"

"It's Christmas, isn't it? It's your birthday, isn't it?"

"Yes, but—"

"If it's Christmas and it's your birthday, then you open presents. But the gift I have for you isn't gift-wrapped. It's sort of like the Christmas dinner we just ate—untraditional."

I looked at the small Christmas tree in the corner.

"It's not under the tree, Montgomery. Like I said, it's not traditional—it's inside information. About the case, I mean."

"Really?"

"It's not much, but you can take it or leave it."

"I'll take it."

"We've interviewed everybody on that computer printout you gave me. Everybody on the Moyers' Visitor Access List checks out. Your thief stole useless information as far as we're concerned. But we did find something in Moyer's dock box. It may have been what Junior was looking for that day he broke into the wrong box."

"What'd you find?"

"A key. Trouble is, we don't know what it's for."

"A safety deposit box?"

"Naw. We checked that out with their bank. And their home safe has a combination lock. Same with Moyer's office safe."

"How 'bout a storage locker of some kind?"

"We haven't been able to find any evidence that the Moyers had a storage locker."

"So that's it? That's my present?"

"Yep. Merry Christmas and Happy Birthday."

"Thank you very much, Detective, but that tells me exactly nothing."

"Maybe so, but now you know as much as I do."

"Come on. You've got to know more than that."

"Not really. Just a theory or two, but you've got one or two of those yourself, so I'm not going to give you something you don't need. Now, where's my present?"

"*Your* present?"

"It's Christmas, Montgomery. I give you a present, you give me a present. Doesn't have to be anything fancy."

"But, I . . . well, how 'bout some inside information of mine?"

He smiled. "Lay it on me."

"Miranda Moyer was involved in baby brokering. From what I've heard, she was quite adept at seeking out young girls and pressuring them to give up their babies for adoption, sometimes before they even knew that's what they wanted. It's possible that someone changed her mind and wanted her baby back. Might be a strong motive for murder, don't you think?"

"I think it's a real nice gift, Montgomery. Not much substance, but, like they say, it's the thought that counts."

TWENTY-ONE

MY CHRISTMAS WITH **Allen Kingston** came to an abrupt ending when he got a call from the precinct to investigate a domestic disturbance that had turned deadly. He dropped me off at the marina on his way to the scene. As I climbed out of the car and thanked him again for the dinner, he got in one last dig. "If you really want to thank me, Red, try keeping your nose out of the Moyer investigation." Right. I waved him off with a smart salute and matching smile.

I awoke early the next morning with Kingston's parting words still ringing in my ears. Despite his admonishment, I was more eager than ever to resume my investigation. I'd missed the gift exchange at Donna's, but the so-called gift Kingston had given me was very much on my mind. And so, too, were the questions it raised: What was the key in the dock box all about? Was Moyer really a blackmailer? Is that what got him killed? Were the police any closer to solving the Moyers' murders than I was?

The feelings that had surfaced when I was with Kingston yesterday puzzled me most of all. I couldn't help smiling as I pictured him aboard *Second Wind*, fussing about the cabin, making tea and holding my hand. And then at his bunga-

low—the hot buttered rum by the warm fire, the music, the
dinner. But it was the way he'd held me on the dock that
stirred me the most. I shook my head, determined not to
dwell on such things. Kingston would've laughed if he'd
known how appealing I found him. After all, he was the
one who said I shouldn't "read anything into" our day together. So I pushed my feelings for him aside, chalking up
the experience to nothing more than the spirit of the season.
Christmas tends to bring out a different side of people. Even
cops.

Bert and Rose weren't expected back until the end of the
week, but I headed for the administration building anyway.
I hoped I could find a phone number for Rose's parents in
her Rolodex. Despite Kingston's assurances about the Missing Link, I couldn't wait to talk to Rose about what she'd
learned from her visit.

Larstad's Marina had a skeleton crew on duty the day
after Christmas, mostly in case of emergencies. All of the
peripheral businesses like the yacht brokerage and apparel
outlet were closed. The harbormaster's office, though, was
open as usual. Holiday or not, someone was required to be
on duty, twenty-four hours a day, three-hundred-sixty-five
days a year. The security guard at the front desk was a
premed student at the university, but thanks to the holidays,
he'd traded his textbooks for a Tom Clancy novel. He turned
it facedown and greeted me.

"What brings you out today, Mrs. M?"

"Gotta check something in Rose's office. Could you give
me the keys? I'll just be a minute."

"You won't need the keys. She's here."

"In her office?"

"Yep. Same with Mr. Foster. Guess someone forgot to
tell them it's a holiday."

Rose's office was on the main floor, down the hall from
the lobby. She was pouring herself a cup of coffee when I
walked through the door.

"Hey! Aren't you supposed to be on vacation?" I asked.

She smiled sheepishly and gestured to the stacks of papers and folders on her desk. "I had to get back—that Nakito audit is coming up soon, and things are a mess. Bert's upstairs. He had work to do, too, so we cut our trip short." She blew on her coffee and took a sip. "Besides, two days with my family is just about two days too many."

"I know what you mean. I spent Christmas Eve at Donna's. Kind of makes me wish I were an orphan."

We both laughed, but it was strained. The humor hit too close to the emotions.

I asked, "Can you take a break for a few minutes?"

"Sure." She motioned to the chair next to her desk. "Just push those folders onto the floor and have a seat. You want some tea?"

I declined with a shake of my head and said, "I'm glad you came back early. I've been dying to talk to you. In fact, I came over here to see if I could find your parents' phone number. Detective Kingston told me that James Preston shut down the Missing Link."

Rose looked surprised. "No way. It's fully operational— at least it was a few days ago. And your friend Yolanda is running the show." She shuddered. "My God, Kellie, the woman's a barracuda."

"Little Yolanda? Guppy maybe, but I'd hardly call her a barracuda."

"I'm serious. She may be little, but she's got that entire office staff shaking in their boots. And she's not taking any guff from James Preston, either."

"Maybe you better start at the beginning. Tell me everything that happened."

"Okay. I called the number you gave me for the Moyer and Preston Law Office. When I asked if I'd reached the Missing Link, the receptionist immediately transferred me to Yolanda. I told her I'd heard about the Missing Link and was interested in making an appointment. That's when I got the third degree."

"Questioned you, did she?"

Rose nodded. "Believe it. She wanted to know where I'd heard about the service. What did I know about it? Who was I trying to locate? How old was I? Etcetera, etcetera. She was friendly enough, but extremely cautious."

"What did you tell her?"

"Just what you told me to say. I'd heard about the Missing Link through an adoption forum on CompuServe. I gave her my correct name and age, but everything else was just like we made up—I'd been adopted as an infant and had great parents and all, but I'd always had a longing to meet my birth parents, particularly my mother."

"And she accepted that?"

"She asked a few more questions first. Where was I born? What had I done to locate my parents before calling the Missing Link? Did I have any information on them at all? Those sorts of questions. I guess I must have passed the test because I got an appointment to see her."

"So what happened at the office?"

"That was very interesting, Kellie. The receptionist called Yolanda to let her know I was waiting and before I could even sit down, she came out to the lobby and hustled me into Donald Moyer's former office herself."

"Moyer's office?"

"Right. His nameplate was still on the door, but it sure felt like her office. Anyway, we had just begun to talk about the service when we were interrupted by a phone call from her secretary. I couldn't hear what she said, of course, but whatever it was, it made Yolanda go ballistic. She said, 'I don't care if it *is* Mr. Preston. I'm with a client right now. And don't disturb me again!' She slammed the phone down. Real nasty. Then she took a deep breath like she was counting to ten and when she turned her attention back to me, she was all buttery and sweet again."

"What did she tell you about the service?"

"She said that since I was born in Washington State, the chances of finding my birth parents were excellent. I asked her why that was, but she demurred, saying that their methods were confidential, but I could be assured that I'd get my money's worth.''

"Let me guess. Ten thousand dollars' worth.''

"How'd you know? Ten thousand dollars for locating one parent. Twenty for two.''

"Donna gave Cassie a check for Christmas. She must have talked to Yolanda or somebody there to know how much to give her.''

Rose whistled. "Some Christmas present. I wondered why Donna was at the office that day. I couldn't believe you'd involve her in one of your ruses, too.'' She set her coffee cup on the desk. "How do you feel about Cassie using the Missing Link?''

"We had a major blow-up over it. I left Donna's right afterward and I haven't heard from Cassie since. I'm really worried.''

"Maybe she'll change her mind. They require half the fee up front. It's nonrefundable, even if they can't locate either parent. Yolanda said not to worry, though. 'We never fail.' Never, I asked? 'Never,' she repeated. It was at that point that Preston came barreling into the office. He was very distinguished-looking in a custom-made suit, but the effect was diminished considerably.''

"How so?''

"He was drunk. Yolanda immediately stood up. Her voice was strained as she said, 'James, this isn't a good time.' She came around her desk and took him firmly by the arm. It was clear she wanted him out of the office, but Preston was having none of it. He shrugged her off saying, 'Don't touch me, you little tramp.' ''

"What'd she do?''

"That's when I stood up. Preston noticed me then and said, 'Who's this? Another sucker on the line?' Yolanda was clearly livid, but she forced a smile and escorted me to the door, saying we'd have to resume our talk later.''

"And Preston? Did he leave, too?''

"No way. Yolanda got me out the door real quick, but

Preston dug in his heels and took up residence. I pretended to be leaving and headed down the hall to the lobby, but as soon as she shut the door, I turned around and came back."

"Good girl. Did you hear anything?"

"I was right outside her office door, but I could've been ten feet down the hall and not missed anything. Preston accused Yolanda of trying to take over Moyer's practice. Yolanda said she was just using his office, but Preston countered with, 'You're just a paralegal—and a lousy one at that.' She told him he had no room to talk, that he was nothing but a lush, that if it weren't for her, the business would go down the tubes. By this time they were both shouting so loud that people started popping out of their offices to check on the commotion. I figured I'd better leave."

"Sounds kind of familiar."

"In what way?"

"Preston had a loud argument with Moyer, too, the night before the murders. I hope Yolanda keeps that in mind."

"From what I saw of Yolanda, I'd be more concerned about Preston's safety than hers."

Rose's description of Yolanda's behavior coupled with Bob Chapman's innuendoes had me shaken. It was hard to square with the eager-to-please young woman I'd known at Horace Mann. Had the competitive corporate world changed her that much? Or was she simply under too much stress over Donald Moyer's death? Worse yet, had his questionable tactics somehow rubbed off on her? Was she really having an affair with Moyer as Emily had insinuated? Had that somehow affected her behavior? Rose and I speculated on the possibilities for a few minutes.

"An affair is possible, I suppose, but maybe she just got hooked on power," suggested Rose. "I've seen it happen before. The ambitious young corporate secretary or assistant is privy to her boss's secret wheeling and dealing and finds it irresistible."

"Could be," I said. "But I think there's something else

going on with Yolanda.'' I was determined to confront my old pal and find out. I called her from Rose's office, but the receptionist said she was unavailable to take my call—she had back-to-back appointments scheduled all day. I left my name and number, but just to be on the safe side, I scheduled an appointment with her, too. The first available time slot was at nine o'clock tomorrow morning.

I wanted to stick around and talk with Rose for a while longer—get her thoughts on *Second Wind*'s break-in and Terri Moyer's revelations about her parents—but I hated to interfere with her work any more than I had. So we said our good-byes and promised to get together as soon as things settled down.

I'd just closed the door to her office when the Weasel sauntered out of the restroom at the far end of the hall. That he was in the building at all surprised me since he never hung around much during the holidays. But then, with the Nakito deal still up in the air, he'd been doing his best to ensure a high profile. He wore tan chinos and a bright red polo shirt, which he was still tucking in when he caught sight of me. I tried to avoid eye contact, but it was too late.

''Kellie! Hold on there!'' He charged down the hall before I could slip away. ''I need to talk to you, Kellie.''

What he really needed to do was zip up his pants. ''I already turned in the boat show plans.''

''Yes, yes, of course you did. But we have a small problem.''

''What problem?''

''Don't worry. It won't take all that much to fix—maybe just a few hours or so.''

''*What* problem, Todd?''

''I thought your sketch for the booth was . . . how should I put this? A little too plain for the image Larstad Marina has cultivated over the years. I think we need something bigger and bolder, something that really makes a statement.''

"Fine, go for it. Do whatever you think best." I turned to leave.

"Hold on, Kellie. This is your project. The advance team from Nakito Enterprises, however, agrees with my opinion of the design. I told Mr. Kano you'd be happy to revise the plans, and he's counting on you to come up with something impressive."

"Since when do you speak for me?"

He scrunched up his nose as though he'd stepped in something foul. "You don't have to get testy. For your information, this project is a very high-priority item. Do it right and you just might improve your status with the team."

I wondered when he'd get around to his real agenda. "My status?"

He cleared his throat and assumed a serious look. "Negotiating the sale of a marina is not like selling a car," he said. "It's a highly complicated and complex undertaking. Exceptional skill is needed to handle the delicate intricacies involved in order to reach a mutually agreeable sale."

"Cut to the chase, Todd. What *about* my status?"

A serious and sober look again. "I'm sure you have nothing to worry about, Kellie, but the advance team is evaluating everyone's role at the marina. The more you demonstrate your willingness to do whatever it takes to make the marina succeed, the more secure your future will be."

How nice. The Weasel looking out for my best interests. "So," he continued, "if you'll follow me back to my office and pick up the original plans, you can get started right away. Mr. Kano is expecting the revisions tomorrow."

The Weasel's manipulations had me fuming, but I wasn't all that surprised. I knew he'd eventually figure out a way to make me pay for the way I'd smart-mouthed him the night of the break-in. As I headed home with the plans, I weighed the pros and cons of ditching the project and running over to the Sports Center. Before the Weasel had saddled me with the extra work, I'd been thinking about getting Sissy's take on the woman Darla Schuster had seen arguing with Miranda. I still hadn't decided what to do when I reached the slip. The phone was ringing, and I scrambled aboard, nearly dropping the Weasel's precious plans into the water in my haste.

"Hi, Kellie. This is Emily."

Damn. I'd forgotten all about returning her call. "Hi, Emily. I got your phone message, but I just haven't had a moment to call."

"That's okay. I've been in and out a lot. What with Christmas and all, things have been rather hectic." She sighed. "Actually, a lot hectic. But that's the case all year long when you're married to a politician." She paused, then added, "Besides, I knew you'd be busy with Christmas, too. And the investigation, of course. How's it going, anyway?"

"I'm not sure what to say. There're too many unanswered questions floating around."

"Oh? What kind of questions?"

"Just the usual—who dunnit and why?"

"There must be something I can do to help."

"I appreciate the offer, Emily, but I think some of the questions will be answered within the next day or so."

"I'm sure they will. In the meantime, how about joining me for lunch? I'm going to be over your way today—a photo-op session with Conrad and the mayor at Westlake Center Mall. I thought we might get together afterward."

I glanced at the boat show plans I'd tossed on the table. "That sounds nice, but I've got a project for the marina that's going to keep me pretty busy." I wanted my options open in case I bagged the Weasel's project and headed for the Sports Center.

"You have to eat, don't you? I could meet you at the Topside, say . . . at noon?"

Her offer was tempting. If I decided to stick around and tackle the revisions, I'd probably be ready for a break by then. Hell, I was ready for a break and I hadn't even started yet.

"Oh, Kellie, please say yes. You have no idea how badly I need to get away from the campaign hoopla for a bit. And if it makes any difference," she said, "I've been thinking about that question you asked me the other night. The one about whether Miranda ever mentioned that someone was following her around, giving her a hard time. Remember?"

"I remember. Did you think of something?"

"I believe I did."

"The Topside at noon will be fine."

TWENTY-TWO

OUR LUNCH CAME and went without any mention of Miranda Moyer. Janey gave us a refill on our tea and hurried off to take care of a group celebrating a birthday.

"You look tired," Emily said after she left.

It took me awhile to respond. It was one of those well-meaning comments that only makes you feel worse. Emily looked anything but tired in her stylish outfit—a cheerful yellow tunic over a dark blue turtleneck and matching tights. She had on the same chic leather boots and gold jewelry that she'd worn the night I'd found her aboard *Second Wind*. I wasn't up on designer labels, but her outfit had to be an expensive, original-name something or other.

And yet, for all her obvious wealth, Emily had a way of making you feel comfortable in her presence. I could see why her husband's political foes called her Conrad Cummings's greatest asset. She had beauty, brains, charm, and, most important, she knew how to listen. "I guess I am a little tired," I admitted.

"This investigation is getting to you, isn't it?"

I nodded, and we both looked out the window, our attention drawn to a young couple walking along the water's edge with a toddler in tow. A sad look crossed Emily's face as the toddler's father showed her how to skip rocks across the water. I wondered if she was thinking of her boys. She'd shared with me that they attended a boarding school and were away from home most of the year. "They're such good kids and a delight to have around," she'd said. "Especially after dealing with some of the phony hangers-on that Conrad's campaign seems to attract." She'd smiled then, one of those disarming dimpled smiles that the photographers loved so much. "In a way, you and the boys are the only real people I know." I admit I was flattered by the comparison.

After a moment, she turned away from the window and said, "So what exactly have you found out?"

"Not a whole heck of a lot. I've been going around in circles mostly. The more I talk to people, the more confusing everything gets. Maybe that's why I look tired."

"You know, Kellie, I've said before that I want to help you in any way I can and I meant it. I need to do something really useful for a change. I've been feeling like such a fifth wheel lately. Take that photo shoot today—it seems as if all I'm good for is serving as a pretty prop on Conrad's arm. I'd feel a whole lot better if I could give you some information about the Moyers that will help steer you in the right direction."

Those were the words I'd been waiting to hear. "Sounds good to me."

She ran her fingers through her thick black hair. "Of course, if I knew what ground you've already covered, it might help jog my memory some more."

That made sense. I hadn't really had an opportunity to discuss my findings (meager as they were) with anyone. Rose usually filled that role, but today's conversation with her had been maddeningly brief. I really did need to talk things over with someone—and Emily seemed the logical choice. Maybe talking to her would help jog my memory, too. "I've interviewed folks here and in Bremerton and basically what I've learned is that Donald Moyer wasn't the honest, upright attorney I used to know. For example, I found out that he didn't have any qualms about not disclosing vital facts when it came to arranging adoptions." I filled her in on my conversation with Bob and Betty Chapman.

"I'm not surprised. Donald had a lot of warts, but he was good at keeping them hidden. Sounds like the Chapmans found a few of them. Do you think they had anything to do with the murders?"

"I'm not sure. Bob Chapman is carrying around a great deal of anger, and his wife is awfully troubled, but whether they're capable of murder is another matter. They both seemed genuinely surprised when I told them that the Moyers had been killed."

"What do you make of Betty Chapman wandering off the way she did?"

"Like I said, she's one troubled woman. So was I when I returned home from Bremerton that day. My boat had been broken into and trashed."

A look of concern flickered across Emily's face. "Oh, my gosh. I'm so sorry to hear that. Was anything stolen?"

"Nothing of value, but I think the break-in was related to the case." I told her about the missing case notes. "No other boats were broken into that night, which also leads me to believe I was specifically targeted."

"I guess that rules out the Chapmans if you were in Bremerton talking to them at the time."

"Not necessarily. I stayed in town playing tourist and doing some last minute Christmas shopping. I didn't make it back to the marina until much later than I'd anticipated."

Emily's eyes caught mine, and she smiled. "Ah, I see. Late enough, perhaps, for one of the Chapmans to have paid you a visit?"

"Bob Chapman told me that the last time his wife wandered off she went to Seattle. She could've done it again— she had plenty of time to hop a ferry and break into the boat before I returned. For that matter, her husband only *said* he was going back to work.''

"So you suspect them?''

"At this point, I suspect everyone.''

"Who's everyone?''

The first person who came to mind was Terri Moyer, but I hesitated to say anything. Although Reba Stanton's phone message had confirmed that Terri Moyer was signed out of Coleman Rehab on the dates her parents and brother were murdered, that didn't necessarily mean she was involved. Until I knew more about Terri and her problems, I decided to keep the information to myself.

"I spoke to a young woman and her husband on Christmas Eve who had a pretty good motive for murder,'' I said. "But Miranda was the target, not Donald.''

The revelation seemed to take her by surprise. She leaned forward, her arms on the table. "What do you mean?''

"Let me ask you something first. How much do you know about Miranda's involvement in her husband's law practice?''

Emily shrugged. "She didn't have anything to do with the Missing Link, if that's what you're suggesting. Like I mentioned the night I met you on *Second Wind*—that was her husband's dirty business.''

"How 'bout the adoption business?''

"What about it?'' she asked.

"I've heard that Miranda was involved in baby brokering.''

"Oh. Well, I guess that's one way of putting it. Miranda believed she was just helping people—you know, offering young girls who had no resources of their own a way out of their difficulties.''

"By pressuring them into giving up their babies for adoption whether they were ready or not?''

"I don't know about that,'' she said. "All I know is that Miranda offered to help when no one else wanted anything to do with the girls—especially their families. Anyway, it always turned out well in the end. The couples that Donald found were eager to adopt the babies and give them a good home. The girls were eager to get on with their lives. Everyone got what they wanted.''

''I'm not so sure about that.''

''Are you referring to the couple you saw on Christmas Eve?''

I gave her a quick rundown on my visit with the Schusters. ''But I've crossed them off my list of suspects.''

''Why?''

''I just can't picture them as murderers—no matter how desperate they were to get their baby back. They're such a sweet couple. And despite Steve Schuster's imposing size, I'm convinced he's just as tender and kindhearted as his gentle wife.''

''You're probably right,'' she said. ''But how many times have you heard those very same words used to describe someone who later turned out to be a brutal serial killer?''

''Every time they interview the shocked neighbors,'' I said.

''I find it hard to think of Miranda as a conniving baby broker, but if it's true then it's also possible that Darla Schuster wasn't the only young woman who later changed her mind about adoption. Perhaps there's another woman out there who wasn't as gentle as Darla.''

''Any ideas?''

''Well, as I said on the phone, I did think of someone who'd bothered Miranda at the Sports Center. I'd forgotten all about the incident because Miranda hadn't seemed too concerned at the time.''

''You think it could be someone who Miranda had helped with an adoption?''

''Maybe there was someone like that bothering her, but the woman I was thinking of was Yolanda Vanasek. I saw Miranda arguing with her at the Sports Center.''

''I didn't know you were a member.''

''I'm not. Conrad and I belong to an athletic club on

Mercer Island, but I've been a guest at the Center often enough. Anyway, I definitely remember the incident—they got kind of loud. I didn't know who Yolanda was at the time and wondered what it was all about. When I asked Miranda about her, she just dismissed the whole thing as office politics.''

"She didn't say why they were arguing?"

"Not really. Just something about how this assistant of her husband's was getting awfully pushy."

"What do you mean by pushy?"

"You know, ambitious. Seems Yolanda Vanasek wanted more out of life than what she could earn on a paralegal's salary. It was only later that I learned that Miranda suspected her of having an affair with Donald. It's possible that's what she really meant by the term 'office politics.' "

"Interesting. Did Miranda ever say anything about Yolanda's relationship with Nancy Preston?"

"Let me think about that a minute," Emily said. She looked out the window again. A lone sailboat that had been tacking back and forth across the bay caught a gust of wind and quickly headed up into it, making the most of the energy burst. "Well," Emily said finally, "I'm not sure what to tell you about Yolanda and Nancy. I can't remember Miranda saying anything about their relationship. Nancy is kind of hard to get to know. She loves tennis, her kids, and presumably James Preston. Those are the only three subjects she'll talk about—getting anything more personal than that out of her is like pulling teeth."

"How long have they been married?"

"A few years. The kids are just toddlers. Preston dumped his first wife for her. You know how it goes—trading in the old model for a newer, sleeker look."

"The trophy wife," I said without thinking.

Emily gave me a knowing look. "Well," she said with a sigh, "I certainly wish you luck in figuring this all out. I have to give you credit. I wouldn't know how to even begin to unravel the mess."

I shrugged and looked out the window, noting the sailboat's progress. She'd resumed tacking, cutting a zigzag course toward her destination. "I guess the way I see it, this investigation is like that little sloop out there," I said, pointing to the sailboat. "The seasoned sailor stays on the same tack as long as it appears advantageous, and then, at the appropriate moment, pushes the tiller toward the sail and changes direction. Each separate piece of information I glean about the Moyers is like a separate tack. It calls for a major readjustment."

"I certainly admire your patience—and courage. I'd have given up long before this. The break-in would've been enough to scare me off. Weren't you just a little bit scared after that?"

"Maybe I'm just plain foolhardy, but as my Grampy used to say, 'Fortune, like the wind, favors the bold. So just keep on tacking, Kellie, darlin', and you'll get there.' "

The birthday bunch was becoming rowdy and demanding, but Janey still found time to come around again to ask if we wanted another refill on our tea. We declined and paid our tab. I thanked Emily for the info, and she said I could thank her by rescheduling our sailing lesson. Her time was at a premium these days—Conrad's campaign was heating up—but she consulted her Day-Timer and switched some prior commitments around so that we could go out the day after tomorrow.

I went home just long enough to grab my workout bag. If anyone knew what Yolanda and Miranda's argument had been about, it would be Sissy. As I expected, the parking lot at the Sports Center was busier than the half-yearly sale at Nordstrom. It happened every holiday—too much eating combined with the club being closed for two days had people standing in line to work out. Since I couldn't find a place to park, I swallowed my pride and pulled into the valet line. The service had always struck me as a bit over the top. The way I looked at it, if you couldn't even walk from the parking lot to the front door, just how serious could you be about physical fitness? Today, though, I was glad it was available.

As soon as I was inside the building, I stashed my workout bag in a locker and made a beeline for the bistro. It was doing a booming business, especially the juice bar. I plopped down on a stool between two men who'd come straight from the weight room. Their shirts were soaked with sweat, and the stench was overpowering, but I toughed it out.

Carmen was behind the counter serving up drinks as fast as she could get them made. Two girls I'd never seen before were bussing tables. Sissy was nowhere in sight. Carmen nodded as I sat down, but I had to wait a couple of minutes before she was free to take my order.

"What'll it be?" she asked.

"I'd like to talk to Sissy. She around?"

"Nope."

"On a break?"

Carmen laughed. "You might say that. She quit."

Damn. As usual, I was a day late and a dollar short. "Finally got her trip jar full, huh?"

"Right to the top and overflowing."

"Good for her."

"Yeah, I suppose, but I'm going crazy here without her." She motioned to the girls bussing tables. "They're still learning the ropes."

The weightlifters paid their tab and left. The empty stools were quickly claimed by two ladies in tennis garb who smelled a whole lot better. "You want to order now?" Carmen asked with a quick nod at the new arrivals. "I don't have time to chew the fat."

"Okay, sure." I gave her my order. When I finished the drink she'd made for me, I slipped a generous tip under my juice glass. Carmen quickly scooped up the bill, tucked it inside her shirt pocket, and smiled her thanks. "Maybe you'd better start a trip jar, too," I said.

"Maybe I better."

Carmen didn't impress me as the gossipy type, but I figured it wouldn't hurt to ask her about Yolanda. "Consider the tip a first deposit. I'd be happy to make an additional deposit if you could spare a few minutes to talk with me."

"I'm a little busy right now," she said. "Come back in an hour or so."

I changed my clothes and spent the hour working out on the treadmill and the rowing machine. It felt great to be in the swing of things without my ankle giving me problems. Afterward, I showered and headed for the bistro.

The juice bar had thinned out considerably during the intervening hour. I sat at a table alongside the window overlooking the tennis courts. Carmen soon joined me. "I've got about five minutes is all—there's a big party coming in later for dinner. I have to help out on the grill." She looked at the tennis courts and sighed. "What a life," she said wistfully.

"You like tennis?"

"Love it! That's the reason I work here—free tennis membership. A lot of good it does me now. I've been so busy since Sissy left I haven't had time to play."

"Tell me about Sissy's leaving. I didn't realize she was so close to her goal."

"She wasn't."

"What happened?"

"She got a windfall. Some woman came in one day and talked to her for quite a while. Sissy was gone the next day—off to Hawaii. She was super happy."

"Who was the woman she talked to?"

"I don't know her name, but I'd seen her before."

"A member?"

"I don't think so, although she played a lot of tennis with Mrs. Moyer."

"What did she look like?"

"I'm not good at describing people."

"Give it a try."

"Well, I'd say she was very pretty."

"How old?"

She twisted a strand of her blond hair around her finger. "Gosh, I'm not sure. She wasn't as old as Mrs. Moyer, if that's what you mean. But her hair was dark—I do know that. And I remember thinking what beautiful skin she had." She poked at a pimple on her chin. "I always notice things like that."

"Anything else you noticed?"

"Well, she was dressed nice."

This was getting nowhere fast. "And you say she talked to Sissy?"

"Right. It was quite a conversation."

"In what way?"

"Well, you know Sissy. She could be kind of crude at times. I thought she'd said something the woman didn't like because she got this sort of shocked look on her face. But then Sissy said something else, and she started smiling."

"And Sissy quit the next day?"

"Yep. Said her ship had come in and she was *aloha* bound." Carmen sighed. "I wish I was with her. I truly do."

I took a ten-spot from my shoulder bag and handed it to her. "This won't get you to Hawaii, but it's a start."

She smiled, tucked the bill inside her shirt pocket, and stood up.

"I know you have to get back to work, Carmen, but I have one more question."

She hesitated, looking over at the juice bar. "Okay," she said, "but make it quick."

"This woman who talked with Sissy. Did you ever see her arguing with Miranda Moyer?"

"No, not that I remember."

"Maybe not an argument. A disagreement, perhaps?"

"No, nothing like that. She seemed to be on good terms with Mrs. Moyer. But the other one—she definitely wasn't."

"The other one?"

"I'd forgotten all about her until you mentioned the arguing. She wasn't what you'd call a bistro regular, but I'd seen her talking to Mrs. Moyer a time or two. They really got into it the last time."

"Do you know what it was about?"

"Not really. Sissy could've told you, though. She had a nose for that sort of thing. All I know is that the woman left in a huff. I never saw her again."

"How would you describe her?"

"I thought you had just one more question."

I pulled another ten-spot from my wallet. "This is important."

"Well, since you put it that way." She snapped up the money. "She was very attractive. Even prettier than the other woman."

I tried to keep the frustration out of my voice and asked, "Could you be just a little more specific?"

"I don't suppose you have a photo or anything I could look at?"

I shook my head. "Try to remember."

"I'm sorry, but like I said, I'm not good at describing people. Besides, I only saw her a couple of times. She was beautiful—that's all I can say."

"How old would you guess she was?"

"I don't know. Youngish."

"Short or tall?"

"Look, I'd really like to help you, but the fact is, I just didn't pay that much attention." She stood up. "I gotta get back to work."

"I understand, Carmen. Thanks for taking the time to talk." I pushed my business card across the table. "If you hear from Sissy or think of anything else about either woman could you give me a call?"

She smiled wearily. "Sure, I can do that."

Now I knew why Allen Kingston favored circumstantial evidence over an eyewitness. Carmen's vague descriptions could've fit any number of women. I looked out at the tennis courts and suddenly realized I hadn't asked about Nancy Preston. Could she be one of the mystery women? I thought about sticking around until Carmen could take another break, but decided to talk to the woman in question herself. Nancy Preston was just finishing up a lesson on court number three.

TWENTY-THREE

I WISH I could say my conversation with Nancy Preston was a pleasant and helpful experience. It was not. The entire exchange reminded me of a blind date I once had—short, ugly, and cheap.

I left the bistro and caught up with her just as she was heading for the locker room. She was dressed all in white—a cute, by-the-numbers tennis outfit that oozed femininity. A perfect showcase for her long legs and sexy figure. She had a white towel slung around her neck and carried her racket in one hand, a plastic water bottle in the other. She'd stopped in the hall to take a drink from the bottle when I approached her. "Nancy Preston?"

She gave me a quick glance and dabbed at a bead of sweat on her forehead with the towel. Her milky white complexion was flushed from the exercise she'd just finished, and it gave her refined facial features a raw, rough-edged quality.

"My name's Kellie Mont—"

"I know who you are," she said sharply.

"You do?"

"And you can forget about pestering me with any of your goddamn questions. I have nothing to say."

"But I just want—"

"I don't give a rat's ass what you want," she said in a mean whisper. Her face clouded up like curdled milk as she tightened her grip on the racket. "I'm not about to run off at the mouth like you've got everyone else doing."

She paused long enough to smile at two tennis–clad women who passed us. I took advantage of the moment and said, "Listen, I don't know what you've heard about me, but I've just been gathering information about the Moyers. To help with the police investigation. That's all."

She snorted. "Then do something really helpful—like get a new hairdo. Or better yet, a facelift. You look like a run-over tennis shoe." She turned around, and I found myself staring at her backside. Flipped off with a quick twist of her head and a swish of her long blond hair. She strode purposefully down the hall toward the locker room.

"Wait a minute!" I called after her. "Would that be a Reebok or a Nike?"

THE NEXT MORNING, I left the marina in plenty of time for my appointment with Yolanda, whom I hoped would be a little more forthcoming than Ms. Gutter-Mouth Preston. The traffic wasn't bad for a change, but I didn't bother to search for a parking meter. Instead, I drove straight to the same underground garage I'd used before, figuring the extra expense would ensure that I got to her office on time—early even. I made the two-block hike to the Columbia Center easily enough, but when I turned the corner in front of the building I ran smack-dab into a sidewalk full of people. The street was lined with police cars, a fire truck, and a Medic One van. Two uniformed officers were screening everyone attempting to enter the building. I had a very uneasy feeling about the scene as I shoved my way through the crowd.

"Sorry, ma'am, but unless you work in the building, you'll have to leave."

"What's going on?"

He tugged at his belt with a self-important air. "Police business, ma'am." He gestured toward the sidewalk. "Move along, now."

I pulled a card from my shoulder bag and handed it to him. "I'm with the harbormaster's office. On official business."

He scrutinized the card, his eyes lingering on the sailing school logo. "Larstad's Marina?" He didn't bother to mask his skepticism. I'm definitely going to have to get different cards.

"I'm here to see Detective Allen Kingston." I didn't know if Kingston was involved in what was going on, but I figured it wouldn't hurt to throw his name around.

"He's a little busy at the moment. We've had an incident on the forty-second floor."

Same floor as the Moyer and Preston office. I managed to keep my voice calm and controlled—a major accomplishment considering the uneasy feeling I'd had earlier had escalated to full-blown anxiety. "Officer, that's why I'm here." I moved closer to the door. "Now are you going to let me through or not?"

He hesitated, and for a moment, I thought my ruse had failed, but then he opened the door. I scooted inside before he could change his mind and took the express elevator to the forty-second floor. Two more uniforms blocked the entrance to the Moyer and Preston Law Office. I tried the same name-dropping routine on them, but was swiftly escorted back to the elevator. "Can't you at least tell me what happened?" I pleaded. My escort was a no-nonsense sort who cut me off with a frown. He punched the down button and then waited with me until the elevator arrived. "Make sure you get off at the lobby," he said. At the lobby, though, I stayed on and rode the elevator back up to the atrium level.

A few office workers were taking an early morning break at Starbucks, but for the most part, the atrium was empty. I walked around for a while, hoping I'd come up with some way to find out what was going on. Had Yolanda and Preston's argument turned deadly? Obviously a homicide had occurred. Why else would Kingston be there? But who'd been killed? After a few minutes of aimless wandering, I decided I might as well have some tea. Lord knows, I didn't need the caffeine jolt—I was already hyped, but old habits die hard. Maybe it would help me think of a plan of action.

I ducked into Starbucks and ordered a cup of Irish Breakfast to go. While I waited for the tea to cool, a couple of dressed-for-success yuppies carrying alligator briefcases passed by my table. Jabbering excitedly about some business deal, they headed for The Office, a small corner pub near the stairway. I couldn't imagine who'd want a drink at nine o'clock in the morning. On second thought, maybe I could.

I left the tea on the table and followed the two men into The Office. It was a dark, intimate place with lots of leather, mahogany, and brass. A man's kind of office. The kind of place where deals were made, troubles shared, and affairs started. James Preston sat hunched over the bar, his long legs awkwardly straddling the stool. He cradled a half-empty martini glass with slender, feminine-looking hands, marred only by the tiniest of liver spots. The impeccably dressed, distinguished gentleman I'd seen at the funeral now looked merely tawdry, a disheveled version of his former self. He was wearing a similar dark-gray pinstripe suit and white shirt, but it looked as though he'd slept the night in them. His tie was soiled, his silver hair mussed.

I sat down on the stool next to him. He gave me no notice, concentrating instead on gulping down the last of his cocktail. He beckoned the bartender with an impatient wave and then wiped his mouth with a bar napkin. The bartender paused just long enough to take my order before whisking Preston's glass away. The delay caused Preston to glance over at me for the first time. It was brief, but we made eye contact.

"Mr. Preston? James Preston?"

He turned slightly and nodded. His blue eyes were glazed and rimmed in red.

"Kellie Montgomery," I said, extending a hand.

He made no move to take it. "I don't mean to be rude," he said, "but I really don't care to engage in conversation. It's been a difficult morning."

The bartender returned with our drinks. Preston relieved the bartender of his part of the burden and quickly took a sip. I squeezed a lemon into my Diet Pepsi and waited a moment before trying again. "Mr. Preston, I understand your reluctance to speak to me, but I need to know what's going on at your office. The police have it cordoned off."

No response.

"Is it Yolanda? Has something happened to Yolanda Vanasek? I used to work with her at Horace Mann before she became a paralegal. I'm worried about her."

Preston took another sip of his drink, his disinterest clear.

Time to up the ante. "I understand you and Yolanda argued recently."

He turned to face me. "Who'd you say you were again?"

"Kellie Montgomery." I pulled a card from my shoulder bag. "I'm with the harbormaster's office."

He took the card and laid it on the counter. "Ah, yes, Larstad's Marina. Nice place." He turned back to his drink.

"Mr. Preston, is Yolanda Vanasek dead?"

His fingers white-knuckled the martini glass, but he said nothing.

"Well, is she?"

"Yes, yes! She committed suicide. Are you satisfied now?"

"Suicide!" My God, I never expected that. "When? When did this happen?"

Preston eyed his empty glass. "Good Lord." He set the glass down and signaled the bartender again. "Listen, young lady, I must not have made myself clear. I'm not in the mood to converse with you about anything, least of all Yolanda Vanasek." He gave me a strained smile. "So why don't you be a nice girl and run along now? Surely there's something more important you could be doing at that marina of yours." He picked up his martini glass. "As for me, the most important item on my agenda is finishing this drink and ordering another."

"I just can't believe she'd kill herself."

Preston tossed back the last of his drink. "Guilty conscience, most likely."

"Mr. Preston, was Yolanda Vanasek blackmailing you?"

He sighed deeply. "Wherever did you get that idea?"

I shrugged. "She took over Moyer's office—perhaps she took over his schemes, too."

"What does it matter now? She's dead. Don's dead. It's all over."

"Except for the police investigation. Have you been questioned yet?"

"Only by you."

The bartender set another drink in front of him. Preston took a hungry sip, then asked, "What's your interest in all of this, anyway?"

"I know that you were opposed to the Missing Link and that Moyer kept the service going over your objections by threatening to reveal something from your past. I suspect Yolanda was attempting to do the same thing."

"Evil. Not to mention unethical, immoral, and illegal."

"Blackmail usually is."

"Quite so, but I was referring to the Missing Link. An evil abomination, pure and simple."

"Helping adoptees locate their birth parents? Some people think that's a needed service, a humane service. They say everyone has a right to know who they are and where they came from."

"Hmmf. And what do these people say about the birth parents' rights? Don't they have a right to their privacy and anonymity?"

"The courts seem to think so."

He nodded. "My point exactly."

"How'd Moyer do it, then? Get the records, I mean. I thought adoption records were sealed by the court."

He shook his head. "My dear, you can't possibly be that naive. Give people enough cold hard cash, and the rules get bent. With one particular court clerk, it didn't take much."

"So Moyer bribed the clerk and got the adoption records he wanted?"

"Only for those people adopted in Washington State. For everyone else, he paid a private detective to track down the parents. Not as quick or as effective as a bribe, but it worked well enough. I have to give Don credit. It was a slick, profitable operation, made even better with cunning and a few dollars thrown in the right direction."

"And Yolanda followed in Moyer's footsteps?"

"I'd have fired her if she hadn't had me over the same barrel as her boss. That scheming little bitch made Don look like a Boy Scout."

"How so?"

"This is getting tedious."

"I think the word is *confusing*. I can't understand why Yolanda would commit suicide if she had such a lucrative deal going."

"Go away, young lady." He motioned to the bartender.

"Just one more question and I'll leave you to your martini. A key was found in the dock box next to the *Merry Maiden*'s slip. Do you have any idea why Moyer would store a key in a dock box at the marina?"

He shook his head. "I've only been to that marina one time—a charity fundraiser at the Pacific Broiler. I don't know a thing about any key in a dock box."

"Your name is listed with the harbormaster's office as a co-owner of the *Merry Maiden*."

"The yacht was a tax write-off. Don and Miranda used it to entertain clients. I have no idea what else he did there. Now, if you don't mind, young lady, I've answered more than enough questions. I have some serious drinking to do."

He reached for the new martini the bartender had brought.

"I think not," said a voice behind us.

Preston and I both turned around at the same time. A stern-looking Detective Allen Kingston put a hand on Preston's arm. "You and I are going for a little ride."

Preston tried to shrug him off, but Kingston had him in a tight grip. "For what purpose, Detective? Am I under arrest?"

"Should you be?"

"Come, come, Detective," Preston said with a frown. "Don't play games with me. I'm hardly in the mood."

"Your mood don't concern me none, but I'll guarantee you it's gonna get a whole lot worse if you don't get your butt off that goddamn stool. You're wanted at the station for questioning. *Now.*"

Preston gave a resigned shrug and untangled his legs from the stool. "Ms. Montgomery."

"Mr. Preston."

Kingston smiled. "See ya around, Red."

I slapped a couple bucks on the counter and caught up with them at the elevator. The down arrow light came on, and when the doors opened, a couple of women stepped out. Kingston guided Preston aboard and kept the door from closing with his hand. I shook my head and stepped back. "Thanks, but I'm going up." Kingston cocked an eyebrow, then dropped his hand and let the doors close.

THE OFFICES OF Dutton, Hoffstedder, and Grimm were on the fifty-first floor. The receptionist was a perky redhead with mint-green eyes. She adjusted her telephone headset and greeted me cheerfully when I came in.

"I'm here to see Mr. Vanasek," I said.

Her perkiness quickly disappeared, replaced with a protective wariness. "Do you have an appointment?"

"No, but I'm a friend of the family."

"I'm afraid Mr. Vanasek isn't seeing anyone today."

"He'll want to see me—I knew his wife."

She hesitated, looking me over carefully. "Well, I . . . what did you say your name is?"

"I didn't." I handed her my card. "Just give him this. He'll understand."

She took her headset off. "Wait here. I'll be right back."

I gave her a head start and then followed her down the hallway. She stopped in front of one of the doors and knocked softly before opening it. "Mr. Vanasek, I hate to bother you, but . . ."

". . . you have a visitor," I said, stepping around her and into the room.

Richard Vanasek stood with his back to us, gazing out his office window. He didn't turn around, as if too captivated by the sight of Mt. Rainier to be distracted by anyone or anything. Besides the snow-capped mountain, he had a perfect view of Elliott Bay, where several dozen sailboats—colorful spinnakers billowing—were competing in some kind of race. I doubted he saw any of it.

"I'm sorry, Mr. Vanasek, but she followed me in here. I asked her to wait."

Vanasek sighed and turned around. I was momentarily startled by the change in his appearance. I'd remembered him from the funeral as a handsome, outdoor type; a kayaker or hiker perhaps, someone who preferred climbing Mt. Rainier to the corporate ladder. But he didn't look capable of hiking or much of anything today. His rugged face was ashen, his eyes dull, and his bearing hunched over and broken looking.

"She says she knew your wife," added the receptionist.

"Have we met?" he asked.

"Briefly, at the Moyers' funeral. I'm Kellie Montgomery. From Larstad's Marina?"

"Ah, yes," he said. "Yolanda's teacher friend from Horace Mann." He slumped into the chair behind his desk. "It's okay, Sally. You can leave us now." As she closed the door, he said, "You'll have to forgive her. Sally's rather protective of me." He offered me a seat in the upholstered arm-chair in front of his desk.

"I just found out about Yolanda. I came here to tell you how very sorry I am."

He glanced at a photo on his desk. "I can't believe she's gone. It's such a shock."

We were both silent for a moment. Vanasek had the same anguished look I'd seen on the faces of victims' relatives when I was a paramedic volunteer. Some liked to talk. Others didn't. I hoped Richard Vanasek was the talking kind. He looked out the window again and asked, "How did you find out so soon?"

"I was supposed to see Yolanda this morning. We had a nine o'clock appointment, but when I arrived, the police were already there."

"They figure it probably happened last night. She didn't come home from work yesterday." He caught my raised eyebrow. "But that's typical for her. I often don't make it home myself when I'm on a case." He motioned to a big leather couch across the room. "Sleep right there, if at all. Yolanda's a workaholic, too." He shrugged. "Was."

"So you didn't think anything was wrong when she didn't come home last night?"

"Not at all. I'd talked to her before I left the office. She said she had some more work to do. I offered to run out and get her something to eat, but she told me not to bother—she'd pick up a pizza on her way home. When she never showed up, I just figured her work was taking longer than she'd expected."

"Who found her?"

"Her secretary, Vivian. She'd arrived early at Yolanda's request. Apparently they were going to get a head start on some project Yolanda was working on. Vivian had offered to work late, but Yolanda told her to go on home—they'd get together first thing in the morning. That's why this whole suicide business makes no sense. Why would she tell Vivian to come in early if she was planning to kill herself?"

"How'd she die?"

"Gunshot to the temple. God, it was awful. The police didn't want me to see her, but I insisted. They prepared me for the worst—if you can ever be prepared for something like that—but poor Vivian had no advance warning and almost passed out." He shook his head. "Jesus."

"A gun's a terrible way to go," I said.

"That's another strange thing. We don't even own a gun. Yolanda was scared to death of them. If she were going to kill herself, she'd have used pills or something like that. Never a gun."

"I agree, it sounds strange. But suicide isn't exactly a rational act."

"I don't care. There's just no way Yolanda would've killed herself. There wasn't even a suicide note."

I'd been on a few suicide calls during my stint with the paramedics and I could've told him that the absence of a note wasn't all that unusual. But Vanasek seemed so miserable that I steered the conversation in another direction. "What about the project Yolanda and Vivian were working on? Do you have any idea what it was?"

"No, why?"

"I just wondered if it had anything to do with the Missing Link."

"You know about that, huh?"

"Yes. In fact, that's what I was coming to see Yolanda about. I understand she's been running things since Moyer's death."

"Over James Preston's strident objections."

"The police have taken him in for questioning."

"Good! I figured they would."

"Why's that?"

"I overheard the officers talking when I viewed her body. From what I could gather, any time there's a violent death, they have to investigate all possibilities before they make a final determination."

"You think Preston might've been involved somehow?"

"I wouldn't rule it out. Especially since Vivian saw Preston go in to Yolanda's office just before she left for the night. Heard loud voices, too—she's sure they were fighting. James Preston was probably the last person to see my wife alive."

"Except for the killer."

"Like I said, the last person to see Yolanda alive."

"You suspect him of killing her?" I asked.

Vanasek ran a hand through his hair. "God, I don't know. There's been so much going on lately, it's hard to know what to think."

"What about Preston's wife, Nancy? Did Yolanda ever mention anything about her?"

"Not that I can recall. Why?"

"It's probably nothing, but I got the impression from something Yolanda said at the Moyers' funeral that she didn't care for the woman very much. I just wondered if it was personal or whether it had anything to do with her job at the law office."

"Well, the only thing I ever heard her say about Preston's wife was that she was jealous."

"Jealous of whom?"

"The Moyers. Nancy Preston didn't think her husband was getting a fair shake in the partnership—financially, I mean. But that was bull. According to Yolanda, James Preston was ruining the business because of his drinking problem. If it weren't for Donald Moyer, there wouldn't have been a business to share at all." He paused a moment and looked at Yolanda's photograph again. "How well did you know her?"

"It's been awhile since we worked together at Horace Mann. Back then she seemed to be very ambitious and hardworking. Raising her son, working full-time, and going to school nights—it couldn't have been easy."

"It wasn't, but that's what attracted me to her. She was so damned ambitious. Career woman, mother, student—nothing seemed impossible for Yolanda. I was kind of surprised when she quit law school, but working as Moyer's paralegal was quite fulfulling for her. She gave it her all and was happy to do it. Then Moyer was killed. That's when everything began to change.''

"In what way?"

"She wasn't just ambitious anymore; she was a woman possessed. Working, working, working. That's all she wanted to do. The Missing Link was like some kind of mission for her.''

"Did she talk much about it?''

"No, that's what was so odd. Before Donald and Miranda were killed, Yolanda and I shared everything. There was nothing she liked better than to come home and talk about what went on at the office. We used to laugh about it. Our favorite hobby was hashing over cases together—we'd sit in front of the fireplace, sip wine, and try to top one another's stories. I thought she was just upset about Moyer's death, that she'd eventually come around to her old self again. Then Moyer's son called her at home one evening, and it got even worse.''

"What did he want?"

"She didn't say, and I didn't press her on it. I figured she'd tell me eventually, but she never did. All I know is that she was not happy with that phone call. She slammed the receiver down and stormed out of the room. She left the house shortly after that, saying only that she had to go back to the office.''

"When was this?"

"The day after his parents were killed.''

"Richard, did Yolanda ever mention anything about a key? Maybe a key Donald Moyer had?''

"The police asked me about a key, too, but I didn't know what to tell them. I can't imagine why Moyer would store a key in a dock box unless it had something to do with their yacht. Why do you ask?''

"I've been involved in the Moyer case ever since their yacht was towed to Larstad's.'' Since the receptionist never gave him my card, I took another one from my shoulder bag and handed it to him. "I run the sailing school at the marina, but I also assist the harbormaster from time to time. The day after his parents were killed, I found Donald, Jr., trying to break into *Merry Maiden*'s dock box."

"Do you think he was looking for the key?"

"I'm not sure what he was looking for. In any event, he got the wrong box and never found it."

"What's the significance of the key anyway? The police wouldn't tell me."

"They wouldn't tell me, either. I'm not convinced the police know, but I think it may be very important. Are you sure Yolanda never said anything about it?"

"Quite sure." He rubbed his temples. "Jesus, this is so hard."

"I lost my husband three years ago. He wasn't killed, so I don't know that kind of grief, but I do know how hard it is to lose someone you love." I stood up. "I have to go now, but I hope that you'll feel free to call me if you need to. Talking it out sometimes helps."

He stood and walked me to the door. "Thanks for stopping by."

As I shook his hand, I got an idea. "Richard, may I ask you a favor?"

"What kind of favor?"

I motioned to the photograph of Yolanda on his desk. "Do you think I could borrow that photo for a while?"

"Sure, but what for?"

"I want to show it to someone. I'll make sure you get it back right away."

He carefully removed the photo from its silver frame. "Here you go," he said, handing it to me.

"Thanks, Richard. If you happen to think of anything Yolanda might have said about the key or the Missing Link or even James Preston, would you give me a call?"

"I've already told you everything I know. The police, too."

"You might think of something later."

"That's what Detective Kingston said. He also said he'd be around to see me again. I know how these things go. The husband is usually the prime suspect."

"Usually," I said. "But in this case it appears that James Preston is number one on their list."

"Mine, too."

TWENTY-FOUR

I HAD AN errand to run after I left Vanasek's office and when I got back to the marina, the red light on my answering machine was blinking. The first message was from the Weasel. I skipped through a long diatribe about how he was still waiting to get something definitive from me on the revised plans. He wanted me to call him back ASAP, but I listened to the second message instead. Emily Cummings had called to confirm our sailing date for tomorrow morning. I put the tea kettle on and returned her call. She'd heard about Yolanda, and we hashed that news over for a while, but reached no conclusions.

After I hung up with Emily, I spent the rest of the afternoon working on the Weasel's project and fending off a couple more phone calls from him demanding a blow-by-blow progress report. I didn't know whether his so-called interest was because of some pressure from the Nakitos or whether he just had nothing better to do than to bug me. I decided it was the latter. After his third call, I said, "Look, Todd, things will go a hell of lot quicker if you just leave me alone so I can work." I'd no sooner hung up the phone when it rang again.

I grabbed the receiver. "What *now*?" I asked irritably.

"Kellie? Is that you?"

"Uh, yes."

"This is Rich Vanasek. I can call back if this isn't a good time."

"No, no. I'm sorry. I thought you were someone else. What can I do for you?"

"I've found something that you might be interested in. Can you come over to the house?"

Ever since the break-in, I'd been trying to temper my curiosity with a certain amount of caution. I didn't think I had anything to fear from Vanasek, but I hesitated before answering and glanced at my watch. It was almost five o'clock. "Is this something we can talk about in a restaurant? If I don't get some food in me soon, I'm going to pass out."

"Well, I guess so, as long as it's a place with some privacy. I have something to show you."

"What is it?"

"I don't want to talk about it on the phone. You pick the restaurant, and I'll meet you there."

"Okay, how about Luigi's? It's a small café in Magnolia with the best pizza and pasta in town. It's also quiet and private."

"Sounds good. Give me the directions, and I'll meet you there in half an hour."

"Make that an hour. I've got something I'm working on that I'd like to get wrapped up first."

I spent a few more minutes putting the finishing touches on what I hoped would satisfy the Weasel's big and bold look and called the project complete—for the second time. I decided to make his day and drop it off at his office on my way to see Vanasek, but when I knocked on his door, there wasn't any answer. Typical Weasel stunt. He gets me working at hyperbolic speed to meet some so-called emergency deadline and then cuts out. I was about to slip the plans under his door when Hiroshi Kano came around the corner.

He bowed politely and said, "Ah, Ms. Montgomery. How nice to see you."

I wasn't much on protocol, but I knew enough to give him a little bow in return. "Mr. Kano."

"Do you, by any chance, know where Mr. Wilmington is?" he asked.

"Haven't a clue. I thought he'd be in his office. He called just a short while ago wanting these plans for the boat show booth. I've revised them as you requested."

Kano's dark eyebrows bunched up like two ripe figs. "As I requested?"

"The Weasel, er, Todd Wilmington said you wanted something bigger and bolder." I handed him the plans. "I think this should do the trick."

He smiled politely and bowed again. I followed suit.

"Please forgive me, Ms. Montgomery, but I'm confused. Mr. Wilmington showed me these plans several days ago. I was very pleased with what he'd done. You say you've made some changes to his plans."

So that was how the Weasel was playing the game. "Mr. Kano, I think we need to have a little talk . . ." Our conversation didn't take long, but I knew Kano had the picture by the time we bowed our good-byes.

WENDELL AND I used to hang out at Luigi's a lot. It was a casual place where folks could linger over their pizza and beer and chat with their tablemates or the owners, Luigi and Lisa. It was a little early for the dinner crowd, but the pizza take-out counter was busy. The room's spicy aroma made my empty stomach growl.

As soon as Lisa saw me she turned the take-out counter over to her teen-age assistant and greeted me with some good-natured ribbing about neglecting old friends. When I told her another person would be joining me shortly, she shifted into her favorite role since Wendell's death—matchmaker. "Male or female?" she asked.

"Male. But don't get any ideas. I knew his wife. She was killed today, and her husband needs to talk to someone. We'd like as much privacy as possible, okay?"

She clucked sympathetically and showed me to a table at the back of the room. "Do you want to order now or wait for him?" I decided to go ahead and order a large pizza—Luigi's Special—and a bottle of Moretti.

Vanasek arrived just as Lisa came back with my beer. He ordered a bottle for himself and took off his raincoat, carefully folding it over the extra chair. He was still dressed in the suit he'd worn at the office, but it hung on him loosely, as if grief had already begun to alter his body. He set a large manila envelope on the table.

"I ordered pizza for us. I hope you don't mind."

"Not at all. I'm not really hungry, though." He looked haggard, even more so than he had earlier in the day. My heart went out to him.

"Are you okay?"

"No."

I came up with what I hoped were some encouraging words and then opened my shoulder bag. "Before I forget, here's Yolanda's photo."

He glanced at it briefly and then tucked it inside his suit jacket.

I pointed to the envelope he'd placed on the table. "What's that?"

"A mystery."

I poured some of the Moretti into a glass while I waited for him to say more, but he just stared at the envelope, a glazed look on his face. Lisa arrived with his beer. "Your pizza will be up in a moment," she said.

I waited until she'd left before pointing to the envelope again. "Are you going to explain?"

"That's just the thing. I can't."

"Maybe you could start by showing me what's inside."

"Oh, yes, of course." He glanced around the cafe before opening the clasp and removing some photos. He pushed one of the photos facedown across the table. "Tell me what you think of this."

I turned the photo over. It was a black-and-white picture of a young girl, maybe thirteen or fourteen, sitting on an unmade bed. She was naked, her legs spread apart in a disturbingly provocative pose. Although the photo was blurred, the girl's face was clearly visible. And despite her blank stare and dull eyes, there was something vaguely familiar about her. "Who is this?"

"I have absolutely no idea."

I motioned to the other photos. "More of the same?"

He nodded and pushed them across the table. I turned them over one at a time. The same girl was in each photo. Different poses, all staged for maximum effect. "Where did you get these?"

"That's the incredible part. They're Yolanda's. I went home right after you left my office. There wasn't any use staying at work. I was a basket case. Anyway, I was sitting at home, trying to make sense of what happened. I guess I was feeling sorry for myself. And guilty, too."

"Guilty?"

"You know, going through all the what-ifs. What if I'd stayed with Yolanda last night instead of going home? What if I'd brought her a sandwich? What if I'd paid more attention to her lately? Maybe if I'd done any of those things, she'd still be alive. All those thoughts were running through my mind when I remembered something you'd said."

"What was that?"

"How the key the police found in Moyer's dock box was important. It reminded me that Yolanda had a key, too. I'd forgotten all about it until this afternoon. We have a safety deposit box at Seafirst, but Yolanda always took care of those kinds of things. Now that she was gone, I decided that I'd better take a look at what was in the box. I was expecting to find our birth certificates, passports, some of her jewels, things like that." He waved his hand over the photos. "Instead, I found these."

Lisa arrived with the pizza, and Vanasek quickly stuffed the photos back inside the envelope. I gobbled down a slice right away, but he just looked at his empty plate and nursed his beer. After helping myself to a second slice I asked, "Why do you think Yolanda had the photos?"

"That's why I called you. I have absolutely no idea. Do you think they're related to her death?"

"Possibly. You?"

"I don't know what to think. I'm going to turn them over to the police, but I wanted to know what you thought first."

"I think Detective Kingston should definitely take a look at them. I also think you should be prepared."

"For what?"

"Richard, I'm not sure how to say this, but Yolanda may have been involved in a blackmailing scheme."

"What in hell are you talking about?"

"I've met a couple of people lately who believe Donald Moyer was a blackmailer. There's a possibility that Yolanda may have taken over where Moyer left off."

"That's crazy!"

"Maybe so, but James Preston confirmed that he was being blackmailed by Moyer. He also made it pretty clear that Yolanda was blackmailing him, too. I'm guessing that's why the police were so anxious to talk to him today. If Yolanda's death wasn't a suicide, Preston might have been responsible."

"I can't believe this. I mean, I thought Preston was involved somehow. But Yolanda a blackmailer? Never."

"It might explain why these photos were in your safety deposit box."

"Why was Preston being blackmailed by Moyer?"

"I don't know what Moyer had on him, but he threatened to reveal whatever it was if Preston tried to shut down the Missing Link. I think Yolanda knew what it was and that's why she was able to keep the operation going after Moyer was killed."

"Jesus." He tapped the envelope. "And just how do you figure these photos relate to all that?"

"Suppose Donald Moyer was blackmailing someone over the photos. If he was blackmailing Preston, it's probable he was blackmailing others. Say the young girl who originally posed for the photos is an adult now with a reputation to protect. Perhaps she was the one who killed Donald and Miranda aboard their boat."

"How does that explain the death of their son?"

"Maybe Junior knew about the photos. Maybe that's what he was looking for in the dock box he thought was his parents'."

"Sounds kind of far-fetched to me. Why would he think his father would store photos in a dock box?"

"Because he didn't know where they were stored. He asked me that day if I knew of any other storage places at the marina. I figure he had looked everywhere else. Detective Kingston said the key they found in the dock box wasn't for their home safe or the office safe—they're both combination locks. Maybe the key was for a storage locker someplace else entirely. You said that Junior called Yolanda at home. It's possible she knew about the storage locker and told him where it was."

"Why would she do that?"

"Perhaps he offered her a deal of some sort. He knew she'd already taken over the Missing Link. Maybe Junior convinced her to tell him where the storage locker was in return for some information she needed. It's possible he knew about some of his father's other blackmail schemes. Could be that's what got them both killed."

Vanasek ran his finger around the rim of his beer glass as he considered the possibility. "I don't know. That just doesn't sound like Yolanda. But then, I'm beginning to think I really didn't know my wife after all. She took Moyer's death awfully hard. So hard, in fact, that I questioned her about it. I thought they might've been having an affair.''

''What'd she say?''

''That she didn't want to talk about it. Just clammed up the way she did that day at the funeral. I guess I'll never know for sure.'' He shook his head. ''And now blackmail. It all seems so impossible.''

''There's something else. I went to the Sports Center to-day—it's a tennis and fitness club that the Moyers belonged to. An employee there identified Yolanda from the photo you gave me. She claims Yolanda was there shortly after Miranda's death, talking to another employee. After their conversation, the employee suddenly quit. It seems she came into quite a bit of money—enough to quit her job and head for Hawaii.''

''I'm not sure what you're getting at.''

''Just this: It's possible that the key in the dock box was for either Donald's or Miranda's locker at the Sports Center. Perhaps that's what Yolanda's conversation with the employee was all about—she paid the employee to help her get into the Moyers' locker.''

''For what purpose? Why would she want inside their club locker?''

I reached for another slice of pizza and offered him one, but he declined. ''That I haven't figured out yet—but I suspect it has something to do with the blackmail. And, as far as that goes, have you checked your bank account lately? Unless Yolanda had a separate account that you didn't know about, she may have deposited the payoffs she received directly into your account.''

''I'll look into it. I was so overwhelmed by finding these photos in the safety deposit box, I left the bank in a daze. When I got home all I could think about was calling you.''

''I'm glad you did, but we need to talk to Detective Kingston.''

''You're right.'' Vanasek checked his watch. ''It's getting late. Do you think he'd still be in?''

"There's only one way to find out."

I used Lisa's private line to call Kingston at police head-quarters. He was in, but couldn't or wouldn't come to the phone. I left an urgent message to call me at Lisa's number. Richard and I finished off the pizza—well, I finished it; he only ate one slice—and had just ordered another round of beer when Kingston finally returned my call. I told him about the photos, but he didn't seem very interested.

"I can't talk right now. How 'bout you and Vanasek come down to the station first thing in the morning? I'll probably still be here."

"Why? What's going on?"

"Let's just say that the Moyer case is about to be re-solved."

"You're arresting Preston?"

"I didn't say that."

"But that's who you're interrogating, right?"

"Gotta go, Red. See ya in the morning."

Richard Vanasek was relieved when I told him that King-ston couldn't see us until tomorrow. It'd been a long and traumatic day for him. "I doubt if I can get any sleep to-night," he said, "but it's probably best if I go home and give it a try."

Before we parted company, I asked to borrow one of the photographs. Vanasek obliged, handing me the packet with a quizzical look. "It's just a hunch I have," I explained. I flipped through the photos until I found the shot I was look-ing for—one with the girl's face looking directly into the camera. "There's someone I'd like to show this to," I said, tucking the photo inside my handbag. "If we're lucky, we may just get a name to go with the picture."

TWENTY-FIVE

COLEMAN REHABILITATION CENTER was a secluded, twenty-acre estate on the outskirts of Woodinville, not far from where the Moyers' funeral had been held. Although it was dark by the time I left Luigi's and the meandering back roads leading to Coleman were about as convoluted as the IRS tax code, I still managed to find the place without getting lost. Okay, so I cheated. I'd called ahead and asked Reba Stanton for detailed directions.

My trek to Coleman had been long overdue. Although I'd promised to call her, I hadn't spoken to Terri Moyer since her sailing lesson at Larstad's. I'd been preoccupied with my own problems, but the truth was I had conflicting feelings about her. On the one hand, I was sympathetic to the suffering she'd experienced as a child and the toll it'd taken on her in the years since; on the other hand, I couldn't help but wonder if her recent emotional problems weren't the result of her possible involvement in her parents' murders.

I'm not sure what I expected a psychiatric social worker to look like—maybe a female version of the elderly gate guard I'd met at the compound entrance—but Reba Stanton was young, maybe twenty-eight at the most. Although casually dressed in a white blouse, bulky red sweater, and jeans, she was very much the professional. Exuding a confidence born of good looks and intelligence, she greeted me with a warm smile. "Hi, Kellie," she said. "Welcome to Coleman." Her handshake was as solid and self-assured as her demeanor. "Let's sit by the fire a moment, shall we?"

The sign in front of the building had simply read ADMINISTRATION, which was like calling the Taj Mahal a cemetery plot. The dull and uninspiring label belied the rugged, Northwest grandeur behind the double-door entry. The lobby was spacious and parklike, featuring a large indoor waterfall and a profusion of hanging plants and other greenery. Several plush leather couches and chairs were arranged conversation-style on big colorful area rugs. The lobby's focal point, though, was the massive river-stone fireplace that Reba had indicated. Its blazing fire cast the entire room in a warm, pleasant glow.

As soon as we'd settled ourselves on one of the couches, Reba asked, "You said on the phone you had something you wanted to show Terri?"

I pulled the photo from my handbag. "This is kind of disturbing to look at," I warned, handing it to her.

Reba examined the photo without comment. When she looked up, a frown creased her otherwise wrinkle-free brow. "What's this got to do with Terri?"

"I'm not sure if it has anything to do with her, actually. An acquaintance of mine found it earlier today under rather mysterious circumstances. We're trying to figure out who the girl is. There's a chance she may be connected somehow to the murder of Terri's parents and brother. I'd like to see if Terri can identify her."

"She hasn't been doing very well lately."

I shifted uncomfortably on the couch. "I'm sorry to hear that." Maybe this hadn't been such a hot idea after all.

"But it's not unexpected," Reba said, noticing my distress. "As I mentioned to you on the phone the other day, backsliding is typical in cases such as Terri's."

"She's using again?"

"Oh, no. She's still drug and alcohol free. I'm referring to her emotional stability. Terri was making progress, you see—almost ready to be discharged—and then her family was murdered. The tragedy has set her back considerably."

"I thought she wasn't very close to the family, especially after what they'd done to her."

"It's true they were estranged—and for very good reasons—but that doesn't mean Terri didn't love them." She caught my surprised look and added, "She had conflicting feelings about them, but yes, she loved them. So, given their traumatic deaths, her behavior is perfectly understandable."

"What kind of behavior are we talking about?"

A spark from the fireplace landed on the rug near our feet. Reba quickly rose from the couch and stomped it out. When she sat down again, she said, "Acting impulsively."

I didn't get what she was implying. "I've been accused of acting rather impulsively myself," I said, thinking that's exactly how Allen Kingston would describe my behavior.

"Most people have at one time or another. But with individuals like Terri, the behavior is potentially much more excessive and self-damaging. For example, they may gamble too much, binge eat, abuse substances, practice unsafe sex. Or, as in Terri's case, self-mutilate."

I pictured the silver rings she wore in her lips. "You mean like body piercing?"

"And tattoos. Terri's backside is a veritable montage of intricate designs. She likes to paint tears on her face, but I wouldn't be surprised to find them permanently affixed one of these days. As far as the body piercing goes, the lip rings are just the latest in a series. She's also pierced her belly button, nipples, and private parts."

"But lots of women are into tattoos and body piercing these days. In fact, it's considered rather trendy in some circles. Surely you're not suggesting that these women have some sort of personality disorder as well?"

"Not at all. But Terri's self-mutilation goes way beyond

a trendy fad. She's cut herself with knives, burned herself with cigarettes.'' Reba threw her hands into the air. ''And that's just what I know about. If you can think of something shocking or of questionable benefit, Terri's probably done it.''

''Makes sailing seem rather boring.''

''Exactly. So when she came up with the idea of taking lessons, I thought she'd finally hit on something worthwhile. But she's been in a funk ever since she got back from the lesson. She'd just sit in her room all day if we'd let her.''

''Where is she now?''

She waved toward the hallway. ''Hobby room.''

''That sounds like progress.''

Reba shook her head. ''It wasn't her idea. I had to practically drag her there. She's not in a friendly mood. Actually, she's in a hostile mood. And I think you may be the reason why.''

''What'd I do?''

''It's more like what you didn't do. After she confided in you, she expected to hear from you again. When you didn't call or come to see her, she felt rejected.''

''But I . . . it was Christmas and—''

Reba held up her hand. ''Kellie, I know. It doesn't matter. To Terri, you'd abandoned her. And abandonment—real or imagined—is a major problem for her. In fact, seeing you might be all it takes to set her off again.''

''Set her off?''

''Make her angry. She has real difficulty with anger management. She may also become extremely sarcastic or verbally abusive. Especially since she feels you've been neglecting her.''

I wasn't keen on confronting Terri with the photo under these circumstances, but I had to at least give it a try. ''It's up to you, of course, but I'd sure like to talk to her. I won't show her the photo if you think that's unwise.''

''Well,'' she said after a moment's hesitation, ''maybe it would help if you talked to her. She seemed to like you—

and she did confide in you that day." She stood up. "Let's go see what happens. But don't be surprised if she doesn't respond appropriately."

There were eight people in the hobby room—four men playing cards, three women painting some ceramic bowls, and Terri. Dressed in dull gray sweats and fuzzy slippers, she sat by herself at a table in the corner. Reba's comment about dragging her to the hobby room seemed right on. She looked as if she'd come straight from her bed without so much as a pass at combing her hair or washing her face. She was staring listlessly at a picture of a square-rigged sailing schooner on the front of a puzzle box. As far as I could tell, most of the puzzle pieces were still in the box.

Reba and I joined her at the table, but if she noticed our arrival, it wasn't obvious. She continued to stare at the schooner, fingering a triangular-shaped piece she held in her left hand. After a moment I said, "I think it goes there." I pointed to a splotch of white in the corner. "It looks like the beginning of one of the sails."

Terri took the suggestion, securing the piece and immediately retrieving another. Without looking up from the puzzle, she asked, "What are *you* doing here?"

Reba said, "Kellie would like to talk to you for a few minutes."

She fidgeted with the puzzle piece but said nothing.

Reba glanced at me and then said, "Did you hear me, Terri?"

Her back stiffened slightly. "This is so stupid," she said, tossing the puzzle piece onto the table.

"Terri," I said. "I'd like to talk to you if—"

"Isn't that sweet?" she said, addressing the card players. "Suddenly the lady has time to chitchat." She pounded her fist on the table. "Well, fuck that!" Puzzle pieces bounced into the air and onto the floor. "Now look what you made me do." Terri hesitated a moment and then grabbed the card table with both hands and upended it, flinging the puzzle box and its contents across the room. The ensuing clamor didn't interrupt the card game, but all three women at the ceramic table turned around in their chairs. Terri glared at them. "Say one word and your artsy-fartsy doodads are history."

Reba's face had "I told you so" written all over it, but I figured I had nothing to lose at this point. I stepped around the upended card table so that I was facing Terri. She refused to look at me, swiveling her chair toward the wall. "I'm sorry I didn't call or come to see you sooner," I said to her back. "I could give you a hundred reasons why, but the fact is, I didn't." I placed my hand gently on her shoulder. "But I'm here now, Terri. And I'd very much like to talk to you."

I fully expected her to pull away from my grasp, but she began to sob instead. I glanced at Reba, who gave me a go-ahead nod. I wasn't sure what to do or say, but I couldn't help feeling sorry for her. "It's all right now," I said soothingly. "I'm here for you." I put both hands on her heaving shoulders. Several moments passed before she'd cried herself out. When she finally turned around, she buried her tear-stained face in my chest. My heart went out to her, and I held her as I'd hold a hurt child, comforting her with whatever words came to mind. All the while, Reba was quietly herding the others out of the room. Afterwards, she came back and sat down next to us.

Terri clung to me for several minutes, then apologized profusely for her outburst and thanked me over and over again for coming to see her. I swallowed my doubts concerning her innocence and told her that it was okay, that I understood her hurt and her anger. When she began to talk, it was as if a dam had burst. The words came tumbling out in a frenzied rush. Her story was similar to what she'd shared after our sailing lesson—Donald and Miranda Moyer had been parents in name only. Although she talked freely of their abuse and neglect, I kept thinking about what Reba had said—that there was something she was still holding back, a secret too painful for words.

As she talked, I debated whether I should show her the photograph. The girl's pose was so provocative, so obscene that I wondered how Terri would react. She was calmer now, her words less hurried, and she'd even laughed a few times, but I questioned whether she could look at something so disturbing without becoming upset again. I'd almost decided to skip the whole thing when she said something that made me change my mind.

"When I left home, Daddy cut me out of their will. But he set up a great trust fund for me. Not that he had any choice—he knew I knew."

"What do you mean?" I asked.

She glanced at Reba. "Well, uh, I don't think I . . ."

"It's okay, Terri," said Reba softly. "Go ahead." This was the first time since we'd begun talking that Reba had interjected a comment. From the look she gave me, I could tell she thought Terri was about to say something important.

But Terri just sat there, nervously twisting a finger around a lock of hair. She was quiet for so long that I figured she wasn't going to finish the thought. "It's no big deal," she finally said with a shrug. "I mean, it happened so long ago. I don't even know where she is anymore. Maybe she's dead, too."

"She?" Reba asked.

"Sunny. Sunny Wilson."

"Why don't you tell us about Sunny?" suggested Reba. She'd slipped into her therapist's role, her voice soothing and encouraging.

"She was my best friend. This was when we lived in the old neighborhood, before we moved to Broadmoor. Sunny and I were inseparable. We did everything together." Terri heaved a deep sigh. "I loved her, I truly did."

"But something happened, didn't it?" asked Reba gently.

"Oh, yes, you could say that." Terri shivered and folded her arms across her chest. "Everything was in boxes, packed up and ready for the movers. Like always, Mama was out— probably getting a facial or something. I wasn't home, either. I mean, I wasn't supposed to be home. I'd taken Donny to the park, but it was cold outside, and he needed a hat. So we came back home to get it.'' She paused.

"And?'' Reba prompted.

"And I heard them.'' She paused again and looked out the window. "They, uh . . . they were in the bedroom. At first, I was confused. I thought Mama had come home or something because I heard Daddy offer her a drink. But it wasn't Mama with Daddy. It was Sunny's voice telling Daddy no, she didn't want a drink. Daddy just laughed and said, 'God, I'm going to miss you.' I couldn't figure out what was going on so I crept up to the door and peeked inside.'' Terri turned from the window and covered her face with both hands. "God, it was awful.''

"What'd you see, Terri?''

"I can't tell you.''

"Yes, you can,'' said Reba. "You saw Sunny and . . .''

"She was naked. Naked and sitting on the bed. Daddy forced a wine glass into her hand and made her drink. She coughed and spilled most of the wine onto the bed sheet. She told him that she had to go, that she didn't feel so good. But Daddy didn't seem to hear. He reached into a cardboard box, one that hadn't been sealed by the movers yet. He told her to stay right where she was. Then he pulled a camera from the box. 'Give me a sexy look, sugar,' he said, aiming it at her.''

I met Reba's eyes, and she nodded. I removed the photograph from my handbag and handed it to Terri. "Is this the picture your father took that day?'' I asked.

"Oh, God. Oh, God.'' She dropped the photo and drew in several great gulps of air.

Reba placed her hand on Terri's back. "You're hyperventilating, Terri. Put your head between your knees,'' she advised.

After she'd calmed down, Terri asked, "Where did you get that picture?''

I explained briefly, leaving out any mention of blackmail.

"Sunny didn't want him to do it, you know. She grabbed

the sheet to cover herself and told Daddy she wasn't kidding, that she really didn't feel good, that she was going to be sick.'' Terri shuddered at the memory. "I shouldn't have stayed. I should've just walked away from the door, but I couldn't. I closed my eyes, but I'll never forget what I heard. Sunny crying. Daddy yelling, 'You ungrateful little cunt. You show me some pussy right now, or everyone in this goddamn town is going to know about you.' ''

"So that's what you meant earlier," said Reba. "When you said you knew, you were referring to your father and your best friend."

"No." Terri stared at the photo, still lying facedown on the floor. "I meant I knew about their baby."

TWENTY-SIX

A BABY. THE essence of sweet innocence, God's most precious gift, had become Terri's albatross. "Don't you see?" she said. "I loved Daddy. Mama didn't love him. Sunny didn't love him. I was the one, the only one who truly loved him."

"And yet he betrayed your love," said Reba.

"I know what he did to me was wrong and I'll never forgive him for that. I still loved him, though. But after Sunny, after she had his baby, it was never the same. I mean, how could he do that to me? I was his baby. His doll baby. His only baby."

Reba and Terri were still talking when I left. I had what I wanted—a name to go with the photo. Reba had what she wanted—the long-awaited breakthrough. And Terri? I believed she had what she wanted, too. What she needed most—no more secrets, no more silence.

CASSIE WAS SITTING in the cabin, her backpack and suitcase on the floor. She'd been reading a paperback, and when

I came in, she set it on the table. "Hi, Mom," she said simply.

"What's going on?" I asked.

"Nothing. I just wanted to come home. I hope you don't mind me barging in like this unannounced."

"Mind? I'm delighted!" I pushed her backpack and suitcase aside, sat down next to her, and put my arm around her shoulder, willing her not to pull away.

"Mom, I'm so sorry."

"It's all right, Cassie. I'm sorry, too."

"You were right about that search firm."

"You've heard about the suicide?"

"Yeah, it's the top story on every channel—but I'd already decided not to use the Missing Link. I gave the check back to Aunt Donna last night."

"Why'd you change your mind?"

"Things were getting a little bizarre."

"What things?"

She hesitated. "Well, Aunt Donna for one."

"Honey, Aunt Donna's always been a little bizarre."

She laughed heartily. "Good one, Mom."

"You hungry?"

"I thought you'd never ask."

I fixed her favorite snack—egg salad sandwich with cucumbers, potato chips, Dr. Pepper, and brownies—then joined her at the table, content just to watch her eat. I figured there was more she had to say about her decision, but I was determined to let it unfold at her own speed. After she'd finished a third brownie, she said, "You know, Mom, Aunt Donna took on this search of mine like it was her own. She was making all of the decisions for me. What to do. How to do it. When to do it. I was beginning to feel like if I ever did find my birth mother, Donna would want to meet her first. After you blew up at her, it got even worse."

"I didn't mean to cause you problems."

"I know that." She sipped her pop. "Anyway, I finally

had to tell her to back off. I appreciated her help and all, but it is my life."

"That must have gone over like a lead balloon."

"She didn't take it well, that's for sure."

I motioned to the suitcase. "She kick you out?"

"No, it was my decision to leave. I was hoping you'd take me in."

I patted her hand. "You're always welcome here."

She looked away from me, her eyes downcast. "I would've come here in the first place, but I didn't want to hurt your feelings." She caught my puzzled look. "I mean, I was worried about how you'd react. I thought if I stayed at Aunt Donna's, my search would be easier on you somehow. I guess I was wrong."

"As far as the search goes, you can relax. You didn't hurt my feelings."

"You're sure?"

"I've done a lot of thinking ever since you told me you were going to look for your birth mother. I guess I've come to realize that what you're doing is okay. No, it's more than okay—it's the right thing to do."

"Do you really mean that?"

"Yes, Cassie, I really do. I have to admit, though, that in the beginning I wasn't so sure. Donna was right about one thing—I was afraid. Terrified, actually."

Cassie looked confused. "What do you mean, terrified? I don't get it."

"I don't think I did, either. Maybe not until just a few minutes ago. I think it was something as simple as having you home again, laughing with you, watching you eat that crazy sandwich."

"What? You think eggs and cucumbers are crazy?" she asked, feigning shock.

I smiled. "No more so than the way I've been acting."

"No, Mom, you haven't been acting crazy at all." She clasped my hand. "But I would like to try and understand how you've been feeling."

"About the only way I know how to explain it is this: Twenty years ago, your birth mother made a decision that was probably the most difficult yet loving decision she ever made. A decision that changed all of our lives forever—hers, mine, your father's, and especially yours. I've given silent thanks for her courage many, many times over the years. And yet when you first told me that you were going to search for her, that you wanted to meet her, I was terrified. You see, you weren't hers anymore. She'd given you to me—the most precious gift anyone can give another. And I loved you with all my heart. You were *my* daughter, *my* baby."

"I still am," said Cassie.

"But don't you see? I was afraid that if you found this woman, she'd steal you from me."

Cassie covered her mouth, as if to suppress a laugh.

"Sounds silly, doesn't it? I realize now how foolish I've been. I think I got everything all mixed up when I lost your father and great-grandfather."

"What do you mean?"

"Death—your great-grandfather's and then your father's—surprised me. They came out of nowhere, and there was nothing I could do about it. Absolutely nothing but watch them leave me. So when you announced that you were going to search for your birth mother, I was afraid you'd leave me, too."

"I just wanted to meet her. It's hardly the same as dying."

"Of course, but I was afraid that if you found this woman, you'd come to love her, and there wouldn't be anything left over for me. So in a way it was like dying—only worse. You'd be here, but your love would be gone."

"I had no idea you felt like this."

"It took me awhile to sort everything out, but, yes, that's how I've been feeling."

"But you said you're okay with my search now. What happened to make you change your mind?"

"I can't point to anything in particular. Maybe it's because of all this stuff that's come up with the Moyer case. I do know that when your father and Grampy died, I was confused for quite a while."

"It didn't seem like it. You made all those decisions and everything—quitting your job, selling the house."

"That's not what I'm talking about. I knew what I wanted to do with the rest of my life. It was this thing called love that had me confused. It took me a long time to understand that love isn't something that has to be held tightly and exclusively for fear that it will be lost. This may sound like some corny bumper sticker, but I've come to believe that it's only when we can let go of the fear of losing that we'll find the joy of loving." I squeezed her hand. "So I guess what I'm trying to say, Cassie, is that if you do find your birth mother, if you do come to know her and maybe even love her, it will be okay with me."

"Really?"

"Really."

She threw her arms around me. "I love you, Mom."

We'd been stalled like a sloop "in irons" under a windless sky for so long that it suddenly felt as though we'd caught a great breath out of the heavens, billowing our sails and sweeping us on our homeward course once again. "I love you, too, Cassie."

When we finally pulled away, she reached for her backpack. "I almost forgot. I have something for you." She pulled out a package wrapped in red and green foil and handed it to me. "I never got a chance to give it to you the other night. Go ahead and open it." It was a book: *Being Adopted—The Lifelong Search for Self.* "I thought this would help you understand what I'm doing. It explains a whole lot of things."

"I'll be sure to read it," I said. "And now I have something for you." I retrieved her present from the bulkhead storage compartment.

But I already opened the presents you gave me—at Aunt

Donna's." She tugged at her sweater sleeve. "See? I'm wearing the ski sweater right now. I love it!"

"And it looks great on you, Cass." I handed her the present. "This is something special. I didn't take it to Donna's because I wanted you to open it when we could be by ourselves."

She tore the wrapping off and grinned as she read the title of the book: *How to Find Almost Anyone, Anywhere* by Norma Mott Tillman and *The Adoption Searchbook: Techniques for Tracing People* by Mary Jo Rillera.

"I thought these might help you. They come highly recommended."

"This is great!" she said, flipping through several pages.

"They say there's a wealth of information on the search process in them."

"Who's they?"

"The folks in the adoption forum. You know, on CompuServe."

"No way. You've actually been chatting on the net?"

"Don't act so shocked. I'm a nineties mom."

"Not shocked. Pleased. It makes what I wanted to ask you a lot easier." She paused, running her fingers over the spine of one of the books. "Do you think you'd be willing to attend a search and reunion support group meeting with me?"

"Cassie, I'll do anything you want. In fact, if you'd like me to help with your search, I'll do that, too. But don't count on any ten-thousand-dollar check!"

We both laughed as the phone rang. I ignored it, but Cassie motioned for me to pick it up. "You better answer that. Some woman has called twice since I got here. That's probably her again. She sounded anxious to talk to you."

I reached for the phone. "Hello?"

"Kellie! I'm so glad I finally caught you at home. I wanted to ask if there's anything special I should bring for tomorrow's lesson. I'm so excited I can hardly wait."

"I'm afraid you'll have to, Emily. I was going to call you, but you beat me to it—I won't be able to make our lesson after all."

"How come?"

"Something important has come up."

"I see." She was silent for a beat and when she spoke again, her voice was shaky. "You know, Kellie, it wasn't easy for me to schedule this lesson. My boys are home from school now, and I'm trying to squeeze in as much time with them as I can. And if you recall, I had to move some important appointments around in order to accommodate you. I'd think the least you could do is accommodate me. I thought you liked me."

I wasn't sure how to respond. I knew politicians sometimes had fragile egos, but I hadn't expected something like this from Emily. According to the papers, her husband's gubernatorial campaign was in difficulty. Maybe the strain had gotten to her. More likely, though, it was grief talking. She'd been awfully close to Miranda, and dealing with death, as I well knew, could give you some strange ideas. I took a gentle approach with her.

"I'm very sorry, Emily. I appreciate your busy schedule. And I do like you. I've really enjoyed getting to know you and I hope we can become good friends. I promise I'll call you and reschedule our lesson just as soon as possible."

"So you'll still give me sailing lessons?"

"Of course. I just can't get together with you tomorrow."

"Okay," she said tentatively. "But you're sure you still like me?"

"Yes, Emily. I still like you."

After I hung up, Cassie asked, "Who the heck was that?"

"Just a woman who needs a friend. It's a long story, and I—" The phone rang again. My hand was still on the receiver, and before I could think about it, I answered. It was the Weasel.

As soon as he heard my voice, he immediately began peppering me with questions about my conversation with

Mr. Kano. "What on earth did you tell him, Kellie? He's been acting very strangely, and I—"

"Look, Todd, I can't talk right now."

"Just when do you think you *can* talk to me?"

When hell freezes over was the thought that came to mind, but I evaded the issue with a vague "soon" and hung up before he could start ragging on me for a specific date and time.

"Sorry about that, Cassie. Now, what were we . . ."

She had curled up on the settee and was snoring softly. I found an extra blanket and spread it over her, then climbed into bed myself.

KINGSTON'S OFFICE WAS located on the fifth floor of the Public Safety Building in downtown Seattle. The city is divided geographically into several precincts, but all of the homicide detectives work out of the headquarters facility as do detectives assigned to various other units such as robbery, bias crimes, missing persons, and emergency response. Besides SPD headquarters and the West Precinct, the facility is home to Seattle's municipal court, the public health department, and a slew of administrative offices. Built in the late 1950s, the ten-story building also housed the city jail until King County built a new facility several years ago.

I stopped at the lobby for the mandatory security inspection. Metal detectors were a rather recent addition to the building. They were installed, not coincidentally, after a gunman went on a shooting spree at the county courthouse and killed three people, including his pregnant wife. I'd just retrieved my bag from the conveyor belt when I spotted Brian Saunders waiting in front of the elevator. Kingston's partner was dressed casually in loafers, jeans, and an ivory cable-knit sweater.

"Hey, Brian! What're you doing here? I thought you were off recuperating."

"You know what they say—you can't keep a good man

down." He flashed a broad smile. "I've just been cleared
for active duty again." He flexed his right arm as proof.
Besides the bulging biceps, his face was deeply tanned for
the middle of winter, and his overall demeanor was more
relaxed than I'd ever seen him.

"That's great, Brian. I was worried about you."

The elevator arrived, and Saunders hit the button for the
fifth floor. "I take it that's where you're headed?"

I nodded. "I'm supposed to meet with Kingston."

His relaxed air disappeared like a puff of smoke.
"Hmmf."

I shot him a raised eyebrow. "Why do I get the feeling
you're not looking forward to teaming up with him again?"

"What can I say?" He shrugged. "The man's got a real
hang-up about college grads in general and me in particular.
But ever since the list came out, he's been really bent out
of shape."

"What list?"

The elevator stopped, and we exited. "The civil service
list for sergeant. I placed number one, and Allen made the
number two spot."

"That's a problem? Sounds like you both have a good
chance for a promotion with ratings that high."

"Not really. There's only one position available—it's up
for grabs, but Allen thinks I've got an inside track or something because of my degree."

"I had no idea Kingston was even interested in making
sergeant."

"That's the other thing. He's always going off about how
I'm on the fast track, like the only reason I want the sergeant's job is because it's a stepping stone to bigger and
better things. The way he talks, you'd think the chief is
already checking the want ads."

I laughed. "It can't be that bad."

"I'm not exaggerating. And the worst part is, I don't
think Allen really wants the sergeant's job."

"But if he went to the trouble of studying for the exam—

I've heard it's not exactly a piece of cake—don't you think that would indicate he was serious, especially since he passed with such a high score?''

"Maybe, but I have a hunch he's just doing it to prove something. Or it could be he just wants to up his pension when he retires. The fifteen percent pay differential is nothing to sneeze at.''

We stopped at the glassed-in counter leading to the homicide unit, and Brian signaled the receptionist to buzz us on through. Once inside the secured area, I signed the log book and was given a visitor's badge. I clipped the badge to my jacket, and we headed down the hall to the unit.

"I don't know what to tell you, Brian. I have noticed, though, that Kingston has been awfully tired lately—more than usual. Maybe he just wants out of the field. He's been a detective for a long time.''

"Sergeant isn't the way to go if you're tired. They still go out on field calls, plus they have overall responsibility for the detectives they supervise. No, I think Allen's got some other agenda in mind.'' He paused at the door to the homicide unit. "This is where I leave you.''

"Aren't you going inside?'' Like the other detectives, Brian shared an office with his partner.

"I have to report to the lieutenant first. But don't worry, Allen should be in a good mood this morning. The Vanasek woman's death has been officially ruled a homicide. And the word is something big's going down on the Moyer case.''

"Can I go in unescorted?'' I asked.

"Yeah, just don't steal anything,'' he said with a wink. "On second thought, help yourself to any of that junk Allen's got crammed into our cubbyhole. It needs a good weeding out.''

Once inside the unit, I passed through a labyrinth of blue and gray partitions until I located the cubicle that Brian and Kingston shared. Most of the detectives had decorated their small work spaces with various personal items and souvenirs from cases they'd handled. Kingston and Saunders's office had a crime scene photograph blown up like a poster. It was a grainy black-and-white view of a brick wall on which someone had scribbled, "I AM DEATH, DESTROIER OF THE WORLD." Evidently you don't have to be a good speller to destroy the world.

Rich Vanasek sat in a chair next to Kingston's desk, a leather briefcase propped on his lap like a table. Both men had paper cups in their hands.

As Brian had insinuated, Kingston's half of the office was a mess. Every conceivable space in the small cubicle was filled with something—an assortment of manuals, books, file folders, and other papers stacked on his desk, his filing cabinet, and most of the floor. Unlike Brian's desk, which had been personalized with family photos and other mementos, Kingston's work space had no personal touches other than an empty donut box and the remnants of Chinese take-out.

I said hello and looked around for a chair. Finding none, I leaned against a two-drawer metal filing cabinet alongside Brian's desk. I stashed my shoulder bag on the floor and shifted my weight against the cabinet, but I still couldn't get comfortable.

"I could round up another chair somewhere," Kingston said with no conviction. "But I'm hoping this won't take long. I'm beat." He yawned as if to drive home the point, then downed some of his coffee and grimaced. "You want some tea or something?" To Vanasek he said, "She's a little fussy how she takes her caffeine."

"Don't bother. As you say, I hope we won't be here that long. Rich, why don't you show him the photos?"

Vanasek set his cup on the floor and snapped open his briefcase. "I found these in our safety deposit box," he said. "Kellie thinks they may be related to the case." He removed the envelope and held it out to Kingston.

When Kingston made no effort to take the envelope, I took it from Vanasek and dumped the contents on the desk, adding the photo I'd shown Terri to the pile. "I think these are what got the Moyers and Yolanda killed," I said. "I understand suicide has been ruled out in Yolanda's case."

Kingston glanced at the photos briefly, yawned again, and propped his head up with one hand. I ignored him and pressed on. "We know Donald Moyer was a blackmailer and—"

Kingston's head jerked up. "We do?"

"Preston admitted to me yesterday that Moyer was blackmailing him." I glanced at Richard Vanasek. "He also said that Yolanda had taken up the same cause."

"Go on."

"Well, I figure it like this: Donald Moyer was blackmailing someone over these photos. The young girl who posed for them is probably an adult now with a reputation to protect. I had an interesting conversation with Terri Moyer last night. Turns out the girl in the photo was her best friend."

"What are you saying?"

"That Donald Moyer was a pedophile. He molested his daughter and her best friend."

"Terri Moyer told you all this?" asked Kingston. "Was she stoned at the time?"

"Don't be so quick to dismiss her credibility," I said irritably. That I'd also been guilty of the same thing—had even considered her a suspect—didn't seem relevant at the moment. "You can check with her therapist. The fact that Terri was able to talk about the incident was a major breakthrough for her." I pointed to the photographs. "Her name is Sunny Wilson, and she had Donald Moyer's baby at age thirteen. Terri found out about it, and that's what sent her over the edge emotionally. She'd kept her father's dirty little secret bottled up inside her for years. And to make certain that she did, Donald Moyer set her up with a generous trust fund. I don't know what happened to the child, but he or she would be around twenty now. It's possible that Moyer was using these photos against Sunny—or maybe even the child. But Sunny wasn't willing or able to pay up like Preston, so she decided to end the threats once and for all by killing Moyer aboard his boat.''

"And Miranda and Junior? How do they figure in all this?''

"Miranda just happened to be in the wrong place at the wrong time. As far as Donald, Jr., goes, the killer didn't count on him knowing about the photos and his father's blackmail scheme. That's probably what he was doing that day I saw him at the marina—looking for someplace where his father might have stashed these photos. Since he opened the wrong dock box, he missed the key. When Junior found out that Yolanda was still running the Missing Link, he figured she must know more about his father's business than she'd let on.''

"He even called our house," added Vanasek. "He'd never done that before.''

"I think he called Yolanda to ask about the photos that he believed she had. They joined forces in the blackmail scheme and wound up getting killed for their trouble.'' I paused and waited for Kingston to respond. His eyes were half closed. "Well?''

He blinked. "That's it? You're done?''

"Yes. What do you think?''

"I think you've painted a nice little scenario, Montgomery. Almost as imaginative as the last one you laid on me.'' Richard cocked his eyebrow at me, which Kingston immediately picked up on. "She didn't tell you about her baby-brokering theory?''

He shook his head.

"It was a beaut. You see, according to Montgomery here, the killer was out to get Miranda Moyer instead of her husband because—''

"Kingston.''

"—Miranda had forced her to give up a baby for adoption against her wishes.''

"Why don't you just drop it?''

"Oh, I will. Right through all the holes in your present theory."

"What holes?" asked Richard. "It's painful to think of my wife as a blackmailer, but the scenario Kellie outlined isn't so far-fetched. Why else would these photos be in our safety deposit box?"

"Any number of reasons, I suppose. But that's not the question you should be asking."

"Here it comes," I said to Vanasek. "He's going to tell us exactly what we should be asking."

"Anything to speed this meeting along." Kingston held up an index finger. "Question number one: How did Junior know about the photos? As far as we can determine, he was just a playboy. A not-so-bright, lazy playboy who couldn't care less about his parents' business, legal or otherwise. He had his money; that's all he cared about."

He held up a second finger. "Question number two: How did Junior, or Yolanda for that matter, know the identity of the girl in the photos?" He turned a couple of the photos over. "I don't see any identifying marks here. Sounds as though even Terri Moyer didn't recall her name until she'd had this so-called therapeutic breakthrough. And, as you said, the girl's all grown up now, probably even married with a different last name. So how'd they contact her?"

A third finger went up. "Question number three: Why would Junior and Yolanda join forces in a blackmail scheme in the first place? Junior inherited a sizable estate, and Yolanda, as you say, was blackmailing James Preston just fine on her own. She didn't need any partners."

Fourth finger. "Which brings us to question number four. When we opened the Moyers' safety deposit box—and their office and home safes—we found no photos, negatives, or anything else inside. Nothing at all to suggest that anyone, besides James Preston, had motive or opportunity to commit the murders." Kingston pushed the photos aside.

"I seem to recall that you once thought Junior had plenty

of motive and opportunity to kill his parents," I said. "Until he turned up dead himself."

"Nice try, Montgomery. But this time we've got an air-tight case."

"You've made an arrest?" asked Vanasek.

Kingston nodded. "Mr. R. James Preston. An hour ago." He glanced at his watch as if confirming the fact. "Now if you'll excuse me, I've gotta go home and crash." He stuffed the last of the photos inside the envelope and handed it back to Vanasek.

"Just a minute, Detective." Vanasek and Kingston both turned to look at me. "I have a couple of questions of my own." I held up my index finger. "Question number one: What possible reason would Preston have to kill Junior?"

Kingston smiled. "Terri Moyer might've had a cushy trust fund to draw on, but she'd been written out of their will years ago. That left Junior as the only heir. With him gone, Preston stood to inherit the entire estate himself."

"He was included in the will?"

"Quite a shocker, huh? The fact is, Moyer and Preston were childhood buddies. Preston was older than Moyer, but they still did everything together—law school, best man at each other's weddings. Hell, Preston was even Junior's god-father."

"But with Moyer gone, he had the law practice all to himself. That had to be worth quite a bit," I said.

"So what? Preston's a lush. He knew he couldn't keep the practice going on his own. Selling it was a chancy deal at best. But with all the Moyers dead, he had no need to keep the practice going."

Vanasek put the envelope back in his briefcase and closed the lid. "Okay, all that makes sense. But what about my wife? Why'd he have to kill her?"

"That's the only part of Montgomery's scenario that holds water. Preston killed her because he was sick and tired of paying money to a blackmailer. He confessed that Moyer *and* Yolanda had been blackmailing him. Seems he got

drunk and killed a kid some years back in a hit-and-run
accident.''

"Did he confess to the murders?" I asked.

Kingston shook his head.

"I didn't think so. And what about that key you found
in the dock box? What was it for?''

"I don't know," said Kingston. He stood up. "But it
doesn't matter anymore. This case is closed."

TWENTY-SEVEN

R. JAMES PRESTON'S arrest was a major news event. The story was given extensive, if not sensational, coverage in both of Seattle's major newspapers as well as the *Eastside Journal*. The local television stations carried the story as their lead on the six and eleven o'clock newscasts for two days running and were still doing daily follow-up pieces. All of which goes to prove my theory that what passes for news these days is directly proportional to the amount of blood, mayhem, and sleaze that can be bilked from a story. Then, too, it's far easier to gloss over what's happening in the Middle East and other hot spots around the world than what's going on at home. Murder in our own backyard gets our attention every time.

Kingston was happy. The weariness he'd been wearing like a heavy coat was gone. In fact, I'd never seen him more energized. The favorable publicity he'd gotten for breaking the Moyer case—while not a factor in the selection process for sergeant—certainly hadn't hurt his chances. It was still unofficial but, according to Kingston, his promotion was a done deal. Once the chief announced his decision and the paperwork made it through the SPD bureaucratic maze, he'd no longer have to, in his words, "wipe the noses of any more college-boy fast-trackers."

Bert was happy. In spite of the Weasel's spurious nay-saying about security, the Nakito team was impressed with the way Bert'd been running the marina—and especially the way he handled the publicity surrounding the gruesome discovery aboard *Merry Maiden.* Rose's successful audit was icing on the cake. But the very day Nakito Enterprises informed him that they wanted him to stay on as harbormaster when the sale was finalized, old man Larstad suddenly had a change of heart. He pulled out of the deal altogether and gave Bert a raise for the professionalism he'd demonstrated during the negotiations.

According to Reba Stanton, Terri Moyer was doing very well since revealing the secret that had haunted her for so long. Her mental outlook was improving on a daily basis, and her anger and self-damaging behaviors were under control. I could see that for myself. She'd shown up for her second sailing lesson looking radiant. I was relieved to see the obvious improvement and, more important, the end to my doubts about her involvement in the murders. Terri was an instructor's dream—enthused, talented, and a fast learner. Unlike last time, she assured me that she would complete the course. Sailing, she said, had made her happier than she could ever remember.

About the only person who wasn't happy these days was the Weasel. Not only had he tried to take all the credit for my boat show plans, but he'd told the team that he'd been responsible for the upgraded security measures that Bert developed. But my little conversation with Mr. Kano had put the kibosh on his attempt to ingratiate himself with the Nakito team. No one knew for sure whether old man Larstad was aware of what his nephew had been up to, but Bert believed that was part of the reason for his raise. I say if the old man had really known about the Weasel's double-dealing, he'd have fired the guy. But, as Bert reminded me, it's kind of hard to fire someone who doesn't have a job.

So, the Weasel was still with us, but he'd been keeping himself out of sight lately—and no one was likely to file a missing person's report.

All in all, I guess I was happy, too. The sailing school was still in business, and Cassie was back home with me again—at least until Christmas break was over and she returned to college. She'd gone skiing today at Stevens Pass with her boyfriend, Tyler, and some other pals, but we'd made plans to take in a movie later.

So my life seemed to be on track once again. What more could I want—world peace? The truth was, I'd have settled for a few answers. I tried forgetting about the case—after all, it was solved. But there were still some questions that wouldn't stop nagging at me: Why was the key in the dock box? Who was the mystery woman who had a fight with Miranda? Why did they fight? Where was Sunny Wilson now? Had Moyer and Yolanda used the photographs to blackmail her? Or had my scenario about the killer been full of holes just as Kingston claimed?

"Permission to come aboard?" Emily Cummings's voice was as cheerful as the morning. We'd finally scheduled a sailing date, and the day couldn't have been better—bright and sunny but crisp enough to remind you that it was still winter thanks to a mild December cold front that had come in overnight, kissing Puget Sound like a playful lover.

I waved her aboard. Emily's grin was wide and her dark eyes sparkling. As usual, she wore no makeup, but her cheeks had a rosy glow, like a freshly scrubbed youngster. She'd exchanged her fancy designer clothes for winter boater's garb—good sturdy deck shoes, heavy wool fisherman's sweater under a windbreaker, waterproof gloves, hat with earflaps, and warm-looking trousers. She had a duffel bag slung over her shoulder.

"You can stow your bag below if you'd like," I said.

She nodded and headed for the hatchway. I was relieved to see that she was in a good mood. After our last telephone conversation, I wasn't sure what to expect. She'd called me a couple of days earlier to arrange another sailing date, and although she didn't come right out and say it, I got the distinct impression that she believed I'd been deliberately avoiding her. She didn't accuse me of not liking her again, but her tone had been less than friendly. I'd been feeling somewhat apprehensive about our get-together ever since. Apparently I'd been worried for nothing—she was as chipper and pleasant as ever.

"Grab some tea while you're down there," I said. "We'll chat awhile before going out." I've found it helps nonsailors like Emily if they know some basic boating nomenclature and terminology up front. Ordinarily we'd have been aboard the J 22 or Santana 20—my boats of preference for beginners—but Emily had been so insistent on sailing *Second Wind* that I'd agreed to the switch.

While she was below, I set my own tea mug aside and did a quick presail check. The routine was fairly simple: After I checked each item to make sure it was in good working order, I penciled in a check mark beside it on the list. Radio and instruments? Check. Fuel? Check. Running rigging? Check. Winch handles? Check. Safety gear? Oops. I pulled a couple of life jackets out of the stowage locker as Emily came topside.

She sat down on a side bench in the cockpit. One hand held a mug of tea, the other was jammed inside her pocket. On the dock behind her, a couple of screeching seagulls played tug o'war with a purple starfish. "So," she said, "I hear your days as a detective are over."

I tossed the life jackets aside, grabbed my mug, and sat down on the bench across from her. "I guess so. The case is solved—at least as far as the police are concerned."

She eyed me over the rim of her mug. "But?"

"I still have a lot of questions," I said, sipping my tea. "It doesn't really matter, though. The police are satisfied, and the district attorney thinks there's enough evidence against Preston to go to trial. The gun he used to make

Yolanda's death look like a suicide was the same type of weapon that killed the Moyers."

"From what I read in the newspapers, his lawyer is claiming anyone could've planted that gun," Emily said. "It didn't even belong to Preston. Sounds like the case is mostly circumstantial."

"The lead detective says he'll take circumstantial over an eyewitness any day."

"So what's still bothering you about the case?"

"The photographs," I said.

"What photographs? There hasn't been anything about photographs in the news."

"They were a set of rather provocative shots. Richard Vanasek found them in their safety deposit box. He turned them over to the police, but Detective Kingston dismissed them as irrelevant."

"But you're convinced they're important?"

I nodded. "We know Moyer was a blackmailer. It's possible he was blackmailing someone over those photographs. Someone who wanted him dead more than Preston did. Tell me something, did Miranda ever mention anything to you about a key?"

"No, why?"

"The police found one in the Moyers' dock box. They never did figure out what it was for."

"You have an idea about that, too?"

"I think the key ties in with the photographs."

"How so?"

"That's one of those questions that still bothers me. I talked to a woman at the Sports Center who told me about an employee who met with Yolanda Vanasek in the bistro. Shortly before she was killed, Yolanda gave the employee a substantial amount of money. Now, I don't know for sure, but Yolanda may have paid the employee for some information about the lockers at the Center. Junior had been searching for anyplace his parents might have stored things. Maybe Moyer was keeping those photographs in his Center locker. Maybe the key that was found in the dock box fits his locker at the Center.''

"Didn't the police search the locker?''

"They searched Moyer's home and office, but I don't think they knew about the lockers at the Sports Center. I'm going there later today to take a look at Donald's and Miranda's lockers. I have a friend at the Center who can pave the way for me.''

"What're you hoping to find?''

"I'm not sure, really. I want to talk to the bistro staff again. You said you saw Yolanda arguing with Miranda at the Center, but when I questioned my source at the bistro, she said they'd always gotten along real well together. She couldn't remember ever seeing them fight.''

"That doesn't mean it didn't happen. I mean, I know what I saw.''

"I agree, but my source saw another woman arguing with Miranda. I'd sure like to know who she was.''

"You don't think this so-called source of yours was just confused? That it was Yolanda and not someone else she saw?''

"Maybe. And that's why I'm going to the Center again— I think the answers are there. I just have to look around some more.''

Emily suddenly stood up. "You know what bothers me about you, Kellie?'' she asked, scowling. "You just can't leave well enough alone. You're not going to stop until you figure things out. You're like that stupid commercial on TV—you just keep going and going and going.''

"What are you talking about?''

"This!'' She pulled her hand from her pocket and thrust a gun inches from my face. It wasn't all that big, but shoved up close and personal it seemed monstrous. And lethal.

Emily moved in closer as if to hug me. "There'll be no more chatting either,'' she said. She leaned down so that her lips almost brushed my ear. "Just get this fuckin' boat moving,'' she whispered, shoving the gun under my ribs.

Even through my jacket the gun felt cold and hard. I couldn't think, couldn't move, couldn't do anything but stare at the gun. And remember the blood-splattered havoc it caused when its bullets ripped through Donald and Miranda Moyer.

She pushed it in deeper. "I said move!"

I looked into her eyes. They weren't sparkling anymore—just dark and mean, like the gun she held in her hand. A killer's eyes. I tried to speak, but the words wouldn't come. She grabbed hold of my arm with her free hand and spun me around. When she let go, she jammed the gun into the small of my back and pushed me toward the console panel.

I stumbled, but she grabbed my arm again and broke my fall. "No tricks!" she barked, cuffing me hard in the jaw.

She pointed to the key I'd placed in the ignition during my presail check. "Okay," she said. "Start 'er up."

My hand shook as I turned the key. I held my breath, hoping somehow that the engine wouldn't turn over. But the reliable Yanmar roared to life.

"Now get the lines," she ordered.

Emily followed close behind me as I stepped out of the cockpit. We inched along the narrow deck together, as if partners in a strange, intimate dance. When we got to the entry gate, I started to step out onto the dock to release the spring lines. She gripped my arm. "No! Don't get off the boat. Just untie us from here."

"But if I do that I'll have to leave the lines on the dock."

"Just do it!"

I worked quickly, untying the spring lines while Emily stood behind me like a shadow, the gun never more than a few inches from my back. Once I had the spring lines clear, we moved to the bow where I freed both ends of the line from the starboard cleat. But I was so jittery that I couldn't flick the line off the dock cleat. "Just let it go," she said, and the line splashed into the water. A gull screamed and took flight, leaving bits of purple starfish littering the dock.

"Where's your shore boat?" she asked suddenly.

I motioned to the portside bow. "Up there." Usually, I keep the Zodiak on top of the forward deck when moored. This morning, though, I'd put the inflatable craft in the water and tied it temporarily to *Second Wind*'s portside bow. Since I didn't have need for a shore boat while giving a sailing lesson, I'd planned to secure it to the dock before casting off.

With the bow line and spring lines unsecured, the wind began to push the sloop away from the dock. We were drifting toward *Forever Young*, moored in the slip alongside us. When Emily saw what was happening, she said, "Leave the dinghy be. Just get us out of here!"

I cast off the stern line and put the engine in reverse. It was too late to miss *Forever Young*, and we hit hard. The fenders, still attached to our port side, offered some protection but not enough. I continued backing out of the slip, scraping, gouging, and bumping into *Forever Young* until we were clear of the dock. A pair of black-and-white ducks skittered out of our way.

Emily stood close by my left side as I steered the boat toward the marina's exit. She pressed the gun into my ribs but didn't speak. The sound of the engine broke the marina's early morning quiet, and I glanced around, hoping that someone might hear or see us leaving. But what if they did? The gun was well hidden, jammed into the folds of my jacket. All they'd see were two women going out for an early morning sail.

I had to think of something quick. My mind raced, but my thoughts were jumbled. Was this the way the Moyers had felt? I couldn't believe what was happening. I'd been so sure of myself, so sure of my instincts about people. I'd liked Emily. She'd acted a bit strange lately, but I hadn't feared her. I'd waved off Kingston's concerns for my safety, boasting that I could take care of myself. Well, Kellie, now's your chance.

Emily nudged me. "Gun it."

"What?"

"The throttle. Gun it!"

We were still within the confines of the marina with dozens of boats peacefully nestled in their slips. "But the wake—"

She thrust the gun deeper into my side. "Just do it!" I pushed the throttle forward, and we picked up speed. Like a baby tsunami, the wake hit the boats we passed and tugged roughly at their mooring lines. Gulls skittered and squawked. Emily took no note. As soon as we were beyond the breakwater—and far enough from the shore that I couldn't jump overboard—she took the wheel. "Now get up to the bow and bring that dinghy back here," she ordered.

When I'd retrieved the Zodiak and had finished tying it to the aft stanchion, Emily had me take the wheel again. "Where're we headed?" I asked. Her mouth twitched, but she said nothing. Was she as nervous as I was?

She pointed toward Bainbridge Island, and my hopes soared. The island was popular with the boating crowd all year round. There were bound to be some boaters out on a day like today. Definitely some fishermen or crabbers. I didn't know how I'd do it, but there had to be a way to get somebody's attention. I turned the wheel toward Bainbridge.

"Not Bainbridge," Emily said. "Potter's Cove."

"We can't," I said quickly. Potter's Cove was a wildlife reserve. Except for rare visits by researchers from the University, no one ever went there. Visitors were strictly prohibited.

Emily laughed, a wretched laugh that chilled me far more than the biting wind off the bay. "Don't worry," she said with a sneer. "All the little duckies will be quite safe."

"Look," I said, shivering, "the waters around that cove are damned treacherous, especially at low tide. If I take *Second Wind* in there, she'll never make it. The rocks will tear up the keel before we know what hit us."

"Sounds perfect. Keep going." She reached over and pushed the throttle forward. Five knots. Six knots. Seven knots. Full speed. We'd be at Potter's Cove in less than an hour. I didn't know what she planned to do when we got there, but I knew it wouldn't be pleasant. I needed a plan, too, but I couldn't think of anything. Maybe if I got her talking.

"Why're you doing this?" I asked. "It makes no sense whatsoever. You're in the clear. James Preston has been arrested for the murders. You don't have to do this. No one suspects you of anything. Think of your husband, your boys. Do you really want to jeopardize your life with them? You've got too much at stake, too much to lose."

"You don't like me, do you?"

Not this again. The woman must be insane. She flashes a gun at me and then worries about whether I like her? "I think you're just swell," I said. "It's the gun I can do without."

She smiled as if I'd paid her a compliment.

"You're Sunny Wilson, the girl in the photographs, aren't you? Donald Moyer was blackmailing you over the photographs, and then his son and Yolanda Vanasek took over where he left off."

"That kid was a stupid asshole. He only found out about me by accident."

"How was that?"

"Moyer left a file at home. Everything was in it—my name, address, the works. The kid found the file and tried to blackmail me even though he didn't have the photos. It runs in the family, I guess. Then he teamed up with that bitch Yolanda—she was smart enough to figure out how to get her hands on the negatives. But I got rid of the file, the negatives, and her, too."

Then I was right. Moyer hid the negatives at the Sports Center, and that's why Yolanda met with Sissy at the bistro. She paid big time for Moyer's locker number. No wonder Sissy quit. She probably got a generous bonus for helping Yolanda get inside the locker without the key.

"You think you're such a hotshot detective, snooping

around, asking questions, getting people all stirred up. Hell, you don't know jack shit. But you're trouble just the same. You keep poking your nose in my business much longer, the whole world will have it figured out before you." She shook her head. "Some fuckin' detective. I bet you don't even know why I searched your fuckin' boat."

How could I have been so dense? Emily had been conning me from the beginning. The refined politician's wife mourning the loss of her close friend had all been an act. She didn't want to help with the case, didn't want sailing lessons, didn't want my friendship. But I'd fallen for everything. I'd even flattered myself that someone like Emily would want to hang out with me, all the time worrying that I was taking advantage of her celebrity for business purposes. She was simply after information. And I'd made the break-in so easy—telling her I couldn't take her sailing because I'd be gone all day. "You were trying to find out what I knew?"

"Wrong! I already had you pegged as a know-nothing. No, I had to get that bitch's letter."

I was confused, but I said nothing. I wasn't about to give her further proof that she was right about me.

"You still don't get it, do you? The Vanasek woman and Junior were two of a kind. I got the photos from Moyer before I made him pay for his crimes, but the negatives were still out there somewhere. So I figured Junior must have them since he was after me for money before they'd even buried his folks. When I popped him, the bitch got nervous and lifted the negatives from Moyer's locker at the Sports Center."

"Then had them developed and stashed in her safety deposit box," I added.

"She never said anything about that part. She just contacted me and made her demands for money. What she did say was that she'd written you a little letter—insurance, so to speak—explaining what was going on. The letter was to be opened in the event of her death, something like that.

Stupid ninny had been watching too many movies.''

''But I never received any such letter.''

''Ha!''

A letter from Yolanda? Where? How? All Emily stole during the break-in were my case notes and a bunch of un-opened . . . Christmas cards! The letter must have been in one of the cards! My God, she was right. I'd been wrong about everyone and everything connected to this case. What a fool I'd been. I should never have gotten myself involved in the investigation in the first place. If I'd listened to Kingston I wouldn't be standing here with a gun in my ribs. I didn't want to die. Not like this. Tears filled my eyes, spilling out over my cheeks like a waterfall. I wiped them away with my jacket sleeve, but they kept coming back.

Emily rolled her eyes at my weakness and sat down on the bench next to the helm. ''Well,'' she said, pointing the gun at me, ''as they say, life's a bitch and then you die.''

In the distance, a Washington State Ferry glided across the bay to the Seattle waterfront. Emily watched it for a moment and then sighed. ''Daddy took me on my first ferry ride when I was five. He took me up to the top deck and gave me some bread. Showed me how to tear it apart and throw it up in the air for the seagulls. I loved it.'' She sighed again. After a moment, she added, ''But that was before it started.''

''Before what started?''

''You don't want to know. It wasn't nice.''

''Neither is murder.''

''Some things are worse, much worse.''

''You were the woman at the bistro, weren't you? The woman who argued with Miranda before the murders. Why were you arguing with her?''

''You just can't stop playing detective, can you?''

''I guess not.''

She shrugged her shoulders. ''Well, for once you're right. Partly right. I did argue with Miranda at the bistro.'' She paused, her eyes staring off into the horizon where her memories were.

I looked from her to the console panel. The VHF radio was so close. If only . . . I glanced at Emily, but her eyes had shifted from the horizon back to me again. I asked, "The worse things, the things you said were worse than murder—did they have something to do with the Missing Link?"

"No!" Emily shouted.

"Maybe something that happened in your past. Like a baby?"

"*No!*"

"Donald Moyer's baby?"

"Damn you."

"Miranda found out, didn't she? Did she take care of her husband's baby for you, Emily? You were so young, maybe alone, too. Did she offer you a way out?"

"You're so full of shit. Miranda didn't know a thing about me back then. Only that asshole husband of hers knew. I was thirteen, okay? He promised me no one would ever find out. The adoption records were sealed. Permanently. But the bastard didn't care about that. All he cared about was money. And destroying lives."

"Why'd you argue with Miranda?"

"It was a stupid idea, my going to see her. I thought maybe she'd help me—you know, convince Moyer not to tell anyone about me. I shouldn't have bothered. The Missing Link was too much of a money maker. The bitch knew how her bread was buttered."

"Where's your child now?"

"I don't know. God . . ." Her voice trailed off, her eyes vacant. Cautiously and slowly, I moved my left hand off the steering wheel. The VHF radio transmitter was just inches away. *Whack!* Using the butt of the gun like a hammer, she smashed my hand. *Whack!* Then the transmitter.

"Storytime's over, bitch! Get both hands on that wheel."

I couldn't move, the pain too intense.

"*Now*! she screamed, pressing the gun to my temple.

Second Wind glided past a green buoy. Two sea lions lounged on its base, unconcerned with the clanging noise of the marker's bell or my plight. Potter's Cove was just minutes away.

TWENTY-EIGHT

IT WAS A good day for sailing but we were running *Second Wind* without her sails. What would Grampy have thought of that? Would anyone but another sailor even notice? Or care? Several fishing boats passed without a backward glance.

I shivered in the wind, chilled despite the sweat between my breasts. Emily sat in the cockpit eyeing me closely, the gun ever vigilant as she waited patiently for her plan to unfold. I still had no plan to match hers. My mind raced desperately as I tried to think of something helpful. Emily obviously knew her way around boats. Didn't she say she'd spent time on a Bayliner? But what about a sailboat? Was she really as inexperienced as she'd led me to believe? We were roaring closer and closer to the rocks. Talk. Talk to her, Kellie. Get her distracted.

"So Moyer took those photos of you," I said. "Why would he risk exposing himself by blackmailing you?"

"Drop it, will you?"

"If you got pregnant at thirteen, you were sexually abused. Moyer abused you and then tried to use that abuse against you."

"Shut up. Just shut the fuck up!"

"You gave up your baby for adoption and started over, burying the past and its painful memories. Buried it deep. Only the past didn't stay buried, did it?"

"*No*!" she shouted above the roar of the engine. Then in a softer voice, "It was supposed to be a secret."

"And Donald Moyer used that secret to blackmail you."

"It was that damn Missing Link. The kid wanted to meet me. She had agreed to pay Moyer ten thousand dollars for my name and address. He'd handled the adoption so he had all the records. Plus he knew exactly where I was now— he'd seen my picture in the paper often enough. He told me he wouldn't disclose my identity if I came up with more cash than the kid—a lot more. He figured I'd be good for it, considering my husband's wealth."

"And the photos?"

"Extra insurance. In case I balked."

"But couldn't you have threatened him with exposure, too? After all, he fathered your baby."

"Where'd you get that idea?"

"From your best friend—Terri Moyer."

"Give me a fuckin' break. Terri's looney tunes."

"But she saw you and Moyer in the bedroom. The day he took the photos."

"So what? That doesn't mean I had his baby."

"Then who was the father?"

"Like it matters now. But if you must know, it was my goddamn stepfather. Terri's so fucked up, she got the part about the baby wrong, too. I had twins. Twin girls."

"So Moyer handled their adoption. He wasn't the father?"

"Just the molester. Terri and I were two little girls with the same problem—predatory fathers. My stepfather and Moyer worked out a little deal. Moyer wouldn't charge him anything for handling the adoption if I'd come visit him from time to time. I even wound up seeing him after they moved to Broadmoor. Terri never did get herself together, but I got out. I survived.''

"How was that?''

"After I had the twins, my stepfather died. My mother couldn't make it on her own, so I wound up in a foster home, a real Beaver Cleaver home. Two little boys and a mother and father who actually loved each other. I was happy for the first time in my life. So friggin' happy that I decided I wanted just what they had—and more. So I studied them.''

"Studied them?''

"You know, how they talked, how they dressed, how they did things. The first time I sat down to dinner with them I didn't even know what a salad fork was. But I took it all in and remade myself. And believe me, it wasn't easy. I had so much to learn. But I was determined to do whatever it took. Hell, I even had plastic surgery on my nose when I was eighteen.'' She laughed bitterly. "Plus a couple of tucks here and there over the years. Must keep up appearances for Conrad. Politics, you know.''

"So that's why Terri Moyer didn't know what had become of you. Your face has been plastered all over the newspapers and TV, but she didn't recognize you.''

Emily laughed again. "What would you expect from someone with scrambled brains? Besides, I'd changed my name, too—even before I became a Cummings. Well, I guess I didn't really change it. I just started going by my real father's name instead of Wilson. I also used my own first name, which was almost like a new name. Terri had always called me Sunny, but everybody else knew me by my middle name. Anyway, that's not important. The important thing is, all my hard work paid off. I went to college, married well, and started living the kind of life I deserved.''

"Until Donald Moyer contacted you.''

"That asshole threatened to ruin everything. He waltzed back into my life out of nowhere, breaking promises, threatening me, turning my whole world upside down. Like a goddamn virus—he infected everything he touched.''

"So you killed him.''

"I did what I had to do. Don't you see? Everything had been set in motion years ago. I had no choice. I never had a choice. Never.''

I glanced to starboard. Potter's Cove was just ahead. I had to act fast. "You have a choice now, Emily. You've been hurt badly, but another killing isn't the answer. You need help. Let me help you.'' We locked eyes, and for a brief moment I thought I'd reached her. "Please, Emily.''

She looked past me. "We're here. It's too late.''

"It's never too late. Put the gun away, and I can go with you to the authorities. I'll see to it that you get the help you need.''

"Ha! Do you think the so-called authorities are going to care about what happened to me twenty years ago? All they'll care about is that I murdered four people. Hell, I'm a one-woman crime wave. It would be the bust of the year. After the Green River fiasco, the cops would be slapping high-fives all over the place—they'd finally have themselves a goddamn serial killer.''

"It doesn't have to be that way. I can talk to Allen King—''

"*No!* This is the way it'll go down: I'll go forward and look for rocks. You'll stay here and steer where I tell you to. And don't get any bright ideas.'' She waved the gun. "Your boat's not so big that I can't get a clear shot at you— even from the bow. And I'm not going that far.''

She stood up and began inching her way along the starboard deck toward the shrouds, all the while keeping the gun pointed back at me. I knew then what her plan was. She'd keep the gun on me until she spotted the rocks. Then she'd have me maneuver *Second Wind* right into them. The end would come quickly. With water pouring into the hold and the radio dead, she'd knock me out and climb into the dinghy for her getaway. The boat would sink and everyone would assume I'd had an accident. A serious misjudgment that had caused my own death. I had to do something—now.

Second Wind's narrow deck had one benefit—Emily had to move carefully to keep from losing her balance as the boat moved. I decided to make things a little more difficult for her. I kept my hands poised where she could see them, but not so that they were actually touching the wheel. Using my foot, I spun the wheel to change the boat's direction just a bit. The slight movement was enough. Emily stumbled on a cleat and dropped her weapon onto the deck. Cursing loudly, she immediately grabbed the lifelines and bent over to retrieve it, at the same time. I rushed around to the front of the wheel and released the main sheet stopper. Then I spun the wheel hard to port.

The effect was immediate. The boom jerked to starboard just as Emily, having fetched the pistol, stood upright again. The boom hit her in the head with such force that she toppled over the safety rails and into the icy water. She sank beneath the surface like a lead weight.

The sharp turn to port had been effective, but it had also put *Second Wind* in a direct course for Bird Rock—a huge dung-stained rock that stuck three feet out of the water. I pulled back on the throttle to slow down just as Emily bobbed to the surface, still clutching the gun. She spit water from her mouth and shot wildly.

I ducked further into the cockpit with one hand still on the wheel. The first bullet hit the mast. The second, the console panel. Then quiet. I cautiously poked my head up. Not seeing Emily, I jerked the wheel away from Bird Rock. A third bullet whizzed by my head. I jammed the throttle forward. I was afraid to look back, expecting one of Emily's wild shots to eventually hit me.

Suddenly realizing that the bullets had stopped, I turned around and looked behind me. Emily had heaved herself into the dinghy while I was busy avoiding Bird Rock. Now she was busy herself—pulling the tether line hand-over-hand toward the stern. Within seconds she'd be close enough to pull herself aboard. I kept one hand on the wheel while I reached for my knife with the other.

But no knife dangled from my belt loop. I'd missed attaching it during my aborted presail check. I looked around for something else, but there wasn't anything useful. Just the two bright orange life jackets that I'd tossed on the deck earlier. Right. I'll just hit her with a PFD and be done with it. The dinghy was within inches of the stern. Frantic now, I looked for anything I could use as a weapon.

I used my foot to hold the wheel steady while I reached over and threw back the lid of the stowage locker. The gear I'd been sorting through during my presail check was still there, including a boat hook. I let go of the wheel with my foot and grabbed the boat hook. Without someone holding the wheel, the boat began to spin in a tight circle, dragging the dinghy behind it like a long umbilical cord.

"Won't work," Emily shouted. She held onto the tether line with one hand and pointed the gun at me with the other. She nodded to the hook. "Throw it overboard. And slow the goddamn boat down."

I tossed the hook over the side and pulled back on the throttle.

"Keep both hands on the fuckin' wheel!" she shouted.

As soon as the boat resumed a straight course, Emily put the gun down and began pulling on the dinghy's tether line once again. I watched over my shoulder as she steadily made her way toward *Second Wind*. I felt tears welling up again. Damn it, be strong. Think. But I was fresh out of ideas and frustrated as hell. I stomped my foot like a two-year old and heard something skitter across the cockpit. The knife? Where'd it go?

I bent down slightly and, with both hands still on the wheel, frantically scanned the cockpit. All I could see were the orange PFDs grinning at me like garish Halloween pumpkins. I kicked them aside and the knife rolled out. I grabbed for it just as Emily reached the stern. She leaned over the dinghy's bow and tried to get a hand-hold on the swim ladder, but I jabbed wildly at her fingers, and she let go of the ladder.

When she scrambled for her gun, I sliced the tether line. Whirling around to the wheel, I jammed the throttle forward again. I glanced back at the dinghy bobbing in *Second Wind*'s wake. Emily got off one more shot. This time the bullet hit its mark. I let go of the wheel and slumped to the cockpit deck.

White waves lapped at my face. Vague images. A big boat. Shouting. Someone holding me. Blood. Then cold. Bone-chilling cold.

TWENTY-NINE

THE NURSE WAS a big woman. She stood next to my bed, fussing with a tube attached to my arm. She caught me staring at her. "Oh, good," she said, flashing a toothy grin. "Glad to see someone's awake around here." She glanced over her shoulder. I followed her gaze to the corner of the room where Allen Kingston sat in an overstuffed chair, snoring loudly.

"He's been camped out in your room ever since they brought you in yesterday," she said as she slipped a new IV bag on the pole. After she checked my arm, she added, "A royal pain in the butt, if you ask me."

"Why? What's he been doing?"

"Just fussing and fuming at everyone who's come near you." She smoothed the covers over me. "That's one concerned fellow you've got there, hon."

I glanced up at the IV bag. "Am I dying?"

She laughed and nodded at Kingston. "He wouldn't let you!" She patted me on the head. "Don't worry. You're doing just fine. The bullet messed up your shoulder a bit, but it didn't hit anything vital."

"Then why am I still here?"

She laughed again. "Ready to check out, are we? You've had surgery to repair the damage, hon. The doctor will be in soon to take a look at you, and he can explain everything. So you might as well get used to the place. You're going to be with us a few days."

I couldn't tell if the bump she gave Kingston's chair on the way out was an accident or calculated, but it didn't matter—it was effective. Kingston bolted upright. "What? What?" he asked.

He was as rumpled and crumpled as ever, which suddenly struck me as terribly funny. I giggled.

"Oh! You're awake." He jumped up and practically sprinted to the bed. "How're you doing, Montgomery?"

I giggled again. Must have been the lingering effects of anesthesia. "Painkillers are a wunnerful thing."

He looked wary. "Good, good."

Another giggle. When I thought I could talk without giggling again, I asked, "What happened out there?"

"I was going to ask you the same thing."

"You mean you've been hanging around here all night just so you could interrogate me?"

"Well, no. I mean, yes." He ran his hand through his hair. "Shit. This isn't coming out right. I was worried, Montgomery. I wanted to make sure that—"

"Relax, Kingston. I'm okay."

He leaned against the bed and gently took hold of my bruised hand. He looked at the IV attached to it. "You were damn lucky, you know. That Colt could've done some serious damage had the bullet hit a bone. It was an officer's model, one that husband of hers—our governor wannabe—brought home for protection. He had quite an arsenal stashed away, and the woman just helped herself to whatever she wanted. He never even realized any weapons were missing. You ask me, they're both nuts." He shook his head. "Are you sure you're okay?"

"I'm sure. And thanks for coming. I appreciate it."

He grinned. "No problem." He let go of my hand and

rounded up the chair he'd been sleeping in earlier. He pulled it next to the bed and sat down. "So what were you doing out there with that crazy woman anyway? She says you were giving her sailing lessons—didn't she like your teaching method?"

"Very funny. She didn't like me nosing around in her business."

"I can relate to that."

"Listen, Kingston. She's the killer—not James Preston. She killed them all. Donald and Miranda, Junior, and Yolanda." I glanced at the IV. "And she almost killed me, too."

"I know. She's in custody, but we haven't got much out of her yet that makes any sense. I think she's looney tunes."

"Maybe so."

"Were you really giving her a sailing lesson?"

"That was my plan, but she had another agenda."

"Obviously." He looked downcast, as if he were to blame for what had happened. "I should've listened to you, Montgomery. You were right about Preston."

"Don't worry about it—Emily Cummings had me fooled completely. I didn't think Preston was the killer, but I sure didn't suspect Emily. When I told her I was still bothered by the case and was planning to do some more investigating, she got worried. Not that she thought I was such a hotshot detective—she made it clear how little she thought of my abilities. She was more afraid that I'd stumble onto her by mistake. So she decided to take me out first."

"She was the girl in those photos, right?"

I nodded. "She was known as Sunny Wilson then. It's sad, really. She was used, abused, and lied to. Then she had twins when she was only thirteen and had to give them up for adoption."

Kingston said, "Whoa, there. You want to run that by me again? I thought you said Donald Moyer molested her."

"Right."

"And that he fathered her baby—Emily's baby. But now

you're telling me she had twins by him, too?''

''Terri Moyer got things a little mixed up. Moyer molested Emily all right, but she didn't have his baby. That dubious honor fell to her stepfather. I don't know all the circumstances surrounding the twins' birth and relinquishment, but it must have been very hard. She survived, though, and made a life for herself. Then Moyer dug it all up again.''

''With the Missing Link?''

I filled him in on Moyer's scheme to blackmail Emily.

''The thing that I don't get is why Moyer kept the key to his club locker at the marina.''

''That puzzled me, too, at first,'' I said. ''Try this scenario: Moyer hides both the negatives and the photos in his locker at the Sports Center. But he only takes the photos with him to the marina, where Emily has agreed to meet for the payoff. He temporarily hides the photos along with the locker key in the dock box, and when Emily arrives, he takes the photos out of the dock box. Instead of handing over the money, though, Emily pulls a gun and demands the negatives, too. Before Moyer can respond, Miranda shows up unexpectedly. Emily forces them both onto their yacht without ever knowing about the club locker or that the key was still in the dock box.''

''Then Junior gets in the act—and starts looking for what? The key?''

''I don't think he knew about it, either.''

''So why was he searching the dock box?''

I related what Emily had told me about Junior and Yolanda. ''Emily thought that by killing Yolanda her troubles would be over. She had stolen the letter Yolanda had sent me explaining everything and—''

''Wait a minute. What letter?''

''Remember those Christmas cards that got stolen?'' I explained why Emily had broken into my boat. ''Anyway, after the break-in, Emily had the letter, the negatives, and no more blackmailers on her back. But she wanted to be sure all her bases were covered. The sailing lessons were just a pretext, a way for her to keep track of the investigation. And a convenient way to get rid of me if need be. She thought she could make my death look like an accident by running *Second Wind* into the rocks at Potter's Cove.''

"How'd she wind up in the dinghy taking pot shots at you?''

"She might've known something about boating, but she sure didn't know much about sailing. I lowered the boom on her when she wasn't looking.''

Kingston laughed. "I always wondered where that expression came from.''

"Okay. Now it's your turn. I don't remember much about what happened after I was shot. You care to fill me in on the rescue?''

"The Coast Guard got a frantic call from Bert.''

"How'd Bert know what was up?''

"I guess you hit a boat on your way out of the marina.''

"Forever Young.''

"Yeah, that's it. Anyway, the owners had spent the night aboard and were still asleep when you so rudely awakened them. They knew something had to be wrong—you'd never bash and run like that. So they called Bert.''

"How'd you find out?''

"Actually I was on my way to the marina when I heard the call on the scanner. I made it down to the pier in time to hitch up with the Harbor Patrol. When we arrived on the scene, the Coast Guard had *Second Wind* secured on a tow. The Cummings woman was still in the dinghy going nowhere fast. She'd run out of bullets and was screaming her head off like a banshee. Had one hell of a time getting her into handcuffs—we all wound up pitching in.''

"The Coast Guard, Harbor Patrol, Seattle PD. So all you guys finally cooperated on a collar, huh?''

"Yep. They got Cummings, and I got you.''

"You did?''

"Didn't I?'' He took my hand—the one without the IV—and squeezed it.

Well, well. I didn't know what to say to that, afraid I might be reading more into it than he intended. Maybe it was the drugs or whatever it was they were feeding me, but I took a chance and squeezed his hand back. He smiled, and my spirits soared. After a moment or two, I asked, "What about James Preston? Has he been released?"

"Nope."

"How come? I thought you arrested Emily?"

"We got Preston on that old hit-and-run case Moyer was blackmailing him over. Just in time, too—statute of limitations had almost run out. As an added bonus, I finally learned what the *R* in his name stands for."

"Rat?"

"Ha! That would've been better than Reginald. Can you believe it? Reginald James Preston."

"And his wife? How's she taking all this?"

"You mean Chatty Nancy?"

"I think my meds are wearing off. Did you say chatty?"

"Oh, yeah. A regular chatterbox, that one. The little woman couldn't wait to dish the dirt on her hubby when she found out that he was gonna walk on the murder charge."

"How come?"

"She'd signed a prenuptial agreement. If they divorced, she got nothing. If Preston died, most of his assets went to his first wife. But if he was incapacitated in some way— and doing jail time is one hell of an incapacitation—she had control of everything. So with the Moyers dead and Preston in jail, she got her hands on the whole ball of wax, including the law firm. She wanted the old man out of the picture for a long, long time."

"Sounds like she owes Emily a debt of gratitude."

"Debt is right. The IRS has been camping out on her doorstep. Seems they're mighty interested in the business practices at the Moyer and Preston Law Office. From what I hear, she'll have a hard time buying a tennis ball after she gets through paying all the back taxes and fines."

"Gee, what a shame," I said, grinning. "But enough about her. What about your promotion? Did Emily's arrest have any effect on that?"

"Naw, the chief had already offered me the job."

"Congratulations, Sergeant."

"Don't be so quick with the congratulations, Montgomery."

"Why not?"

He shifted in his chair. "It's no big deal. I changed my mind, that's all—turned the job down yesterday. I never could see myself as sergeant, but after twenty years on the force it just seemed like a logical move. Moving up the old career ladder has never been a goal of mine. I guess I took the exam just to see if I could pass the damn thing."

"From what I hear, you did more than just pass."

"Yeah, well." He shrugged. "Shocked quite a few people, not to mention myself, when I came out number two on the list. But as far as I'm concerned, Saunders is welcome to the job."

"He made sergeant, then?"

"Yep. I'll be reporting to the college boy now."

"How do you feel about that?"

He rubbed at the stubble on his face. "Time will tell, but at least Saunders knows his stuff—hell, he ought to, I've taught him everything he knows."

I smiled. "Maybe you'll get a woman partner this time around—someone who already knows her stuff."

Kingston smiled and looked down at our hands, still clasped together. "Maybe. Maybe I just will at that, Red."

THIRTY

"ARE YOU SURE you're up to this?" asked Cassie. She took her eyes off the traffic edging its way toward the Ballard bridge long enough to give me a quick once-over. My arm was in a sling and my jaw a mass of purple bruises where Emily had hit me. I couldn't blame her for asking.

"Piece of cake." I fingered the prescription bottle in my pocket. One more hour and I could take another pill. I eased my head against the car seat and closed my eyes.

"Mom, you don't have to do this. I mean, we could go another time. I'll be back home for spring break. We could go then."

A boat horn tooted below the bridge. I opened my eyes and spotted the problem. A sailboat with a too-tall mast needed to pass underneath. The bridge tender rang a bell and lowered the traffic barriers. Cassie shifted and brought the Miata to a stop.

"God knows I don't feel much better than I look, but you can stop your fussing. You invited me to this support group meeting, and I want to go now, Cassie. Not tomorrow, not next spring. But right now." I took her hand in mine. "Getting shot and winding up in the hospital tends to make one acutely aware of what's really important in life." I squeezed her hand. "And, in case you didn't know it, that's you."

She leaned over and kissed my cheek. "I know that, Mom. I've always known that."

There was a lot more I wanted to say, but I needed some time to get the words right. I closed my eyes again and leaned my head against the seat. My thoughts drifted back to yesterday's phone call from Kingston. He'd called to give me the information I'd asked for. He said it didn't take him long—all of Moyer's files had been seized with a search warrant the day they arrested Preston—and our file was right there, too, including the name of Cassie's birth mother. It was just her maiden name, of course, but it was a start.

"Any other information on her?" I'd asked.

"Naw, the file's rather thin on details. No father listed or anything like that. Doesn't say how old she was at the time, but my guess is that she was an attorney."

"How do you figure?"

"Her name—it's E. Renée Stryker."

"You have a real hang-up about initials, don't you?"

"Hey, wait a minute. There is something else here. Did you know Cassie has a twin sister?"

My God. Why wasn't I told? "Are you sure?"

"Yeah, says so right here, plain as day. She was adopted, too. Some family in Portland, Oregon."

"Kingston," I said, "Emily Cummings had twin girls. You don't think . . ."

"Naw. That'd have to be one hell of a coincidence."

He was right. Still, there was something else. "Think about this: Emily told me she'd changed her name."

"So?"

"She said Sunny was just a nickname. Except for Terri Moyer, everyone else called her by her middle name. It was only later on, after she'd been in foster care, that she started going by her first name."

"And your point is?"

"The name on Cassie's records: E. Renée Stryker."

"E as in Emily?"

"It's a possibility."

"But I thought her maiden name was Wilson."

"Wilson was her stepfather's name. She told me she dropped it and started using her real father's name."

"Stryker?"

"I have no idea. No idea at all."

"Then let's find out," Kingston said. "I'll call you back in a minute." It took more than a minute, but when he called back, he said, "Well, Red, you can relax."

"Why? What did you find out?"

"Emily Cummings isn't Cassie's mother."

"How do you know?"

"Simple. She got married, didn't she? The county has Cummings's marriage certificate on file—with her maiden name listed. It's a public record, and I had a friend who works there check it out."

"And?"

"Emily's name was listed on the marriage certificate as E. Marie Freemont. Not Stryker."

"So Emily had twin girls, but—"

"Cassie wasn't one of them."

CASSIE GENTLY TAPPED my arm. "Mom, wake up. We're here."

"Huh?"

"The meeting. It's time to go inside." She unlocked her door and reached for the door handle.

"Uh, Cassie, wait. Could we sit here for just a few minutes?"

She turned and looked at me carefully. "Are you all right, Mom? Because I meant it when I said we don't have to—"

"Relax. I'm doing just fine, but I need to share something with you before we go inside."

"Can't it wait? We're late now."

"Oh, Cassie darling, you're right. It is late—twenty years late. But like the wind, it was something we couldn't control. All we can do now is adjust the sails and see where they take us."